The Profession of
A Collection of Articles on New
    Publishing, Taken From the Atlantic Monthly

Editor: Willard Grosvenor Bleyer

Alpha Editions

This edition published in 2024

ISBN 9789362518002

Design and Setting By
Alpha Editions
www.alphaedis.com
Email - info@alphaedis.com

As per information held with us this book is in Public Domain.
This book is a reproduction of an important historical work.
Alpha Editions uses the best technology to reproduce historical work
in the same manner it was first published to preserve its original nature.
Any marks or number seen are left intentionally to preserve.

Contents

PREFACE	- 1 -
INTRODUCTION	- 2 -
II	- 4 -
III	- 6 -
IV	- 7 -
V	- 8 -
VI	- 9 -
VII	- 10 -
VIII	- 11 -
IX	- 12 -
X	- 13 -
XI	- 15 -
I	- 17 -
II	- 22 -
III	- 27 -
PRESS TENDENCIES AND DANGERS	- 31 -
THE WANING POWER OF THE PRESS	- 38 -
I	- 38 -
II	- 43 -
NEWSPAPER MORALS	- 53 -
I	- 53 -
II	- 60 -
NEWSPAPER MORALS: A REPLY	- 64 -
THE SUPPRESSION OF IMPORTANT NEWS	- 71 -

I	- 71 -
II	- 72 -
III	- 75 -
IV	- 78 -
V	- 81 -
THE PERSONAL EQUATION IN JOURNALISM	- 84 -
I	- 84 -
II	- 86 -
IV	- 94 -
V	- 96 -
THE PROBLEM OF THE ASSOCIATED PRESS	- 97 -
I	- 97 -
III	- 103 -
THE ASSOCIATED PRESS: A REPLY	- 106 -
CONFESSIONS OF A PROVINCIAL EDITOR	- 112 -
I	- 114 -
II	- 117 -
III	- 121 -
THE COUNTRY EDITOR OF TO-DAY	- 125 -
I	- 125 -
II	- 129 -
III	- 132 -
IV	- 135 -
SENSATIONAL JOURNALISM AND THE LAW	- 138 -
I	- 138 -
II	- 142 -
THE CRITIC AND THE LAW	- 148 -

I	- 148 -
III	- 156 -
HONEST LITERARY CRITICISM	- 161 -
I	- 161 -
II	- 166 -
III	- 171 -
IV	- 175 -
DRAMATIC CRITICISM IN THE AMERICAN PRESS	- 178 -
THE HUMOR OF THE COLORED SUPPLEMENT	- 184 -
I	- 184 -
II	- 188 -
THE AMERICAN GRUB STREET	- 191 -
I	- 191 -
II	- 194 -
III	- 198 -
IV	- 201 -
V	- 204 -
JOURNALISM AS A CAREER	- 207 -
I	- 207 -
III	- 214 -
BIBLIOGRAPHY	- 217 -
1. Books on Principles of Journalism	- 217 -
2. What Typical Newspapers Contain	- 218 -
3. What the Public Wants	- 219 -
4. What Is News?	- 220 -
5. The Reporter and the News	- 221 -
7. Yellow and Sensational Journalism	- 223 -

8. Inaccuracy	- 224 -
10. Coloring the News	- 226 -
12. Editorial Policy and Influence	- 228 -
13. The Associated Press and the United Press	- 229 -
15. Dramatic Criticism	- 231 -
16. Book-Reviewing in Newspapers	- 232 -
17. Newspaper Style	- 233 -
19. The Country Newspaper	- 235 -
20. Newspapers of the Future	- 236 -
NOTES ON THE WRITERS	- 237 -

PREFACE

The purpose of this book is to bring together in convenient form a number of significant contributions to the discussion of the newspaper and its problems which have appeared in the *Atlantic Monthly* in recent years. Although these articles were intended only for the readers of that magazine at the time of their original publication, they have permanent value for the general reader, for newspaper workers, and for students of journalism.

Practically every phase of journalism is taken up in these articles, including newspaper publishing, news and editorial policies, the influence of the press, yellow and sensational journalism, the problems of the newspaper in small cities, country journalism, the Associated Press, the law of libel, book-reviewing, dramatic criticism, "comics," free-lance writing, and the opportunities in the profession. For readers who desire to make a further study of any of the important aspects of the press, a bibliography of such books and magazine articles as are generally available in public libraries has been appended.

Most of the authors of the articles in this volume are newspaper and magazine writers and editors whose long experience in journalism gives particular value to their analysis of conditions, past and present. Brief notes on the journalistic work of the writers are given in the Appendix.

For permission to reprint the articles the editor is indebted to the writers and to the editor of the *Atlantic Monthly*.

W. G. B.

UNIVERSITY OF WISCONSIN,

January 12, 1918.

INTRODUCTION

BY WILLARD GROSVENOR BLEYER

I

"The food of opinion," as President Wilson has well said, "is the news of the day." The daily newspaper, for the majority of Americans, is the sole purveyor of this food for thought. Citizens of a democracy must read and assimilate the day's news in order to form opinions on current events and issues. Again, for the average citizen the newspaper is almost the only medium for the interpretation and discussion of questions of the day. The composite of individual opinions, which we call public opinion, must express itself in action to be effective. The newspaper, with its daily reiteration, is the most powerful force in urging citizens to act in accordance with their convictions. By reflecting the best sentiment of the community in which it is published, the newspaper makes articulate intelligent public opinion that might otherwise remain unexpressed. Since the success of democracy depends not only upon intelligent public opinion but upon political action in accordance with such opinion, it is not too much to say that the future of democratic government in this country depends upon the character of its newspapers.

Yet most newspaper readers not unnaturally regard the daily paper as an ephemeral thing to be read hurriedly and cast aside. Few appreciate the extent to which their opinions are affected by the newspaper they read. Nevertheless, to every newspaper reader—which means almost every person in this country—the conditions under which newspapers are produced and the influences that affect the character of news and editorials, should be matters of vital concern.

To newspaper workers and students of journalism the analysis of the fundamental questions of their profession is of especial importance. Discussion of current practices must precede all effort to arrive at definite standards for the profession of journalism. Only when the newspaper man realizes the probable effect of his work on the ideas and ideals of thousands of readers, and hence on the character of our democracy, does he appreciate the full significance of his news story, headline, or editorial.

The modern newspaper has developed so recently from simple beginnings into a great, complex institution that no systematic and extensive study has been made of its problems. Journalism has won recognition as a profession only within the last seventy-five years, and professional schools for the training of newspaper writers and editors have been in existence less than fifteen years. In view of these conditions, it is not surprising that definite principles and a generally accepted code of ethics for the practice of the profession have not been formulated.

Ideal conditions of newspaper editing and publishing are not likely to be brought about by legislation. So jealous are the American people of the liberty of their press that they hesitate, even when their very existence as a nation is threatened, to impose legal restrictions on the printing of news and opinion. If regulation does come, it should be the result, as it has been in the professions of law and medicine, of the creation of an enlightened public opinion in support of professional standards adopted by journalists themselves.

The present is an auspicious time to discuss such standards. The world war has put to the test, not only men and machinery, but every institution of society. Of each organized activity we ask, Is it serving most effectively the common good? Not simply service to the state, but service to society, is being demanded more and more of every individual and every institution. "These are the times which try men's souls," and that try no less the mediums through which men's souls find expression. The newspaper, as the purveyor of "food of opinion" and as the medium for expressing opinion, must measure up to the test of the times.

II

The first step in a systematic analysis of the principles of journalism must be a consideration of the function of the newspaper in a democracy. In the varied and voluminous contents of a typical newspaper are to be found news of all kinds, editorial comment, illustrations of current events, recipes, comic strips, fashions, cartoons, advice on affairs of the heart, short stories, answers to questions on etiquette, dramatic criticism, chapters of a serial, book reviews, verse, a "colyum," and advertisements. What in this mélange is the one element which distinguishes the newspaper from all other publications? It is the daily news. Weekly and monthly periodicals do everything that the newspaper does, except print the news from day to day.

Whatever other aims a newspaper may have, its primary purpose must be to give adequate reports of the day's news. Although various inducements other than news may be employed to attract some persons to newspapers who would not otherwise read them regularly, nevertheless these features must not be so prominent or attractive that readers with limited time at their disposal will neglect the day's news for entertainment.

To assist the public to grasp the significance of the news by means of editorial interpretation and discussion, to render articulate the best public sentiment, and to persuade citizens to act in accordance with their opinions, constitute an important secondary function of the newspaper. Even though the editorial may seem to exert a less direct influence upon the opinions and political action of the average citizen than it did in the period of great editorial leadership, nevertheless the interpretation and discussion of timely topics in the editorial columns of the daily press are a force in democratic government that cannot be disregarded.

Newspapers by their editorials can perform two peculiarly important services to the public. First, they can show the relation of state, national, and international questions to the home and business interests of their readers. Only as the great issues of the day are brought home to the average reader is he likely to become keenly interested in their solution. Second, newspapers in their editorials can point out the connection between local questions and state-wide, nation-wide, or world-wide movements. Only as questions at issue in a community are shown in their relation to larger tendencies will the average reader see them in a perspective that will enable him to think and act most intelligently.

In addition to fulfilling these two functions, the newspaper may supply its readers with practical advice and useful information, as well as with entertaining reading matter and illustrations. There is more justification for wholesome advice and entertainment in newspapers that circulate largely among classes whose only reading matter is the daily paper than there is in papers whose readers obtain these features from other periodicals. In view of the numberless cheap, popular magazines in this country, the extent to which daily newspapers should devote space and money to advice and entertainment deserves careful consideration. That without such consideration these features may encroach unjustifiably on news and editorials seems evident.

III

Since the primary function of the newspaper is to give the day's news, the question arises, What is news? If from the point of view of successful democracy the value of news is determined by the extent to which it furnishes food for thought on current topics, we are at once given an important criterion for defining news and measuring news-values. Thus, news is anything timely which is significant to newspaper readers in their relation to the community, the state, and the nation.

This conception of news is not essentially at variance with the commonly accepted definition of it as anything timely that interests a number of readers, the best news being that which has greatest interest for the greatest number. The most vital matters for both men and women are their home and their business interests, their success and their happiness. Anything in the day's news that touches directly or indirectly these things that are nearest and dearest to them, they will read with eagerness. As they may not always be able to see at once the relation of current events and issues to their home, business, and community interests, it is the duty of the newspaper to present news in such a way that its significance to the average reader will be clear. Every newspaper man knows the value of "playing up" the "local ends" of events that take place outside of the community in which his paper is published, but this method of bringing home to readers the significance to them of important news has not been as fully worked out as it will be. On this basis the best news is that which can be shown to be most closely related to the interests of the largest number of readers.

"But newspapers must publish entertaining news stories as well as significant ones," insists the advocate of things as they are. This may be conceded, but only with three important limitations. First, stories for mere entertainment that deal with events of little or no news-value must not be allowed to crowd out significant news. Second, such entertaining news-matter must not be given so much space and prominence, or be made so attractive, that the average reader with but limited time in which to read his paper will neglect news of value. Third, events of importance must not be so treated as to furnish entertainment primarily, to the subordination of their true significance. To substitute the *hors d'œuvres*, relishes, and dessert of the day's happenings for nourishing "food of opinion" is to serve an unbalanced, unwholesome mental diet. The relish should heighten, not destroy, a taste for good food.

IV

In order to furnish the average citizen with material from which to form opinions on all current issues, so that he may vote intelligently on men and measures, newspapers must supply significant news in as complete and as accurate a form as possible. The only important limitations to completeness are those imposed by the commonly accepted ideas of decency embodied in the phrase, "All the news that's fit to print," and by the rights of privacy. Carefully edited newspapers discriminate between what the public is entitled to know and what an individual has a right to keep private.

Inaccuracy, due to the necessity for speed in getting news into print, most newspapers agree must be reduced to a minimum. The establishment of bureaus of accuracy, and constant emphasis on such mottoes as "Accuracy First," "Accuracy Always," and "If you see it in the *Sun*, it's so," are steps in that direction.

Deliberate falsification of news for any purpose, good or bad, must be regarded as an indefensible violation of the fundamental purpose of the press. Any cause, no matter how worthy it may be, which cannot depend on facts and truth for its support does not deserve to have facts and truth distorted in its behalf.

The "faking" of news can never be harmless. Even though the fictitious touches in an apparently innocent "human-interest" or "feature" story may be recognized by most readers, yet the effect is harmful. "It's only a newspaper story," expresses the all-too-common attitude of a public whose confidence in the reliability of newspapers has been undermined by news stories wholly or partially "faked."

The "coloring," adulteration, and suppression of news as "food of opinion" is as dangerous to the body politic as similar manipulation of food-stuffs was to the physical bodies of our people before such practices were forbidden by law. How completely the opinions and moral judgments of a whole nation may be perverted by deliberate "coloring" and suppression of news, in this case by its own government, was demonstrated in Germany immediately before and during the world war.

The jury of newspaper readers must have "the truth, the whole truth, and nothing but the truth," if it is to give an intelligent verdict.

V

The so-called "yellow journals" are glaring examples of newspapers built up on news and editorial policies shaped to attract undiscriminating readers by sensational methods. By constantly emphasizing sensational news and by "sensationalizing" and "melodramatizing" news that is not sufficiently startling, as well as by editorials stirring up class feeling among the masses against the monied and ruling classes, "yellow journals" have been able to outstrip all other papers in circulation.

Unquestionably the most serious aspect of the influence of sensational and yellow journalism is the distorted view of life thus given. Because these papers are widely read by the partially assimilated groups of foreign immigrants in large centres of population, like New York and Chicago, they exert a particularly dangerous influence by giving these future citizens a wrong conception of American society and government. That the false ideas of our life and institutions given to foreign elements of our population while they are in the process of becoming Americanized are a serious menace to this country, requires no proof. No matter who the readers may be, however, news that is "colored" to appear "yellow," and misleading editorials, will always be dangerous to the public welfare.

VI

The treatment of sensational events, particularly those involving crime and scandal, undoubtedly constitutes one of the difficult problems of all newspapers. The demoralizing effect of accounts of criminal and vicious acts, when read by immature and morally unstable individuals, is generally admitted. On the other hand, fear of publicity and consequent disgrace to the wrong-doer and his family, is a powerful deterrent. Moreover, if newspapers suppressed news of crime and vice, citizens might remain ignorant of the extent to which they existed in the community, and consequently, with the aid of a corrupt local government, wrong-doing might flourish until it was a menace to every member of the community.

To give sufficient publicity to news of crime and scandal in order to provide the necessary deterrent effect, to furnish readers with the information to which they are entitled, and at the same time to present such news so that it will not give offense or encourage morally weak readers to emulate the criminal and the vicious, define the middle course which exponents of constructive journalism must steer.

VII

Criticisms of the newspaper of the present day should not leave us with the impression that the American press is deteriorating. No one who compares the newspaper of to-day with its predecessors of fifty, seventy-five, or a hundred years ago, can fail to appreciate how immeasurably superior in every respect is the press of the present day. In our newspapers now there is much less of narrow political partisanship, much less of editorial vituperation and personal abuse, much less of objectionable advertising, and relatively less news of crime and scandal. Viewed from a distance of more than half a century, great American editors loom large, but a critical study of the papers they edited shows their limitations. They were pioneers in a new land,—for modern journalism began but eighty-five years ago,—and as such, they deserve all honor for blazing the trail; but we must not be blind to the defects of the papers that they produced, any more than we may overlook the faults of the press of our own day.

The period of the struggle against slavery culminating in the Civil War was one of great editorial leadership. To say that it was the era of great "views-papers" and that the present is the day of great "news-papers" is to sum up the essential difference between the two periods. In terms of democratic government, this means that citizens of the older day were accustomed to accept as their own, political opinions furnished them ready-made by their favorite editor, whereas voters to-day want to form their own opinions on the basis of the news and editorials furnished them by their favorite paper. This greater independence of judgment, with its corollary, greater independence in voting, is a long step forward toward a more complete democracy.

VIII

The recent development of community spirit as a means of realizing more fully the ideals of democracy by fostering greater solidarity among the diverse elements of our population, has been reflected in the news policies of many papers. By "playing up" news that tends to the upbuilding of the community, and by "playing down," and even eliminating entirely, news that tends to exert an unwholesome influence, newspapers in various parts of the country have developed a type of constructive journalism. Such consideration for the effect of news on readers as members of the community, and hence on community life, is one of the most important forward steps taken by the modern newspaper.

Although occasion may arise from time to time for newspapers to turn the searchlight of publicity on social and political corruption, the feeling is gaining strength that newspaper crusades in the interests of institutions and movements making for community uplift are even more important than the continued exposure of evils. Many aggressive, crusading papers, accordingly, have turned from a policy of exposing such conditions to the constructive purpose of showing how various agencies may be used for community development. "Searchlight" journalism is thus giving way to "sunlight" journalism. A constructive policy that aims to handle local news and "local ends" of all news in such a manner that they will exert a wholesome, upbuilding influence on the community, is one of the most potent forces making for a better democracy.

IX

With the entry of the United States into world-affairs in coöperation with other nations, a new duty was placed upon the American press. For a number of years before the world war the amount of foreign news in the average American newspaper was very limited. With the decline of weekly letters from foreign countries written by well-known correspondents, and the reliance by newspapers on the great press associations for foreign news, readers had had relatively less news of importance from abroad than formerly. The world war naturally changed this condition completely.

Unless the United States decides finally to return to its former policy of isolation, American citizens must be kept in touch with important movements in other nations, so that they can form intelligent opinions in regard to the relation of this country to these nations. Since the daily newspaper is the principal medium for presenting such news, it is clear that newspapers must be prepared to present significant foreign news in such a manner that it will attract readers, by connecting it with their interests as American citizens.

X

How the future will solve the problems of journalism must be largely a matter of conjecture. Temporarily the world war has given rise to peculiar problems, none of which, however, seems likely to have permanent effects on our newspapers. Censorship of news and of editorial discussion has precipitated anew the ever-perplexing question of the exact limits of the liberty of the press in war times. War, too, has made clearer the pernicious influence resulting from the dissemination throughout the world of "colored" news by means of semi-official news agencies subsidized and controlled by some of the European nations. The extent to which a whole nation may be kept in the dark by government control of news and discussion, as well as the impossibility of other nations getting important information to the people of such a country, has been strikingly exemplified by Germany and Austro-Hungary. The need of definite provision for international freedom of the press has been pointed out as an essential factor in any programme for permanent peace.

The rise in the price of print paper and increased cost of production, largely the result of war conditions, have led so generally to the raising of the price of papers from one to two cents that the penny paper bids fair to disappear entirely. This increase in price has not appreciably reduced circulation. To economize in the use of paper during the war, many papers have reduced the number of pages by cutting down the amount of reading matter. Whether or not these changes will continue when normal conditions of business are restored cannot be predicted.

Endowed newspapers, municipal newspapers, and even university newspapers, have been proposed as possible solutions of the problems of the press. Of these proposals only one, the municipal newspaper, has had a trial, and even that has not been tried under conditions that permit any conclusions as to its feasibility. Although there has been a marked tendency, hastened by the war, toward government ownership or control of railroad, telegraph, and telephone lines, which, like newspapers, are private enterprises that perform a public function, there has been no corresponding movement looking toward ownership or control of newspapers by the federal, state, or local government.

Effective organization of newspaper writers and editors has been urged as a means of establishing definite standards for the profession. It seems remarkable that in this age of organization newspaper workers are the only members of a great profession who have no national association. Newspaper publishers, circulation managers, advertising men, and the editor-publishers of weekly and small daily newspapers have such organizations. For free-lance writers there is the Authors' League of

America. In several Middle Western states organizations of city editors have been effected; but a movement to unite them into a national association has not as yet made much progress.

Two national newspaper conferences have been held under academic auspices to discuss the problems of journalism, the first at the University of Wisconsin in 1912, and the second at the University of Kansas, two years later. Although a number of leaders in the profession took part in the programmes and interesting discussion resulted, the attendance of newspaper workers was not sufficiently large to be representative of the country as a whole, and no permanent organization was effected.

That a national organization of newspaper men and women is neither impossible nor ineffectual has been demonstrated in Great Britain, where three of such associations have been active for a number of years. The Institute of Journalists of Great Britain, an association of newspaper editors and proprietors, holds an annual conference for the discussion of current questions in journalism and has had as its head such distinguished journalists as Robert Donald of the London *Daily Chronicle*, A. G. Gardiner of the London *Daily News*, and J. L. Garvin, formerly editor of the *Pall Mall Gazette* and now editor of the *Observer*. The other associations are the National Union of Journalists, composed exclusively of newspaper workers, which maintains "branches" and "district councils" in addition to the national association; and the Society of Women Journalists.

XI

There is no one simple solution for the complex problems of journalism. In so far as the newspaper is a private business enterprise, it will continue to adjust itself to the steadily advancing standards of the business world. "Service," the new watchword in business, is already being taken up by the business departments of newspapers in relation to both advertisers and readers. The rejection of objectionable advertising and the guaranteeing of all advertising published have been among the first steps taken toward serving both readers and honest business men by protecting them against unscrupulous advertisers. When it is generally accepted in the business world that service, as well as honesty, is the best policy, no newspaper can long afford to pursue any other.

Nor need private ownership be a menace to the completeness and accuracy with which newspapers present news and opinion. Just as business men are coming to realize that truthful advertising is most effective and that a satisfied customer is the best advertiser, so newspapers are coming more and more to appreciate the fact that accuracy and fair play in news and editorials are also "good business." Neither the public nor a majority of editors and publishers can afford to permit unscrupulous private ownership to impair seriously the usefulness and integrity of any newspaper.

In so far as the newspaper performs a public function, its usefulness will be measured by the character of the service that it renders. Its standing will be determined by the extent to which it serves faithfully the community, the state, and the nation. Whatever principles are formulated and whatever code is adopted for the profession of journalism will be based on the fundamental idea of service to the people—to the masses as well as to the classes.

Newspaper workers, from the "cub" reporter to the editor-in-chief, will be recognized as public servants, not as mere employees of a private business. The high standards maintained by them in newspaper offices will reinforce the ideal of public service held up before college men and women preparing themselves for journalism. The public will understand more fully than it ever has done the necessity of supporting heartily the standards established by newspapers themselves. Requests to "keep it out of the paper" and threats of "stop my paper" will be less frequent when advertisers, business men, and readers see that such attempts at coercion are an indefensible interference with an institution whose first duty is to the public.

With an ever-increasing appreciation of the value of its service in business relations and with an ever-broadening conception of its duties and responsibilities, the newspaper of to-morrow may be depended on to do its part in the greatest of all national and international tasks, that of "making the world safe for democracy."

SOME ASPECTS OF JOURNALISM

BY ROLLO OGDEN

I

It is, in a way, a form of flattery, in the eyes of modern journalism, that it should be put on its defense—added to the fascinating list of "problems." This is a tribute to its importance. The compliment may often seem oblique. An editor will, at times, feel himself placed in much the same category as a famous criminal—a warning, a horrible example, a target for reproof, but still an interesting object. That last is the redeeming feature. If the newspaper of to-day can only be sure that it excites interest in the multitude, it is content. For to force itself upon the general notice is the main purpose of its spirit of shrill insistence, which so many have noted and so many have disliked.

But the clamorous and assertive tone of the daily press may charitably be thought of as a natural reaction from its low estate of a few generations back. Upstart families or races usually have bad manners, and the newspaper, as we know it, is very much of an upstart. For long, its lot was contempt and contumely. In the first half of the eighteenth century, writing in general was reduced to extremities. Dr. Johnson says of Richard Savage that, "having no profession, he became by necessity an author." But there was a lower deep, and that was journalism. Warburton wrote of one who is chiefly known by being pilloried in the *Dunciad* that he "ended in the common sink of all such writers, a political newspaper." Even later it was recorded of the Rev. Dr. Dodd, author of the *Beauties of Shakespeare*, that he "descended so low as to become editor of a newspaper." After that, but one step remained—to the gallows; and this was duly taken by Dr. Dodd in 1777, when he was hanged for forgery. A calling digged from such a pit may, without our special wonder, display something of the push and insolence natural in a class whose privileges were long so slender or so questioned that they must be loudly proclaimed for fear that they may be forgotten.

This flaunting and over-emphasis also go well with the charge that the press of to-day is commercialized. That accusation no one undertaking to comment on newspapers can pass unnoticed. Yet why should journalism be exempt? It is as freely asserted that colleges are commercialized; the theatre is accused of knowing no standard but that of the box-office; politics has the money-taint upon it; and even the church is arraigned for ignoring the teachings of St. James, and being too much a respecter of the persons of the rich. If it is true that the commercial spirit rules the press, it is at least in good company. In actual fact, occasional instances of gross and unscrupulous financial control of newspapers for selfish or base ends must be admitted to exist. There are undoubtedly some editors who bend their conscience to their dealing. Newspaper proprietors exist who sell themselves for gain. But this is not what is ordinarily meant by the charge of commercialization. Reference is, rather, to the newspaper as a money-making institution. "When shall we have a journal," asked a clergyman not long ago, "that will be published without advertisements?"

The answer is, never—at least, I hope so, for the good of American journalism. We have no official press. We have no subsidized press. We have not even an endowed press. What that would be in this country I can scarcely imagine, but I am sure it would have little or no influence. A newspaper carries weight only as it can point to evidence of public sympathy and support. But that means a business side; it means patronage; it means an eye to money. A newspaper, like an army, goes upon its belly—though it does not follow that it must eat dirt. The dispute about being commercialized is always a question of more or less. When Horace Greeley founded the *Tribune* in 1841, he had but a thousand dollars of his own in cash. Yet his struggle to make the paper a going concern was just as intense as if he were starting it to-day with a capital (and it would be needed) of a million. Greeley, to his honor be it said, refused from the beginning to take certain advertisements. But so do newspaper proprietors to-day whose expenses per week are more than Greeley's were for the first year.

The immensely large capital now required for the conduct of a daily newspaper in a great city has had important consequences. It has made the newspaper more of an institution, less of a personal organ. Men no longer designate journals by the owner's or editor's name. It used to be Bryant's paper, or Greeley's paper, or Raymond's, or Bennett's. Now it is simply *Times, Herald, Tribune,* and so on. No single personality can stamp itself upon the whole organism. It is too vast. It is a great piece of property, to be administered with skill; it is a carefully planned organization which best produces the effect when the personalities of those who work for it are swallowed up. The individual withers, but the newspaper is more and more. Journalism becomes impersonal. There are no more "great editors," but there is a finer *esprit de corps*, better "team play," an institution more and more firmly established and able to justify itself.

Large capital in newspapers, and their heightened earning power, tend to steady them. Freaks and rash experiments are also shut out by lack of means. Greeley reckoned up a hundred or more newspapers that had died in New York before 1850. Since that time it would be hard to name ten. I can remember but two metropolitan dailies within twenty-five years that have absolutely suspended publication. Only contrast the state of things in Parisian journalism. There must be at least thirty daily newspapers in the French capital. Few of them have the air of living off their own business. Yet the necessary capital and the cost of production are so much smaller than ours that their various backers can afford to keep them afloat. But this fact does not make their sincerity or purity the more evident. On the contrary, the rumor of sinister control is more frequently circulated in connection with the French press than with our own. Our higher capitalization helps us. Just because a great sum is invested, it cannot be imperiled by allowing unscrupulous men to make use of the newspaper property; for that way ruin lies, in the end. The corrupt employment has to be concealed. If it had been known surely, for example, that Mr. Morgan, or Mr. Ryan, or Mr. Harriman owned a New York newspaper, and was utilizing it as a means of furthering his schemes, support would speedily have failed it, and it would soon have dried up from the roots.

This give and take between the press and the public is vital to a just conception of American journalism. The editor does not nonchalantly project his thoughts into the void. He listens for the echo of his words. His relation to his supporters is not unlike Gladstone's definition of the intimate connection between the orator and his audience. As the speaker gets from his hearers in mist what he gives back in shower, so the newspaper receives from the public as well as gives to it. Too often it gets as dust what it gives back as mud; but that does not alter the relation. Action and reaction are all the while going on between the press and its patrons. Hence it follows that the responsibility for the more crying evils of journalism must be divided.

I would urge no exculpation for the editor who exploits crime, scatters filth, and infects the community with moral poison. The original responsibility is his, and it is a fearful one. But it is not solely his. The basest and most demoralizing journal that lives, lives by public approval or tolerance. Its readers and advertisers have its life in their hands. At a word from them, it would either reform or die. They have the power of "recall" over it, as it is by some proposed to grant the people a power of recall over bad representatives in legislature or Congress. The very dependence of the press upon support gives its patrons the power of life and death over it.

Advertisers are known to go to a newspaper office to seek favors, sometimes improper, often innocent. Why should they, and mere readers, too, not exercise their implied right to protest against vulgarity, the exaggeration of the trivial, hysteria, indecency, immorality, in the newspaper which they are asked to buy or to patronize? To a journalist of the offensive class they could say: "You excuse yourself by alleging that you simply give what the public demands; but we say that your very assertion is an insult to us and an outrage upon the public. You say that nobody protests against your course; well, we are here to protest. You point to your sales; we tell you that, unless you mend your columns, we will buy no more." There lies here, I am persuaded, a vast unused power for the toning up of our journalism. At any rate, the reform of a free press in a free people can be brought about only by some such reaction of the medium upon the instrument. Legislation direct would be powerless. Sir Samuel Romilly perceived this when he argued in Parliament against proposals to restrict by law the "licentious press." He said that, if the press were more licentious than formerly, it was because it had not yet got over the evils of earlier arbitrary control; and the only sure way to reform it was to make it still more free. Romilly would doubtless have agreed that a free people will, in the long run, have as good newspapers as it wants and deserves to have.

As it is, public sentiment has a way, on occasion, of speaking through the press with astonishing directness and power. All the noise and extravagance, the ignorance and the distortion, cannot obscure this. There is a rough but great value in the mere publicity which the newspaper affords. The free handling of rulers has much for the credit side. When Senior was talking with Thiers in 1856, the conversation fell upon the severe press laws under Napoleon III. The Englishman said that perhaps these were due to the license of newspapers in the time of the foregoing republic, when their attacks on public men were often the extreme of scurrility. "C'était horrible," said Thiers; "mais, pour moi, j'aime mieux être gouverné par des honnêtes gens qu'on traite comme des voleurs, que par des voleurs qu'on traite en honnêtes gens."[1] And when you have some powerful robbers to invoke the popular verdict upon, there is nothing like modern journalism for doing the job thoroughly. Those great names in our business and political firmament which lately have fallen like Lucifer, dreaded exposure in the press most of all. Courts and juries they could have faced with equanimity; or, rather, their lawyers would have done it for them in the most beautiful illustration of the law's delay. But the very clamor of newspaper publicity was like an embodied public conscience pronouncing condemnation—every headline an officer. I know of no other power on earth that could have stripped away from these rogues every shelter which their money could buy, and have been to them such an advance section of the Day of Judgment. In the immense publicity that dogged them they saw that worst of all punishments described by Shelley:—

—when thou must *appear* to be

That which thou art internally;

And after many a false and fruitless crime,

Scorn track thy lagging fall.

1. "It is terrible, but for my part, I would rather be governed by honest men who are treated as though they were thieves, than by thieves who are treated as though they were honest men."—ED.

II

It is, no doubt, a belief in this honestly and wholesomely scourging power of newspapers which has made the champions of modern democracy champions also of the freedom of the press. It has not been seriously hampered or shackled in this country; but the history of its emancipation from burdensome taxation in England shows how the progressive and reactionary motives or temperaments come to view. When Gladstone was laboring, fifty years ago, to remove the last special tax upon newspapers, Lord Salisbury—he was then Lord Robert Cecil—opposed him with some of his finest sneers. Could it be maintained that a person of any education could learn anything from a penny paper? It might be said that the people would learn from the press what had been uttered by their representatives in Parliament, but how much would that add to their education? They might even discover the opinions of the editor. All this was very interesting, but it did not carry real instruction to the mind. To talk about a tax on newspapers being a tax on knowledge was a prostitution of real education. And so on. But contrast this with John Bright's opinion. In a letter written in 1885, but not published till this year, he said: "Few men in England owe so much to the press as I do. Its progress has been very great. I was one of those who worked earnestly to overthrow the system of taxation which from the time of Queen Anne had fettered, I might almost say, strangled it out of existence.... I hope the editors and conductors of our journals may regard themselves as under a great responsibility, as men engaged in the great work of instructing and guiding our people.... On the faithful performance of their duties, on their truthfulness and their adherence to the moral law, the future of our country depends."

To pass from these ideals to the tendencies and perplexities of newspapers as they are is not possible without the sensation of a jar. For specimens of the faults found in even the reputable press by fair-minded men we may turn to a recent address before a university audience by Professor Butcher. Admitting that journalism had never before been "so many-sided, so well informed, so intellectually alert," he yet noted several literary and moral defects. Of these he dwelt first upon "hasty production." "Formerly, the question was, who is to have the last word; now it is a wild race between journalists as to who will get the *first* word." The professor found the marks of hurry written all over modern newspapers. Breathless haste could not but affect the editorial style. "It is smartly pictorial, restless, impatient, emphatic." This charge no editor of a daily paper can find it in his heart confidently to attempt to repel. His work has to be done under narrow and cramping conditions of time. The hour of going to press is ever before him as an inexorable fate. And that judgments formed and opinions expressed under such stress are often of a sort that one would fain withdraw, no sane writer for the press thinks of denying. This ancient handicap of the pressman was described by Cowper in 1780. "I began to think better of his [Burke's] cause," he wrote to the Rev. Mr. Unwin, "and burnt my verses. Such is the lot of the man who writes upon the subject of the day; the aspect of affairs changes in an hour or two, and his opinion with it; what was just and well-deserved satire in the morning, in the evening becomes a libel; the author commences his own judge, and, while he condemns with unrelenting severity what he so lately approved, is sorry to find that he has laid his leaf gold upon touchwood, which crumbled away under his finger."

While all this is sorrowfully true,—to none so sorrowful as those who have it frequently borne in upon them by personal experience,—it is, after all, *du métier*. It is a condition under which the work must be done, or not at all. A public which occasionally disapproves of a newspaper too quick on the trigger would not put up at all with one which held its fire too long. And there is, when all is said, a good deal of the philosophy of life in the compulsion to "go to press." Only in that spirit can the rough work of the world get done. The artist may file and polish endlessly; the genius may brood; but the newspaper man must cut short his search for the full thought or the perfect phrase, and get into type with the best at the moment attainable. At any rate, this makes for energy decision, and a ready practicality. Life is made up of such compromises, such forced adjustments, such constant striving for the ideal with the necessitated acceptance of the closest approach to it possible, as are of the very atmosphere in the office of a daily newspaper. But the result is got. The pressure may be bad for literary technique but at all events it forces out the work. If Lord Acton had known something of the driving motives of a journalist, he would not have spent fifty years collecting material for a great history of liberty, and then died before being quite persuaded in his own mind that he was ready to write it. The counsel of wisdom which Mr. Brooke gives in *Middlemarch* need never be addressed to a newspaper writer; that he must "pull up" in time, every day teaches him.

Professor Butcher also drew an ingenious parallel between the Sophists of ancient Greece and present-day journalists. It was not very flattering to the latter. One of the points of comparison was that "their pretensions were high and their basis of knowledge generally slight." Now, "ignorance," added the uncomplimentary professor, "has its own appropriate manner, and most journalists, being very clever fellows, are, when they are ignorant, conscious of their ignorance. A fine, elusive manner is therefore adopted; it is enveloped in a haze." To this charge, also, a bold and full plea of not guilty cannot be entered by a newspaper man. If his own conscience would allow it, he knows that too many of his own calling would rise up to confute him. The jokes, flings, stories, confessions are too numerous about the easy and empty assumptions of omniscience by the press. Mr. Barrie has, in his reminiscential *When a Man's Single*, told too many tales out of the sanctum. Some of them bear on the point in hand. For example:—

"'I am not sure that I know what the journalistic instinct precisely is,' Rob said, 'and still less whether I possess it.'

"'Ah, just let me put you through your paces,' replied Simms. 'Suppose yourself up for an exam. in journalism, and that I am your examiner. Question One: The house was soon on fire; much sympathy is expressed with the sufferers. Can you translate that into newspaper English?'

"'Let me see,' answered Rob, entering into the spirit of the examination. 'How would this do: In a moment the edifice was enveloped in shooting tongues of flame; the appalling catastrophe has plunged the whole street into the gloom of night'?

"'Good. Question Two: A man hangs himself; what is the technical heading for this?'

"'Either "Shocking Occurrence" or "Rash Act."'

"'Question Three: *Pabulum, Cela va sans dire, Par excellence, Ne plus ultra*. What are these? Are there any more of them?'

"'They are scholarships,' replied Rob; 'and there are two more, namely, *Tour de force* and *Terra firma*.'

"'Question Four: A. (a soldier) dies at 6 P.M. with his back to the foe; B. (a philanthropist) dies at 1 A.M.; which of these, speaking technically, would you call a creditable death?'

"'The soldier's, because time was given to set it.'

"'Quite right. Question Five: Have you ever known a newspaper which did not have the largest circulation and was not the most influential advertising medium?'

"'Never.'

"'Well, Mr. Angus,' said Simms, tiring of the examination, 'you have passed with honors.'"

Many cynical admissions by the initiate could be quoted. The question was recently put to a young man who had a place on the staff of a morning newspaper: "Are you not often brought to a standstill for lack of knowledge?" "No," he replied, "as a rule I go gayly ahead, and without a pause. My only difficulty is when I happen to know something of the subject." But no one takes these sarcasms too seriously. They are a part of the Bohemian tradition of journalism. But Bohemianism has gone out of the newspaper world, as the profession has become more specialized, more of a serious business. Even in his time, Jules Janin, writing to Madame de Girardin apropos of her *École des Journalistes*, happily exposed the "assumption that good leading articles ever were or ever could be produced over punch and broiled bones, amidst intoxication and revelry."

Editors may still be ignorant, but at any rate they are not unblushingly devil-may-care about it. They do not take their work as a pure lark. They try to get their facts right. And the appreciation of accurate knowledge, if not always the market for it, is certainly higher now in newspaper offices than it used to be. The multiplied apparatus of information has done at least that for the profession. Much of its knowledge may be "index-learning," but at any rate it gets the eel by the tail. And the editor has a fairish retort for the general writer in the fact that the latter might more often be caught tripping if he had to produce his wisdom on demand and get it irrevocably down in black and white and in a thousand hands without time for consideration or amendment. This truth was frankly put by Motley in a letter to Holmes in 1862: "I take great pleasure in reading your prophecies, and intend to be just as free in hazarding my own.... If you make mistakes, you shall never hear of them again, and I promise to forget them. Let me ask the same indulgence from you in return. This is what makes letter-writing a comfort, and journalism dangerous."

It is a distinction which an editor may well lay to his soul when accused of being a mere Gigadibs—

You, for example, clever to a fault,

The rough and ready man who write apace,

Read somewhat seldomer, think, perhaps, even less.

Even in journalism, the Spanish proverb holds that knowing something does not take up any room—*el saber no ocupa lugar*. Special information is, as I often have occasion to say to applicants for work, the one thing that gives a stranger a chance in a newspaper office. The most out-of-the-way knowledge has a trick of falling pat to the day's need. A successful London journalist got his first foothold by knowing all about Scottish Disruption, when that struggle between the Established and Free churches burst upon the horizon. The editor simply had to have the services of a man who could tell an interested English public all about the question which was setting the heather afire. Similarly, not long since, a young American turned up in New York with apparently the most hopeless outfit for journalistic work. He had spent eight years in Italy studying mediæval church history—and that was his basis for thinking he could write for a daily paper of the palpitating present! But it happened just then that the aged Leo XIII drew to his end, and here was a man who knew all the *Papabili*—cardinals and archbishops; who understood thoroughly the ceremony and procedure of electing a pope; who was drenched in all the actualities of the situation, and who could, therefore, write about it with an intelligence and sympathy which made his work compel acceptance, and gave him entrance into journalism by the unlikely Porta Romana. It is but an instance of the way in which a profession growing more serious is bound to take knowledge more seriously.

III

It is, however, what Sir Wemyss Reid called the "Wegotism" of the press that some fastidious souls find more offensive than its occasional betrayals of crass ignorance. Lecky remarked upon it, in his chapters on the rise of newspapers in England. "Few things to a reflecting mind are more curious than the extraordinary weight which is attached to the anonymous expression of political opinion. Partly by the illusion of the imagination, partly by the weight of emphatic assertion, a plural pronoun, conspicuous type, and continual repetition, unknown men are able, without exciting any surprise or sense of incongruity, to assume the language of the accredited representatives of the nation, and to rebuke, patronize, or insult its leading men with a tone of authority which would not be tolerated from the foremost statesmen of their time."

A remedy frequently suggested is signed editorials. Let the Great Unknown come out from behind his veil of anonymity, and drop his "plural of majesty." Then we should know him for the insignificant and negligible individual he is. It is true that some hesitating attempts of that kind have been made in this country, mostly in the baser journalism, but they have not succeeded. There is no reason to think that this practice will ever take root among us. It arose in France under conditions of rigorous press censorship, and really goes in spirit with the wish of government or society to limit that perfect freedom of discussion which anonymous journalism alone can enjoy. Legal responsibility is, of course, fixed in the editor and proprietors. Nor is the literary disguise, as a rule, of such great consequence, or so difficult to penetrate. Most editors would feel like making the same answer to an aggrieved person that Swift gave to one of his victims. In one of his short poems he threw some of his choicest vitriol upon one Bettesworth, a lawyer of considerable eminence, who in a rage went to Swift and demanded whether he was the author of that poem. The Dean's reply was: "Mr. Bettesworth, I was in my youth acquainted with great lawyers who, knowing my disposition to satire, advised me that, if any scoundrel or blockhead whom I had lampooned should ask, 'Are you the author of this paper?' I should tell him that I was not the author; and therefore I tell you, Mr. Bettesworth, that I am not the author of these lines."

But the real defense of impersonal journalism lies in the conception of a newspaper, not as an individual organ, but as a public institution. Walter Bagehot, in his *Physics and Politics*, uses the newspaper as a good illustration of an organism subduing everything to type. Individual style becomes blended in the common style. The excellent work of assistant editors is ascribed to their chief, just as his blunders are shouldered off upon them. It becomes impossible to dissect out the separate personalities which contribute to the making up of the whole. The paper represents, not one man's thought, but a body of opinion. Behind what is said each day stands a long tradition. Writers, reviewers, correspondents, clientele, add their mite, but it is little more than Burns's snowflake falling into the river. The great stream flows on. I would not minimize personality in journalism. It has counted enormously; it still counts. But the institutional, representative idea is now most telling. The play of individuality is much restricted; has to do more with minor things than great policies. John Stuart Mill, in a letter of 1863 to Motley, very well hit off what may be called the chance rôle of the individual in modern journalism: "The line it [the London *Times*] takes on any particular question is much more a matter of accident than is supposed. It is sometimes better than the public, and sometimes worse. It was better on the Competitive Examinations and on the Revised Educational Code, in each case owing to the accidental position of a particular man who happened to write on it—both which men I could name to you."

Wendell Phillips told of once taking a letter to the editor of a Boston paper, whom he knew, with a request that it be published. The editor read it over, and said, "Mr. Phillips, that is a very good and interesting letter, and I shall be glad to publish it; but I wish you would consent to strike out the last paragraph."

"Why," said Phillips, "that paragraph is the precise thing for which I wrote the whole letter. Without that it would be pointless."

"Oh, I see that," replied the editor; "and what you say in it is perfectly true,—the very children in the streets know that it is true. I fully agree with it all myself. Yet it is one of those things which it will not do to say publicly. However, if you insist upon it, I will publish the letter as it stands."

It was published the next morning, and along with it a short editorial reference to it, saying that a letter from Mr. Phillips would be found in another column, and that it was extraordinary that so keen a mind as his should have fallen into the palpable absurdity contained in the last paragraph.

The story suggests the harmful side of the interaction between press and public. It sometimes puts a great strain upon the intellectual honesty of the editor. He is doubtful how much truth his public will bear. His audience may seem to him, on occasions, minatory, as well as, on others, encouraging. So hard is it for the journalist to be sure, with Dr. Arnold, that the times will always bear what an honest man has to say. At this point, undoubtedly, we come upon the moral perils of the newspaper man. And when outsiders believe that he writes to order, or without conviction, they naturally hold a low view of his occupation.

Journalism, wrote Mrs. Mark Pattison in 1879, "harms those, even the most gifted, who continue in it after early life. They cannot honestly write the kind of thing required for their public if they are really striving to reach the highest level of thought and work possible to themselves." If this were always and absolutely true, little could be said for the Fourth Estate. We should all have to agree with James Smith, of *Rejected Addresses* fame:—

Hard is his lot who edits, thankless job!

A Sunday journal for the factious mob.

With bitter paragraph and caustic jest,

He gives to turbulence the day of rest,

Condemn'd this week rash rancor to instil,

Or thrown aside, the next, for one who will.

Alike undone, or if he praise or rail

(For this affects his safety, that his sale),

He sinks, alas, in luckless limbo set—

If loud for libel, and if dumb for debt.

The real libel, however, would be the assertion that the work of American journalism is done to any large extent in that spirit of the galley slave. With all its faults, it is imbued with the desire of being of public service. That is often overlaid by other motives—money-making, timeserving, place-hunting. But at the high demand of a great moral or political crisis, it will assert itself, and editors will be found as ready as their fellows to hazard their all for the common weal. To show what sort of fire may burn at the heart of the true journalist, I append a letter never before published:—

"NEW YORK, *April 23, 1867.*

"There is a man here named Barnard, on the bench of the Supreme Court. Some years ago he kept a gambling saloon in San Francisco, and was a notorious blackleg and *vaurien*. He came then to New York, plunged into the basest depths of city politics, and emerged Recorder. After two or three years he got by the same means to be a judge of the Supreme Court. His reputation is now of the very worst. He is unscrupulous, audacious, barefaced, and corrupt to the last degree. He not only takes bribes, but he does not even wait for them to be offered him. He sends for suitors, or rather for their counsel, and asks for the money as the price of his judgments. A more unprincipled scoundrel does not breathe. There is no way in which he does not prostitute his office, and in saying this I am giving you the unanimous opinion of the bar and the public. His appearance on the bench I consider literally an awful occurrence. Yet the press and bar are muzzled,—for that is what it comes to,—and this injurious scoundrel has actually got possession of the highest court in the State, and dares the Christian public to expose his villainy.

"If I were satisfied that, if the public knew all this, it would lie down under it, I would hand the *Nation* over to its creditors and take myself and my children out of the community. I will not believe that yet. I am about to say all I dare say—as yet—in the *Nation* to-morrow. Barnard is capable of ruining us, if he thought it worth his while, and could of course imprison me for contempt, if he took it into his head, and I should have no redress. You have no idea what a labyrinth of wickedness and chicane surrounds him. Moreover, I have no desire either for notoriety or martyrdom, and am in various ways not well fitted to take a stand against rascality on such a scale as this. But this I do think, that it is the duty of every honest man to do something. Barnard has now got possession of the courts, and if he can silence the press also, where is reform to come from?... I think some movement ought to be set on foot having for its object the hunting down of corrupt politicians, the exposure of jobs, the sharpening of the public conscience on the whole subject of political purity. If this cannot be done, the growing wealth will kill—not the nation, but the form of government without which, as you and I believe, the nation would be of little value to humanity."

This was written to Professor Charles Eliot Norton by the late Edwin Lawrence Godkin. The Barnard referred to was, of course, the infamous judge from whom, a few years later, the judicial robes were stripped. Mr. Godkin's attack upon him was, so far as I know, the first that was made in print. But the passion of indignation which glowed in that great journalist, with his willingness to hazard his own fortunes in the public behalf, only sets forth conspicuously what humbler members of the press feel as their truest motive and their noblest reward.

PRESS TENDENCIES AND DANGERS

BY OSWALD GARRISON VILLARD

The passing of the *Boston Journal*, in the eighty-fourth year of its age, by merger with the *Boston Herald* has rightly been characterized as a tragedy of journalism. Yet it is no more significant than the similar merger of the *Cleveland Plain Dealer* and the *Cleveland Leader*, or the *New York Press* and the *New York Sun*. All are in obedience to the drift toward consolidation which has been as marked in journalism as in other spheres of business activity—for this is purely a business matter. True, in the cases of the Sun and the *Press* Mr. Munsey's controlling motive was probably the desire to obtain the Associated Press service for the *Sun*, which he could have secured in no other way. But Mr. Munsey was not blind to the advantages of combining the circulation of the *Press* and the *Sun*, and has profited by it.

It is quite possible that there will be further consolidations in New York and Boston before long; at least conditions are ripe for them. Chicago has now only four morning newspapers, including the *Staats-Zeitung*, but one of these has an uncertain future before it. The *Herald* of that city is the net result of amalgamations which successively wiped out the *Record*, the *Times*, the *Chronicle*, and the *Inter-Ocean*. It is only a few years ago that the *Boston Traveler* and the *Evening Herald* were consolidated, and Philadelphia, Baltimore, New Orleans, Portland (Oregon), and Philadelphia are other cities in which there has been a reduction in the number of dailies.

In the main it is correct to say that the decreasing number of newspapers in our larger American cities is due to the enormously increased costs of maintaining great dailies. This has been found to limit the number which a given advertising territory will support. It is a fact, too, that there are few other fields of enterprise in which so many unprofitable enterprises are maintained. There is one penny daily in New York which has not paid a cent to its owners in twenty years; during that time its income has met its expenses only once. Another of our New York dailies loses between $400,000 and $500,000 a year, if well-founded report is correct, but the deficit is cheerfully met each year. It may be safely stated that scarcely half of our New York morning and evening newspapers return an adequate profit.

The most striking fact about the recent consolidations is that this leaves Cleveland with only one morning newspaper, the *Plain Dealer*. It is the sixth city in size in the United States, yet it has not appeared to be large enough to support both the *Plain Dealer* and the *Leader*, not even with the aid of what is called "foreign," or national, advertising, that is, advertising which originates outside of Cleveland. There are now many other cities in which the seeker after morning news is compelled to take it from one source only, whatever his political affiliations may be: in Indianapolis, from the *Star*; in Detroit, from the *Free Press*; in Toledo, from the *Times*; in Columbus, from the *State Journal*; in Scranton, from the *Republican*; in St. Paul, from the *Pioneer Press*; and in New Orleans, from the *Times-Picayune*. This circumstance comes as a good deal of a shock to those who fancy that at least the chief political parties should have their representative dailies in each city—for that is the old American tradition.

Turning to the State of Michigan, we find that the development has gone even further, for here are some sizable cities with no morning newspaper and but one in the evening field. In fourteen cities whose population has more than doubled during the last twenty-five years the number of daily newspapers printed in the English language has shrunk from 42 to only 23. In nine of these fourteen cities there is not a single morning newspaper; they have but one evening newspaper each to give them the news of the world, unless they are content to receive their news by mail from distant cities. On Sunday they are better off, for there are seven Sunday newspapers in these towns. In the five cities having more than one newspaper, there are six dailies that are thought to be unprofitable to their owners, and it is believed that, within a short time, the number of one-newspaper cities will grow to twelve, in which case Detroit and Grand Rapids will be the only cities with morning dailies. It is reported by competent witnesses that the one-newspaper towns are not only well content with this state of affairs, but that they actively resist any attempt to change the situation, the merchants in some cases banding together voluntarily to maintain the monopoly by refusing advertising to those wishing to start competition.

It is of course true that in the larger cities of the East there are other causes than the lack of advertising to account for the disappearance of certain newspapers. Many of them have deserved to perish because they were inefficiently managed or improperly edited. The *Boston Transcript* declares that the reason for the *Journal's* demise was lack "of that singleness and clearness of direction and purpose which alone establish confidence in and guarantee abiding support of a newspaper." If some of the Hearst newspapers may be cited as examples of successful journals that have neither clearness nor honesty of purpose, it is not to be questioned that a newspaper with clear-cut, vigorous personalities behind it is far more likely to survive than one that does not have them. But it does not help the situation to point out, as does the *Columbia* (S. C.) *State*, that "sentiment and passion" have been responsible for the launching of many of the newspaper wrecks; for often sentiment and the righteous passion of indignation have been responsible for the foundation of notable newspapers such as the *New York Tribune*, whose financial success was, for a time at least, quite notable. It is the danger that newspaper conditions, because of the enormously increased costs and this tendency to monopoly, may prevent people who are actuated by passion and sentiment from founding newspapers, which is causing many students of the situation much concern. What is to be the hope for the advocates of new-born and unpopular reforms if they cannot have a press of their own, as the Abolitionists and the founders of the Republican party set up theirs in a remarkably short time, usually with poverty-stricken bank accounts?

If no good American can read of cities having only one newspaper without concern,—since democracy depends largely upon the presenting of both sides of every issue,—it does not add any comfort to know that it would take millions to found a new paper, on a strictly business basis, in our largest cities. Only extremely wealthy men could undertake such a venture,—precisely as the rejuvenated *Chicago Herald* has been financed by a group of the city's wealthiest magnates,—and even then the success of the undertaking would be questionable if it were not possible to secure the Associated Press service for the newcomer.

The "journal of protest," it may be truthfully said, is to-day being confined, outside of the Socialistic press, to weeklies of varying types, of which the *Survey*, the *Public*, and the *St. Louis Mirror*, are examples; and scores of them fall by the wayside. The large sums necessary to establish a journal of opinion are being demonstrated by the *New Republic*. Gone is the day when a *Liberator* can be founded with a couple of hundred dollars as capital. The struggle of the *New York Call* to keep alive, and that of some of our Jewish newspapers, are clear proof that conditions to-day make strongly against those who are fired by passion and sentiment to give a new and radical message to the world.

True, there is still opportunity in small towns for editorial courage and ability; William Allen White has demonstrated that. But in the small towns the increased costs due to the war are being felt as keenly as in the larger cities. *Ayer's Newspaper Directory* shows a steady shrinkage during the last three years in the weeklies, semi-weeklies, tri-weeklies, and semi-monthlies, there being 300 less in 1916 than in 1914. There lies before me a list of 76 dailies and weeklies over which the funeral rites have been held since January 1, 1917; to some of them the government has administered the *coup de grace*. There are three Montreal journals among them, and a number of little German publications, together with the notorious *Appeal to Reason* and a couple of farm journals: 21 states are represented in the list, which is surely not complete.

Many dailies have sought to save themselves by increasing their price to two cents, as in Chicago, Pittsburg, Buffalo, and Philadelphia; and everywhere there has been a raising of mail-subscription and advertising rates, in an effort to offset the enormous and persistent rise in the cost of paper and labor. It is indisputable, however, that, if we are in for a long war, many of the weaker city dailies and the country dailies must go to the wall, just as there have been similar failures in every one of the warring nations of Europe.

Surveying the newspaper field as a whole, there has not been of late years a marked development of the tendency to group together a number of newspapers under one ownership in the manner of Northcliffe. Mr. Hearst, thanks be to fortune, has not added to his string lately; his group of *Examiners, Journals,* and *Americans* is popularly believed not to be making any large sums of money for him, because the weaker members offset the earnings of the prosperous ones, and there is reputed to be great managerial waste.[2] When Mr. Munsey buys another daily, he usually sells an unprosperous one or adds another grave to his private and sizable newspaper cemetery. The Scripps-McRae Syndicate, comprising some 22 dailies, has not added to its number since 1911.

2. Mr. Hearst acquired the *Boston Advertiser* in November 1917, shortly after this article was written.-ED.

In Michigan the Booth Brothers control six clean, independent papers, which, for the local reasons given above, exercise a remarkable influence. The situation in that state shows clearly how comparatively easy it would be for rich business men, with selfish or partisan purpose, to dominate public opinion there and poison the public mind against anything they disliked. It is a situation to cause much uneasiness when one looks into the more distant future and considers the distrust of the press because of a far-reaching belief that the large city newspaper, being a several-million-dollar affair, must necessarily have managers in close alliance with other men in great business enterprises,—the chamber of commerce, the merchants' association group,—and therefore wholly detached from the aspirations of the plain people.

Those who feel thus will be disturbed by another remarkable consolidation in the field of newspaper-making—the recent absorption of a large portion of the business of the American Press Association by the Western Newspaper Union. The latter now has an almost absolute monopoly in supplying "plate" and "ready to print" matter to the small daily newspapers and the country weeklies—"patent insides" is a more familiar term. The Western Newspaper Union to-day furnishes plate matter to nearly fourteen thousand newspapers—a stupendous number. In 1912 a United States court in Chicago forbade this very consolidation as one in restraint of trade; to-day it permits it because the great rise in the cost of plate matter, from four to seventeen cents a pound, seems to necessitate the extinction of the old competition and the establishment of a monopoly. The court was convinced that this field of newspaper enterprise will no longer support two rival concerns. An immense power which could be used to influence public opinion is thus placed in the hands of the officers of a money-making concern, for news matter is furnished as well as news photogravures.

Only the other day I heard of a boast that a laudatory article praising a certain astute Democratic politician had appeared in no less than 7,000 publications of the Union's clients. Who can estimate the value of such an advertisement? Who can deny the power enormously to influence rural public opinion for better or for worse? Who can deny that the very innocent aspect of such a publication makes it a particularly easy, as well as effective, way of conducting propaganda for better or for worse? So far it has been to the advantage of both the associations to carry the propaganda matter of the great political parties,—they deny any intentional propaganda of their own,—but one cannot help wondering whether this will always be the case, and whether there is not danger that some day this tremendous power may be used in the interest of some privileged undertaking or some self-seeking politicians. At least, it would seem as if our law-makers, already so critical of the press, might be tempted to declare the Union a public-service corporation and, therefore, bound to transmit all legitimate news offered to it.

In the strictly news-gathering field there is probably a decrease of competition at hand. The Allied governments abroad and our courts at home have struck a hard blow at the Hearst news-gathering concern, the International News Association, which has been excluded from England and her colonies, Italy, and France, and has recently been convicted of news-stealing and falsification on the complaint of the Associated Press. The case is now pending an appeal in the Supreme Court, when the decision of the lower court may be reversed. If, as a result of these proceedings, the association eventually goes out of business, it will be to the public advantage, that is, if honest, uncolored news is a desideratum. This will give to the Associated Press—the only press association which is altogether coöperative and makes no profit by the sale of its news—a monopoly in the morning field. If this lack of organized competition—it is daily competing with the special correspondents of all the great newspapers—has its drawbacks, it is certainly reassuring that throughout this unprecedented war the Associated Press has brought over an enormous volume of news with a minimum of just complaints as to the fidelity of that news—save that it is, of course, rigidly censored in every country, and particularly in passing through England. It has met vast problems with astounding success.

But it is in considerable degree dependent upon foreign news agencies, like Reuter's, the Havas Agency in France, the Wolf Agency in Germany, and others, including the official Russian agency. Where these are not frankly official agencies, they are the creatures of their governments and have been either deliberately used by them to mislead others, and particularly foreign nations, or to conceal the truth from their own subjects. As Dean Walter Williams, of the University of Missouri School of Journalism, has lately pointed out, if there is one thing needed after this war, it is the abolition of these official and semi-official agencies with their frequent stirring up of racial and international hatreds. A free press after the war is as badly needed as freedom of the seas and freedom from conscienceless kaisers and autocrats.

At home, when the war is over, there is certain to be as relatively striking a slant toward social reorganization, reform, and economic revolution as had taken place in Russia, and is taking place in England as related by the *London Times*. When that day comes here, the deep smouldering distrust of our press will make itself felt. Our Fourth Estate is to have its day of overhauling and of being muckraked. The perfectly obvious hostility toward newspapers of the present Congress, as illustrated by its attempt to impose a direct and special tax upon them; its rigorous censorship in spite of the profession's protest of last spring; and the heavy additional postage taxes levied upon some classes of newspapers and the magazines, goes far to prove this. But even more convincing is the dissatisfaction with the metropolitan press in every reform camp and among the plain people. It has grown tremendously because the masses are, rightly or wrongly, convinced that the newspapers with heavy capital investments are a "capitalistic" press and, therefore, opposed to their interests.

This feeling has grown all the more because so many hundreds of thousands who were opposed to our going to war and are opposed to it now still feel that their views—as opposed to those of the prosperous and intellectual classes—were not voiced in the press last winter. They know that their position to-day is being misrepresented as disloyal or pro-German by the bulk of the newspapers. In this situation many are turning to the Socialistic press as their one refuge. They, and multitudes who have gradually been losing faith in the reliability of our journalism, for one reason or another, can still be won back if we journalists will but slake their intense thirst for reliable, trustworthy news, for opinions free from class bias and not always set forth from the point of view of the well-to-do and the privileged. How to respond to this need is the greatest problem before the American press. Meanwhile, on the business side we drift toward consolidation on a resistless economic current, which foams past numberless rocks, and leads no man knows whither.

THE WANING POWER OF THE PRESS

BY FRANCIS E. LEUPP

I

After the last ballot had been cast and counted in the recent mayoralty contest in New York, the successful candidate paid his respects to the newspapers which had opposed him. This is equivalent to saying that he paid them to the whole metropolitan press; for every great daily newspaper except one had done its best to defeat him, and that one had given him only a left-handed support.[3] The comments of the mayor-elect, although not ill-tempered, led up to the conclusion that in our common-sense generation nobody cares what the newspapers say.

3. The conditions here referred to in the election of Mayor Gaynor in 1909 were almost duplicated in 1917, when Mayor Mitchel was defeated for reëlection, although all the New York newspapers, except the two Hearst papers and the Socialist daily, supported him.—ED.

Unflattering as such a verdict may be, probably a majority of the community, if polled as a jury, would concur in it. The airy dismissal of some proposition as "mere newspaper talk" is heard at every social gathering, till one who was brought up to regard the press as a mighty factor in modern civilization is tempted to wonder whether it has actually lost the power it used to wield among us. The answer seems to me to depend on whether we are considering direct or indirect effects. A newspaper exerts its most direct influence through its definite interpretation of current events. Its indirect influence radiates from the amount and character of the news it prints, the particular features it accentuates, and its method of presenting these. Hence it is always possible that its direct influence may be trifling, while its indirect influence is large; its direct influence harmless, but its indirect influence pernicious; or *vice versa*.

A distinction ought to be made here like that which we make between credulity and nerves. The fact that a dwelling in which a mysterious murder has been committed may for years thereafter go begging in vain for a tenant, does not mean that a whole cityful of fairly intelligent people are victims of the ghost obsession; but it does mean that no person enjoys being reminded of midnight assassination every time he crosses his own threshold; for so persistent a companionship with a discomforting thought is bound to depress the best nervous system ever planted in a human being.

So the constant iteration of any idea in a daily newspaper will presently capture public attention, whether the idea be good or bad, sensible or foolish. Though the influence of the press, through its ability to keep certain subjects always before its readers, has grown with its growth in resources and patronage, its hold on popular confidence has unquestionably been loosened during the last forty or fifty years. To Mayor Gaynor's inference, as to most generalizations of that sort, we need not attach serious importance. The interplay of so many forces in a political campaign makes it impracticable to separate the influence of the newspapers from the rest, and either hold it solely accountable for the result, or pass it over as negligible; for if we tried to formulate any sweeping rules, we should find it hard to explain the variegated records of success and defeat among newspaper favorites. But it may be worth while to inquire why an institution so full of potentialities as a free press does not produce more effect than it does, and why so many of its leading writers today find reason to deplore the altered attitude of the people toward it.

Not necessarily in their order of importance, but for convenience of consideration, I should list the causes for this change about as follows: the transfer of both properties and policies from personal to impersonal control; the rise of the cheap magazine; the tendency to specialization in all forms of public instruction; the fierceness of competition in the newspaper business; the demand for larger capital, unsettling the former equipoise between counting-room and editorial room; the invasion of newspaper offices by the universal mania of hurry; the development of the news-getting at the expense of the news-interpreting function; the tendency to remould narratives of fact so as to confirm office-made policies; the growing disregard of decency in the choice of news to be specially exploited; and the scant time now spared by men of the world for reading journals of general intelligence.

In the old-style newspaper, in spite of the fact that the editorial articles were usually anonymous, the editor's name appeared among the standing notices somewhere in every issue, or was so well known to the public that we talked about "what Greeley thought" of this or that, or wondered "whether Bryant was going to support" a certain ticket, or shook our heads over the latest sensational screed in "Bennett's paper." The identity of such men was clear in the minds of a multitude of readers who might sometimes have been puzzled to recall the title of the sheet edited by each. We knew their private histories and their idiosyncrasies; they were to us no mere abstractions on the one hand, or wire-worked puppets on the other, but living, moving, sentient human beings; and our acquaintance with them enabled us, as we believed, to locate fairly well their springs of thought and action. Indeed, their very foibles sometimes furnished our best exegetical key to their writings.

When a politician whom Bryant had criticised threatened to pull his nose, and Bryant responded by stalking ostentatiously three times around the bully at their next meeting in public, the readers of the *Evening Post* did not lose faith in the editor because he was only human, but guessed about how far to discount future utterances of the paper with regard to his antagonist. When Bennett avowed his intention of advertising the *Herald* without the expenditure of a dollar, by attacking his enemies so savagely as to goad them into a physical assault, everybody understood the motives behind the warfare on both sides, and attached to it only the significance that the facts warranted. Knowing Dana's affiliations, no one mistook the meaning of the *Sun's* dismissal of General Hancock as "a good man, weighing two hundred and fifty pounds, but ... not Samuel J. Tilden." And Greeley's retort to Bryant, "You lie, villain! willfully, wickedly, basely lie!" and his denunciation of Bennett as a "low-mouthed, blatant, witless, brutal scoundrel," though not preserved as models of amenity for the emulation of budding editors, were felt to be balanced by the delicious frankness of the *Tribune's* announcement of "the dissolution of the political firm of Seward, Weed & Greeley by the withdrawal of the junior partner."

With all its faults, that era of personal journalism had some rugged virtues. In referring to it, I am reminded of a remark made to me, years ago, by the oldest editor then living,—so old that he had employed Weed as a journeyman, and refused to hire Greeley as a tramp printer,—that "in the golden age of our craft, every editor wore his conscience on his arm, and carried his dueling weapon in his hand, walked always in the light where the whole world could see him, and was prepared to defend his published opinions with his life if need be." Without going to that extreme, it is easy to sympathize with the veteran's view that a man of force, who writes nothing for which he is not ready to be personally responsible, commands more respect from the mass of his fellows than one who shields himself behind a rampart of anonymity, and voices only the sentiments of a profit-seeking corporation.

Of course, the transfer of our newspapers from personal to corporate ownership and control was not a matter of preference, but a practical necessity. The expense of modernizing the mechanical equipment alone imposed a burden which few newspaper proprietors were able to carry unaided. Add to that the cost of an ever-expanding news-service, and the higher salaries demanded by satisfactory employees in all departments, and it is hardly wonderful that one private owner after another gave up his single-handed struggle against hopeless financial odds, and sought aid from men of larger means. Partnership relations involve so many risks, and are so hard to shift in an emergency, that resort was had to the form of a corporation, which afforded the advantage of a limited liability, and enabled a shareholder to dispose of his interest if he tired of the game. Since the dependence of a newspaper on the favor of an often whimsical public placed it among the least attractive forms of investment, even under these well-guarded conditions, the capitalists who were willing to take large blocks of stock were usually men with political or speculative ends to gain, to which they could make a newspaper minister by way of compensating them for the hazards they faced.

These newcomers were not idealists, like the founders and managers of most of the important journals of an earlier period. They were men of keen commercial instincts, evidenced by the fact that they had accumulated wealth. They naturally looked at everything through the medium of the balance-sheet. Here was a paper with a fine reputation, but uncertain or disappearing profits; it must be strengthened, enlarged, and made to pay. Principles? Yes, principles were good things, but we must not ride even good things to death. The noblest cause in creation cannot be promoted by a defunct newspaper, and to keep its champion alive there must be a net cash income. The circulation must be pushed, and the advertising patronage increased. More circulation can be secured only by keeping the public stirred up. Employ private detectives to pursue the runaway husband, and bring him back to his wife; organize a marine expedition to find the missing ship; send a reporter into the Soudan to interview the beleaguered general whose own government is powerless to reach him with an army. Blow the trumpet, and make ringing announcements every day. If nothing new is to be had, refurbish something so old that people have forgotten it, and spread it over lots of space. Who will know the difference?

What one newspaper did, that others were forced to do or be distanced in the competition. It all had its effect. A craving for excitement was first aroused in the public, and then satisfied by the same hand that had aroused it. Nobody wished to be behind the times, so circulations were swelled gradually to tenfold their old dimensions. Rivalry was worked up among the advertisers in their turn, till a half-page in a big newspaper commanded a price undreamed of a few years before. Thus one interest was made to foster another, each increase of income involving also an increase of cost, and each additional outlay bringing fresh returns. In such a race for business success, with such forces behind the runners, can we marvel at the subsidence of ideals which in the days of individual control and slower gait were uppermost? With the capitalists' plans to promote, and powerful advertisers to conciliate by emphasizing this subject or discreetly ignoring that, is not the wonder rather that the moral quality of our press has not fallen below its present standard?

Even in our day we occasionally find an editor who pays his individual tribute to the old conception of personal responsibility by giving his surname to his periodical or signing his leading articles himself. In such newspaper ventures as Mr. Bryan and Mr. La Follette have launched within a few years, albeit their motives are known to be political and partisan, more attention is attracted by one of their deliverances than by a score of impersonal preachments. Mr. Hearst, the high priest of sensational journalism, though not exploiting his own authority in the same way, has always taken pains to advertise the individual work of such lieutenants as Bierce and Brisbane; and he, like Colonel Taylor of Boston, early opened his editorial pages to contributions from distinguished authors outside of his staff, with their signatures attached. A few editors I have known who, in whatever they wrote with their own hands, dropped the diffusive "we" and adopted the more direct and intimate "I." These things go to show that even journalists who have received most of their training in the modern school appreciate that trait in our common human nature which prompts us to pay more heed to a living voice than to a talking-machine.

II

The importance of a responsible personality finds further confirmation in the evolution of the modern magazine. From being what its title indicates, a place of storage for articles believed to have some permanent value, the magazine began to take on a new character about twenty years ago. While preserving its distinct identity and its originality, it leaped boldly into the newspaper arena, and sought its topics in the happenings of the day, regardless of their evanescence. It raised a corps of men and women who might otherwise have toiled in obscurity all their lives, and gave them a chance to become authorities on questions of immediate interest, till they are now recognized as constituting a limited but highly specialized profession. One group occupied itself with trusts and trust magnates; another with politicians whose rise had been so meteoric as to suggest a romance behind it; another with the inside history of international episodes; another with new religious movements and their leaders, and so on.

What was the result? The public following which the newspaper editors used to command when they did business in the open, but which was falling away from their anonymous successors, attached itself promptly to the magazinists. The citizen interested in insurance reform turned eagerly to all that emanated from the group in charge of that topic; whoever aspired to take part in the social uplift bought every number of every periodical in which the contributions of another group appeared; the hater of monopoly paid a third group the same compliment. What was more, the readers pinned their faith to their favorite writers, and quoted Mr. Steffens and Miss Tarbell and Mr. Baker on the specialty each had taken, with much the same freedom with which they might have quoted Darwin on plant-life, or Edison on electricity. If any anonymous editor ventured to question the infallibility of one of these prophets of the magazine world, the common multitude wasted no thought on the merits of the issue, but sided at once with the teacher whom they knew at least by name, against the critic whom they knew not at all. The uncomplimentary assumption as to the latter always seemed to be that, as only a subordinate part of a big organism, he was speaking, not from his heart, but from his orders; and that he must have some sinister design in trying to discredit an opponent who was not afraid to stand out and face his fire.

Apropos, let us not fail to note the constant trend, of recent years, toward specialization in every department of life and thought. There was a time when a pronouncement from certain men on nearly any theme would be accepted by the public, not only with the outward respect commanded by persons of their social standing, but with a large measure of positive credence. One who enjoyed a general reputation for scholarship might set forth his views this week on a question of archæology, next week on the significance of the latest earthquake, and a week later on the new canals on the planet Mars, with the certainty that each outgiving would affect public opinion to a marked degree; whereas nowadays we demand that the most distinguished members of our learned faculty stick each to his own hobby; the antiquarian to the excavations, the seismologist to the tremors of our planet, the astronomer to our remoter colleagues of the solar system. It is the same with our writers on political, social, and economic problems. Whereas the old-time editor was expected to tell his constituency what to think on any subject called up by the news overnight, it is now taken for granted that even news must be classified and distributed between specialists for comment; and the very sense that only one writer is trusted to handle any particular class of topics inspires a desire in the public to know who that writer is before paying much attention to his opinions.

The intense competition between newspapers covering the same field sometimes leads to consequences which do not strengthen the esteem of the people at large for the press at large. Witness the controversy which arose over the conflicting claims of Commander Peary and Dr. Cook as the original discoverer of the North Pole. One newspaper syndicate having, at large expense, procured a narrative directly from the pen of Cook, and another accomplished a like feat with Peary, to which could "we, the people," look for an unbiased opinion on the matters in dispute? An admission by either that its star contributor could trifle with the truth was equivalent to throwing its own exploit into bankruptcy. So each was bound to stand by the claimant with whom it had first identified itself, and fight the battle out like an attorney under retainer; and what started as a serious contest of priority in a scientific discovery threatened to end as a wrangle over a newspaper "beat."

Then, too, we must reckon with the progressive acceleration of the pace of our twentieth-century life generally. Where we walked in the old times, we run in these; where we ambled then, we gallop now. It is the age of electric power, high explosives, articulated steel frames, in the larger world; of the long-distance telephone, the taxicab, and the card-index, in the narrower. The problem of existence is reduced to terms of time-measurement, with the detached lever substituted for the pendulum because it produces a faster tick.

What is the effect of all this on the modernized newspaper? It must be first on the ground at every activity, foreseen or unforeseeable, as a matter of course. Its reporter must get off his "story" in advance of all his rivals. Never mind strict accuracy of detail—effect is the main thing; he is writing, not for expert accountants, or professional statisticians, or analytic philosophers, but for the public; and what the public wants is, not dry particulars, but color, vitality, heat. Pictures being a quicker medium of communication with the reader's mind than printed text, nine-tenths of our daily press is illustrated, and the illustrations of distant events are usually turned out by artists in the home office from verbal descriptions. What signifies it if only three cars went off the broken bridge, and the imaginative draftsman put five into his picture because he could not wait for the dispatch of correction which almost always follows the lurid "scoop"? Who is harmed if the telegram about the suicide reads "shots" instead of "stabs," and the artist depicts the self-destroyer clutching a smoking pistol instead of a dripping dirk?

It is the province of the champion of the up-to-date cult to minimize the importance of detail. The purpose of the picture, he argues, is to stamp a broad impression instantaneously on the mind, and thus spare it the more tedious process of reading. And if one detail too many is put in, or one omitted which ought to have been there, whoever is sufficiently interested to read the text will discover the fault, and whoever is not will give it no further thought anyway. As to the descriptive matter, suppose it does contain errors? The busy man of our day does not read his newspaper with the same solemn intent with which he reads history. What he asks of it is a lightning-like glimpse of the world which will show him how far it has moved in the last twelve hours; and he will not pause to complain of a few deviations from the straight line of truth, especially if it would have taken more than the twelve hours to rectify them.

This would perhaps be good logic if the pure-food law were broadened in scope so as to apply to mental pabulum, and every concocter of newspaper stories and illustrations were compelled to label his adulterated products. Then the consumer who does not object to a diet of mixed fact and falsehood, accuracy and carelessness, so long as the compound is so seasoned as to tickle his palate, could have his desire, while his neighbor who wishes an honest article or nothing at all could have his also. As it is, with no distinguishing marks, we are liable to buy one thing and get another.

The new order of "speed before everything" has brought about its changes at both ends of a newspaper staff. The editorial writer who used to take a little time to look into the ramifications of a topic before reducing his opinions to writing, feels humiliated if an event occurs on which he cannot turn off a few comments at sight; but he has still a refuge in such modifying clauses as "in the light of the meagre details now before us," or "as it appears at this writing," or "in spite of the absence of full particulars, which may later change the whole aspect of affairs."

No such covert offers itself to the news-getter in the open field. What he says must be definite, outright, unqualified, or the blue pencil slashes remorselessly through his "it is suspected," or "according to a rumor which cannot be traced to its original source." What business has he to "suspect"? He is hired to know. For what, pray, is the newspaper paying him, if not for tracing rumors to their original source; and further still, if so instructed? He is there to be, not a thinker, but a worker; a human machine like a steam potato-digger, which, supplied with the necessary energizing force from behind, drives its prods under nature's mantle, and grubs out the succulent treasures she is trying to conceal.

III

Nowhere is the change more patent than in the department of special correspondence. At an important point like Washington, for instance, the old corps of writers were men of mature years, most of whom had passed an apprenticeship in the editorial chair, and still held a semi-editorial relation to the newspapers they represented. They had studied political history and economics, social philosophy, and kindred subjects, as a preparation for their life-work, and were full of a wholesome sense of responsibility to the public as well as to their employers. Poore, Nelson, Boynton, and others of their class, were known by name, and regarded as authorities, in the communities to which they daily ministered. They were thoughtful workers as well as enterprising. They went for their news to the fountain-head, instead of dipping it out of any chance pool by the wayside. When they sent in to their home offices either fact or prophecy, they accompanied it with an interpretation which both editors and public knew to be no mere feat in lightning guesswork; and the fame which any of them prized more than a long calendar of "beats" and "exclusives" was that which would occasionally move a worsted competitor to confess, "I missed that news; but if —— sent it out, it is true."

When, in the later eighties, the new order came, it came with a rush. The first inkling of it was a notice received, in the middle of one busy night, by a correspondent who had been faithfully serving a prominent Western newspaper for a dozen years, to turn over his bureau to a young man who up to that time had been doing local reporting on its home staff. Transfers of other bureaus followed fast. A few were left, and still remain, undisturbed in personnel or character of work. Here and there, too, an old-fashioned correspondent was retained, but retired to an emeritus post, with the privilege of writing a signed letter when the spirit moved him; while a nimbler-footed successor assumed titular command and sent the daily dispatches. The bald fact was that the newspaper managers had bowed to the hustling humor of the age. They no longer cared to serve journalistic viands, which required deliberate mastication, to patrons who clamored for a quick lunch. So they passed on to their representatives at a distance the same injunction they were incessantly pressing upon their reporters at home: "Get the news, and send it while it is hot. Don't wait to tell us what it means or what it points to; we can do our own ratiocinating."

Is the public a loser by this obscuration of the correspondent's former function? I believe so. His appeal is no longer put to the reader directly: he becomes the mere tool of the newspaper, which in its turn furnishes to the reader such parts of his and other communications as it chooses, and in such forms as best suit its ulterior purposes. Doubtless this conduces to a more perfect administrative coördination in the staff at large, but it greatly weakens the correspondent's sense of personal responsibility. Poore had his constituency, Boynton had his, Nelson had his. None of these men would, under any conceivable stress of competition, have wittingly misled the group of readers he had attached to himself; nor would one of them have tolerated any tampering in the home office with essential matters in a contribution to which he had signed his name. Indeed, so well was this understood that I never heard of anybody's trying to tamper with them. It occasionally happened that the correspondent set forth a view somewhat at variance with that expressed on the editorial page of the same paper; but each party to this disagreement respected the other, and the public was assumed to be capable of making its own choice between opposing opinions clearly stated. A special virtue of the plan of independent correspondence lay in the opportunity it often afforded the habitual reader of a single newspaper to get at least a glance at more than one side of a public question.

Among the conspicuous fruits of the new régime is the direction sometimes sent to a correspondent to "write down" this man or "write up" that project. He knows that it is a case of obey orders or resign, and it brings to the surface all the Hessian he may have in his blood. If he is enough of a casuist, he will try to reconcile good conscience with worldly wisdom by picturing himself as a soldier commanded to do something of which he does not approve. Disobedience at the post of duty is treachery; resignation in the face of an unwelcome billet is desertion. So he does what he is bidden, though it may be at the cost of his self-respect and the esteem of others whose kind opinion he values. I have had a young correspondent come to me for information about something under advisement at the White House, and apologize for not going there himself by showing me a note from his editor telling him to "give the President hell." As he had always been treated with courtesy at the White House, he had not the hardihood to go there while engaged in his campaign of abuse.

Another, who had been intimate with a member of the administration then in power, was suddenly summoned one day to a conference with the publisher of his paper. He went in high spirits, believing that the invitation must mean at least a promotion in rank or an increase of salary. He returned crestfallen. Several days afterward he revealed to me in confidence that the paper had been unsuccessfully seeking some advertising controlled by his friend, and that the publisher had offered him one thousand dollars for a series of articles—anonymous, if he preferred—exposing the private weaknesses of the eminent man, and giving full names, dates, and other particulars as to a certain unsavory association in which he was reported to find pleasure! Still another brought me a dispatch he had prepared, requesting me to look it over and see whether it contained anything strictly libelous. It proved to be a forecast of the course of the Secretary of the Treasury in a financial crisis then impending. "Technically speaking," I said, after reading it, "there is plenty of libelous material in this, for it represents the Secretary as about to do something which, to my personal knowledge, he has never contemplated, and which would stamp him as unfit for his position if he should attempt it. But as a matter of fact he will ignore your story, as he is putting into type to-day a circular which is to be made public to-morrow, telling what his plan really is, and that will authoritatively discredit you."

"Thank you," he answered, rather stiffly. "I have my orders to pitch into the Secretary whenever I get a chance. I shall send this to-day, and to-morrow I can send another saying that my exclusive disclosures forced him to change his programme at the last moment."

These are sporadic cases, I admit, yet they indicate a mischievous tendency; just as each railway accident is itself sporadic, but too frequent fatalities from a like cause on the same line point to something wrong in the management of the road. It is not necessary to call names on the one hand, or indulge in wholesale denunciation on the other, in order to indicate the extremes to which the current pace in journalism must inevitably lead if kept up. The broadest-minded and most honorable men in our calling realize the disagreeable truth. A few of the great newspapers, too, have the courage to cling still to the old ideals, both in their editorial attitude and in their instructions to their news-gatherers. Possibly their profits are smaller for their squeamishness; but that the better quality of their patronage makes up in a measure for its lesser quantity, is evident to any one familiar with the advertising business. Moreover, in the character of its employees and in the zeal and intelligence of their service, a newspaper conducted on the higher plane possesses an asset which cannot be appraised in dollars and cents. Of one such paper a famous man once said to me, "I disagree with half its political views; I am regarded as a personal enemy by its editor; but I read it religiously every day, and it is the only daily that enters the front door of my home. It is a paper written by gentlemen for gentlemen; and, though it exasperates me often, it never offends my nostrils with the odors of the slums."

This last remark leads to another consideration touching the relaxed hold of the press on public confidence: I refer to the topics treated in the news columns, and the manner of their presentation. Its importance is attested by the sub-titles or mottoes adopted by several prominent newspapers, emphasizing their appeal to the family as a special constituency. In spite of the intense individualism, the reciprocal independence of the sexes, and the freedom from the trammels of feudal tradition of which we Americans boast, the social unit in this country is the family. Toward it a thousand lines of interest converge, from it a thousand lines of influence flow. Public opinion is unconsciously moulded by it, for the atmosphere of the home follows the father into his office, the son into his college, the daughter into her intimate companionships. The newspaper, therefore, which keeps the family in touch with the outside world, though it may have to be managed with more discretion than one whose circulation is chiefly in the streets, finds its compensation in its increased radius of influence of the subtler sort. For such a field, nothing is less fit than the noisome domestic scandals and the gory horrors which fill so much of the space in newspapers of the lowest rank, and which in these later years have made occasional inroads into some of a higher grade. Unfortunately, these occasional inroads do more to damage the general standing of the press than the habitual revel in vulgarity. For a newspaper which frankly avows itself unhampered by niceties of taste can be branded and set aside as belonging in the impossible category; whereas, when one with a clean exterior and a reputation for respectability proves unworthy, its faithlessness arouses in the popular mind a distrust of all its class.

And yet, whatever we may say of the modern press on its less commendable side, we are bound to admit that newspapers, like governments, fairly reflect the people they serve. Charles Dudley Warner once went so far as to say that no matter how objectionable the character of a paper may be, it is always a trifle better than the patrons on whom it relies for its support. I suspect that Mr. Warner's comparison rested on the greater frankness of the bad paper, which, by very virtue of its mode of appeal, is bound to make a brave parade of its worst qualities; whereas the reader who is loudest in proclaiming in public his repugnance for horrors, and his detestation of scandals, may in private be buying daily the sheet which peddles both most shamelessly.

This sort of conventional hypocrisy among the common run of people is easier to forgive than the same thing among the cultivated few whom we accept as mentors. I stumbled upon an illuminating incident about five years ago which I cannot forbear recalling here. A young man just graduated from college, where he had attracted some attention by the cleverness of his pen, was invited to a position on the staff of the *New York Journal*. Visiting a leading member of the college faculty to say farewell, he mentioned this compliment with not a little pride. In an instant the professor was up in arms, with an earnest protest against his handicapping his whole career by having anything to do with so monstrous an exponent of yellow journalism. The lad was deeply moved by the good man's outburst, and went home sorrowful. After a night's sleep on it, he resolved to profit by the admonition, and accordingly called upon the editor, and asked permission to withdraw his tentative acceptance. In the explanation which followed he inadvertently let slip the name of his adviser. He saw a cynical smile cross the face of Mr. Hearst, who summoned a stenographer, and in his presence dictated a letter to the professor, requesting a five-hundred-word signed article for the next Sunday's issue and inclosing a check for two hundred and fifty dollars. On Sunday the ingenuous youth beheld the article in a conspicuous place on the *Journal's* editorial page, with the professor's full name appended in large capitals.

We have already noted some of the effects produced on the press by the hurry-skurry of our modern life. Quite as significant are sundry phenomena recorded by Dr. Walter Dill Scott as the result of an inquiry into the reading habits of two thousand representative business and professional men in a typical American city. Among other things, he discovered that most of them spent not to exceed fifteen minutes a day on their newspapers. As some spent less, and some divided the time between two or three papers, the average period devoted to any one paper could safely be placed at from five to ten minutes. The admitted practice of most of the group was to look at the headlines, the table of contents, and the weather reports, and then apparently at some specialty in which they were individually interested. The editorial articles seem to have offered them few attractions, but news items of one sort or another engaged seventy-five per cent of their attention.

In an age as skeptical as ours, there is nothing astonishing in the low valuation given, by men of a class competent to do their own thinking, to anonymous opinion; but it will strike many as strange that this class takes no deeper interest in the news of the day. The trained psychologist may find it worth while to study out here the relation of cause and effect. Does the ordinary man of affairs show so scant regard for his newspaper because he no longer believes half it tells him, or only because his mind is so absorbed in matters closer at hand, and directly affecting his livelihood? Have the newspapers perverted the public taste with sensational surprises till it can no longer appreciate normal information normally conveyed?

Professor Münsterberg would doubtless have told us that the foregoing statistics simply justify his charge against Americans as a people; that we have gone leaping and gasping through life till we have lost the faculty of mental concentration, and hence that few of us can read any more. Whatever the explanation, the central fact has been duly recognized by all the yellow journals, and by some also which have not yet passed beyond the cream-colored stage. The "scare heads" and exaggerated type which, as a lure for purchasers, filled all their needs a few years ago, are no longer regarded as sufficient, but have given way to startling bill-board effects, with huge headlines, in block-letter and vermilion ink, spread across an entire front page.

The worst phase of this whole business, however, is one which does not appear on the surface, but which certainly offers food for serious reflection. The point of view from which all my criticisms have been made is that of the citizen of fair intelligence and education. It is he who has been weaned from his faith in the organ of opinion which satisfied his father, till he habitually sneers at "mere newspaper talk"; it is he who has descended from reading to simply skimming the news, and who consciously suffers from the errors which adulterate, and the vulgarity which taints, that product. But there is another element in the community which has not his well-sharpened instinct for discrimination; which can afford to buy only the cheapest, and is drawn toward the lowest, daily prints; which, during the noon hour and at night, finds time to devour all the tenement tragedies, all the palace scandals, and all the incendiary appeals designed to make the poor man think that thrift is robbery. Over that element we find the vicious newspaper still exercising an enormous sway; and, admitting that so large a proportion of the outwardly reputable press has lost its hold upon the better class of readers, what must we look for as the resultant of two such unbalanced forces?

Not a line of these few pages has been written in a carping, much less in a pessimistic spirit. I love the profession in whose practice I passed the largest and happiest part of my life; but the very pride I feel in its worthy achievements makes me, perhaps, the more sensitive to its shortcomings as these reveal themselves to an unprejudiced scrutiny. The limits of this article as to both space and scope forbid my following its subject into some inviting by-paths: as, for instance, the distinction to be observed between initiative and support in comparing the influence of the modern newspaper with that of its ancestor of a half-century ago. I am sorry, also, to put forth so many strictures without furnishing a constructive sequel. It would be interesting, for example, to weigh such possibilities as an endowed newspaper which should do for the press, as a protest against its offenses of deliberation and its faults of haste and carelessness, what an endowed theatre might do for the rescue of the stage from a condition of chronic inanity. But it must remain for a more profound philosopher, whose function is to specialize in opinion rather than to generalize in comment, to show what remedies are practicable for the disorders which beset the body of our modern journalism.

NEWSPAPER MORALS

BY H. L. MENCKEN

I

Aspiring, toward the end of my nonage, to the black robes of a dramatic critic, I took counsel with an ancient whose service went back to the days of *Our American Cousin*, asking him what qualities were chiefly demanded by the craft.

"The main idea," he told me frankly, "is to be interesting, to write a good story. All else is dross. Of course, I am not against accuracy, fairness, information, learning. If you want to read Lessing and Freytag, Hazlitt and Brunetière, go read them: they will do you no harm. It is also useful to know something about Shakespeare. But unless you can make people *read* your criticisms, you may as well shut up your shop. And the only way to make them read you is to give them something exciting."

"You suggest, then," I ventured, "a certain—ferocity?"

"I do," replied my venerable friend. "Read George Henry Lewes, and see how *he* did it—sometimes with a bladder on a string, usually with a meat-axe. Knock somebody on the head every day—if not an actor, then the author, and if not the author, then the manager. And if the play and the performance are perfect, then excoriate someone who doesn't think so—a fellow critic, a rival manager, the unappreciative public. But make it hearty; make it hot! The public would rather be the butt itself than have no butt in the ring. That is Rule Number 1 of American psychology—and of English, too, but more especially of American. You must give a good show to get a crowd, and a good show means one with slaughter in it."

Destiny soon robbed me of my critical shroud, and I fell into a long succession of less æsthetic newspaper berths, from that of police reporter to that of managing editor, but always the advice of my ancient counselor kept turning over and over in my memory, and as chance offered I began to act upon it, and whenever I acted upon it I found that it worked. What is more, I found that other newspaper men acted upon it too, some of them quite consciously and frankly, and others through a veil of self-deception, more or less diaphanous. The primary aim of all of them, no less when they played the secular Iokanaan than when they played the mere newsmonger, was to please the crowd, to give a good show; and the way they set about giving that good show was by first selecting a deserving victim, and then putting him magnificently to the torture.

This was their method when they were performing for their own profit only, when their one motive was to make the public read their paper; but it was still their method when they were battling bravely and unselfishly for the public good, and so discharging the highest duty of their profession. They lightened the dull days of midsummer by pursuing recreant aldermen with bloodhounds and artillery, by muckraking unsanitary milk-dealers, or by denouncing Sunday liquor-selling in suburban parks—and they fought constructive campaigns for good government in exactly the same gothic, melodramatic way. Always their first aim was to find a concrete target, to visualize their cause in some definite and defiant opponent. And always their second aim was to shell that opponent until he dropped his arms and took to ignominious flight. It was not enough to maintain and to prove: it was necessary also to pursue and overcome, to lay a specific somebody low, to give the good show aforesaid.

Does this confession of newspaper practice involve a libel upon the American people? Perhaps it does—on the theory, let us say, that the greater the truth, the greater the libel. But I doubt if any reflective newspaper man, however lofty his professional ideals, will ever deny any essential part of that truth. He knows very well that a definite limit is set, not only upon the people's capacity for grasping intellectual concepts, but also upon their capacity for grasping moral concepts. He knows that it is necessary, if he would catch and inflame them, to state his ethical syllogism in the homely terms of their habitual ethical thinking. And he knows that this is best done by dramatizing and vulgarizing it, by filling it with dynamic and emotional significance, by translating all argument for a principle into rage against a man.

In brief, he knows that it is hard for the plain people to *think* about a thing, but easy for them to *feel*. Error, to hold their attention, must be visualized as a villain, and the villain must proceed swiftly to his inevitable retribution. They can understand that process; it is simple, usual, satisfying; it squares with their primitive conception of justice as a form of revenge. The hero fires them too, but less certainly, less violently than the villain. His defect is that he offers thrills at second-hand. It is the merit of the villain, pursued publicly by a *posse comitatus*, that he makes the public breast the primary seat of heroism, that he makes every citizen a personal participant in a glorious act of justice. Wherefore it is ever the aim of the sagacious journalist to foster that sense of personal participation. The wars that he wages are always described as the people's wars, and he himself affects to be no more than their strategist and *claque*. When the victory has once been gained, true enough, he may take all the credit without a blush; but while the fight is going on he always pretends that every honest yeoman is enlisted, and he is even eager to make it appear that the yeomanry began it on their own motion, and out of the excess of their natural virtue.

I assume here, as an axiom too obvious to be argued, that the chief appeal of a newspaper, in all such holy causes, is not at all to the educated and reflective minority of citizens, but frankly to the ignorant and unreflective majority. The truth is that it would usually get a newspaper nowhere to address its exhortations to the former; for, in the first place, they are too few in number to make their support of much value in general engagements, and, in the second place, it is almost always impossible to convert them into disciplined and useful soldiers. They are too cantankerous for that, too ready with embarrassing strategy of their own. One of the principal marks of an educated man, indeed, is the fact that he does not take his opinions from newspapers—not, at any rate, from the militant, crusading newspapers. On the contrary, his attitude toward them is almost always one of frank cynicism, with indifference as its mildest form and contempt as its commonest. He knows that they are constantly falling into false reasoning about the things within his personal knowledge,—that is, within the narrow circle of his special education,—and so he assumes that they make the same, or even worse, errors about other things, whether intellectual or moral. This assumption, it may be said at once, is quite justified by the facts.

I know of no subject, in truth, save perhaps baseball, on which the average American newspaper, even in the larger cities, discourses with unfailing sense and understanding. Whenever the public journals presume to illuminate such a matter as municipal taxation, for example, or the extension of local transportation facilities, or the punishment of public or private criminals, or the control of public-service corporations, or the revision of city charters, the chief effect of their effort is to introduce into it a host of extraneous issues, most of them wholly emotional, and so they contrive to make it unintelligible to all earnest seekers after the truth.

But it does not follow thereby that they also make it unintelligible to their special client, the man in the street. Far from it. What they actually accomplish is the exact opposite. That is to say, it is precisely by this process of transmutation and emotionalization that they bring a given problem down to the level of that man's comprehension, and, what is more important, within the range of his active sympathies. He is not interested in anything that does not stir him, and he is not stirred by anything that fails to impinge upon his small stock of customary appetites and attitudes. His daily acts are ordered, not by any complex process of reasoning, but by a continuous process of very elemental feeling. He is not at all responsive to purely intellectual argument, even when its theme is his own ultimate benefit, for such argument quickly gets beyond his immediate interest and experience. But he is very responsive to emotional suggestion, particularly when it is crudely and violently made; and it is to this weakness that the newspapers must ever address their endeavors. In brief, they must try to arouse his horror, or indignation, or pity, or simply his lust for slaughter. Once they have done that, they have him safely by the nose. He will follow blindly until his emotion wears out. He will be ready to believe anything, however absurd, so long as he is in his state of psychic tumescence.

In the reform campaigns which periodically rock our large cities,—and our small ones, too,—the newspapers habitually make use of this fact. Such campaigns are not intellectual wars upon erroneous principles, but emotional wars upon errant men: they always revolve around the pursuit of some definite, concrete, fugitive malefactor, or group of malefactors. That is to say, they belong to popular sport rather than to the science of government; the impulse behind them is always far more orgiastic than reflective. For good government in the abstract, the people of the United States seem to have no liking, or, at all events, no passion. It is impossible to get them stirred up over it, or even to make them give serious thought to it. They seem to assume that it is a mere phantasm of theorists, a political will-o'-the-wisp, a utopian dream—wholly uninteresting, and probably full of dangers and tricks. The very discussion of it bores them unspeakably, and those papers which habitually discuss it logically and unemotionally— for example, the *New York Evening Post*—are diligently avoided by the mob. What the mob thirsts for is not good government in itself, but the merry chase of a definite exponent of bad government. The newspaper that discovers such an exponent—or, more accurately, the newspaper that discovers dramatic and overwhelming evidence against him—has all the material necessary for a reform wave of the highest emotional intensity. All that it need do is to goad the victim into a fight. Once he has formally joined the issue, the people will do the rest. They are always ready for a man-hunt, and their favorite quarry is the man of politics. If no such prey is at hand, they will turn to wealthy debauchees, to fallen Sunday-school superintendents, to money barons, to white-slave traders, to un-sedulous chiefs of police. But their first choice is the boss.

In assaulting bosses, however, a newspaper must look carefully to its ammunition, and to the order and interrelation of its salvos. There is such a thing, at the start, as overshooting the mark, and the danger thereof is very serious. The people must be aroused by degrees, gently at first, and then with more and more ferocity. They are not capable of reaching the maximum of indignation at one leap: even on the side of pure emotion they have their rigid limitations. And this, of course, is because even emotion must have a quasi-intellectual basis, because even indignation must arise out of facts. One fact at a time! If a newspaper printed the whole story of a political boss's misdeeds in a single article, that article would have scarcely any effect whatever, for it would be far too long for the average reader to read and absorb. He would never get to the end of it, and the part he actually traversed would remain muddled and distasteful in his memory. Far from arousing an emotion in him, it would arouse only ennui, which is the very antithesis of emotion. He cannot read more than three columns of any one subject without tiring: 6,000 words, I should say, is the extreme limit of his appetite. And the nearer he is pushed to that limit, the greater the strain upon his psychic digestion. He can absorb a single capital fact, leaping from a headline, at one colossal gulp; but he could not down a dissertation in twenty. And the first desideratum in a headline is that it deal with a single and capital fact. It must be, "McGinnis Steals $1,257,867.25," not, "McGinnis Lacks Ethical Sense."

Moreover, a newspaper article which presumed to tell the whole of a thrilling story in one gargantuan installment would lack the dynamic element, the quality of mystery and suspense. Even if it should achieve the miracle of arousing the reader to a high pitch of excitement, it would let him drop again next day. If he is to be kept in his frenzy long enough for it to be dangerous to the common foe, he must be led into it gradually. The newspaper in charge of the business must harrow him, tease him, promise him, hold him. It is thus that his indignation is transformed from a state of being into a state of gradual and cumulative becoming; it is thus that reform takes on the character of a hotly contested game, with the issue agreeably in doubt. And it is always as a game, of course, that the man in the street views moral endeavor. Whether its proposed victim be a political boss, a police captain, a gambler, a fugitive murderer, or a disgraced clergyman, his interest in it is almost purely a sporting interest. And the intensity of that interest, of course, depends upon the fierceness of the clash. The game is fascinating in proportion as the morally pursued puts up a stubborn defense, and in proportion as the newspaper directing the pursuit is resourceful and merciless, and in proportion as the eminence of the quarry is great and his resultant downfall spectacular. A war against a ward boss seldom attracts much attention, even in the smaller cities, for he is insignificant to begin with and an inept and cowardly fellow to end with; but the famous war upon William M. Tweed shook the whole nation, for he was a man of tremendous power, he was a brave and enterprising antagonist, and his fall carried a multitude of other men with him. Here, indeed, was sport royal, and the plain people took to it with avidity.

But once such a buccaneer is overhauled and manacled, the show is over, and the people take no further interest in reform. In place of the fallen boss, a so-called reformer has been set up. He goes into office with public opinion apparently solidly behind him: there is every promise that the improvement achieved will be lasting. But experience shows that it seldom is. Reform does not last. The reformer quickly loses his public. His usual fate, indeed, is to become the pet butt and aversion of his public. The very mob that put him into office chases him out of office. And after all, there is nothing very astonishing about this change of front, which is really far less a change of front than it seems. The mob has been fed, for weeks preceding the reformer's elevation, upon the blood of big and little bosses; it has acquired a taste for their chase, and for the chase in general. Now, of a sudden, it is deprived of that stimulating sport. The old bosses are in retreat; there are yet no new bosses to belabor and pursue; the newspapers which elected the reformer are busily apologizing for his amateurish errors—a dull and dispiriting business. No wonder it now becomes possible for the old bosses, acting through their inevitable friends on the respectable side,—the "solid" business men, the takers of favors, the underwriters of political enterprise, and the newspapers influenced by these pious fellows,—to start the rabble against the reformer. The trick is quite as easy as that but lately done. The rabble wants a good show, a game, a victim: it doesn't care who that victim may be. How easy to convince it that the reformer is a scoundrel himself, that he is as bad as any of the old bosses, that he ought to go to the block for high crimes and misdemeanors! It never had any actual love for him, or even any faith in him; his election was a mere incident of the chase of his predecessor. No wonder that it falls upon him eagerly, butchering him to make a new holiday!

This is what has happened over and over again in every large American city—Chicago, New York, St. Louis, Cincinnati, Pittsburg, New Orleans, Baltimore, San Francisco, St. Paul, Kansas City. Every one of these places has had its melodramatic reform campaigns and its inevitable reactions. The people have leaped to the overthrow of bosses, and then wearied of the ensuing tedium. A perfectly typical slipping back, to be matched in a dozen other cities, is going on in Philadelphia to-day [1914]. Mayor Rudolph Blankenberg, a veteran war-horse of reform, came into office through the downfall of the old bosses, a catastrophe for which he had labored and agitated for more than thirty years. But now the old bosses are getting their revenge by telling the people that he is a violent and villainous boss himself. Certain newspapers are helping them; they have concealed but powerful support among financiers and business men; volunteers have even come forward from other cities—for example, the Mayor of Baltimore. Slowly but surely this insidious campaign is making itself felt; the common people show signs of yearning for another *auto-da-fé*. Mayor Blankenberg, unless I am the worst prophet unhung, will meet with an overwhelming defeat in 1915.[4] And it will be a very difficult thing to put even a half-decent man in his place: the victory of the bosses will be so nearly complete that they will be under no necessity of offering compromises. Employing a favorite device of political humor, they may select a harmless blank cartridge, a respectable numskull, what is commonly called a perfumer. But the chances are that they will select a frank ringster, and that the people will elect him with cheers.

4. This was written in 1914. The overthrow of Blankenberg took place as forecast, and Philadelphia has since enjoyed boss rule again, with plentiful scandals.—H. L. M.

II

Such is the ebb and flow of emotion in the popular heart—or perhaps, if we would be more accurate, the popular liver. It does not constitute an intelligible system of morality, for morality, at bottom, is not at all an instinctive matter, but a purely intellectual matter: its essence is the control of impulse by an ideational process, the subordination of the immediate desire to the distant aim. But such as it is, it is the only system of morality that the emotional majority is capable of comprehending and practicing; and so the newspapers, which deal with majorities quite as frankly as politicians deal with them, have to admit it into their own system. That is to say, they cannot accomplish anything by talking down to the public from a moral plane higher than its own: they must take careful account of its habitual ways of thinking, its moral thirsts and prejudices, its well-defined limitations. They must remember clearly, as judges and lawyers have to remember it, that the morality subscribed to by that public is far from the stern and arctic morality of professors of the science. On the contrary, it is a mellower and more human thing; it has room for the antithetical emotions of sympathy and scorn; it makes no effort to separate the criminal from his crime.

The higher moralities, running up to that of Puritans and archbishops, allow no weight to custom, to general reputation, to temptation; they hold it to be no defense of a ballot-box stuffer, for example, that he had scores of accomplices and that he is kind to his little children. But the popular morality regards such a defense as sound and apposite; it is perfectly willing to convert a trial on a specific charge into a trial on a general charge. And in giving judgment it is always ready to let feeling triumph over every idea of abstract justice; and very often that feeling has its origin and support, not in matters actually in evidence, but in impressions wholly extraneous and irrelevant.

Hence the need of a careful and wary approach in all newspaper crusades, particularly on the political side. On the one hand, as I have said, the astute journalist must remember the public's incapacity for taking in more than one thing at a time, and on the other hand, he must remember its disposition to be swayed by mere feeling, and its habit of founding that feeling upon general and indefinite impressions. Reduced to a rule of everyday practice, this means that the campaign against a given malefactor must begin a good while before the capital accusation—that is, the accusation upon which a verdict of guilty is sought—is formally brought forward. There must be a shelling of the fortress before the assault; suspicion must precede indignation. If this preliminary work is neglected or ineptly performed, the result is apt to be a collapse of the campaign. The public is not ready to switch from confidence to doubt on the instant; if its general attitude toward a man is sympathetic, that sympathy is likely to survive even a very vigorous attack. The accomplished mob-master lays his course accordingly. His first aim is to arouse suspicion, to break down the presumption of innocence—supposing, of course, that he finds it to exist. He knows that he must plant a seed, and tend it long and lovingly, before he may pluck his dragon-flower. He knows that all storms of emotion, however suddenly they may seem to come up, have their origin over the rim of consciousness, and that their gathering is really a slow, slow business. I mix the figures shamelessly, as mob-masters mix their brews!

It is this persistence of an attitude which gives a certain degree of immunity to all newcomers in office, even in the face of sharp and resourceful assault. For example, a new president. The majority in favor of him on Inauguration Day is usually overwhelming, no matter how small his plurality in the November preceding, for common self-respect demands that the people magnify his virtues: to deny them would be a confession of national failure, a destructive criticism of the Republic. And that benignant disposition commonly survives until his first year in office is more than half gone. The public prejudice is wholly on his side: his critics find it difficult to arouse any indignation against him, even when the offenses they lay to him are in violation of the fundamental axioms of popular morality. This explains why it was that Mr. Wilson was so little damaged by the charge of federal interference in the Diggs-Caminetti case—a charge well supported by the evidence brought forward, and involving a serious violation of popular notions of virtue. And this explains, too, why he survived the oratorical pilgrimages of his Secretary of State at a time of serious international difficulty—pilgrimages apparently undertaken with his approval, and hence at his political risk and cost. The people were still in favor of him, and so he was not brought to irate and drum-head judgment. No roar of indignation arose to the heavens. The opposition newspapers, with sure instinct, felt the irresistible force of public opinion on his side, and so they ceased their clamor very quickly.

But it is just such a slow accumulation of pin-pricks, each apparently harmless in itself, that finally draws blood; it is by just such a leisurely and insidious process that the presumption of innocence is destroyed, and a hospitality to suspicion created. The campaign against Governor Sulzer in New York offers a classic example of this process in operation, with very skillful gentlemen, journalistic and political, in control of it. The charges on which Governor Sulzer was finally brought to impeachment were not launched at him out of a clear sky, nor while the primary presumption in his favor remained unshaken. Not at all. They were launched at a carefully selected and critical moment—at the end, to wit, of a long and well-managed series of minor attacks. The fortress of his popularity was bombarded a long while before it was assaulted. He was pursued with insinuations and innuendoes; various persons, more or less dubious, were led to make various charges, more or less vague, against him; the managers of the campaign sought to poison the plain people with doubts, misunderstandings, suspicions. This effort, so diligently made, was highly successful; and so the capital charges, when they were brought forward at last, had the effect of confirmations, of corroborations, of proofs. But if Tammany had made them during the first few months of Governor Sulzer's term, while all doubts were yet in his favor, it would have got only scornful laughter for its pains. The ground had to be prepared; the public mind had to be put into training.

The end of my space is near, and I find that I have written of popular morality very copiously, and of newspaper morality very little. But, as I have said before, the one is the other. The newspaper must adapt its pleading to its clients' moral limitations, just as the trial lawyer must adapt *his* pleading to the jury's limitations. Neither may like the job, but both must face it to gain a larger end. And that end, I believe, is a worthy one in the newspaper's case quite as often as in the lawyer's, and perhaps far oftener. The art of leading the vulgar, in itself, does no discredit to its practitioner. Lincoln practiced it unashamed, and so did Webster, Clay, and Henry. What is more, these men practiced it with frank allowance for the naïveté of the people they presumed to lead. It was Lincoln's chief source of strength, indeed, that he had a homely way with him, that he could reduce complex problems to the simple terms of popular theory and emotion, that he did not ask little fishes to think and act like whales. This is the manner in which the newspapers do their work, and in the long run, I am convinced, they accomplish about as much good as harm thereby. Dishonesty, of course, is not unknown among them: we have newspapers in this land which apply a truly devilish technical skill to the achievement of unsound and unworthy ends. But not as many of them as perfectionists usually allege. Taking one with another, they strive in the right direction. They realize the massive fact that the plain people, for all their poverty of wit, cannot be fooled forever. They have a healthy fear of that heathen rage which so often serves their uses.

Look back a generation or two. Consider the history of our democracy since the Civil War. Our most serious problems, it must be plain, have been solved orgiastically, and to the tune of deafening newspaper urging and clamor. Men have been washed into office on waves of emotion, and washed out again in the same manner. Measures and policies have been determined by indignation far more often than by cold reason. But is the net result evil? Is there even any permanent damage from those debauches of sentiment in which the newspapers have acted insincerely, unintelligently, with no thought save for the show itself? I doubt it. The effect of their long and melodramatic chase of bosses is an undoubted improvement in our whole governmental method. The boss of to-day is not an envied first citizen, but a criminal constantly on trial. He himself is debarred from all public offices of honor, and his control over other public officers grows less and less. Elections are no longer boldly stolen; the humblest citizen may go to the polls in safety and cast his vote honestly; the machine grows less dangerous year by year; perhaps it is already less dangerous than a *camorra* of utopian and dehumanized reformers would be. We begin to develop an official morality which actually rises above our private morality. Bribe-takers are sent to jail by the votes of jurymen who give presents in their daily business, and are not above beating the street-car company.

And so, too, in narrower fields. The white-slave agitation of a year or so ago was ludicrously extravagant and emotional, but its net effect is a better conscience, a new alertness. The newspapers discharged broadsides of 12-inch guns to bring down a flock of buzzards—but they brought down the buzzards. They have libeled and lynched the police—but the police are the better for it. They have represented salicylic acid as an elder brother to bichloride of mercury—but we are poisoned less than we used to be. They have lifted the plain people to frenzies of senseless terror over drinking-cups and neighbors with coughs—but the death-rate from tuberculosis declines. They have railroaded men to prison, denying them all their common rights—but fewer malefactors escape to-day than yesterday.

The way of ethical progress is not straight. It describes, to risk a mathematical pun, a sort of drunken hyperbola. But if we thus move onward and upward by leaps and bounces, it is certainly better than not moving at all. Each time, perhaps, we slip back, but each time we stop at a higher level.

NEWSPAPER MORALS: A REPLY

BY RALPH PULITZER

The striking article in the March *Atlantic* by Mr. Henry L. Mencken, on "Newspaper Morals," is so full of palpable facts supporting plausible fallacies that simple justice to press and "proletariat" seems to render proper a few thoughts in answer to it.

Mr. Mencken's main facts, summarized, are as follows: that press and public often approach public questions too superficially and sentimentally; that the sense of proportion is too often lost in the heat of campaigns; that the truth is too often obscured by the intrusion of irrelevant personalities; and that after the intemperate extremes of reform waves there always come reactions into indifference to the evils but yesterday so furiously fought.

Mr. Mencken's fallacies are: the supercilious assumption that these weaknesses are not matters of human temperament running up and down through a certain proportion of every division of society, but that, on the contrary, they are class affairs, never tainting the educated classes, but limited to "the man in the street," "the rabble," "the mob"; that apparently the emotionalizing of public questions by the press is to be censured in principle and sneered at in practice; that it means a deliberate truckling by the newspapers to the ignorant tastes of the masses when the press fights a public evil by attacking, with argument and indignation mingled, a man who personifies that evil, instead of opposing the general principle of that evil with a wholly passionless intellectualism.

A general fallacy which affects Mr. Mencken's whole article lies in criticising as offenses against "newspaper morals" those imperfections which, where they exist at all, could properly be criticised only under such criteria as suggested by "Newspaper Intellectuals," or "Newspapers as the Exponents of Pure Reason."

Mr. Mencken first exposes and deprecates the "aim" of the newspapers to "knock somebody on the head every day," "to please the crowd, to give a good show, by first selecting a deserving victim and then putting him magnificently to the torture," and even to fight "constructive campaigns for good government in exactly the same gothic, melodramatic way."

Now "muck-raking" rather than incense-burning is not a deliberate aim so much as a spontaneous instinct of the average newspaper. Nor is there anything either mysterious or reprehensible about this. The public, of all degrees, is more interested in hitting Wrong than in praising Right, because fortunately we are still in an optimistic state of society, where Right is taken for granted and Wrong contains the element of the unusual and abnormal. If the day shall ever come when papers will be able to "expose" Right and regard Wrong as a foregone conclusion, they will doubtless quickly reverse their treatment of the two. In an Ali Baba's cave it might be natural for a paper to discover some man's honesty; in a *yoshiwara* it might be reasonable for it to expatiate on some woman's virtue. But while honesty and virtue and rightness are assumed to be the normal condition of men and women and things in general, it does not seem either extraordinary or culpable that people and press should be more interested in the polemical than in the platitudinous; in blame than in painting the lily; in attack than in sending laudatory coals to Newcastle. It scarcely needs remark, however, that when the element of surprise is introduced by some deed of exceptional heroism or abnegation or inspiration, the newspapers are not slow in giving it publicity and praise.

Mr. Mencken finds it deplorable that "a very definite limit is set, not only upon the people's capacity for grasping intellectual concepts, but also upon their capacity for grasping moral concepts"; that, therefore, it is necessary "to visualize their cause in some definite and defiant opponent ... by translating all arguments for a principle into rage against a man." Far be it from me to deny that people and papers are too prone to get diverted from the pursuit of some principle by acrimonious personalities wholly ungermane to that principle. But the protest against this should not lead to unfair extremes in the opposite direction. If Mr. Mencken's ideal is a nation of philosophers calmly agreeing on the abstract desirability of honesty while serenely ignoring the specific picking of their own pockets, we have no ground for argument. But until we reach such a semi-imbecile Utopia, it would seem to be no reflection on "the people's" intellectual or moral concepts that they should refuse to excite themselves over any theoretical wrong until their attention is focused on some practical manifestation of it, in the concrete acts of some specific individual.

May I add, parenthetically, that some papers and many acutely intellectual gentlemen find it far more convenient and comfortable to generalize virtuously than to particularize virtuously? Nor does it require merely moral or physical courage to reduce the safely general to the disagreeably personal. It requires no despicable amount of intellectual acumen as well.

Mr. Mencken next proceeds to "assume here, as an axiom too obvious to be argued, that the chief appeal of a newspaper in all such holy causes is not at all to the educated and reflective minority of citizens, but to the ignorant and unreflective majority." On the contrary, it is very far from being "too obvious to be argued." A great many persons of guaranteed education are sadly destitute of any reflectiveness whatsoever, while an appalling number of "the ignorant" have the effrontery to be able to reflect very efficiently. This is apart from the fact that the general intelligence among many of the ignorant is matched only by the abysmal stupidity of many of the educated.

Thus it is that the decent paper makes its appeal on public questions to the numerically large body of reflective "ignorance" and to the numerically small body of reflective education, leaving it to the demagogic papers, which are the exception at one end, to inflame the unreflective ignorant, and to the sycophantic papers at the other end to pander to the unreflective educated.

As to Mr. Mencken's charge that he knows of "no subject, save perhaps baseball, on which the average American newspaper discourses with unfailing sense and understanding," I know of no subject at all, even including baseball, on which the most exceptionally gifted man in the world discourses with unfailing sense and understanding. But I do know this: that, considering the immense range of subjects which the American paper is called upon to discuss, and its meagre limits of time in which to prepare for such discussion, the failings of that paper in sense and understanding are probably rarer than would be those under the same conditions of Mr. Mencken's most fastidious selection.

"But," Mr. Mencken continues, "whenever the public journals presume to illuminate such a matter as municipal taxation, for example, or the extension of local transportation facilities, or the punishment of public or private criminals, or the control of public-service corporations, or the revision of city charters, the chief effect of their effort is to introduce into it a host of extraneous issues, most of them wholly emotional, and so they continue to make it unintelligible to all earnest seekers after truth." Here again it is all a matter of point of view. If Mr. Mencken's earnest seekers after truth wish to evolve ideological schemes of municipal taxation, or supramundane extensions of transportation facilities, or transcendental control of public-service corporations, or academic revisions of city charters, then, indeed, the newspaper discussions of these questions would be bewildering to these visionary workers in the realms of pure reason. For the newspapers "presume" to regard these questions, not as theoretical problems, to be solved under theoretical conditions, on theoretical populations, to theoretical perfection, but as workable projects for a workaday world, in which the most beautiful abstract reasoning must stand the test of flesh-and-blood conditions; they regard emotional issues as so far, indeed, from being extraneous that the human nature of the humblest men and women must be weighed in the balance against the nicest syllogisms of the precisest logic. And this is nothing that Mr. Mencken need condescend to apologize for so long as "newspaper morals" are under discussion. For it must be obvious that the honest exposition and analysis of public questions from a human as well as a scientific point of view is a higher moral service to the community than an exclusively scientific, wholly unsympathetic search after truth by those who regard populations as mere subjects for the demonstration of principles.

It is precisely the honorable prerogative of newspapers not only to clarify but to vivify, to galvanize dead hypotheses into living questions, to make the educated and the ignorant alike feel that public questions should interest and stir all good citizens and not merely engross social philosophers and political theorists.

But here let me avoid joining Mr. Mencken in the pitfall of generalizations, by drawing a sharp distinction between the great run of decent papers which do honestly emotionalize public questions and the relatively few papers which unscrupulously *hystericalize* these questions.

Mr. Mencken is entirely correct when he admits that this emotionalizing brings these problems down to a "man's comprehension, and, what is more important, within the range of his active sympathies." But he again shows a very unfortunate class arrogance when he identifies this man as "the man in the street." If Mr. Mencken searched earnestly enough after truth, he would find this man to be about as extensively the man at the ticker, the man in the motor-car, the man at the operating table, the man in the pulpit. In the same vein he continues that the only papers which discuss good government unemotionally "are diligently avoided by the *mob*." If Mr. Mencken only included with his proletariat the mob of stockbrokers and doctors and engineers and lawyers and college graduates generally, who refuse to read these logical and unemotional discussions, he would unfortunately be quite right. It would be a beautiful thing indeed if we had with us to-day one hundred millions of "earnest seekers after truth," all busily engaged in discussing "good government in the abstract," "logically and unemotionally." If they were only thus dispassionately busied, it is quite true that things would not be as at present, when "they are always ready for a man hunt and their favorite quarry is a man of politics. If no such prey is at hand, they will turn to wealthy debauchees, to fallen Sunday-school superintendents, to money barons, to white-slave traders." In those halcyon times the one hundred million calm abstractionists would discuss the influence of Beaumont and Fletcher on bosses, or, failing this, the ultimate effect of wealth on eroticism, the obscure relations between proselyting and decadence, or the effect of the white-slave traffic on the gold reserve.

But in our present unregenerate epoch Mr. Mencken is quite right in holding that it is generally the specific evils of government or society which bring about reform waves, which in turn crystallize themselves into general principles. It is a shockingly practical process, I admit; but then, we are a shockingly practical people, who prefer sordid results to inspired theories. And at that we are not in such bad company. For in no country in the world is there such a thing as a "revealed" civilization. On the contrary, civilization has always been for the most part purely empirical, and progress will ever remain so.

There is, therefore, cause not for shame but for pride when a newspaper reveals some specific iniquity, and by not merely expounding its isolated character to the public intelligence, but also by interpreting its general menace to the public imagination and bringing home its inherent evil to the public conscience, arouses that public to social legislation, criminal prosecution, or political reform.

Mr. Mencken next assaults once more his unfortunate "man in the street" by declaring that "it is always as a game, of course, that the man in the street views moral endeavor.... His interest in it is almost always a sporting interest." On the contrary, here at last we have a case where a class distinction can fairly be drawn. "The man in the street" is a naïve man who takes his melodrama seriously, who believes robustly in blacks and whites without subtilizing them into intermediate shades, for whom villains and heroes really exist. He is the last person on earth to view the moral endeavor of a political or social campaign as a game. It is the supercilious class, with its sophistication and attendant cynicism, to whom such campaigns tend to take on the aspect of sporting events and games of skill.

But it is not necessary to go into the details of Mr. Mencken's theory as to the depraved nature of popular participation in political reform. Its gist is contained in his truly shocking statement that the war on the Tweed ring and its extirpation was to the "plain people" nothing but "sport royal"! Any one who can take one of the most inspiring civic victories in the history, not alone of a city, but of a nation, and degrade the spirit that brought it about to the level of the cockpit or the bull ring, supplies an argument that needs no reinforcing against his prejudices on this whole subject.

Mr. Mencken justly deplores the reactions which follow upon reform successes, but unjustly concentrates the blame on the fickleness of "the rabble." This evil is not a matter of mob-psychology but of unstable human nature, high and low. These revulsions and reactions are the shame, impartially, of all classes of our communities. They permeate the educated atmosphere of fastidious clubs as extensively as they do the ignorant miasma of vulgar saloons. If they induce the "ignorant and unreflective" plebeian to sit in his shirt-sleeves with his legs up, resting his feet, on election day, instead of doing his duty at the polls, do they not equally congest the golf links with "earnest seekers after truth" busily engaged in sacrificing ballots to Bogeys?

I wholly agree with Mr. Mencken's strictures on the public morality which holds it to be a relevant defense for a ballot-box stuffer "that he is kind to his little children." The sentimentalism which so frequently perverts a proper public conception of public morality is sickening. But here again the indictment should be against average human nature, educated or ignorant, and not against the "man in the street" as a class and alone. To this man the fact that the ballot-box stuffer is kind to his little children may carry more weight than to the man of education and culture. To the latter the fact that some monopoly-breeding, law-defying, legislation-bribing, railroad-wrecking gentleman is kind to his fellow citizens by donating to them picture galleries and free libraries may carry more weight than to the former. Is not the one just as much as the other "ready to let feeling triumph over every idea of abstract justice"?

Again, with Mr. Mencken's prescription for making a successful newspaper crusade there can be no quarrel, save that here once more he suggests, by referring to the newspaper as a "mob-master," that these methods are exclusively applicable to the same long-suffering "man in the street." These methods on which Mr. Mencken elaborates are the rather obvious ones used by every lawyer, clergyman, statesman, or publicist the world over who has a forensic fight to make and win against some public evil—accusation, iteration, cumulation, and climax. If these methods are used by "mob-masters," they are equally used by snob-servants, and incidentally by the great mass of honest newspapers which are neither the one thing nor the other.

At the end of his article, having set up a man of straw which he found it impossible to knock down, Mr. Mencken patronizingly pats it on the back:—

"The newspaper must adapt its pleading to its client's moral limitations, just as the trial lawyer must adapt his pleading to the jury's limitations. Neither may like the job, but both must face it to gain a larger end. And that end is a worthy one in the newspaper's case quite as often as in the lawyer's, and perhaps far oftener. The art of leading the vulgar in itself does no discredit to its practitioner. Lincoln practised it unashamed, and so did Webster, Clay, and Henry."

Alas for this well-intentioned effort at amends! It is impossible to agree with Mr. Mencken even here when he praises press and public with such faint damnation.

A decent newspaper does not and must not adapt its pleadings to its clients' moral limitations. Intellectual limitations? Yes. It is restricted by a line beyond which intelligence and education alike would be at sea, and which only specialists and experts would understand. But moral limitations? No.

The paper in this regard is less like the lawyer and more like the judge. A judge can properly adapt his charge in simplicity of form to the intellectual limitations of the jury, but it will scarcely be contended that he may adapt his charge in its substance to the moral limitations of the jury. No more can any self-respecting paper palter with what it believes to be the right and the truth because of any moral limitations in its constituency. Demagogic papers may do it. Class-catering papers may do it. But the decent press which lies between does not thus stultify itself.

And now to Mr. Mencken's condescending conclusion:—

"Our most serious problems, it must be plain, have been solved orgiastically and to the tune of deafening newspaper urging and clamor.... But is the net result evil?... I doubt it.... The way of ethical progress is not straight.... But if we thus move onward and upward by leaps and bounces, it is certainly better than not moving at all. Each time, perhaps, we slip back, but each time we stop at a higher level."

Why, then, sweepingly reflect on the morals of the press, if by humanizing abstract principles, by emotionalizing academic doctrines, by personifying general theories, it has accomplished this progress? Granted that in the heat of battle it fails to handle the cold conceptions of austere philosophers with proper scientific etiquette. Granted that it makes blunders in technical statements which to the preciosity of specialists seem inexcusable. Granted that it mixes its science and its sentiment in a manner to shock the gentlemen of disembodied intellects. Granted that the press has many more such intellectual peccadilloes on its conscience.

But if the press does these things honestly, it does them morally, and does not need to excuse them by their results, even though these results are in very truth infinitely more precious to humanity than could be those obtained by the chill endeavors of what Mr. Mencken himself, with the perfect accuracy of would-be irony, describes as "a Camorra of Utopian and dehumanized reformers."

THE SUPPRESSION OF IMPORTANT NEWS

BY EDWARD ALSWORTH ROSS

I

Most of the criticism launched at our daily newspapers hits the wrong party. Granted that they sensationalize vice and crime, "play up" trivialities, exploit the private affairs of prominent people, embroider facts, and offend good taste with screech, blare, and color. All this may be only the means of meeting the demand, of "giving the public what it wants." The newspaper cannot be expected to remain dignified and serious now that it caters to the common millions, instead of, as formerly, to the professional and business classes. To interest errand-boy and factory-girl and raw immigrant, it had to become spicy, amusing, emotional, and chromatic. For these, blame, then, the American people.

There is just one deadly, damning count against the daily newspaper as it is coming to be, namely, *it does not give the news.*

For all its pretensions, many a daily newspaper is not "giving the public what it wants." In spite of these widely trumpeted prodigies of costly journalistic "enterprise," these ferreting reporters and hurrying correspondents, these leased cables and special trains, news, good "live" news, "red-hot stuff," is deliberately being suppressed or distorted. This occurs oftener now than formerly, and bids fair to occur yet oftener in the future.

And this in spite of the fact that the aspiration of the press has been upward. Venality has waned. Better and better men have been drawn into journalism, and they have wrought under more self-restraint. The time when it could be said, as it was said of the Reverend Dr. Dodd, that one had "descended so low as to become editor of a newspaper," seems as remote as the Ice Age. The editor who uses his paper to air his prejudices, satisfy his grudges, and serve his private ambitions, is going out. Sobered by a growing realization of their social function, newspaper men have come under a sense of responsibility. Not long ago it seemed as if a professional spirit and a professional ethics were about to inspire the newspaper world; and to this end courses and schools of journalism were established, with high hopes. The arrest of this promising movement explains why nine out of ten newspaper men of fifteen years' experience are cynics.

As usual, no one is to blame. The apostasy of the daily press is caused by three economic developments in the field of newspaper publishing.

II

In the first place, the great city daily has become a blanket sheet with elaborate presswork, printed in mammoth editions that must be turned out in the least time. The necessary plant is so costly, and the Associated Press franchise is so expensive, that the daily newspaper in the big city has become a capitalistic enterprise. To-day a million dollars will not begin to outfit a metropolitan newspaper. The editor is no longer the owner, for he has not, and cannot command, the capital needed to start it or buy it. The editor of the type of Greeley, Dana, Medill, Story, Halstead, and Raymond, who owns his paper and makes it his astral body, the projection of his character and ideals, is rare. Perhaps Mr. Watterson and Mr. Nelson [the late William R. Nelson of the *Kansas City Star*] are the best recent representatives of the type.

More and more the owner of the big daily is a business man who finds it hard to see why he should run his property on different lines from the hotel proprietor, the vaudeville manager, or the owner of an amusement park. The editors are hired men, and they may put into the paper no more of their conscience and ideals than comports with getting the biggest return from the investment. Of course, the old-time editor who owned his paper tried to make money,—no sin that!—but just as to-day the author, the lecturer, or the scholar tries to make money, namely, within the limitations imposed by his principles and his professional standards. But, now that the provider of the newspaper capital hires the editor instead of the editor hiring the newspaper capital, the paper is likelier to be run as a money-maker pure and simple—a factory where ink and brains are so applied to white paper as to turn out the largest possible marketable product. The capitalist-owner means no harm, but he is not bothered by the standards that hamper the editor-owner. He follows a few simple maxims that work out well enough in selling shoes or cigars or sheet-music. "Give people what *they* want, not what *you* want." "Back nothing that will be unpopular." "Run the concern for all it is worth."

This drifting of ultimate control into the hands of men with business motives is what is known as "the commercialization of the press."

The significance of it is apparent when you consider the second economic development, namely, the growth of newspaper advertising. The dissemination of news and the purveying of publicity are two essentially distinct functions, which, for the sake of convenience, are carried on by the same agency. The one appeals to subscribers, the other to advertisers. The one calls for good faith, the other does not. The one is the corner-stone of liberty and democracy, the other a convenience of commerce. Now, the purveying of publicity is becoming the main concern of the newspaper, and threatens to throw quite into the shade the communication of news or opinions. Every year the sale of advertising yields a larger proportion of the total receipts, and the subscribers furnish a smaller proportion. Thirty years ago, advertising yielded less than half of the earnings of the daily newspapers. To-day, it yields at least two thirds. In the larger dailies the receipts from advertisers are several times the receipts from the readers, in some cases constituting ninety per cent of the total revenues. As the newspaper expands to eight, twelve, and sixteen pages, while the price sinks to three cents, two cents, one cent, the time comes when the advertisers support the newspaper. The readers are there to *read*, not to provide funds. "He who pays the piper calls the tune." When news columns and editorial page are a mere incident in the profitable sale of mercantile publicity, it is strictly "businesslike" to let the big advertisers censor both.

Of course, you must not let the cat out of the bag, or you will lose readers, and thereupon advertising. As the publicity expert, Deweese, frankly puts it, "The reader must be flimflammed with the idea that the publisher is really publishing the newspaper or magazine for him." The wise owner will "maintain the beautiful and impressive bluff of running a journal to influence public opinion, to purify politics, to elevate public morals, etc." In the last analysis, then, the smothering of facts in deference to the advertiser finds a limit in the intelligence and alertness of the reading public. Handled as "a commercial proposition," the newspaper dares not suppress such news beyond a certain point, and it can always proudly point to the unsuppressed news as proof of its independence and public spirit.

The immunity enjoyed by the big advertiser becomes more serious as more kinds of business resort to advertising. Formerly, readers who understood why accidents and labor troubles never occur in department stores, why dramatic criticisms are so lenient, and the reviews of books from the publishers who advertise are so good-natured, could still expect from their journal an ungloved freedom in dealing with gas, electric, railroad, and banking companies. But now the gas people advertise, "Cook with gas," the electric people urge you to put your sewing-machine on their current, and the railroads spill oceans of ink to attract settlers or tourists. The banks and trust companies are buyers of space, investment advertising has sprung up like Jonah's gourd, and telephone and traction companies are being drawn into the vortex of competitive publicity. Presently, in the news-columns of the sheet that steers by the cash-register, every concern that has favors to seek, duties to dodge, or regulations to evade, will be able to press the soft pedal.

A third development is the subordination of newspapers to other enterprises. After a newspaper becomes a piece of paying property, detachable from the editor's personality, which may be bought and sold like a hotel or mill, it may come into the hands of those who will hold it in bondage to other and bigger investments. The magnate-owner may find it to his advantage not to run it as a newspaper pure and simple, but to make it—on the sly—an instrument for coloring certain kinds of news, diffusing certain misinformation, or fostering certain impressions or prejudices in its clientele. In a word, he may shape its policy by non-journalistic considerations. By making his paper help his other schemes, or further his political or social ambitions, he will hurt it as a money-maker, no doubt, but he may contrive to fool enough of the people enough of the time. Aside from such thraldom, newspapers are subject to the tendency of diverse businesses to become tied together by the cross-investments of their owners. But naturally, when the shares of a newspaper lie in the safe-deposit box cheek by jowl with gas, telephone, and pipeline stock, a tenderness for these collateral interests is likely to affect the news columns.

III

That in consequence of its commercialization, and its frequent subjection to outside interests, the daily newspaper is constantly suppressing important news, will appear from the instances that follow. They are hardly a third of the material that has come to the writer's attention.

A prominent Philadelphia clothier visiting New York was caught perverting boys, and cut his throat. His firm being a heavy advertiser, not a single paper in his home city mentioned the tragedy. One New York paper took advantage of the situation by sending over an extra edition containing the story. The firm in question has a large branch in a Western city. There too the local press was silent, and the opening was seized by a Chicago paper.

In this same Western city the vice-president of this firm was indicted for bribing an alderman to secure the passage of an ordinance authorizing the firm to bridge an alley separating two of its buildings. Representatives of the firm requested the newspapers in which it advertised to ignore the trial. Accordingly the five English papers published no account of the trial, which lasted a week and disclosed highly sensational matter. Only the German papers sent reporters to the trial and published the proceedings.

In a great jobbing centre, one of the most prominent cases of the United States District Attorney was the prosecution of certain firms for misbranding goods. The facts brought out appeared in the press of the smaller centres, but not a word was printed in the local papers. In another centre, four firms were fined for selling potted cheese which had been treated with preservatives. The local newspapers stated the facts, but withheld the names of the firms—a consideration they are not likely to show to the ordinary culprit.

In a trial in a great city it was brought out by sworn testimony that, during a recent labor struggle which involved teamsters on the one hand and the department stores and the mail-order houses on the other, the employers had plotted to provoke the strikers to violence by sending a long line of strike-breaking wagons out of their way to pass a lot on which the strikers were meeting. These wagons were the bait to a trap, for a strong force of policemen was held in readiness in the vicinity, and the governor of the state was at the telephone ready to call out the militia if a riot broke out. Fortunately, the strikers restrained themselves, and the trap was not sprung. It is easy to imagine the headlines that would have been used if labor had been found in so diabolical a plot. Yet the newspapers unanimously refused to print this testimony.

In the same city, during a strike of the elevator men in the large stores, the business agent of the elevator-starters' union was beaten to death, in an alley behind a certain emporium, by a "strong-arm" man hired by that firm. The story, supported by affidavits, was given by a responsible lawyer to three newspaper men, each of whom accepted it as true and promised to print it. The account never appeared.

In another city the sales-girls in the big shops had to sign an exceedingly mean and oppressive contract which, if generally known, would have made the firms odious to the public. A prominent social worker carried these contracts, and evidence as to the bad conditions that had become established under them, to every newspaper in the city. Not one would print a line on the subject.

On the outbreak of a justifiable street-car strike the newspapers were disposed to treat it in a sympathetic way. Suddenly they veered, and became unanimously hostile to the strikers. Inquiry showed that the big merchants had threatened to withdraw their advertisements unless the newspapers changed their attitude.

In the summer of 1908 disastrous fires raged in the northern Lake country, and great areas of standing timber were destroyed. A prominent organ of the lumber industry belittled the losses and printed reassuring statements from lumbermen who were at the very moment calling upon the state for a fire patrol. When taxed with the deceit, the organ pleaded its obligation to support the market for the bonds which the lumber companies of the Lake region had been advertising in its columns.

On account of agitating for teachers' pensions, a teacher was summarily dismissed by a corrupt school board, in violation of their own published rule regarding tenure. An influential newspaper published the facts of school-board grafting brought out in the teacher's suit for reinstatement until, through his club affiliations, a big merchant was induced to threaten the paper with the withdrawal of his advertising. No further reports of the revelations appeared.

During labor disputes the facts are usually distorted to the injury of labor. In one case, strikers held a meeting on a vacant lot enclosed by a newly-erected billboard. Forthwith appeared, in a yellow journal professing warm friendship for labor, a front-page cut of the billboard and a lurid story of how the strikers had built a "stockade," behind which they intended to bid defiance to the bluecoats. It is not surprising that, when the van bringing these lying sheets appeared in their quarter of the city, the libeled men overturned it.

During the struggle of carriage-drivers for a six-day week, certain great dailies lent themselves to a concerted effort of the liverymen to win public sympathy by making it appear that the strikers were interfering with funerals. One paper falsely stated that a strong force of police was being held in reserve in case of "riots," and that policemen would ride beside the non-union drivers of hearses. Another, under the misleading headline, "Two Funerals stopped by Striking Cabmen," described harmless colloquies between hearse-drivers and pickets. This was followed up with a solemn editorial, "May a Man go to his Long Rest in Peace?" although, as a matter of fact, the strikers had no intention of interfering with funerals.

The lying headline is a favorite device for misleading the reader. One sheet prints on its front page a huge "scare" headline, "'Hang Haywood and a Million Men will march in Revenge,' says Darrow." The few readers whose glance fell from the incendiary headline to the dispatch below it found only the following: "Mr. Darrow, in closing the argument, said that 'if the jury hangs Bill Haywood, one million willing hands will seize the banner of liberty by the open grave, and bear it on to victory.'" In the same style, a dispatch telling of the death of an English policeman, from injuries received during a riot precipitated by suffragettes attempting to enter a hall during a political meeting, is headed, "Suffragettes kill Policeman!"

The alacrity with which many dailies serve as mouthpieces of the financial powers came out very clearly during the recent industrial depression. The owner of one leading newspaper called his reporters together and said in effect, "Boys, the first of you who turns in a story of a lay-off or a shut-down gets the sack." Early in the depression the newspapers teemed with glowing accounts of the resumption of steel mills and the revival of business, all baseless. After harvest time they began to cheep, "Prosperity," "Bumper Crops," "Farmers buying Automobiles." In cities where banks and employers offered clearing-house certificates instead of cash, the press usually printed fairy tales of the enthusiasm with which these makeshifts were taken by depositors and workingmen. The numbers and sufferings of the unemployed were ruthlessly concealed from the reading public. A mass meeting of men out of work was represented as "anarchistic" or "instigated by the socialists for political effect." In one daily appeared a dispatch under the heading "Five Thousand Jobs Offered; only Ten apply." It stated that the Commissioner of Public Works of Detroit, misled by reports of dire distress, set afoot a public work which called for five thousand men. Only ten men applied for work, and all these expected to be bosses. Correspondence with the official established the fact that the number of jobs offered was five hundred, and that three thousand men applied for them!

IV

On the desk of every editor and sub-editor of a newspaper run by a capitalist promoter now [1910] under prison sentence lay a list of sixteen corporations in which the owner was interested. This was to remind them not to print anything damaging to these concerns. In the office these corporations were jocularly referred to as "sacred cows."

Nearly every form of privilege is found in the herd of "sacred cows" venerated by the daily press.

The railroad company is a "sacred cow." At a hearing before a state railroad commission, the attorney of a shippers' association got an eminent magnate into the witness chair, with the intention of wringing from him the truth regarding the political expenditures of his railroad. At this point the commission, an abject creature of the railroads, arbitrarily excluded the daring attorney from the case. The memorable excoriation which that attorney gave the commission to its face was made to appear in the papers as the *cause* instead of the *consequence* of this exclusion. Subsequently, when the attorney filed charges with the governor against the commission, one editor wrote an editorial stating the facts and criticising the commissioners. The editorial was suppressed after it was in type.

The public-service company is a "sacred cow." In a city of the Southwest, last summer [1909], while houses were burning from lack of water for the fire hose, a lumber company offered to supply the firemen with water. The water company replied that they had "sufficient." Neither this nor other damaging information concerning the company's conduct got into the columns of the local press. A yellow journal conspicuous in the fight for cheaper gas by its ferocious onslaughts on the "gas trust," suddenly ceased its attack. Soon it began to carry a full-page "Cook with gas" advertisement. The cow had found the entrance to the sacred fold.

Traction is a "sacred cow." The truth about Cleveland's fight for the three-cent fare has been widely suppressed. For instance, while Mayor Johnson was superintending the removal of the tracks of a defunct street railway, he was served with a court order enjoining him from tearing up the rails. As the injunction was not indorsed, as by law it should be, he thought it was an ordinary communication, and put it in his pocket to examine later. The next day he was summoned to show reason why he should not be found in contempt of court. When the facts came out, he was, of course, discharged. An examination of the seven leading dailies of the country shows that a dispatch was sent out from Cleveland stating that Mayor Johnson, after acknowledging service, pocketed the injunction, and ordered his men to proceed with their work. In the newspaper offices this dispatch was then embroidered. One paper said the mayor told his men to go ahead and ignore the injunction. Another had the mayor intimating in advance that he would not obey an order if one were issued. A third invented a conversation in which the mayor and his superintendent made merry over the injunction. Not one of the seven journals reported the mayor's complete exoneration later.

The tax system is a "sacred cow." During a banquet of two hundred single-taxers, at the conclusion of their state conference, a man fell in a fit. Reporters saw the trifling incident, yet the morning papers, under big headlines, "Many Poisoned at Single-Tax Banquet," told in detail how a large number of banqueters had been ptomaine-poisoned. The conference had formulated a single-tax amendment to the state constitution, which they intended to present to the people for signature under the new Initiative law. One paper gave a line and a half to this most significant action. No other paper noticed it.

The party system is a "sacred cow." When a county district court declared that the Initiative and Referendum amendment to the Oregon constitution was invalid, the item was spread broadcast. But when later the Supreme Court of Oregon reversed that decision, the fact was too trivial to be put on the wires.

The "man higher up" is a "sacred cow." In reporting Prosecutor Heney's argument in the Calhoun case, the leading San Francisco paper omitted everything on the guilt of Calhoun and made conspicuous certain statements of Mr. Heney with reference to himself, with intent to make it appear that his argument was but a vindication of himself, and that he made no points against the accused. The argument for the defense was printed in full, the "points" being neatly displayed in large type at proper intervals. At a crisis in this prosecution a Washington dispatch quoted the chairman of the Appropriations Committee as stating in the House that "Mr. Heney received during 1908 $23,000, for which he performed no service whatever for the Government." It was some hours before the report was corrected by adding Mr. Tawney's concluding words, "during that year."

In view of their suppression and misrepresentation of vital truth, the big daily papers, broadly speaking, must be counted as allies of those whom— as Editor Dana reverently put it—"God has endowed with a genius for saving, for getting rich, for bringing wealth together, for accumulating and concentrating money." In rallying to the side of the people they are slower than the weeklies, the magazines, the pulpit, the platform, the bar, the literati, the intellectuals, the social settlements, and the universities.

Now and then, to be sure, in some betrayed and misgoverned city, a man of force takes some little sheet, prints all the news, ventilates the local situation, arouses the community, builds up a huge circulation, and proves that truth-telling still pays. But such exploits do not counteract the economic developments which have brought on the glacial epoch in journalism. Note what happens later to such a newspaper. It is now a valuable property, and as such it will be treated. The editor need not repeat the bold strokes that won public confidence; he has only to avoid anything that would forfeit it. Unconsciously he becomes, perhaps, less a newspaper man, more a business man. He may make investments which muzzle his paper here, form social connections which silence it there. He may tire of fighting and want to "cash in." In any case, when his newspaper falls into the hands of others, it will be run as a business, and not as a crusade.

V

What can be done about the suppression of news? At least, we can refrain from arraigning and preaching. To urge the editor, under the thumb of the advertiser or of the owner, to be more independent, is to invite him to remove himself from his profession. As for the capitalist-owner, to exhort him to run his newspaper in the interests of truth and progress is about as reasonable as to exhort the mill-owner to work his property for the public good instead of for his private benefit.

What is needed is a broad new avenue to the public mind. Already smothered facts are cutting little channels for themselves. The immense vogue of the "muck-raking" magazines is due to their being vehicles for suppressed news. Non-partisan leaders are meeting with cheering response when they found weeklies in order to reach their natural following. The Socialist Party supports two dailies, less to spread their ideas than to print what the capitalistic dailies would stifle. Civic associations, municipal voters' leagues, and legislative voters' leagues, are circulating tons of leaflets and bulletins full of suppressed facts. Within a year [1909–10] five cities have, with the tax-payers' money, started journals to acquaint the citizens with municipal happenings and affairs. In many cities have sprung up private non-partisan weeklies to report civic information. Moreover, the spoken word is once more a power. The demand for lecturers and speakers is insatiable, and the platform bids fair to recover its old prestige. The smotherers are dismayed by the growth of the Chautauqua circuit. Congressional speeches give vent to boycotted truth, and circulate widely under the franking privilege. City clubs and Saturday lunch clubs are formed to listen to facts and ideas tabooed by the daily press. More is made of public hearings before committees of councilmen or legislators.

When all is said, however, the defection of the daily press has been a staggering blow to democracy.

Many insist that the public is able to recognize and pay for the truth. "Trust the public" and *in the end* merit will be rewarded. Time and again men have sunk money in starting an honest and outspoken sheet, confident that soon the public would rally to its support. But such hopes are doomed to disappointment. The editor who turns away bad advertising or defies his big patrons cannot lay his copy on the subscriber's doorstep for as little money as the editor who purveys publicity for all it is worth; and the masses will not pay three cents when another paper that "looks just as good" can be had for a cent. In a word, the art of simulating honesty and independence has outrun the insight of the average reader.

To conclude that the people are not able to recognize and pay for the truth about current happenings simply puts the dissemination of news in a class with other momentous social services. Because people fail to recognize and pay for good books, endowed libraries stud the land. Because they fail to recognize and pay for good instruction, education is provided free or at part cost. Just as the moment came when it was seen that private schools, loan libraries, commercial parks, baths, gymnasia, athletic grounds, and playgrounds would not answer, so the moment is here for recognizing that the commercial news-medium does not adequately meet the needs of democratic citizenship.

Endowment is necessary, and, since we are not yet wise enough to run a public-owned daily newspaper, the funds must come from private sources. In view of the fact that in fifteen years large donations aggregating more than a thousand million of dollars have been made for public purposes in this country, it is safe to predict that, if the usefulness of a non-commercial newspaper be demonstrated, funds will be forthcoming. In the cities, where the secret control of the channels of publicity is easiest, there are likely to be founded financially independent newspapers, the gift of public-spirited men of wealth.

The ultimate control of such a foundation constitutes a problem. A newspaper free to ignore the threats of big advertisers or powerful interests, one not to be bought, bullied, or bludgeoned, one that might at any moment blurt out the damning truth about police protection to vice, corporate tax-dodging, the grabbing of water frontage by railroads, or the non-enforcement of the factory laws, would be of such strategic importance in the struggle for wealth that desperate efforts would be made to chloroform it. If its governing board perpetuated itself by coöptation, it would eventually be packed with "safe" men, who would see to it that the newspaper was run in a "conservative" spirit; for, in the long run, those who can watch for an advantage *all* the time will beat the people, who can watch only *some* of the time.

Chloroformed the endowed newspaper will be, unless it be committed to the onward thought and conscience of the community. This could be done by letting vacancies on the governing board be filled in turn by the local bar association, the medical association, the ministers' union, the degree-granting faculties, the federated teachers, the central labor union, the chamber of commerce, the associated charities, the public libraries, the non-partisan citizens' associations, the improvement leagues, and the social settlements. In this way the endowment would rest ultimately on the chief apexes of moral and intellectual worth in the city.

While giving, with headline, cut, and cartoon, the interesting news,—forgeries and accidents, society and sports, as well as business and politics,—the endowed newspaper would not dramatize crime, or gossip of private affairs; above all, it would not "fake," "doctor," or sensationalize the news. Too self-respecting to use keyhole tactics, and too serious to chronicle the small beer of the wedding trousseau or the divorce court, such a newspaper could not begin to match the commercial press in circulation. But it would reach those who reach the public through the weeklies and monthlies, and would inform the teachers, preachers, lecturers, and public men, who speak to the people eye to eye.

What is more, it would be a *corrective newspaper*, giving a wholesome leverage for lifting up the commercial press. The big papers would not dare be caught smothering or "cooking" the news. The revelations of an independent journal that everybody believed, would be a terror to them, and, under the spur of a competitor not to be frightened, bought up, or tired out, they would be compelled, in sheer self-preservation, to tell the truth much oftener than they do.

The Erie Canal handles less than a twentieth of the traffic across the State of New York, yet, by its standing offer of cheap transportation, it exerts a regulative pressure on railway rates which is realized only when the canal opens in the spring. On the same principle, the endowed newspaper in a given city might print only a twentieth of the daily press output, and yet exercise over the other nineteen twentieths an influence great and salutary.

THE PERSONAL EQUATION IN JOURNALISM

BY HENRY WATTERSON

I

The daily newspaper, under modern conditions, embraces two parts very nearly separate and distinct in their requirements—the journalistic and the commercial.

The aptitude for producing a commodity is one thing, and the aptitude for putting this commodity on the market is quite another thing. The difference is not less marked in newspaper-making than in other pursuits. The framing and execution of contracts for advertising, for printing-paper and ink, linotyping and press-work; the handling of money and credits; the organization of the telegraphic service and postal service; the supervision of machinery—in short, the providing of the vehicle and the power that turns its wheels—is the work of a single mind, and usually it is engrossing work. It demands special talent and ceaseless activity and attention all day long, and every day in the year. Except it be sufficient, considerable success is out of the question. Sometimes its sufficiency is able to float an indifferent product. Without it the best product is likely to languish.

The making of the newspaper, that is, the collating of the news and its consistent and uniform distribution and arrangement, the representation of the mood and tense of the time, a certain continuity, more or less, of thought and purpose,—the popularization of the commodity,—call for energies and capacities of another sort. The editor of the morning newspaper turns night into day. When others sleep he must be awake and astir. His is the only vocation where versatility is not a hindrance or a diversion; where the conventional is not imposed upon his personality. He should be many-sided, and he is often most engaging when he seems least heedful of rule. Yet nowhere is ready and sound discretion in greater or more constant need. The editor must never lose his head. Sure, no less than prompt, judgment is required at every turning. It is his business to think for everybody. Each subordinate must be so drilled and fitted to his place as to become in a sense the replica of his chief. And, even then, when at noon he goes carefully over the work of the night before, he will be fortunate if he finds that all has gone as he planned it, or could wish it.

I am assuming that the make-up of the newspaper is an autocracy: the product of one man, the offspring of a policy; the man indefatigable and conscientious, the policy fixed, sober, and alert. In the famous sea-fight the riffraff of sailors from all nations, whom Paul Jones had picked up wherever he could find them, responded like the parts of a machine to the will of their commander. They seemed inspired, the British Captain Pearson testified before the Court of Inquiry. So in a well-ordered newspaper office, when at midnight wires are flashing and feet are hurrying, and to the onlooking stranger chaos seems to reign, the directing mind and hand have their firm grip upon the tiller-ropes, which extend from the editorial room to the composing-room, from the composing-room to the press-room, and from the press-room to the breakfast-table.

II

Personal journalism had its origin in the crude requirements of the primitive newspaper. An editor, a printer, and a printer's devil, were all-sufficient. For half a century after the birth of the daily newspaper in America, one man did everything which fell under the head of editorial work. The army of reporters, telegraphers, and writers, duly officered and classified, which has come to occupy the larger field, was undreamed of by the pioneers of Boston, New York, Philadelphia, and Baltimore.

Individual ownership was the rule. Little money was embarked. Commonly it was "So-and-So's paper." Whilst the stories of private war, of pistols and coffee, have been exaggerated, the early editors were much beset; were held to strict accountability for what appeared in their columns; sometimes had to take their lives in their hands. In certain regions the duello flourished—one might say became the fashion. Up to the War of Secession, the instance of an editor who had not had a personal encounter, indeed, many encounters, was a rare one. Not a few editors acquired celebrity as "crack shots," gaining more reputation by their guns than by their pens.

The familiar "Stop my paper" was personally addressed, an ebullition of individual resentment.

"Mr. Swain," said an irate subscriber to the founder of the *Philadelphia Ledger*, whom he met one morning on his way to his place of business, "I have stopped your paper, sir—I have stopped your paper."

Mr. Swain was a gentleman of dignity and composure. "Indeed," said he, with a kindly intonation; "come with me and let us see about it."

When the two had reached the spot where the office of the *Ledger* stood, nothing unusual appeared to have happened: the building was still there, the force within apparently engaged in its customary activities. Mr. Swain looked leisurely about him, and turning upon his now expectant but thoroughly puzzled fellow townsman, he said,—

"Everything seems to be as I left it last night. Stop my paper, sir! How could you utter such a falsehood!"

Mr. James Gordon Bennett, the elder, was frequently and brutally assailed. So was Mr. Greeley. Mr. Prentice, though an expert in the use of weapons, did not escape many attacks of murderous intent. Editors fought among themselves, anon with fatal result, especially about Richmond in Virginia, and Nashville in Tennessee, and New Orleans. So self-respecting a gentleman, and withal so peaceful a citizen, as Mr. William Cullen Bryant, fell upon a rival journalist with a horsewhip on Broadway, in New York. The prosy libel suit has come to take the place of the tragic street duel,—

the courts of law to settle what was formerly submitted to the code of honor,—the star part of "fighting editor" having come to be a relic of bygone squalor and glory. The call to arms in 1861 found few of the editorial bullies ready for the fray, and no one of them made his mark as a soldier in battle. They were good only on parade. Even the South had its fill of combat, valor grew too common to be distinguished, and, out of a very excess of broil and blood, along with multiplied opportunities for the display of courage, gun-play got its quietus. The good old times, when it was thought that a man who had failed at all else could still keep a hotel and edit a newspaper, have passed away. They are gone forever. If a gentleman kills his man nowadays, even in honest and fair fight, they call it murder. Editors have actually to be educated to their work, and to work for their living. The soul of Bombastes has departed, and journalism is no longer irradiated and advertised by the flash of arms.

We are wont to hear of the superior integrity of those days. There will always be in direct accountability a certain sense of obligation lacking to the anonymous and impersonal. Most men will think twice before they commit their thoughts to print where their names are affixed. Ambition and vanity, as well as discretion, play a restraining part here; they play it, even though there be no provocation to danger. Yet, seeing that somebody must be somewhere back of the pen, the result would appear still to be referable to private character.

Most of the personal journalists were in alliance with the contemporary politicians; all of them were the slaves of party. Many of them were without convictions, holding to the measures of the time the relation held by the play-actors to the parts that come to them on the stage. Before the advent of the elder Bennett, independent journalism was unknown. In the "partnership" of Seward, Weed, and Greeley,—Mr. Greeley himself described it, he being "the junior member,"—office, no less than public printing, was the object of two members at least of the firm. Lesser figures were squires instead of partners, their chiefs as knights of old. Callender first served, then maligned, Jefferson. Croswell was the man-at-arms of the Albany Regency, valet to Mr. Van Buren. Forney played majordomo to Mr. Buchanan until Buchanan, becoming President, left his poor follower to hustle for himself; a signal, but not anomalous, piece of ingratitude. Prentice held himself to the orders of Clay. Even Raymond, set up in business by the money of Seward's friends, could call his soul his own only toward the end of his life, and then by a single but fatal misstep brought ruin upon the property his genius had created.

Not, indeed, until the latter third of the last century did independent journalism acquire considerable vogue, with Samuel Bowles and Charles A. Dana to lead it in the East, and Murat Halstead and Horace White, followed by Joseph Medill, Victor F. Lawson, Melville E. Stone, and William R. Nelson, in the West.

III

The new school of journalism, sometimes called impersonal and taking its lead from the counting-room, which generally prevails, promises to become universal in spite of an individualist here and there uniting salient characteristics to controlling ownership—a union which in the first place created the personal journalism of other days.

Here, however, the absence of personality is more apparent than real. Control must be lodged somewhere. Whether it be upstairs, or downstairs, it is bound to be—if successful—both single-minded and arbitrary, the embodiment of the inspiration and the will of one man; the expression made to fit the changed conditions which have impressed themselves upon the writing and the speaking of our time.

Eloquence and fancy, oratory and rhetoric, have for the most part given place in our public life to the language of business. More and more do budgets usurp the field of affairs. As fiction has exhausted the situations possible to imaginative writing, so has popular declamation exhausted the resources of figurative speech; and just as the novel seeks other expedients for arousing and holding the interest of its readers, do speakers and publicists, abandoning the florid and artificial, aim at the simple and the lucid, the terse and incisive, the argument the main point, attained, as a rule, in the statement. To this end the counting-room, with its close kinship to the actualities of the world about it, has a definite advantage over the editorial room, as a school of instruction. Nor is there any reason why the head of the counting-room should not be as highly qualified to direct the editorial policies as the financial policies of the newspaper of which, as the agent of a corporation or an estate, he has become the executive; the newspaper thus conducted assuming something of the character of the banking institution and the railway company, being indeed in a sense a common carrier. At least a greater show of stability and respectability, if not a greater sense of responsibility, would be likely to follow such an arrangement, since it would establish a more immediate relation with the community than that embraced by the system which seems to have passed away, a system which was not nearly so accessible, and was, moreover, hedged about by a certain mystery that attaches itself to midnight, to the flare of the footlights and the smell of printers' ink.

I had written thus far and was about to pursue this line of thought with some practical suggestion emanating from a wealth of observation and reminiscence when, reading the *Atlantic Monthly* for March, I encountered the following passage from the very thoughtful paper of Mr. Edward Alsworth Ross, entitled "The Suppression of Important News":—

"More and more the owner of the big daily is a business man who finds it hard to see why he should run his property on different lines from the hotel proprietor, the vaudeville manager, or the owner of an amusement park. The editors are hired men, and they may put into the paper no more of their conscience and ideals than comports with getting the biggest return from the investment. Of course, the old-time editor who owned his paper tried to make money—no sin, that!—but just as to-day the author, the lecturer, or the scholar, tries to make money, namely, within the limitations imposed by his principles and his professional standards. But, now that the provider of the newspaper capital hires the editor instead of the editor hiring the newspaper capital, the paper is likelier to be run as a money-maker pure and simple—a factory where ink and brains are so applied to white paper as to turn out the largest possible marketable product. The capitalist-owner means no harm, but he is not bothered by the standards that hamper the editor-owner. He follows a few simple maxims that work out well enough in selling shoes or cigars or sheet-music."

There follow many examples of the "suppression" of "news." Some of these might be called "important." Others are less so. Here enters a question as to what is "news" and what is not; a question which gives rise to frequent and sometimes considerable differences of opinion.

If the newspaper manager is to make no distinction between vaudeville and journalism, between the selling of white paper disfigured by printer's ink and the selling of shoes, or sheet-music, comment would seem superfluous. I venture to believe that such a manager would nowhere be able long to hold his own against one of an ambition and intelligence better suited to supplying the requirement of the public demand for a vehicle of communication between itself and the world at large. Now and then we see a very well-composed newspaper fail of success because of its editorial character and tone. Now and then we see one succeed, having no editorial character and tone. But the rule is otherwise. The leading dailies everywhere stand for something. They are rarely without aspiration. Because of the unequal capabilities of those who conduct them, they have had their ups and downs: great journals, like the *Chicago Times*, passing out of existence through the lack of an adequate head; failing journals, like the *New York World*, saved from shipwreck by the timely arrival of an adequate head.

My own observation leads me to believe that more is to be charged against the levity and indifference of the average newspaper—perhaps I should say its ignorance and indolence—than against the suppression of important news. As a matter of fact, suppression does not suppress. Conflicting interests attend to that. Mr. Ross relates that on the desk of every editor and sub-editor of a newspaper run by a certain capitalist, who was also a promoter, lay a list of sixteen corporations in which the owner was interested. This was to remind them not to print anything damaging to those particular concerns. In the office the exempted subjects were jocularly referred to as "sacred cows."

This case, familiar to all newspaper men, was an extreme one. The newspaper proved a costly and ignominious failure. Its owner, who ran it on the lines of an "amusement park," landed first in a bankruptcy and then in a criminal court, finally to round up in the penitentiary. Before him, and in the same city, a fellow "journalist" had been given a state-prison sentence. In another and adjacent city the editor and owner of a famous and influential newspaper who had prostituted himself and his calling escaped the stripes of a convict only through executive clemency.

The disposition to publish everything, without regard to private feeling or good neighborhood, may be carried to an excess quite as hurtful to the community as the suppressions of which Mr. Ross tells us in his interesting résumé. The newspaper which constitutes itself judge and jury, which condemns in advance of conviction, which, reversing the English rule of law, assumes the accused guilty instead of innocent,—the newspaper, in short, which sets itself up as a public prosecutor,—is likely to become a common scold and to arouse its readers out of all proportion to any good achieved by publicity. As in other affairs of life, the sense of decency imposes certain reserves, and also the sense of charity.

The justest complaint which may be laid at the door of the modern newspaper seems to me its invasion of the home, and the conversion of its reporters into detectives. Pretending to be the defender of liberty, it too often is the assailant of private right. Each daily issue should indeed aim to be the history of yesterday, but it should be clean as well as truthful; and as we seek in our usual walks and ways to avoid that which is nasty and ghastly, so should we, in the narration of scandal and crime, guard equally against exaggeration and pruriency, nor be ashamed to suppress that which may be too vile to tell.

In a recent article Mr. Victor Rosewater, the accomplished editor of the *Omaha Bee*, takes issue with Mr. Ross upon the whole line of his argument, which he subjects to the critical analysis of a practical journalist. The muckraking magazines, so extolled by Mr. Ross, are shown by Mr. Rosewater to be the merest collection of already printed newspaper material, the periodical writer having time to put them together in more connected form. He also shows that the Chautauqua circuits are but the emanations of newspaper advertising; and that, if newspapers of one party make suppressions in the interest of their party, the newspapers of the other are ready with the antidote. Obviously, Mr. Ross is either a newspaper subaltern, or a college professor. In either case he is, as Mr. Rosewater shows, a visionary.

In nothing does this betray itself so clearly as in the suggestion of "an endowed newspaper," which is Mr. Ross's remedy for the evils he enumerates.

"Because newspapers, as a rule, prefer construction to destruction," says Mr. Rosewater, "they are accused by Mr. Ross of malfeasance for selfish purposes. True, a newspaper depends for its own prosperity upon the prosperity of the community in which it is published. The newspaper selfishly prefers business prosperity to business adversity. A panic is largely psychological, and the newspapers can do much to aggravate or to mitigate its severity. There is no question that to the willful efforts of the newspapers as a body to allay public fear and to restore business confidence is to be credited the short duration and comparative mildness of the last financial cataclysm. Would an endowed newspaper have acted differently? Most people would freely commend the newspapers for what they did to start the wheels of industry again revolving, and this is the first time I have seen them condemned for suppressing 'important news' of business calamity and industrial distress in subservience to a worship of advertising revenue."

The truth of this can hardly be denied. Most fair-minded observers will agree with Mr. Rosewater that "a few black sheep in the newspaper fold do not make the whole flock black, nor do the combined imperfections of all newspapers condemn them to failure"; and I cannot resist quoting entire the admirable conclusion with which a recognized newspaper authority disposes of a thoroughly theoretic newspaper critic.

"Personally," says Mr. Rosewater, "I would like to see the experiment of an endowed newspaper tried, because I am convinced comparison would only redound to the advantage of the newspaper privately conducted as a commercial undertaking. The newspaper most akin to the endowed newspaper in this country is published in the interest of the Christian Science Church. With it, 'important news' is news calculated to promote the propaganda of the faith, and close inspection of its columns would disclose news-suppression in every issue. On the other hand, a daily newspaper, standing on its own bottom, must have readers to make its advertising space valuable, and without a reasonable effort to cover all the news and command public confidence, the standing and clientage of the paper cannot be successfully maintained. The endowed paper pictured to us as the ideal paper, run by a board of governors filled in turn by representatives of the various uplift societies enumerated by Professor Ross, would blow hot and would blow cold, would have no consistent policy or principles, would be unable to alter the prevailing notion of what constitutes important news, and would be from the outset busily engaged in a work of news-suppression to suit the whims of the particular hobby-riders who happened for the moment to be in dominating control."

In journalism, as in statesmanship, the doctrinaire is more confident than the man of affairs. So, in war, the lieutenant is bolder in the thought than the captain in the action. Often the newspaper subaltern, distrusting his chief, calls that "mercenary" which is in reality "discrimination." It is a pity that there is not more of this latter in our editorial practice.

IV

Disinterestedness, unselfish devotion to the public interest, is the soul of true journalism as of true statesmanship; and this is as likely to proceed from the counting-room as from the editorial room; only, the business manager must be a journalist.

The journalism of Paris is personal, the journalism of London is impersonal—that is to say, the one illustrates the self-exploiting, individualized star-system, the other the more sedate and orderly, yet not less responsible, commercial system; and it must be allowed that, in both dignity and usefulness, the English is to be preferred to the French journalism. It is true that English publishers are sometimes elevated to the peerage. But this is nowise worse than French and American editors becoming candidates for office. In either case, the public and the press are losers in the matter of the service rendered, because journalism and office are so antipathetic that their union must be destructive to both.

The upright man of business, circumspect in his everyday behavior and jealous of his commercial honor, needs only to be educated in the newspaper business to bring to it the characteristic virtues which shine and prosper in the more ambitious professional and business pursuits. The successful man in the centres of activity is usually a worldly-wise and prepossessing person. Other things being equal, success of the higher order inclines to those qualities of head and heart, of breeding and education and association, which go to the making of what we call a gentleman. The element of charm, scarcely less than the elements of energy, integrity, and penetration, is a prime ingredient. Add breadth and foresight, and we have the greater result of fortune and fame.

All these essentials to preëminent manhood must be fulfilled by the newspaper which aspires to preëminence. And there is no reason why this may not spring from the business end, why they may not exist and flourish there, exhaling their perfume into every department; in short, why they may not tempt ambition. The newspapers, as Hamlet observes of the players, are the abstracts and brief chronicles of the time. It were indeed better to have a bad epitaph when you die than their ill report while you live, even from those of the baser sort; how much more from a press having the confidence and respect—and yet more than these, the affection—of the community? Hence it is that special college training is beginning to be thought of, and occasionally tried; and, while this is subject to very serious disadvantage on the experimental side, its ethical value may in the long run find some way to give it practical application and to make it permanent as an arm of the newspaper service. Assuredly, character is an asset, and nowhere does it pay surer and larger dividends than in the newspaper business.

V

We are passing through a period of transition. The old system of personal journalism having gone out, and the new system of counting-room journalism having not quite reached a full realization of itself, the editorial function seems to have fallen into a lean and slippered state, the matters of tone and style honored rather in the breach than in the observance. Too many ill-trained, uneducated lads have graduated out of the city editor's room by sheer force of audacity and enterprise into the more important posts. Too often the counting-room takes no supervision of the editorial room beyond the immediate selling value of the paper the latter turns out. Things upstairs are left at loose ends. There are examples of opportunities lost through absentee landlordism.

These conditions, however, are ephemeral. They will yield before the progressive requirements of a process of popular evolution which is steadily lifting the masses out of the slough of degeneracy and ignorance. The dime novel has not the vogue it once had. Neither has the party organ. Readers will not rest forever content under the impositions of fake or colored news; of misleading headlines; of false alarums and slovenly writing. Already they begin to discriminate, and more and clearly they will learn to discriminate, between the meretricious and the true.

The competition in sensationalism, to which we owe the yellow press, as it is called, will become a competition in cleanliness and accuracy. The counting-room, which is next to the people and carries the purse, will see that decency pays, that good sense and good faith are good investments, and it will look closer to the personal character and the moral product of the editorial room, requiring better equipment and more elevated standards. There will never again be a Greeley, or a Raymond, or a Dana, playing the rôle of "star" and personally exploited by everything appearing in journals which seemed to exist mainly to glorify them. Each was in his way a man of superior attainments. Each thought himself an unselfish servant of the public. Yet each had his limitations—his ambitions and prejudices, his likes and dislikes, intensified and amplified by the habit of personalism, often unconscious. And, this personal element eliminated, why may not the impersonal head of the coming newspaper—proud of his profession, and satisfied with the results of its ministration—render a yet better account to God and the people in unselfish devotion to the common interest?

THE PROBLEM OF THE ASSOCIATED PRESS

BY AN OBSERVER

I

The question of suppressed or tainted news has in recent years been repeatedly agitated, and reformers of all brands have urged that the majority of the newspapers of the country are business-tied—that they are ruled according to the sordid ambition of the counting-house rather than by the untrammeled play of the editorial intellect. Capitalism is alleged to be playing ducks and drakes with the Anglo-Saxon tradition of a free press.

The most important instance of criticism of this kind is afforded by current attacks upon the Associated Press. The Associated Press, as everybody knows, is the greatest news-gathering organization in the world; it supplies with their daily general information more than half the population of the United States. That it should be accused, in these times of class controversy and misunderstanding, of being a "news trust," and of coloring its news in the interest of capital and reaction, is therefore an excessively grave matter. Yet in the last six months it has been accused of both those things. So persistent has been the assertion of certain socialists that the Associated Press colors industrial news in the interest of the employer, that its management has sued them for libel. That it is a trust is the contention of one of its rivals, the Sun News Bureau of New York, whose prayer for its dissolution under the Sherman law, as a monopoly in restraint of trade, is now before the Department of Justice in Washington.[5]

5. This charge made by the *New York Sun*, in February, 1914, was not sustained in an opinion given by the Attorney General of the United States on March 17, 1915.—ED.

To the writer, the main questions at issue, so far as the public is concerned, seem to be as follows:—

1. Is the business of collecting and distributing news in bulk essentially monopolistic? 2. If it is, and if it can not be satisfactorily performed by an unlimited number of competitive agencies (that is, individual newspapers), is the Associated Press in theory and practice the best type of centralized organization for the purpose?

The first question presents little difficulty to the practical journalist. A successful agency for the gathering of news must be monopolistic. No newspaper is rich enough, the attention of no editor is ubiquitous enough, to be able to collect at first hand a tithe of the multitudinous items which a public of catholic curiosity expects to find neatly arranged on its breakfast table. Take the large journals of New York and Boston, with their columns of news from all parts of the United States and the world. Their bills for telegrams and cablegrams alone would be prohibitive of dividends, to say nothing of their bills for the collection of the news. A public educated by a number of newspapers with their powers of observation and instruction whetted to superlative excellence by keen competition would no doubt be ideal; but a journalistic Utopia of that kind is no more feasible than other Utopias. Unlimited and unassisted competition between, say, six newspapers in the same city or district would be about as feasible economically as unlimited competition between six railway lines running from Boston to New York. The need for a common service of foreign and national news must therefore be admitted. To supply such a service, even in these days of especially cheap telegraph and cable rates for press matter, requires a great deal of money, and a press agency has a great deal of money to spend only if it has also a large number of customers.

As the number of newspapers is limited, it is clear that the press agency has strong claims to be recognized as a public service, and to be classed with railways, telephones, telegraphs, waterworks, and many other forms of corporate venture which even the wildest radical admits cannot be subjected to the anarchy of unrestricted competition. Thus the simple charge that the Associated Press is a monopoly cannot be held to condemn it. But, to invert Mr. Roosevelt's famous phrase, there are bad trusts as well as good trusts. That the Associated Press is powerful enough to be a bad trust if those who control it so desire must be admitted offhand. It is a tremendously effective organization. Its service is supplied to more than 850 of the leading newspapers, with a total circulation of, probably, about 20,000,000 copies a day.

The Associated Press is the child of the first effort at coöperative news-gathering ever made. Back in the forties of the last century, before the Atlantic cable was laid, newspapers began to spend ruinous sums in getting the earliest news from Europe. Those were the days in which the first ship-news dispatch-boats were launched to meet vessels as they entered New York harbor, and to race back with the news to their respective offices. The competition grew to the extent even of sending fast boats all the way to Europe, and soon became extravagant enough to cause its collapse. Then seven New York newspapers organized a joint service. This service, which was meant primarily to cover European news, grew slowly to cover the United States. Newspapers in other cities were taken into it on a reciprocal basis. The news of the Association was supplied at that time in return for a certain sum, the newspapers undertaking on their part to act as the local correspondents of the Association. A reciprocal arrangement with Reuter's, the great European agency, followed, whereby it supplied the Associated Press with its foreign service, and the Associated Press gave to Reuter's the use of its American service.

Even so, the Associated Press did not carry all before it. In the seventies a number of Western newspapers formed the Western Associated Press. A period of sharp competition followed, but in 1882 the two associations signed a treaty of partnership for ten years. They were not long in supreme control of the field, however. The Associated Press of those days, like its successor to-day, was a close corporation in the sense that its members could and did veto the inclusion of rivals. As the West grew, new newspapers sprang up and were kept in the cold by their established rivals. The result was the United Press, which soon worked up an effective service. The Associated Press tried to cripple it by a rule that no newspaper subscribing to its service should have access to the news of the Associated Press; but in spite of the rule the United Press waxed strong and might have become a really formidable competitor had not the Associated Press been able to buy a controlling share in it. A harmonious business agreement followed; but in accordance with the business methods of those days the public was not apprized of the agreement, and when, in 1892, its existence became known, there was a row and a readjustment. The United Press absorbed the old Associated Press of New York, and the Western Associated Press again became independent. Reuter's agency continued to supply both associations with its European service.

But the ensuing period of competition did not last. Three years later, the Western Associated Press achieved a monopolistic agreement with Reuter's, carried the war into the United Press territory,—the South and the country east of the Alleghanies,—got a number of New York newspapers to join it, and effected a national organization.

II

That national organization is, to all intents and purposes, the Associated Press of to-day. The only really important change has been in its transference as a company from the jurisdiction of Illinois to that of New York. This change was accomplished in 1900, owing to an adverse judgment of the Supreme Court of Illinois. To grasp the significance of that judgment, and indeed the current agitation against the Associated Press, it is necessary to sketch briefly its rules and methods.

The Associated Press is not a commercial company in the sense that it is a dividend-hunting concern. Under the terms of its present charter, the corporation "is not to make a profit or to make or declare dividends and is not to engage in the selling of intelligence or traffic in the same." It is simply meant to be the common agent of a number of subscribing newspapers, for the interchange of news which each collects in its own district, and for the collection of news such as subscribers cannot collect singlehanded: that is, foreign news and news concerning certain classes of domestic happenings. Its board of directors consists of journalists and publishers connected with subscribing newspapers, who serve without payment. Its executive work is done by a salaried general manager and his assistants. It is financed on a basis of weekly assessments levied, according to their size and custom, upon newspapers which are members. The sum thus collected comes to about $3,000,000 a year. It is spent partly for the hire of special wires from the telegraph companies, and partly for the maintenance of special news-collecting staffs. The mileage of leased wires is immense, amounting to about 22,000 miles by day and 28,000 miles by night. Nor does the organization, as some of its critics seem to imagine, get any special privileges from the telegraph companies. Such privileges belonged to its early history, when business standards were lower than they are now.

The Associated Press has at least one member in every city of any size in the country. That in itself insures it a good news-service; but, as indicated above, it has in all important centres a bureau of its own. Important events, whether fixed, like national conventions, or fortuitous, like strikes or floods or shipwrecks, it covers more comprehensively than any single newspaper can do. Its foreign service is ubiquitous. It no longer depends upon its arrangement with Reuter's, and other foreign news-agencies: early in the present century the intelligence thus collected was found to lack the American point of view, and an extensive foreign service was formed, with local headquarters in London, Paris, and other European capitals, Peking, Tokyo, Mexico, and Havana, and with scores of correspondents all over the world.

Enough has been said to show that its efficiency and the manner of its organization combine to give the Associated Press a distinct savor of monopoly. As the Sun News Bureau and other rivals have found, it cannot be effectively competed against. Too many of the richest and most powerful newspapers belong to it.

Is it a harmful monopoly? Its critics, as explained above, are busy proving that it is. They urge that, being a close corporation, it stifles trade in the selling of news, and that it is not impartial.

The first argument is based upon the following facts. Membership in the Associated Press is naturally valuable. An Associated Press franchise to a newspaper in New York or Chicago is worth from $50,000 to $200,000.[6] To share such a privilege is not in human or commercial nature. One of the first rules of the organization is, therefore, that no new newspaper can be admitted without the consent of members within competitive radius. Naturally, that assent is seldom given. This "power of protest" has not been kept without a struggle. The law-suit of 1900 was due to it. The *Chicago Inter-Ocean* was refused admission,[7] and went to law. The case went to the Supreme Court of Illinois, which ruled that a press agency like the Associated Press was in the nature of a public service and as such ought to be open to everybody. To have yielded to the judgment would have smashed the Associated Press, so it reorganized under the laws of New York, with the moral satisfaction of knowing that the courts of Missouri had upheld what the Illinois court had condemned. Its new constitution, which is that of to-day, keeps in effect the right of protest, the only difference being that a disappointed applicant for membership gets the not very useful consolation of being able to appeal to the association in the slender hope that four-fifths of the members will vote for his admission.

6. In the appraisal of the estate of Joseph Pulitzer in 1914, the two Associated Press franchises held by the *New York World*, one for the morning and one for the evening edition, were valued at $240,000 each.— ED.

7. This is an error which is corrected in Mr. Stone's reply, cf. p. 124.

The practical working of the rule has undoubtedly been monopolistic; not so much because it has rendered the Associated Press a monopoly, but because it has rendered it the mother, potential and sometimes actual, of countless small monopolies. On account of the size of the United States and the diverse interests of the various sections, there is in our country no daily press with a national circulation. Newspapers depend primarily upon their local constituencies. In each journalistic geographic unit, if the expression may be allowed, one or more newspapers possess the Associated Press franchise. Such newspapers have in the excellent and comparatively cheap Associated Press service an instrument for monopoly hardly less valuable than a rebate-giving railway may be to a commercial corporation. It is also alleged by some of its enemies that the Associated Press still at times enjoins its members against taking simultaneously the service of its rival.

It is easy to argue that, because the Associated Press is a close corporation, it cannot be a monopoly, and that those who are really trying to make a "news trust" of it are they who insist that it ought to be open to all comers; but in practice the argument is a good deal of a quibble. The facts remain that, as shown above, an effective news-agency has to be tremendously rich; that to be tremendously rich it has to have prosperous constituents; and that the large majority of prosperous newspapers of the country belong to the Associated Press. In the writer's opinion it would be virtually impossible, as things stand, for any of the Associated Press's rivals to become the Associated Press's equal, upon either a commercial or a coöperative basis.

III

The tremendous importance of the question of the fairness of the Associated Press service is now apparent. If it is deliberately tainted, as the socialists and radicals aver, there is virtually no free press in the country. The question is a very delicate one. Enemies of the Associated Press assert in brief that its stories about industrial troubles are colored in the interest of the employer; that its political news shows a similar bias in favor of the plutocratic party, whatever that may be; that, in fact, it is used as a class organ. In the Presidential campaign of 1912, Mr. Roosevelt's followers insisted that the doings of their candidates were blanketed. In the recent labor troubles [1914] in West Virginia, Michigan, and Colorado, the friends of labor have made the same complaint of one-sidedness in the interest of the employer.

Not only do the directors of the Associated Press deny all insinuations of unfairness, but they argue that partisanship, and especially political partisanship, would be impossible in view of the multitudinous shades of political opinion represented by their constituents. They can also adduce with justice the fact that in nearly every campaign more than one political manager has accused them of favoritism, only to retract when the heat of the campaign was over. The charge of industrial and social partisanship they meet with a point-blank denial. It is impossible in the space of this paper to sift the evidence pro and con. Pending action by the courts the only safe thing to do is to look at the question in terms of tendencies rather than of facts.

The Associated Press, it has been shown, tends to be a monopoly. Does it tend to be a one-sided monopoly? The writer believes that it does. He believes that it may fairly be said that the Associated Press as a corporation is inclined to see things through conservative spectacles, and that its correspondents, despite the very high average of their fairness, tend to do the same thing. It could hardly be otherwise, although it is possible that there is nothing deliberate in the tendency. Nearly all the subscribers to the Associated Press are the most respectable and successful newspaper publishers in their neighborhoods. They belong to that part of the community which has a stake in the settled order of things; their managers are business men among business men; they have relations with the local magnates of finance and commerce: naturally, whatever their political views may be (and the majority of the powerful organs of the country are conservative), their aggregate influence tends to be on the side of conservatism.

The tendency, too, is enhanced by the articles under which the Associated Press is incorporated. There is special provision against fault-finding on the part of members. The corporation is given the right to expel a member "for any conduct on his part or the part of any one in his employ or connected with his newspaper, which in its absolute discretion it shall deem of such a character as to be prejudicial to the interest and welfare of the corporation and its members, or to justify such expulsion. The action of the members of the corporation in such regard shall be final, and there shall be no right of appeal or review of such action." The Associated Press rightly prides itself upon the standing of its correspondents. The majority of them are drawn from the ranks of the matter-of-fact respectable. In the nature of their calling, they are not likely to be economists or theoretical politicians. In the case of a strike, for instance, their instinct might well be to go to the employer or the employer's lieutenant for news rather than to the strike-leader.

Whether the Associated Press is a monopoly within the meaning of the anti-trust law, whether it actually colors news as the socialists aver, must be left to the courts to decide. The point to be noticed here is that it might color news if it wanted to, and that it does exercise certain monopolistic functions. That in itself is a dangerous state of affairs: but it seems to be one that might be rectified. The Illinois Supreme Court has pointed the way. The news-agency is essentially monopolistic. It has much in common with the ordinary public-utility monopoly. It should therefore be treated like a public-utility corporation. It should be subject to government regulation and supervision, and its service should be open to all customers. Were this done, the Associated Press would be altered but not destroyed. Its useful features would surely remain and its drawbacks as surely be lessened. The right of protest would be entirely swept away; membership would be unlimited; the threat of expulsion for fault-finding would be automatically removed from above the heads of members; all newspapers of all shades would be free to apply the corrective of criticism; and if its news were none the less unfair, some arrangement could presumably be made for government restraint.

The Press Association of England is an unlimited coöperative concern. Any newspaper can subscribe to it, and new subscribers are welcome. Especially in the provincial field, it is as powerful a factor in British journalism as the Associated Press is in the journalism of the United States, yet its very openness has saved it from the taint of partiality. To organize the Associated Press on the same lines would, of course, entail hardship to its present constituents. They would be exposed to fierce local competition. The value of their franchises would dwindle. Such rival agencies as exist might be ruined, for they could hardly compete with the Associated Press in the open market. But it is difficult to see how American journalism would suffer from a regulated monopoly of that kind; and the public would certainly be benefited, for it would continue to enjoy the excellent service of the Associated Press, with its invaluable foreign telegrams and its comprehensive domestic news; it would be safeguarded to no small extent from the danger of local or national news-monopolies and from insidiously tainted news.

Such a reform, if reform there has to be, would, in a word, be constructive. The alternatives to it, as the writer understands the situation, would be destructive and empirical. The organization of the Associated Press would either be cut to pieces or destroyed. There would thus be a chaos of ineffective competition among either coöperative or commercial press agencies. Equal competition among a number of coöperative associations would, for reasons already explained, mean comparatively ineffective and weak services. Competition among commercial agencies would have even less to recommend it. The latter must by their nature be more susceptible to special influences than the coöperative agency. They are controlled by a few business men, not by their customers. Competing commercial agencies would almost inevitably come to represent competing influences in public life; while, if worse came to worst, a commercialized "news trust" would clearly be more dangerous than a coöperative news trust. The great reactionary influences of business would have freer play upon its directors than they can have upon the directors of an organization like the Associated Press. If it be decided that even the Associated Press is not immune from such influences, the public should, the writer believes, think twice before demanding its destruction, instead of its alteration to conform with the modern conception of the public-service corporation.

THE ASSOCIATED PRESS: A REPLY

BY MELVILLE E. STONE

[*A letter to the Editor of the Atlantic Monthly, dated August 1, 1914.*]

An article under the title, "The Problem of The Associated Press," appeared in the July issue of the Atlantic. It was anonymous and may be without claim to regard. It is marred by several mistakes of fact. Some of them are inexcusable: the truth might so easily have been learned. Nevertheless it is desirable that everybody should know all about the Associated Press, whether it is an unlawful and dangerous monopoly, or whether it is in the business of circulating "tainted news." Its telegrams are published in full or in abbreviated form, in nearly 900 daily newspapers having an aggregate circulation of many millions of copies. Upon the accuracy of these news dispatches, one half of the people of the United States depend for the conduct of their various enterprises, as well as for the facts upon which to base their opinions of the activities of the world. With a self-governing nation, it is all important that such an agency as the Associated Press furnish as nearly as may be the truth. To mislead is an act of treason.

The writer's history is at fault. For instance, the former Associated Press never bought a controlling share of the old-time United Press, as he alleges. Nor did the *Chicago Inter-Ocean* go to law because it was refused admission. It was a charter member; it admittedly violated a by-law, discipline was administered and against this discipline the law was invoked, and a decision adverse to the then existing Associated Press resulted. The assertion that a "franchise to a newspaper in New York or Chicago is worth from $50,000 to $200,000," will amuse thousands of people who know that five morning Associated Press newspapers of Chicago, the *Chronicle*, the *Record*, the *Times*, the *Freie Presse*, and the *Inter-Ocean*, have ceased publication in the somewhat recent past, and their owners have not received a penny for their so-called "franchises." The *Boston Traveler* and *Evening Journal* were absorbed and their memberships thrown away. The *Christian Science Monitor* voluntarily gave up its membership and took another service which it preferred. The *Hartford Post*, *Bridgeport Post*, *New Haven Union*, and *Schenectady Union* did the same. Cases where Associated Press papers have ceased publication have not been infrequent. Witness the *Worcester Spy*, *St. Paul Globe*, *Minneapolis Times*, *Denver Republican*, *San Francisco Call*, *New Orleans Picayune*, *Indianapolis Sentinel*, and *Philadelphia Times*, as well as many others.

The statement that the Press Association of England is an unlimited coöperative organization betrays incomplete information. Instead, it is a share company with an issued capital of £49,440 sterling. On this capital, in 1913, it made £3,708. 9. 10, or nearly eight per cent. And it had in its treasury at the end of that year a surplus of £23,281. 19. 6, or a sum nearly equal to fifty per cent. of its capitalization. It sells news to newspapers, clubs, hotels, and newsrooms. It is not, as is the Associated Press, a clearing-house for the exchange of news. It gathers all its information by its own employees and sells it outright. Finally, it does not serve all applicants, but declines, as it always has, to furnish its news to the London papers.

But there is a more important matter. It is said that the business of collecting and distributing news is essentially monopolistic. But how can this be? The field is an open one. A single reporter may enter it, and so may an association of reporters. The business in any case may be confined to the news of a city or it may be extended to include a state, a nation, or the world. The material facilities for the transmission of news, so far as they are of a public or quasi-public nature, the mail or the telegraph, are open to the use of all on the same terms. The subject-matter of news, events of general interest, are not property and cannot be appropriated. The element of property exists only in the story of the event which the reporter makes and the diligence which he uses to bring it to the place of publication. This element of property is simply the right of the reporter to the fruit of his own labor.

The "Recessional" was a report of the Queen's Jubilee. It was made by Rudyard Kipling and was his property for that reason, to be disposed of by him as he thought proper. He might have copyrighted it and reserved to himself the exclusive right of publication during the period of the copyright. He chose rather to use his common-law right of first publication and he did this by selling it to the *London Times*. He was not under obligation, moral or legal, to sell it at the same time to any other publisher.

Every other reporter stands upon the same footing and, as the author of his story, is, by every principle of law and equity, entitled to a monopoly of his manuscript until he voluntarily assigns it or surrenders it to the public. He does not monopolize the news. He cannot do that, for real news is as woman's wit, of which Rosalind said, "Make the doors upon [it] and it will out at the casement; shut that and 'twill out at the keyhole; stop that, 'twill fly with the smoke out at the chimney." The reporter as a mere laborer, engaged in personal service, is simply free from compulsion to give or sell his labor to one seeking it. Such is the state of the law to-day.

And the English courts go further and uniformly hold that news telegrams may not be pirated, even after publication. In a dozen British colonies statutory protection of such despatches is given for varying periods. In this country there have been a number of decisions looking to the same end. The output of the Associated Press is not the news; it is a story of the news, written by reporters employed to serve the membership. The organization issues no newspaper; it prints nothing. As a reporter, it brings its copy to the editor, who is free to print it, abbreviate it, or throw it away. And to this reporter's work, the reporter and the members employing him have, by law and morals, undeniably an exclusive right.

The next question involves the integrity of the Associated Press service. The cases of alleged bias he cites are unfortunate. Any claim that the doings of the Progressives in 1912 were "blanketed" by the Associated Press is certainly unwarranted. Our records show that the organization reported more than three times as many words concerning the activities of the Progressives as it did concerning those of all their opponents combined. There were reasons for this. It was a new party in the field, and naturally awakened unusual interest. But also, it should be said that Colonel Roosevelt has expert knowledge of newspaper methods. He understands the value of preparing his speeches in advance and furnishing them in time to enable the Associated Press to send them to its members by mail. They are put in type in the newspaper offices leisurely and the proofs are carefully read. When one of his speeches is delivered, a word or two by telegraph "releases" it, and a full and accurate publication of his views results. While he was President he often gave us his messages a month in advance; they were mailed to Europe and to the Far East, and appeared in the papers abroad the morning after their delivery to Congress. Before he went to Africa, the speeches he delivered a year later at Oxford and in Paris were prepared, put in type, proof-read, and laid away for use when required. This is not an unusual or an unwise practice. It assures a speaker wide publicity and saves him the annoyance of faulty reporting. Neither Mr. Wilson nor Mr. Taft was able to do this, although frequently urged to do so. They spoke extemporaneously, often late in the evening, and under conditions which made it physically impossible to make a satisfactory report, or to transmit it by wire broadcast over the country.

As to the West Virginia coal strike: a magazine charged that the Associated Press had suppressed the facts and that as a consequence no one knew there had been trouble. The authors were indicted for libel. One witness only has yet been heard. He was called by the defense, and in the taking of his deposition it was disclosed that at the date of the publication over 93,000 words had been delivered by the Associated Press to the New York papers. Something like 60 columns respecting the matter had been printed.

However, "The point to be noticed," says your writer, "is that it [the Associated Press] might color news if it wanted to, and that it does exercise certain monopolistic functions. That in itself is a dangerous state of affairs; but it seems to be one that might be rectified." And, as a remedy, he proposes that "its service should be open to all customers." This is most interesting. If the news-service is untrustworthy, it would naturally seem plain that the activities of the agency should be restricted, not extended. Instead of enlarging its field of operations, there should be, if possible, a law forbidding it to take in any new members, or, indeed, summarily putting it out of business. If the Associated Press is corrupt, it is too large now, and no other newspaper should be subjected to its baleful influence.

Your critic adds that then, "if its news were none the less unfair, some arrangement could presumably be made for government restraint." Since the battle against government control of the press was fought nearly two centuries ago, it seems scarcely worth while to waste much effort over this suggestion. Censorship by the king's agents was the finest flower of mediæval tyranny. It is hard to believe that anyone, in this hour, should suggest a return to it.

Under the closely censored method of this coöperative organization, notwithstanding the wide range of its operations, and although its service has included millions of words every month, it is proper to say that there has never been a trial for libel, nor have the expenses in connection with libel suits exceeded a thousand dollars in the aggregate. This should be accepted as some evidence of the standard of accuracy maintained.

As to the refusal of the Associated Press to admit to membership every applicant, the suggestion is made that this puts such a limit on the number of newspapers as to "stifle trade in the selling of news." Thus, says your critic, the Association is "the mother, potential and sometimes actual, of countless small monopolies." In reply, it may be said that we are in no danger of a dearth of newspapers. There are more news journals in the United States than in all the world beside. If the whole foreign world were divided into nations of the size of this country, each nation would have but 80 daily newspapers, while we have over 2,400. And as to circulation, we issue a copy of a daily paper for every three of our citizens who can read and are over ten years of age. With our methods of rapid transportation, hundreds of daily papers might be discontinued, and still leave every citizen able to have his morning paper delivered at his breakfast table. Every morning paper between New York and Chicago might be suppressed, and yet, by the fast mail trains, papers from the two terminal cities could be delivered so promptly that no one in the intervening area would be left without the current world's news. Every angle of every fad, or *ism*, outside the walls of Bedlam, finds an advocate with the largest freedom of expression. Our need is not for more papers, but for better papers—papers issuing truthful news and with clearer sense of perspective as to news.

Entirely independent of the Associated Press, or any influence it might have upon the situation, there has been a noticeable shrinkage in the number of important newspapers in the recent past. One reason has been the lack of demand by the public for the old-time partisan journal. Instead, the very proper requirement has been for papers furnishing the news impartially, and communities therefore no longer divide, as formerly, on political lines in their choice of newspapers. The increased cost of white paper and of labor has also had an effect.

Since there are some 500 or more daily newspapers getting on very well without the advantage of the Associated Press "franchises," it can hardly be said that we have reached a stage where this service is indispensable. This is strikingly true in the light of the fact that in a number of cities the papers making the largest profits are those that have not, nor have ever had, membership in the Associated Press.

It will be agreed at once that private right must ever give way to public good. If it can be shown that, as contended, the national welfare requires that those who, without any advantage over their fellow editors, have built up an efficient coöperative news-gathering agency, must share the accumulated value of the good-will they have achieved, with those who have been less energetic, we may have to give heed to the claim. Such a contention, so persistently urged as it has been, is certainly flattering to the membership and management of the Associated Press.

But, however agreeable it always is to divide up other people's property, before settling the matter there are some things to think of. First, it must be the public good that forces this invasion of private right, not the desire of someone who, with an itch to start a newspaper, feels that he would prefer the Associated Press service. Second, the practical effect of a rule such as was laid down by the Illinois Supreme Court, requiring the organization to render service to all applicants, must be carefully considered. News is not a commodity of the nature of coal, or wood. It is incorporeal. It does not pass from seller to buyer in the way ordinary commodities do. Although the buyer receives it, the seller does not cease to possess it. In order to make a news-gathering agency possible, it has been found necessary to limit, by stringent rules, the use of the service by the member. Thus each member of the Associated Press is prohibited from making any use of the dispatches furnished him, other than to publish them in his newspaper. If such a restriction were not imposed, any member, on receipt of his news service, might at once set up an agency of his own and put an end to the general organization. This rule, as well as all disciplinary measures, would disappear under the plan proposed by the critic in the *Atlantic.* A buyer might be expelled, but to-morrow he could demand readmission. There would in practice no longer be members with a right of censorship over the management; instead, there would be one seller and an unlimited number of buyers. Then, indeed, there would be a monopoly of the worst sort. And government censorship, with all of its attendant and long since admitted evils, would follow. Under a Republican administration, we should have a Republican censor; under a Democratic administration, a Democratic censor. And a free press would no longer exist.

Absolute journalistic inerrancy is not possible. But we are much nearer it to-day than ever before. And it is toward approximate inerrancy in its despatches that the Associated Press is striving. If in its method of organization, or in its manner of administration, it is violating any law, or is making for evil, then it should be punished, or suppressed. If any better method for securing an honest, impartial news service can be devised, by all means let us have it. But that the plan proposed would better the situation, is clearly open to doubt.

CONFESSIONS OF A PROVINCIAL EDITOR

BY PARACELSUS

There is something at once deliciously humorous and pathetic, to the editor of a small daily in the provinces, about that old-fashioned phrase, "the liberty of the press." It is another one of those matters lying so near the marge-land of what is mirthful and what is sad that a tilt of the mood may slip it into either. To the general, doubtless, it is a truth so obvious that it is never questioned, a bequest from our forefathers that has paid no inheritance tax to time. In all the host of things insidiously un-American which have crept into our life, thank Heaven! say these unconscious Pharisees, the "press," if somewhat freakish, has remained free. So it is served up as a toast at banquets, garnished with florid rhetoric; it is still heard from old-fashioned pulpits; it cannot die, even though the conditions which made the phrase possible have passed away.

The pooh-poohing of the elders, the scoffing of the experienced, has little effect upon a boy's mind when it tries to do away with so palpable a truth as that concerning the inability of a chopped-up snake to die until sunset, or that matter-of-fact verity that devil's darning needles have little aim in life save to sew up the ears of youths and maidens. So with that glib old fantasy, "America's free and untrammeled press": it needs a vast deal of argument to convince an older public that, as a matter to be accepted without a question, it has no right to exist. The conditioning clause was tacked on some years ago, doubtless when the old-time weekly began to expand into the modern small daily. The weekly was a periodic pamphlet; the daily disdained its inheritance, and subordinated the expression of opinion to the printing of those matters from which opinion is made. The cost of equipment of a daily newspaper, compared to the old-fashioned weekly, as a general thing makes necessary for the launching of such a venture a well-organized stock company, and in this lies much of the trouble.

Confessions imply previous wrong-doing. Mine, while they are personal enough, are really more interesting because of the vast number of others they incriminate. If two editors from lesser cities do not laugh in each other's faces, after the example of Cicero's augurs, it is because they are more modern, and choose to laugh behind each other's backs. So, in turning state's evidence, I feel less a coward than a reformer.

What circumstance has led me to believe concerning the newspaper situation in a hundred and one small cities of this country is so startling in its unexplained brevity, that I scarce dare parade it as a prelude to my confessions. So much of my experience is predicated upon it that I do not dare save it for a peroration. Here it is, then, somewhat more than half-truth, somewhat less than the truth itself: "A newspaper in a small city is not a legitimate business enterprise." That seems bold and bare enough to stamp me as sensational, does it not? Hear, then, the story of my *Herald*, knowing that it is the story of other Heralds. The *Herald's* story is mine, and my story, I dare say, is that of many others. To the facts, then. I speak with authority, being one of the scribes.

I

I chose newspaper work in my native city, Pittsburg, mainly because I liked to write. I went into it after my high-school days, spent a six months' apprenticeship on a well-known paper, left it for another, and in five years' hard work had risen from the reportorial ranks to that of a subordinate editorial writer—a dubious rise. Hard work had not threshed out ambition: the few grains left sprouted. The death of an uncle and an unexpected legacy fructified my desire. I became zealous to preach crusades; to stamp my own individuality, my own ideals, upon the "people"; in short, to own and run a newspaper. It was a buxom fancy, a day-dream of many another like myself. A rapid rise had obtained for me the summit of reasonable expectation in the matter of salary; but I then thought, as indeed I do still, that the sum in one's envelope o' Mondays is no criterion of success. Personal ambition to "mould opinion," as the quaint untruth has it, as well as the commercial side of owning a newspaper, made me look about over a wide field, seeking a city which really needed a new newspaper. The work was to be in a chosen field, and to be one's own taskmaster is worth more than salary. As I prospected, I saw no possible end to the venture save that of every expectation fulfilled.

I found a goodly town (of course I cannot name it) that was neither all future nor all past; a growing place, believed in by capitalists and real-estate men. It was well railroaded, in the coal fields, near to waterways and to glory. It was developing itself and being developed by outside capital. It had a newspaper, a well-established affair, whose old equipment I laughed at. It needed a new one. My opening was found. The city would grow; I would grow up with it. The promise of six years ago has been in part fulfilled. I have no reason to regret my choosing the city I did.

I went back to Pittsburg, consulted various of the great, obtained letters to prominent men high in the political faith I intended to follow, went back to my town armed with the letters, and talked it over. They had been considering the matter of a daily paper there to represent their faith and themselves, and after much dickering a company was formed. I found I could buy the weekly *Herald*, a nice property whose "good will" was worth having. Its owner was not over-anxious to sell, so drove a good bargain. As a weekly the paper for forty-three years had been gospel to many; I would make it daily gospel to more. In giving $5,500 for it I knew I was paying well, but it had a great name and a wide circulation.

I saw no necessity of beginning on a small scale. People are not dazzled in this way. I wanted a press that folk would come in and see run, and as my rival had no linotypes, that was all the more reason why I should have two. Expensive equipments are necessary for newspapers when they intend to do great works and the public is eager to see what is going to happen. All this took money, more money than I had thought it would. But, talking the matter over with my new friends and future associates, I convinced them that any economy was false economy at the start. But when I started I found that I owned but forty per cent of the Herald Publishing Company's stock. I was too big with the future to care. The sixty per cent was represented by various politicians. That was six years ago.

It does not do in America, much less in the *Atlantic*, to be morosely pessimistic. At most one can be regretful. And yet why should I be regretful? You have seen me settle in my thriving city; see me now. I have my own home, a place of honor in the community, the company of the great. You see me married, with enough to live on, enough to entertain with, enough to afford a bit of travel now and then. I still "run" the *Herald*: it pays me my own salary (my stockholders have never interfered with the business management of the paper), and were I insistent, I might have a consular position of importance, should the particular set of politicians I uphold (my "gang," as my rival the *Bulletin* says) revert to power. There is food in my larder, there are flowers in my garden. I carry enough insurance to enable my small family to do without me and laugh at starvation. I am but thirty-four years old. In short, I have a competence in a goodly little city. Why should I not rejoice with Stevenson that I have "some rags of honor left," and go about in middle age with my head high? Who of my schoolmates has done better?

Is it nothing, then, to see hope dwindle and die away? My regret is not pecuniary: it is old-fashionedly moral. Where are those high ideals with which I set about this business? I dare not look them in their waxen faces. I have acquired immunity from starvation by selling underhandedly what I had no right to sell. Some may think me the better American. But P. T. Barnum's dictum about the innate love Americans have for a hoax is really a serious matter, when the truth is told. Mr. Barnum did not leave a name and a fortune because he befooled the public. If now and then he gave them Cardiff giants and white elephants, he also gave them a brave display in three crowded rings. I have dealt almost exclusively with the Cardiff giants.

My regret is, then, a moral one. I bought something the nature of which did not dawn upon me until late; I felt environment adapt me to it little by little. The process was gradual, but I have not the excuse that it was unconscious. There is the sting in the matter. I can scarcely plead ignorance.

Somewhere in a scrapbook, even now beginning to yellow, I have pasted, that it may not escape me (as if it could!), my first editorial announcing to the good world my intent with the *Herald*. Let me quote from the mocking, double-leaded thing. I know the words. I know even now the high hope which gave them birth. I know how enchanting the vista was unfolding into the future. I can see how stern my boyish face was, how warm my blood. With a blare of trumpets I announced my mission. With a mustering day of the good old stock phrases used on such occasions I marshaled my metaphors. In making my bow, gravely and earnestly, I said, among other things:—

"Without fear or favor, serving only the public, the *Herald* will be at all times an intelligent medium of news and opinions for an intelligent community. Bowing the knee to no clique or faction, keeping in mind the great imperishable standards of American manhood, the noble traditions upon which the framework of our country is grounded, the *Herald* will champion, not the weak, not the strong, but the right. It will spare no expense in gathering news, and it will give all the news all of the time. It will so guide its course that only the higher interests of the city are served, and will be absolutely fearless. Independent in politics, it will freely criticise when occasion demands. By its adherence to these principles may it stand or fall."

But why quote more? You have all read them, though I doubt if you have read one more sincere. I felt myself a force, the *Herald* the expression of a force; an entity, the servant of other forces. My paper was to be all that other papers were not. My imagination carried me to sublime heights. This was six years ago.

II

Events put a check on my runaway ambition in forty-eight hours. The head of the biggest clothing house, and the largest advertiser in the city, called on me. I received him magnificently in my new office, motioning him to take a chair. I can see him yet—stout, prosperous, and to the point. As he talked, he toyed with a great seal that hung from a huge hawser-like watch-chain.

"Say," said he, refusing my chair, "just keep out a little item you may get hold of to-day." His manner was the same with me as with a salesman in his "gents'" underclothing department.

"Concerning?" I asked pleasantly.

"Oh, there's a friend of mine got arrested to-day. Some farmer had him took in for fraud or something. He'll make good, I guess; I know, in fact. He ain't a bad fellow, and it would hurt him if this got printed."

I asked him for particulars; saw a reporter who had the story; learned that the man was a sharp-dealer with a bad reputation, who had been detected in an attempt to cheat a poor farmer out of $260—a bare-faced fraud indeed. I learned that the man had long been suspected by public opinion of semi-legal attempts to rob the "widow and the orphan," and that at last there was a chance of "showing him up." I went back with a bold face.

"I find, though the case has not been tried, that the man is undoubtedly guilty."

"Guilty?" said my advertiser. "What of that? He'll settle."

"That hardly lessens the guilt." I smiled.

The clothing man looked astounded. "But if you print that he'll be ruined," he sputtered.

"From all I can learn, so much the better," I answered.

Then my man swore. "See here," he said, when he got back to written language. "He's just making his living; you ain't got no right to stop a man's earning his living. It ain't none of any newspaper's business. Just a private affair between him and the farmer, and he'll settle."

"I don't see how," I put in somewhat warmly, "it isn't the business of a newspaper to tell its public of a dangerous man, arrested for fraud, caught in his own net so badly that he is willing to settle, as you claim. It is my obvious duty to my constituents to print such a case. From the news point of view—" I was going on smoothly, but he stepped up and shook his fist in my face.

"Constituents? Ain't I a constituent? Don't I pay your newspaper for more advertising than any one else? Ain't I your biggest constituent? Say, young man, you're too big for this town. Don't try to bully me!" he suddenly screamed. "Don't you dare bully me! Don't you dare try it. I see what you want. You're trying to blackmail me, you are; you're trying to work me for more advertising; you want money out of me. That game don't go; not with me it don't. I'll have you arrested."

And he talked as though he believed it!

Then he said he'd never pay me another cent, might all manner of things happen to his soul if he did. He'd go to the *Bulletin*, and double his space. The man was his friend, and he had asked but a reasonable request, and I had tried to blackmail him. He worked that blackmail in every other sentence. Then he strode out, slamming the door.

The "little item" was not printed in the *Herald* (nor in the *Bulletin*, more used to such requests), and, as he had said, he was my biggest advertiser. It was my first experience with the advertiser with a request: for this reason I have given the incident fully. It recurred every week. I grew to think little of it soon. "Think of how his children will feel," say the friends of some one temporarily lodged in the police station. "Think of what the children of some one this man will swindle next will say," is what I might answer. But I don't,—not if an advertiser requests otherwise. As I have grown to phrase the matter, a newspaper is a contrivance which meets its pay-roll by selling space to advertisers: render it therefore agreeable to those who make its existence possible. Less jesuitically it may be put—the ultimate editor of a small newspaper is the advertiser, the biggest advertiser is the politician. This is a maxim that experience has ground with its heel into the fabric of my soul.

We all remember Emerson's brilliantly un-New-England advice, "Hitch your wagon to a star." This saying is of no value to newspapers, for they find stars poor motive power. Theoretically, it must be granted that newspapers, of all business ventures, should properly be hitched to a star. Yet I have found that, if any hitching is to be done, it must be to the successful politician. Amending Mr. Emerson, I have found it the best rule to "yoke your newspaper to the politician in power."

This, then, is what a small newspaper does: sells its space to the advertiser, its policy to the politician. It is smooth sailing save when these two forces conflict, and then Scylla and Charybdis were joys to the heart. Let us look into the advertiser part of the business a bit more closely.

The advertiser seeks the large circulation. The biggest advertiser seeks the cheapest people. Thus is a small newspaper (the shoe will pinch the feet of the great as well) forced, in order to survive, to pander to the Most Low. The man of culture does not buy $4.99 overcoats, the woman of culture 27–cent slippers. The newspaper must see that it reaches those who do. This is one of the saddest matters in the whole business. The *Herald* started with a circulation slightly over 2,000. I found that my town was near enough to two big cities for the papers published there to enter my field. I could not hope to rival their telegraphic features, and I soon saw that, if the *Herald* was to succeed, it must pay strict attention to local news. My rival stole its telegraphic news bodily; I paid for a service. The people seemed to care little for attempted assassinations of the Shah, but they were intensely interested in pinochle parties in the seventh ward. I gave them pinochle parties. Still my circulation diminished. My rival regained all that I had taken from him at the start. I wondered why, and compared the papers. I "set" more matter than he. The great difference was that my headlines were smaller and my editorial page larger than his. Besides, his tone was much lower: he printed rumor, made news to deny it—did a thousand and one things that kept his paper "breezy."

I put in bigger headlines—outdid him, in fact. I almost abolished my editorial page, making of it an attempt to amuse, not to instruct. I printed every little personality, every rumor that my staff could get hold of in their tours. The result came slowly, but surely. Success came when I exaggerated every little petty scandal, every row in a church choir, every hint of a disturbance. I compromised four libel suits, and ran my circulation up to 3,200 in eleven months.

Then I formed some more conclusions. I evolved a newspaper law out of the matter and the experience of some brothers in the craft in small cities near by. Briefly, I stated it in this wise: The worse a paper is, the more influence it has. To gain influence, be wholly bad.

This is no paradox, nor does it reflect particularly upon the public. There is reason for it in plenty. Take the ably edited paper, which glories in its editorial page, in the clean exposition of an honest policy, in high ideas put in good English, and you will find a paper which has a small clientele in a provincial town; or, if it has readers, it will have small influence. Say that it strikes the reader at breakfast, and the person who has leisure to breakfast is the person who has time for editorials, and the expression of that paper's opinion is carefully read. Should these opinions square with the preconceived ideas of the reader, the editorials are "great"; if not, they are "rotten." In other words, the man who reads carefully written editorials is the man whose opinion is formed—the man of culture, and therefore of prejudice. Doubtless he is as well acquainted with conditions as the writer; perhaps better acquainted. When a man does have opinions in a small city, he is quite likely to have strong ones. A flitting editorial is not the thing to change them. On the other hand, the man who has little time to read editorials, or perhaps little inclination, is just the man who might be influenced by them if read. Hence well-written editorials on a small daily are wasted thunder in great part, an uneconomic expenditure of force.

When local politics are at fever-heat, a different aspect of affairs is often seen: editorials are generally read, not so much as expressions of opinion, but as party attack and defense. During periods of political quiet the aim of most editorial pages is to amuse or divert. The advertiser has noted the decadence of the editorial page, and as a general thing makes a violent protest if the crying of his wares is made to emanate from this poor, despised portion of the paper. An advertisement on a local page is worth much more, and he pays more for the privilege.

So I learned another lesson. I shifted, as my successful contemporaries have done, my centre of editorial gravity from its former high position to my first and local pages. I now editorialize by suggestion. News now carries its own moral, the bias I wish it to show. This requires no less skill than the writing of editorials, and, greatly as I deplore it, I find the results pleasing. Does the *Herald* wish to denounce a public official? Into a dozen articles is the venom inserted. Slyly, subtly, and ofttimes openly do news articles point the obvious moral. The "Acqua Tofana" of journalism is ready to be used when occasion demands, and this is very often. Innuendo is common, the stiletto is inserted quietly and without warning, and tactics a man would shun may be used by a newspaper with little or no adverse comment. I mastered the philosophy of the indirect. I gained my ends by carefully coloring my news to the ends and policies of the paper. Nor am I altogether to blame. My paper was supposed to have influence. When I wrote careful and patient editorials, it had none. I saw that the public mind must be enfiladed, ambushed, and I adopted those primary American tactics of Indian warfare: shot from behind tree trunks, spared not the slain, and from the covert of a news item sent out screeching savages upon the unsuspecting public. Editorial warfare as conducted fifty years ago is obsolete; its methods are as antiquated to-day as is the artillery of that age.

III

I have called the *Herald* my own at different times in this article. I conceived it, established it, built it up. It stands to-day as the result of my work. True, my money was not the only capital it required, but mine was the hand that reared it. I found, to my great chagrin, that few people in the city considered me other than a hired servant of the political organization that aided in establishing the *Herald*. It was an "organ," a something which stood to the world as the official utterance of this political set. "Organs," in newspaper parlance, properly have but one function. Mine was evidently to explain or attack, as the case might be. To the politicians who helped start the *Herald* the paper was a political asset. It could on occasion be a club or a lever, as the situation demanded. I had been led to expect no personal intrusion. "Just keep straight with the party" was all that was asked. But never was constancy so unfaltering as that expected of the *Herald*. It must not print this because it was true; it must print that because it was untrue.

I had been six months in the city, when I overheard a conversation in a street car. "Oh, I'll fix the *Herald* all right. I know Johnny X," said one man. That was nice of Johnny X's friend, I thought. The *Bulletin* accused me of not daring to print certain matters. I was ashamed, humiliated. Between the friends of Johnny X and the friends of others, I saw myself in my true light. Johnny X, by the way, a noisy ward politician, owned just one share in the *Herald*; but that gave his friends the right to ask him to "fix" it, nevertheless.

I consulted with a wise man, a real leader, a man of experience and a warm heart. He heard me and laughed, patting me on the shoulder to humor me. "You want that printing, don't you?" he asked.

I admitted that I did. I had counted on it.

"Then," said my adviser, "I wouldn't offend Johnny X, if I were you. He controls the supervisor in his ward."

I began to see a great light, and I have needed no other illumination since. This matter of public printing had been promised me. I knew it was necessary. I saw that, inasmuch as it was given out by the lowest politicians in the town, I escaped easily if I paid as my price the indulgence of the various Johnnies X who had "influence." I was the paid supernumerary of the party, yet had to bear its mistakes and follies, its weak men and their weaker friends, upon my poor editorial back. I realized it from that moment; I should have seen it before. But for all that, my cheeks burned for days, and my teeth set whenever I faced the thought. I don't mind it in the least now.

So at the end of a year and a half I saw a few more things. I saw that by being a good boy and adaptable to "fixing" I could earn thirty-five dollars a week with less work than I could earn forty-five dollars in a big city. I saw that the *Herald* as a business proposition was a failure; that is, it was not, even under the most advantageous conditions, the money-maker that I at first thought it to be. I saw that if the city grew, and if there were no more rivals, if there were a hundred advantageous conditions, it might make several thousand dollars a year, besides paying me a bigger salary. I was very much disheartened. Then there came a turn.

I saw the business part of the proposition very clearly. I must play in with my owners, the party; and in turn my owners would support me nearly as well when they were out of power as they could when ruling. Revenue came from the city, the county, the state, all at "legal" rates. I began to see why these "legal" rates were high, some five times higher than those of ordinary advertising for such a paper as the *Herald*. The state, when paying its advertising bill, must pay the *Herald* five times the rate any clothing advertiser could get. The reason is not difficult to see. All over the state and country there are papers just like the *Herald*, controlled by little cliques of politicians, who, too miserly to support the necessary losses, make the people pay for them. Any attempt to lower the legal rate in any state legislature would call up innumerable champions of the "press," gentlemen all interested in their newspapers at home. The people pay more than a cent for their penny papers. It is the tax-payer who supports a thousand and one unnecessary "organs." The politicians are wise, after all.

So I got my perspective. I was paid to play the political game of others. I had to play it supported by indirect bribes. As a straight business proposition,—that is, without any state or city advertising, tax sales, printing of the proceedings, and the like,—the *Herald* could not live out a year. But by refusing to say many things, and by saying many more, I could get such share of these matters as would support the paper. In my second year, near its close, I saw that I was really a property, a chattel, a something bought and sold. I was being trafficked with to my loss. My friends bought me with public printing, and sold me for their own ends. I saw that they had the best of the bargain.

I could do better without the middlemen. I determined to make my own bargain with the devil for my own soul. It was a brilliant thought, but a bitter one. I determined to be a Sir John Hawkwood, and sell my editorial mercenaries to the highest bidder. Only the weak are gregarious, I thought with Nietzsche. If I could not put a name upon my actions, at least I could put a price. I made a loan, grabbed up some *Herald* stock cheaply, and owned at last over fifty per cent of my own paper. Now, I thought, I will at least make money.

I knew at just that time, that my own party, joined with the enemy, was much interested in a contract the city was about to make with a lighting company, a longterm contract at an exorbitant price. No opposition was expected. The city council had been "seen," the reformers silenced. I knew some of the particulars. I knew that both parties were gaining at the public expense, to their own profit and the tremendous profit of the gas company. I, fearless in my new control, sent out a small editorial feeler, a little suggestion about municipal ownership. This time my editorial did have influence. No mango tree of an Indian juggler blossomed quicker. I was called upon one hour after the paper was out. What in the name of all unnamable did I mean? I laughed. I pointed out the new holdings of stock I had acquired. What did the gentlemen mean? They didn't know—not then.

I had a very pleasant call from the gas company's attorney the next day. He was a most agreeable fellow, a man of parts, assuredly. I, a conscious chattel, would now appraise myself. I waited, letting the pleasantry flow by in a gentle stream. By the way, suggested my new friend, why didn't I try for the printing of the gas company? It was quite a matter. My friend was surprised that the *Herald* had so complete a job-printing plant. The gas company had all of its work done out of town, at a high rate, he thought. He would use his influence, etc., etc. Actually, I felt very important! All this to come out of a little editorial on municipal ownership! The *Herald* didn't care for printing so very much, I said. But I would think it over.

The next day I followed up my municipal ownership editorial. It was my answer. I waited for theirs. I waited in vain. I had overreached myself. This was humiliation indeed, and it aroused every bit of ire and revenge in me. I boldly launched out on a campaign against the dragon. I would see if the "press" could be held so cheaply. I printed statistics of the price of lighting in other cities. I exposed the whole scheme. I stood for the people at last! My early fire came back. We would see: the people and the *Herald* against a throttling corporation and a gang of corrupt aldermen.

Then the other side got into the war. I went to the bank to renew a note. I had renewed it a dozen times before. But the bank had seen the Gorgon and turned to stone. I digged deep and met the note. A big law firm which had given me all its business began to seek out the *Bulletin*. One or two advertisers dropped out. Some unseen hand began to foment a strike. Were the banks, the bar, and, worst of all, the labor unions, in the pay of a gas company? It was exhilarating to be with "the people," but exhilaration does not meet pay-rolls. I may state that I am now doing the gas company's printing at a very fair rate.

I saw that the policy was a good one, nevertheless. I also saw that it could not be carried to the extreme. So I have become merely threatening. I have learned never to overstep my bounds. I take my lean years and my fat years, still a hireling, but having somewhat to say about my market value. What provincial paper does not have the same story to tell?

My public doesn't care for good writing. It has no regard for reason. During one political campaign I tried reason. That is, I didn't denounce the adversary. Admitting he had some very good points, I showed why the other man had better ones. The general impression was that the *Herald* had "flopped," just because I did not abuse my party's opponent, but tried to defeat him with logic! A paper is always admired for its backbone, and backbone is its refusal to see two sides to a question.

I have reached the "masses." I tell people what they knew beforehand, and thus flatter them. Aiming to instruct them, I should offend. God is with the biggest circulations, and we must have them, even if we appeal to class prejudice now and then.

I can occasionally foster a good work, almost underhandedly, it would seem. I take little pleasure in it. The various churches, hospitals, the library, all expect to be coddled indiscriminately and without returning any thanks whatever. I formerly had as much railroad transportation as I wished. I still have the magazines free of charge and a seat in the theatre. These are my "perquisites." There is no particular future for me. The worst of it is that I don't seem to care. The gradual falling away from the high estate of my first editorial is a matter for the student of character, which I am not. In myself, as in my paper, I see only results.

I think these confessions are ample enough and blunt enough. When I left the high school, I would have wished to word them in Stevensonian manner. That was some time ago. We who run small dailies have little care for the niceties of style. There are few of our clientele who know the nice from the not-nice. In our smaller cities we "suicide" and "jeopardize." We are visited by "agriculturalists," and "none of us are" exempt from little iniquities and uniquities of style and expression. We go right on: "commence" where we should "begin," use "balance" for "remainder," never think of putting the article before "Hon." and "Rev.," and some of us abbreviate "assemblyman" into "ass," meaning nothing but condensation. Events still "transpire" in our small cities, and inevitably we "try experiments." We have learned to write "trousers," and "gents" appears only in our advertisements. In common with the very biggest and best papers we always say "leniency." That I do these things, the last coercion of environment, is the saddest, to me, of all.

THE COUNTRY EDITOR OF TO-DAY

BY CHARLES MOREAU HARGER

I

Eulogies and laudatory paragraphs, alternating with sneers, ridicule, and deprecations, long have been the lot of the country editor. Pictured in the comic papers as an egotistic clown, exalted by the politicians as a mighty "moulder of public opinion," occasionally chastised by angry patrons, and sometimes remembered by delighted subscribers, he has put his errors where they could be read of all men and has modestly sought a fair credit for his merits.

At times he has rebelled—not at treatment from his constituency but at patronizing remarks of the city journalist who sits at a mahogany desk and dictates able articles for the eighteen-page daily, instead of writing local items at a pine table in the office of a four-page weekly. Thus did one voice his protest: "When you consider that the country weekly is owned by its editor and that the man who writes the funny things about country papers in the city journals is owned by the corporation for which he writes, it doesn't seem so sad. When you see an item in the city papers poking fun at the country editor for printing news about John Jones' new barn, you laugh and laugh—for you know that on one of the pages of that same city daily is a two-column story in regard to the trimmings on the gowns of the Duchess of Wheelbarrow. And it is all the more amusing because you know the duchess does not even know of the existence of the aforesaid city paper, while John Jones and many of his neighbors take and pay for the paper which mentioned his new barn. Don't waste your pity on the country newspaper worker. He will get along."

Little money is needed to start a country paper. There are those who claim that it does not require any money,—that it can be done on nerve alone,—and they produce evidence to support the statement. True, some of the editors who have the least money and the poorest plants are most successful in their efforts to live up to the conception developed by the professional humorist; but it is not fair to judge the country editor by these—any more than it would be fair to judge the workers on the great city dailies by the publishers of back-street fake sheets that exist merely to rob advertisers; or to judge the editors of reputable magazines by the promoters of nauseous monthlies whose stock in trade is a weird and sickening collection of mail-order bargains and quack medicine advertisements.

The country editor of to-day is far removed from his prototype of two or three decades ago. It would be strange if an age that gives to the farmer his improved self-binder, to the physician his X-ray machine, and to the merchant his loose-leaf ledger, had done nothing for the town's best medium of publicity. The perfection of stereotype plate manufacture by which a page of telegraph news may be delivered ready for printing at a cost of approximately twenty cents a column, and the elaboration of the "ready print," or "patent inside," by which half the paper is printed before delivery, yet at practically no expense over the unprinted sheets, have been the two great labor-savers for the country editor. Thereby he is relieved, if he desire, of the tedious and expensive task of setting much type in order to give the world's general news, and the miscellaneous matter that "fills up" the paper. His energies then may be devoted to reporting the happenings of his locality and to giving his opinions on public affairs. By his doing of these, and by his relations toward the public interests, is he to be judged.

After all, no one man in the community has so large an opportunity to assist the town in advancement as the editor. It is not because he is smarter than others, not because he is wealthy—but because he is the spokesman to the outside world.

He is eager to print all the news in his own paper. Does he do it? Hardly. "This would be a very newsy paper," explained a frank country editor to his subscribers, "were it not for the fact that each of the four men who work on it has many friends. By the time all the items that might injure some of their friends are omitted, very little is left."

"I wish you would print a piece about our schoolteacher," said a farmer's wife to me one afternoon. "Say that she is the best teacher in the county."

"But I can't do that—two hundred other teachers would be angry. You write the piece, sign it, and I'll print it."

"What are you running a newspaper for if you can't please your subscribers?" she demanded—and canceled her subscription.

So the country editor leaves out certain good things and certain bad things for the very simple reason that the persons most interested are close at hand and can find the individual responsible for the statements. He becomes wise in his generation and avoids chastisements and libel suits. He finds that there is no lasting regard in a sneer, no satisfaction in gratifying the impulse to say things that bring tears to women's eyes, nothing to gloat over in opening a wound in a man's heart. If he does not learn this as he grows older in the service, he is a poor country editor.

His relations to his subscribers are intimate. There is little mystery possible about the making of the paper; it is as if he stood in the market-place and told his story. Of course, the demands upon him are many and some of them preposterous. Men with grafts seek to use the paper, people with schemes ask free publicity. The country editor is criticised for charging for certain items that no city paper prints free. The churches and lodges want free notices of entertainments by which they hope to make money; semi-public entertainments prepared under the management of a traveling promoter ask free advertising "for the good of the cause." Usually they get it, and when the promoter passes on, the editor is found to be the only one in town who received nothing for his labor.

It is characteristic of the country town to engage in community quarrels. These absorb the attention of the citizens, and feeling becomes bitter. The cause may be trifling: the location of a schoolhouse, the building of a bridge, the selection of a justice of the peace, or some similar matter, is enough. To the newspaper office hurry the partisans, asking for *ex parte* reports of the conditions. One leader is, perhaps, a liberal advertiser; to offend him means loss of business. Another is a personal friend; to anger him means the loss of friendship. The editor of the only paper in the town must be a diplomat if he is to guide safely through the channel. In former times he tried to please both sides and succeeded in making enemies of every one interested. Now the well-equipped editor takes the position that he is a business man like the others, that he has rights as do they, and he states the facts as he sees them, regardless of partisanship, letting the public do the rest. If there be another paper in town, the problem is easy, for the other faction also has an "organ."

Out of the public's disagreement may come a newspaper quarrel—though this is a much rarer thing than formerly. The old-time country newspaper abuse of "our loathed but esteemed contemporary" is passing away, it being understood that such a quarrel, with personalities entangled in the recriminations, is both undignified and ungentlemanly. "But people will read it," says the man who by gossip encourages these attacks. So will people listen to a coarse street controversy carried on in a loud and angry tone,—but little is their respect for the principals engaged. Country editors of the better class now treat other editors as gentlemen, and the paper that stoops to personal attacks is seldom found. Many a town has gone for years without other than kindly mention in any paper of the editors of the other papers, and in such towns you will generally find peace and courtesy among the citizens.

Of course, there are politics and political arguments, but few are the editors so lacking in the instincts of a gentleman as to bring into these the opposing editor's personal and family affairs. It has come to be understood that such action is a reflection on the one who does it, not on the object of his attack. This is another way of saying that more real gentlemen are running country newspapers to-day than ever before. This broadening of character has broadened influence. The country paper is effecting greater things in legislation than the county conventions are.

"The power of the country press in Washington surprises me," said a Middle West congressman last winter. "During my two terms I have been impressed with it constantly. I doubt if there is a single calm utterance in any paper in the United States that does not carry some weight in Washington among the members of Congress. You might think that what some little country editor says does not amount to anything, but it means a great deal more than most people realize. When the country editor, who is looking after nothing but the county printing, gives expression to some rational idea about a national question, the man off here in Congress knows that it comes from the grass-roots. The lobby, the big railroad lawyers, and that class of people, realize the power of the press, but they hate it. I have heard them talk about it and shake their heads and say, 'Too much power there!' The press is more powerful than money."

This was not said in flattery, but because he had seen on congressmen's desks the heaps of country weeklies, and he knew how closely they were read. The smallest editorial paragraph tells the politician of the condition in that paper's community, for he knows that it is put there because the editor has gathered the idea from some one whom he trusts as a leader—and the politician knows approximately who that leader is. So the country editor often exerts a power of which he knows little.

II

But politics is only a part of the country editor's life. The social affairs of the community are nearest to him. The proud father who brings in a cigar with a notice of the seventh baby's arrival (why cigars and babies should be associated in men's minds I never understood), the fruit farmer who presents some fine Ben Davis apples in the expectation that he will get a notice, are but types. The editor may have some doubts concerning the need of a seventh child in the family of the proud father, and he may not be particularly fond of Ben Davis apples; but he gives generous notices because he knows that the gifts were prompted by kind hearts and that the givers are his friends.

When joy comes to the household, it is but the working of the heart's best impulses to desire that all should share it. The news that the princess of the family has, after many years of waiting, wedded a prosperous merchant of the neighboring county, brings the family into prominence in the home paper. Seldom in these busy times does the editor get a piece of wedding-cake, but nevertheless he fails not to say that the bride is "one of our loveliest young ladies and the groom is worthy of the prize he has won." The city paper does not do that. Here and there a country editor tries to put on city airs and give the bare facts of "social functions," without a personal touch to the lines. But infrequently does he succeed in reaching the hearts of his readers, and somehow he finds that his contemporary across the street, badly printed, sprinkled with typographical errors and halting in its grammar, but profuse in its laudations, is getting an unusual number of new subscribers. Even you, though you may pretend to be unmindful, are not displeased when on the day after your party you read that the guests "went home feeling that a good time had been had."

The time has not yet come for the country paper to assume city airs; nor is it likely to arrive for many years. The reason is a psychological one. The city journal is the paper of the masses; the country weekly or small daily is the paper of the neighborhood. One is general and impersonal; the other, direct and intimate. One is the market-place; the other, the home. The distinction is not soon to be wiped out.

And when sorrow comes! Into the home of a city friend of mine death entered, taking the wife and mother. The family had been prominent in social circles, and columns were printed in the city papers, columns of cold, biographical facts—born, married, died. But the news went back to the small country town where in their early married life the husband and wife had spent many happy years, and in the little country weekly was quite another sort of story. It told how much her friends loved her, how saddened they were by her passing away, how sweet and womanly had been her character. The husband did not send the city papers to distant acquaintances; he sent copy after copy of the little country weekly, the only place where, despite his prominence in the world, appeared a sympathetic relation of the loss that had come to him.

Week after week the country paper does this. From issue after issue clippings are stowed away in bureau drawers or pasted in family Bibles, because they picture the loved one gone. It may not be a very high mission; but no part of the country editor's work has in it more of satisfaction and recompense.

After the funeral comes the real test of the editor's good-nature. Long resolutions adopted by lodges and church organizations are handed in for publication, each bristling with the forms of ritual or creed, and each signed with the names of the committee members upon whom devolved the task of composition. A few country editors are brave enough to demand payment at advertising rates for these publications; generally they are printed without charge.

Nor is there a halt at this step in the proceeding. One day a sad-faced farmer, with a heavy band of crape around his battered soft hat, accompanied by a woman whose heavy veil and black dress are sufficient insignia of woe, comes to the office.

"We would like to put in a 'card of thanks,'" begins the man, "and we wish you would write it for us. We ain't very good at writing pieces, and you know how."

Does the editor tell them how bad is the taste that indulges the stereotyped card of thanks? Does he haughtily refuse to be a party to such violation of form's canons? Scarcely. He knows the formula by heart and "the kind friends and neighbors who assisted us in our late bereavement" comes to him as easily as the opening words of a mayor's proclamation.

Occasionally there is literary talent in the family, and the "card" is prepared without the editor's assistance. Here is one verbatim as it came to the desk:—

"We extend our thanks to the good people who assisted us in the sickness and death of our wife and daughter: The doctor who was so faithful in attendance and effort to bring her back to health, the pastor who visited and prayed with her and us, the students who watched with us and waited on her, the neighbors who did all they could in helping care for her, the dormitory students, the faculty, the literary societies and the A.O.U.W. who furnished such beautiful flowers, we thank them all. Then the undertaker who was so kind, the liveryman and other friends who furnished carriages for us to go to the cemetery—yes, we thank you all."

Doubtless he feels that he should do something toward conserving the best taste in social usage, and that the "card of thanks" should be ruthlessly frowned down; but he sees also the other side. It is unquestionably prompted by a spirit of sincere gratitude, and survives as a concession to a supposed public opinion. Like other things that are self-perpetuating, this continues—and the country editor out of the goodness of his heart assists in its longevity. In no path is the progress of the reformer so difficult as in that of social custom; and this is as true on the village street as on the city boulevard.

III

The past half-decade has brought to the country editor a new problem and a new rival,—the rural delivery route. Until this innovation came, few farmers took daily papers. The country weekly, or the weekly from the city, furnished the news.

Out in the Middle West the other morning, a dozen miles from town, a farmer rode on a sulky plough turning over brown furrows for the new crop. "I see by to-day's Kansas City papers," he began, as a visitor came alongside, "that there is trouble in Russia again." "What do you know about what is in to-day's Kansas City papers?" "Oh, we got them from the carrier an hour ago."

It was not yet noon, but he was in touch with the world's news up to one o'clock that morning—and this twelve miles from a railroad and two hundred miles west of the Missouri River! In that county every farmhouse has rural delivery of mail; and one carrier makes his round in an automobile, covering the thirty miles in four hours or less.

The country editor has viewed with alarm this changing condition. He has feared that he would be robbed of his subscribers through the familiar excuse, "I'm takin' more papers than I can read." But nothing of the kind has happened. Although the rural carriers take each morning great packages of daily papers, brought to the village by the fast mail, the people along the routes are as eager as ever for the weekly visit of the home paper. If by accident one copy is missing from the carrier's supply on Thursday, great is the lamentation. It is doubtful if a single country paper has been injured by the rural route; in most instances the reading habit has been so stimulated as to increase the patronage.

This it has done: it has impressed on the editor the necessity of giving much attention to home news and less to the happenings afar. This is, indeed, the province of the country paper, since it is of the home and the family, not of the market-place. This feature will grow, and the country paper will become more a chronicle of home news and less a purveyor of outside happenings, for soon practically every farmer will have his daily paper with the regularity of the sunrise. On the whole, instead of being an injury this is helpful to the rural publisher; it relieves him of responsibility for a broad field of information and allows him to devote his energy to that news which gives the greatest hold on readers,—the doings of the immediate community. With this will come more generally the printing of the entire paper at home and the decline of the "patent inside," now so common, which has served its purpose well. If it exist, it will be in a modified form, devoted chiefly to readable articles of a literary rather than of a news value.

The city daily may give the telegraph news of the world in quicker and better service, the mail-order house may occasionally undersell the home merchant, the glory of the city's lights may dazzle; but, at the end of the week, home and home institutions are best; so only one publication gives the news we most wish to know,—the country paper. The city business man throws away his financial journal and his yellow "extra," and tears open the pencil-addressed home paper that brings to him memories of new-mown hay and fallow fields and boyhood. Regardless of its style, its grammar, or its politics, it holds its reader with a grip that the city editor may well envy.

In these times the country editor is, like the publisher of the city, a business man. Scores of offices of country weeklies within two hundred miles of the Rockies (which is about as far inland as we can get nowadays) have linotypes or type-setting machines, run the presses with an electric motor, and give the editor an income of three thousand dollars or more a year for labor that allows many a vacation day. The country editor gets a good deal out of life. He lives well; he travels much; he meets the best people of his state; and, if he be inclined, he can accomplish much for his own improvement. Added to this is the joy of rewarding the honorable, decent people of the town with good words and helpful publicity, and the satisfaction of seeing that the rascals get their dues,—and get them they do if the editor lives and the rascals live, for in the country town the editor's turn always comes. It may be long delayed, but it arrives. If he use his power with honesty and intelligence, he can do much good for the community.

In the opinion of some this danger threatens: the increased rapidity of transportation, the multitude of fast trains, and the facilities for placing the big city papers within a zone of one hundred miles of the office of publication, mean the large representation of particular localities, or even the establishment of editions devoted to them. The city paper tries to absorb the local patronage through the competent correspondent who practically edits certain columns or pages of the journal. In the thickly settled East this is more successful than in the West, where distance helps the local paper. But the zone is widening with every improvement in transportation of mails, and soon few sections of the country will be outside the possibilities of some city paper's enterprise in this direction.

When this happens, will the local weekly go out of existence and its subscribers be attached to the big city paper whose facilities for getting news and whose enterprise in reaching the uttermost parts of the world far outstrip the slow-going weekly's best efforts? It is not likely. The county-seat weekly to-day, with its energetic correspondent in the town of Centreville, adds to its list in that section because it gives the news fully and crisply; but it does not drive out of business the Centreville *Palladium*, whose editor has a personal acquaintance with every subscriber and who caters to the home pride of the community. It is probable that the *Palladium* will be more enterprising and will devote more attention to the doings of the dwellers in Centreville in order to keep abreast with the competition; but it cannot be driven out, nor its editor forced from his position by dearth of business. The life of a forceful paper is long. One such paper was sold and its name changed eighteen years ago; yet letters and subscriptions still are addressed to the old publication. A hold like that on a community's life cannot be broken by competition.

IV

The evolution of the country weekly into the country daily is becoming easier as telephone and telegraph become cheaper, and transportation enables publishers to secure at remote points a daily "plate" service that includes telegraph news up to a few hours of the time of publication. The publishing of an Associated Press daily, which twenty years ago always attended a town's boom and generally resulted in the suspension of a bank or two and the financial ruin of several families, has become simplified until it is within reach of modest means.

Instead of the big city journals extending their sway to crush out the country paper, it is more probable that the country papers will take on some of the city's airs, and that, with the added touch of personal familiarity with the people and their affairs, the country editor will become a greater power than in the past. For it is recognized to-day that the publication of a paper is a business affair and not a matter of faith or revenge. If the publication be not a financial success, it is not much of a success of any kind.

The old-time editor who prided himself on his powers of vituperation, who thundered through double-leaded columns his views on matters of world-importance and traded space for groceries and dry goods, has few representatives to-day. The wide-awake, clean-cut, well-dressed young men, paying cash for their purchases and demanding cash for advertising, alert to the business and political movements that make for progress, and taking active part in the interests of the town, precisely as though they were merchants or mechanics, asking no favors because of their occupation, are taking their places. This sort of country editor is transforming the country paper and is making of it a business enterprise in the best sense of the term,—something it seldom was under the old régime.

This eulogy is one often quoted by the country press: "Every year every local paper gives from five hundred to five thousand lines for the benefit of the community in which it is located. No other agency can or will do this. The editor, in proportion to his means, does more for his town than any other man. To-day editors do more work for less pay than any men on earth."

Like other eulogies it has in it something of exaggeration. It assumes the country editor to be a philanthropist above his neighbors. The new type of country editor makes no such claim. To be sure, he prints many good things for the community's benefit,—but he does it because he is a part of the community. What helps the town helps him. His neighbor, the miller, would do as much; his other neighbor, the hardware man, is as loyal and in his way works as hard for the town's upbuilding. In other words, the country editor of to-day assumes no particular virtue because his capital is invested in printing-presses, paper, and a few thousand pieces of metal called type. He does realize that because of his avocation he is enabled to do much for good government, for progress, and for the betterment of his community. Unselfishly and freely he does this. He starts movements that bring scoundrels to terms, that place flowers where weeds grew before, that banish sorrow and add to the world's store of joy; but he does not presume that because of this he deserves more credit than his fellow business men. He is indeed fallen from grace who makes a merit of doing what is decent and honest and fair.

It is often remarked that the ambition of the country editor is to secure a position on a city paper. I have had many city newspapermen confide to me that their fondest hope was to save enough money to buy a country weekly in a thriving town. At first thought it would seem that the city journalist would fail in the new field, having been educated in a vastly different atmosphere and being unacquainted with the conditions under which the country editor must make friends and secure business. But two of the most successful newspapers of my acquaintance are edited by men who served their apprenticeship on city dailies, and finally realized their heart's desire and bought country weeklies in prosperous communities. They are not only making more money than ever before, but both tell me that they have greater happiness than came in the old days of rush, hurry, and excitement.

So long as a country paper can be issued without the expenditure of more than a few hundred dollars, so long as the man with ambition and money can satisfy his desire to "edit," the country paper will be fruitful of jocose remarks by the city journalist. There will be columns of odd reprint from the backwoods of Arkansas, and queer combinations of grammar and egotism from the Egypt of Illinois. The exchange editor will find in his rural mail much food for humorous comment, but he will not find characterizing the country editor a lack of independence, or a lack of ability to look out for himself. The country editor is doing very well, and the trend of his business affairs is in the direction of better financial returns and wider influence. He is a greater power now than ever before in his history, and he will become more influential as the years go by. He will not be controlled by a syndicate, or modeled after a machine-made pattern, but will exert his individuality wherever he may be.

The country editor of to-day is coming into his own. He asks fewer favors and brings more into the store of common good. He does not ask eulogies nor does he resent fair criticisms; he is content to be judged by what he is and what he has accomplished. As the leader of the hosts must hold his place by the consent of his followers, so must the town's spokesman prove his worth. Closest to the people, nearest to their home life, its hopes and its aspirations, the country editor is at the foundation of journalism. Here and there is a weak and inefficient example; but in the main he measures up to as high a standard as does any class of business men in the nation,—and it is as a business man that he prefers to be classed.

SENSATIONAL JOURNALISM AND THE LAW

BY GEORGE W. ALGER

I

So much has been said in recent years concerning the methods and policies of sensational journalism that a further word upon a topic so hackneyed would seem almost to require an explanation or an apology. Current criticism, however, for the most part, has been confined to only one of its many characteristics,—its bad taste and its vulgarizing influence on its readers by daily offenses against the actual, though as yet ideal, right of privacy, by its arrogant boastfulness, mawkish sentimentality, and a persistent and systematic distortion of values in events.

This, the most noticeable feature of yellow journalism, is indicative rather of its character than of its purpose. In considering, however, the present subject,—sensational journalism in its relation to the making, enforcing, and interpreting of law,—we enter a different field, that of the conscious policies and objects with and for which these papers are conducted. The main business of a newspaper as defined by journalists of the old school is the collection and publication of news of general interest coupled with editorial comment upon it. The old-time editor was a ruminative and critical observer of public events. This definition of the functions of a newspaper was long ago scornfully cast aside as absurdly antiquated and insufficient to include the myriad circulation-making enterprises of yellow journalism. These papers are not simply purveyors of news and comment, but have what, for lack of a better term, may be called constructive policies of their own. In the making of law, for example, not content with mere criticism of legislators and their measures, the new journalism conceives and exploits measures of its own, drafted by its own counsel, and introduced as legislative bills by statesmen to whom flattering press notices and the publication of an occasional blurred photograph are a sufficient reward. Not infrequently measures thus conceived and drafted are supported by specially prepared "monster petitions," containing thousands of names, badly written and of doubtful authenticity, of supposed partisans, and by special trains filled with orators and a heterogeneous rabble described in the news columns as "committees of citizens," who at critical periods are collected together and turned loose upon the assembled lawmakers as an impressive object lesson of the public interest fervidly aroused on behalf of the newspaper's bill.

The ethics of persuasion is an interesting subject. It falls, however, outside the scope of this article. It is impossible to lay down any hard and fast rule by which to determine in all cases what form of newspaper influence is legitimate and what illegitimate. The most obvious characteristic of yellow journalism in its relation to lawmaking is that it prefers ordinarily to obtain its ends by the use of intimidation rather than by persuasion. The monster petition scheme just referred to is merely one illustrative expression of this preference. When a newspaper of this type is interested in having some official do some particular thing in some particular way, it spends little of its space or time in attempting to show the logical propriety or necessity for the action it desires. It seeks first and foremost to make the official see that *the eyes of the people are on him*, and that any action by him contrary to that which the newspaper assures him the people want would be fraught with serious personal consequences. The principal point with these papers is always "the people demand" (in large capitals) this or that, and the logic or reason of the demand is obscured or ignored. It is the headless Demos transformed into printer's ink. If by any chance any official, so unfortunate as to have ideas of his own as to how his office should be conducted, proves obdurate to the demands of the printed voice of the people, he becomes the target for newspaper attacks, calculated to destroy any reputation he may previously have had for intelligence, sobriety of judgment, or public efficiency, his tormentor, so far as libel is concerned, keeping, however, as Fabian says, "on the windy side of the law."

An amusing illustration of this kind of warfare occurred in New York some years ago, when for several weeks one of these newspapers published daily attacks upon the President of the Board of Police Commissioners, because he refused to follow the newspaper theories of the proper way of enforcing, or rather not enforcing, the Excise Law. The newspaper took the position that, while the powers of the Police Department were being largely turned to ferreting out saloon-keepers who were keeping open after hours or on Sundays, the detection of serious crimes was being neglected, and that a "carnival of crime," to use the picturesque wording of its headlines, was being carried on in the city. Finally, in one of its issues the paper published a list of thirty distinct criminal offenses of the most serious character,— murder, felonious assault, burglary, grand larceny, and the like,—all alleged to have been committed within a week, in none of which, it asserted, had any criminal been captured or any stolen property recovered. Events which followed immediately upon this last publication showed that the newspaper had erred grievously in its estimate of this particular official under attack. A few days later the Police Commissioner, Mr. Roosevelt, published in the columns of all the other newspapers in New York the result of his own personal investigation of these thirty items of criminal news, showing conclusively that twenty-eight of them were canards pure and simple, and that in the remaining two police activity had brought about results of a most satisfactory kind. Following this statement of the facts was appended an adaptation of some fifteen or twenty lines from Macaulay's merciless essay on Barrère,—perhaps the finest philippic against a notorious and inveterate liar which the English language affords,—so worded that they should apply, not only to the newspaper which published this spurious list of alleged crimes, but to the editor and proprietor personally. The carnival of crime ended at once.

It is, of course, impossible to determine accurately the extent of newspaper influence upon legislation and the conduct of public officials by these systematic attempts at bullying. Making all due allowance, however, there have been within recent years many significant illustrations of the influence of yellow journalism upon the shaping of public events. Mr. Creelman is quite right in saying, as he does in his interesting book, *On the Great Highway*, that the story of the Spanish war is incomplete which overlooks the part that yellow journalism had in bringing it on. He tells us that, some time prior to the commencement of hostilities, a well-known artist, who had been sent to Cuba as a representative of one of these papers and had there grown tired of inaction, telegraphed his chief that there was no prospect of war, and that he wished to come home. The reply he received was characteristic of the journalism he represented: "You furnish the pictures, we will furnish the war." It is characteristic because the new journalism aims to direct rather than to influence, and seeks, to an extent never attempted or conceived by the journalism it endeavors so strenuously to supplant, to create public sentiment rather than to mould it, to make measures and find men.

The larger number of the readers of the great sensational newspapers live at or near the place of publication, where the half-dozen daily editions can be placed in their hands hot from the press. The news furnished in them is, for the most part, of distinctively local interest. In their columns the horizon is narrow and inexpressibly dingy. Detailed narrations of sensational local happenings, preferably crimes and scandals, are given conspicuous places, while more important events occurring outside the city limits are treated with telegraphic brevity. These papers constitute beyond question the greatest provincializing influence in metropolitan life.

The particular local functions of sensational journalism which bring it in close relation to the courts result from its self-imposed responsibilities as detective and punisher of crime and as director of municipal officials. So far as the latter are concerned, yellow journalism has apparently a good record. Many recent instances might, for example, be cited where these newspapers, acting under the names of "dummy" plaintiffs, have sought and obtained preliminary or temporary injunctions against threatened official malfeasance, or where they have instituted legal proceedings to expose corrupt jobbery. As to the actual results thus accomplished, other than the publicity obtained, the general public is not in a position to judge. Temporary injunctions granted merely until the merits of the case can be heard and determined are of no particular value if, when the trial day comes, the newspaper plaintiff fails to appear, the case is dismissed, and the temporary injunction vacated. On such occasions, and they are more frequent than the general public is aware, the newspaper takes little pains to inform its readers of the final results of the matter over which it made such hue and cry months before.

But, however fair-minded persons may differ as to the results actually obtained by these newspaper law enterprises in the civil courts, there is less room for difference of opinion as to the methods with which they are conducted. They are almost invariably so managed as to convey to the minds of their readers the idea that the decision obtained, if a favorable one, has not come as the result of a just rule of law laid down by a wise and fair-minded judge, but has been obtained rather in spite of both law and judge, and wholly because a newspaper of enormous circulation, championing the cause of the people, has wrested the law to its clamorous authority. The attitude of mind thus created is well exemplified in a remark made to me by a business man of more than ordinary intelligence, in discussing an injunction granted in one of these newspaper suits arising out of a water scandal: "Why, of course Judge ———— granted the injunction. Everybody knew he would. There is not a judge on the bench who would have the nerve to decide the other way with all the row the newspapers have made about it. He knows where his bread is buttered."

II

One of the great features of counting-house journalism is its real or supposed ability in the detection and punishment of crime. Whether this field is a legitimate one for a newspaper to enter need not be discussed here. It goes without saying that an interesting murder mystery sells many papers, and if as a result of skillful detective work the guilty party is finally brought to the gallows or the electric chair, it is a triumph for the paper whose reporters are the sleuths. While such efforts, when crowned with success, are the source probably of much credit and revenue, there are various disagreeable possibilities connected with failure which the astute managers of these papers can never afford to overlook. While verdicts in libel suits are in this country generally small (compared with those in England), and the libel law itself is filled with curious and antiquated technicalities by which verdicts may be avoided or reversed, nevertheless there is always the possibility that an innocent victim of newspaper prosecution will turn the tables and draw smart money from the enterprising journal's coffers. The acquittal of the person who has been thrust into jeopardy by newspaper detectives is obviously a serious matter for the paper. On the other hand, there are no important consequences from conviction except, of course, to the person condemned. Is it to be expected that the newspaper, under such circumstances, will preserve a disinterested and impartial tone in its news columns while the man in the dock is fighting for his life before the judge and jury? Is it remarkable that during the course of such a trial the newspaper should fill its pages with ghastly cartoons of the defendant, with murder drawn in every line of his face, or that it should by its reports of the trial itself seek to impress its readers with his guilt before it be proved according to law? that it should send its reporters exploring for new witnesses for the prosecution, and should publish in advance of their appearance on the witness stand the substance of the damaging testimony it is claimed they will give? that it should go even further, and (as was recently shown in the course of a great poisoning case in New York City, the history of which forms a striking commentary on all these abuses) actually pay large sums of money to induce persons to make affidavits incriminating the defendant on trial?

Unfortunately, too often these efforts receive aid from prosecuting officers whose sense of public duty is impaired or destroyed by the itch for reputation and a cheap and tawdry type of forensic triumph. Despicable enough is the district attorney who grants interviews to newspaper reporters during the progress of a criminal trial, and who makes daily statements to them of what he intends to prove on the morrow unless prevented by the law as expounded by the trial judge. A careful study of the progress of more than one great criminal trial in New York City would show how illegal and improper matter prejudicial to the person accused of crime has been ruled out by the trial court, only to have the precise information spread about in thousands upon thousands of copies of sensational newspapers, with a reasonable certainty of their scare headlines, at least, being read by some of the jury.

The pernicious influence of these journals upon the courts of justice in criminal trials (and not merely in the comparatively small number in which they are themselves the instigators of the criminal proceedings) is that they often make fair play an impossibility. The days and weeks that are now not infrequently given to selecting jurors in important criminal cases are spent in large measure by counsel in examining talesmen in an endeavor to find, if possible, twelve men in whose minds the accused has not been already "tried by newspaper" and condemned or acquitted. When the public feeling in a community is such that it will be impossible for a party to an action to obtain an unprejudiced jury, a change of venue is allowed to some other county where the state of the public mind is more judicial. It is a significant fact that nearly all applications for such change in the place of trial from New York City have been for many years based mainly upon complaints of the inflammatory zeal of the sensational press.

The courts in Massachusetts (where judges are not elected by the people, but are appointed by the governor) have been very prompt in dealing in a very wholesome and summary way with editors of papers publishing matter calculated to affect improperly the fairness of jury trials. Whether it be from better principles or an inspiring fear of jail, the courts of public justice in that state receive little interference from unwarranted newspaper stories. Some of the cases in which summary punishment has been meted out from the bench to Massachusetts editors will impress New York readers rather curiously. For example, just before the trial of a case involving the amount of compensation the owner of land should receive for his land taken for a public purpose, a newspaper in Worcester informed its readers that "the town offered Loring [the plaintiff] $80 at the time of the taking, but he demanded $250, and not getting it, went to law." Another paper published substantially the same statement, and both were summarily punished by fine, the court holding that these articles were calculated to obstruct the course of justice, and that they constituted contempt of court. During the trial of a criminal prosecution in Boston a few years ago against a railway engineer for manslaughter in wrecking his train, the editor of the *Boston Traveler* intimated editorially that the railway company was trying to put the blame on the engineer as a scapegoat, and that the result of the trial would probably be in his favor. The editor was sentenced to jail for this publication. The foregoing are undoubtedly extreme cases, and are chosen simply to show the extent to which some American courts will go in punishing newspaper contempts. All of these decisions were taken on appeal to the highest court of the state and were there affirmed. The California courts have been equally vigorous in several cases of recent years, notably in connection with publications made during the celebrated Durant murder trial in San Francisco.

The English courts are, if anything, even more severe in this class of cases, a recent decision of the Court of King's Bench being a noteworthy illustration. During the trial of two persons for felony, the "special crime investigator" of the *Bristol Weekly Dispatch* sent to his paper reports, couched in a fervid and sensational form, containing a number of statements relating to matters as to which evidence would not have been admissible in any event against the defendants on their trial, and reflecting severely on their characters. Both of the defendants referred to were convicted of the crime for which they were indicted, and sentenced to long terms of imprisonment. Shortly after their conviction and sentence the editor of the *Dispatch* and this special crime investigator were prosecuted criminally for perverting the course of justice, and each of them was sentenced to six weeks in prison. Lord Alverstone, who rendered the opinion on the appeal taken by the editor and reporter, in affirming the judgment of conviction, expresses himself in language well worth repeating. He says:[8]—

8. 1 K. B. (1902), 77.—G. W. A.

"A person accused of crime in this country can properly be convicted in a court of justice only upon evidence which is legally admissible, and which is adduced at his trial in legal form and shape. Though the accused be really guilty of the offense charged against him, the due course of law and justice is nevertheless perverted and obstructed if those who have to try him are induced to approach the question of his guilt or innocence with minds into which prejudice has been instilled by published assertions of his guilt, or imputations against his life and character to which the laws of the land refuse admission as evidence."

In the state of New York the courts have permitted themselves to be deprived of the greater portion of the power which the courts of Massachusetts, in common with those of most of the states, exercise of punishing for contempt the authors of newspaper publications prejudicial to fair trials. Some twenty-five years ago the state legislature passed an act defining and limiting the cases in which summary punishment for contempt should be inflicted by the courts. Similar legislation has been attempted in other states, only to be declared unconstitutional by the courts themselves, which hold that the power to punish is inherent in the judiciary independently of legislative authority, and that, as the Supreme Court of

Ohio says, "The power the legislature does not give, it cannot take away." But while the courts of Ohio, Virginia, Georgia, Indiana, Kentucky, Arkansas, Colorado, and California have thus resisted legislative encroachment upon their constitutional powers, the highest court of New York has submitted to having its power to protect its own usefulness and dignity shorn and curtailed by the legislature. The result is that while by legislative permission they may punish the editor or proprietor of a paper for contempt, it can be *only* when the offense consists in publishing "a false or grossly inaccurate report of a judicial proceeding." The insufficiency of such a power is apparent when one considers that the greater number of the cartoons and comments contained in publications fairly complained of as prejudicing individual legal rights are not, and do not pretend to be, reports of judicial proceedings at all, but are entirely accounts of matters "outside the record." If the acts done, for example, in any of the cases cited as illustrations above, had been done under similar circumstances in New York, the New York courts would have been powerless to take any proceeding whatever in the nature of contempt against the respective offenders. The result is that in the state which suffers most from the gross and unbridled license of a sensational and lawless press the courts possess the least power to repress and restrain its excesses. A change of law which shall give New York courts power to deal summarily with trial by newspaper is imperatively needed.

To the two examples which have just been given of the direct influence which counting-house journalism seeks to exert upon judges and jurors, might be added others of equal importance, would space permit. But all improper influences upon legislators or other public officials, or upon judges or jurors, which these papers may exercise or attempt to exercise, are as naught in comparison with their systematic and constant efforts to instill into the minds of the ignorant and poor, who constitute the greater part of their readers, the impression that justice is not blind but bought; that the great corporations own the judges, particularly those of the Federal courts, body and soul; that American institutions are rotten to the core, and that legislative halls and courts of justice exist as instruments of oppression, to preserve the rights of property by denying or destroying the rights of man. No greater injury can be done to the working people than to create in their minds this false and groundless suspicion concerning the integrity of the judiciary. In a country whose political existence, in the ultimate analysis, depends so largely upon the intelligence and honesty of its judges, the general welfare requires, not merely that judges should be men of integrity, but that the people should believe them to be so. It is this confidence which counting-house journalism has set itself deliberately at undermining. It is not so important that the people should believe in the wisdom of their judges. The liberty of criticism is not confined to the bar and what Judge

Grover used to call "the lawyer's inalienable privilege of damning the adverse judge—out of court." There is no divinity which hedges a judge. His opinions and his personality are proper subjects for criticism, but the charge of corruption should not be made recklessly and without good cause.

It is noticeable that this charge of corruption which yellow journalism makes against the courts is almost invariably a wholesale charge, never accompanied by any specific accusation against any definite official. These general charges are more frequently expressed by cartoon than by comment. The big-chested Carthaginian labeled "The Trusts," holding a squirming Federal judge in his fist, is a cartoon which in one form or another appears in some of these papers whenever an injunction is granted in a labor dispute at the instance of some great corporation. Justice holding her scales with a workingman unevenly balanced by an immense bag of gold; a human basilisk with dollar marks on his clothes, a judge sticking out of his pocket, and a workingman under his foot; Justice holding her scales in one hand while the other is conveniently open to receive the bribe that is being placed in it—these and many other cartoons of similar character and meaning are familiar to all readers of sensational newspapers. If their readers believe the cartoons, what faith can they have left in American institutions? What alternative is offered but anarchy if wealth has poisoned the fountains of justice; if reason is powerless and money omnipotent? If the judges are corrupt, the political heavens are empty.

There is no occasion to defend the American judiciary from charges of wholesale corruption. They might be passed over in silence if they were addressed merely to the educated and intelligent, or to those familiar by personal contact with the actual operations of the courts. That there are many judicial decisions rendered which are unsound in their reasoning may be readily granted. That some of the Federal judges are men of very narrow gauge, and that, during the recent coal strike for example, in granting sweeping, wholesale injunctions against strikers they have accompanied their decrees at times with opinions so unjudicial, so filled with mediæval prejudice and rancor against legitimate organizations of working people as to rouse the indignation of right-minded men, may be admitted. But prejudice and corruption are totally dissimilar. There is always hope that an honest though prejudiced man may in time see reason. This hope inspires patience and forbearance. Justice can wait with confidence while the prejudiced or ultra-conservative judge grows wise, and the principles of law are strongest and surest when they have been established by surmounting the prejudice and doubts of many timid and over-conservative men. But justice and human progress should not and will not wait until the corrupt judge becomes honest. To thoughtful men the severest charge yet to be made against this new journalism is not merely the influence it attempts to exert, and perhaps does exert, in particular cases, but that, wantonly and without just cause, it endeavors to destroy in the hearts and minds of thousands of newspaper readers a deserved confidence in the integrity of the courts and a patient faith in the ultimate triumph of justice by law.

THE CRITIC AND THE LAW

BY RICHARD WASHBURN CHILD

I

A recent prosecution by the People of New York, represented by Mr. Jerome, of a suit for criminal libel, attracted the attention of the entire nation. The alleged libel set forth in the complaint had appeared in *Collier's Weekly*, stating the connection of a certain judge with a certain unwholesome publication. The defense to this action was that the statement was true; and, somewhat to the joy of all concerned, excepting the judge, the unwholesome publication, and those who were exposed in the course of trial as being its creatures, the jury were obliged to find that this defense was sound.[9] From a lawyer's point of view it was surprising to find that even professional critics and editorial writers looked upon this case as involving that part of the Common Law which prescribes the limits of criticism. It only needs to be pointed out that the statement relied upon as defamation was a statement of fact, to show that the case against the Collier editors involved no question of a critic's right to criticise or an editor's right to express his opinion. If the suit had been founded on the criticism of the contents of the unwholesome publication which had been offered to the public for those to read who would, then the law of fair comment would have controlled. No doubt, however, even the trained guides to the public taste seldom realize the presence of a law governing their freedom of comment. Such law is in force none the less, and, though the instinct to express only fair and honest opinion will generally suffice to prevent a breach of legal limits, it is evident that the consideration of the law upon the subject is important, not only to the professional critic, but to any man who has enough opinion on matters of public interest to be worth an expression.

9. The verdict for *Collier's Weekly*, the defendant, was rendered on January 26, 1906. Cf. *Collier's Weekly*, February 10, 1906, vol. 36, p. 23.—ED.

It is public policy that the free expression of opinion on matters of public interest should be as little hampered as possible. Fair comment, says the law, is the preventive of affectation and folly, the educator of the public taste and ethics, and the incentive to progress in the arts. Often fair comment is spoken of as privileged. But privilege in its legal sense means that some statement is allowed to some particular person on some particular occasion—a statement that would be libel or slander unless it came within the realm of privilege. On the other hand, fair comment is not the right of any particular person or class, or the privilege of any particular occasion; it is not exclusively the right of the press or of one who is a critic in the sense that he is an expert. Doubtless the newspaper or professional critic is given a greater latitude by juries, who share the prevalent and not ill-advised view that opinion expressed by the public press is usually more sound than private comment. The law, however, recognizes no such distinction. Any one may be a critic.

In civil actions of defamation, truth in a general way is always a defense; whether the person against whom the suit is brought has made a statement of fact or opinion, if he can prove his words to be true, he is safe from liability. Such was the defense of the Collier editors in the criminal case mentioned above. Fair comment, however, does not need to be true to be defended, for it is, if we may use the phrase, its own defense. Then what is fair comment?

The right to comment is confined to matters which are of interest to the public. To endeavor to give a list of matters answering this requirement would be an endless task; even the courts of England and this country have passed upon only a few. Instances when the attention, judgment, and taste of the public are called upon are, however, most frequent in the fields of politics and of the arts. Such are the acts of those entrusted with functions of government, the direction of public institutions and possibly church matters, published books, pictures which have been exhibited, architecture, theatres, concerts, and public entertainments. Two reasons prohibit comment upon that which has not become the affair of the public nor has been offered to the attention of the public:—the public is not benefited by the criticism of that which it does not know, and about which it has no concern, and the act of the doer or the work of the artist against which the comment is directed cannot be said to have been submitted to open criticism.

The requirement, which seems right in principle, and which has been laid down many times in the remarks of English judges, was perhaps overlooked in Battersby vs. Collier, a New York case. Colonel Battersby, it appeared, was a veteran of the Civil War, and for six years had been engaged in painting a picture representing the dramatic meeting of General Lee and General Grant, at which Colonel Battersby was present. This painting was intended for exhibition at the Columbian Exposition. Unfortunately, a few days before Christmas, a young woman of a literary turn of mind had an opportunity to view this immense canvas, and was less favorably impressed with the painting than with the pathos surrounding its inception and development. Accordingly she wrote a story headed by that handiest of handy titles, *The Colonel's Christmas*, but she did not sufficiently conceal the identity of her principal character. Colonel Battersby sued the publishers, and for damages relied upon the aspersions cast upon his picture, which in the story was called a "daub." More than that, there occurred in the narrative these words: "What matters it if the Colonel's ideas of color, light, and shade were a trifle hazy, if his perspective was a something extraordinary, his 'breadth' and 'treatment' and 'tone' truly marvelous, the Surrender was a great, vast picture, and it was the Colonel's life." The court held that this was a fair criticism; but it does not plainly appear that Colonel Battersby had yet submitted his six-year painting to the attention of the public, or that it had at the time become an object of general public interest; and if it had not, the decision would seem doubtful in principle.

On the other hand, in Gott vs. Pulsifer there was involved the "Cardiff Giant," which all remember as the merriest of practical jokes in rock, which made Harvard scientists rub their eyes and called forth from one Yale professor a magazine article to prove that the man of stone was the god Baal brought to New York State by the Phœnicians. The court said that all manner of abuse might be heaped on the Giant's adamant head. "Anything made subject of public exhibition," said they, "is open to fair and reasonable comment, no matter how severe." So you might with impunity call the Cardiff Giant, or Barnum's famous long-haired horse, a hoax; they were objects of general public interest, and any one might have passed judgment upon them.

Letters written to a newspaper may be criticised most severely, as often happens when Constant Reader enters into a warfare of communication with Old Subscriber; and so long as the contention is free from actionable personalities, and remains within the bounds of fair comment, neither will find himself in trouble. Nor is the commercial advertisement immune from caustic comment, if the comment is sincere. The rhymes in the street cars, the posters on the fences, the handbill that is thrust over the domestic threshold, and the signboard, that has now become a factor in every rural sunset or urban sunrise, must bear the comment upon their taste, their efficiency, and their ingenuity, which by their very nature they invite. In England a writer was sued by the maker of a commodity for travelers advertised as the "Bag of Bags." The writer thought the commercial catch-name was silly, vulgar, and ill-conceived, and he said so. The manufacturer in court urged that the comment injured his trade; but the judges were inclined to think that an advertisement appealing to the public was subject to the public opinion and its fair expression. What is of interest to the general public, so that comment thereon will be a right of the public, may, however, in certain cases trouble the jury. A volume of love sonnets printed and circulated privately, and the architecture of a person's private dwelling, might furnish very delicate cases.

In a time when those who desire to be conspicuous succeed so well in becoming so, it is rather amusing to wonder just what may be the difference between the right to comment on the dancer on the stage, and on the lady who, if she has her way, will sit in a box. Both court public notice—the dancer by her penciled eyebrows, her tinted cheeks, her jewelry, her gown, and her grace; the lady in the box, perhaps, by all these things except the last; both wish favorable comment, and perhaps ought to bear ridicule, if their cheeks are too tinted, their eyebrows too penciled, their jewelry too generous, and their gowns too ornate. A more sober view, however, will show that the matter is one of proof. The dancer who exhibits herself and her dance for a consideration necessarily invites expressions of opinion, but it would be difficult to show in a court of law that the gala lady in the box meant to seek either commendation—or disapproval.

A vastly more important and interesting query, and one which must arise from the present state and tendency of industrial conditions, is whether the acts of men in commercial activity may ever become so prominent, and so far-reaching in their effect, that it can well be said that they compel a universal public interest, and that public comment is impliedly invited by reason of their conspicuous and semi-public nature. It may be said that at no time have private industries become of such startling interest to the community at large as at present in the United States. At least a few have had an effect more vital to citizens, perhaps, than the activities of some classes of public officials which are open to fair comment, and certainly more vital than the management of some semi-public institutions, which also are open to honest criticism.

As to corporations, it would seem that, as the public, through the chartering power of legislation, gives them a right to exist and act, an argument that the public retains the right to comment upon their management must have some force; in the case of other forms of commercial activity, whose powers are inherent and not delegated, the question must rest on the determination of the best public policy—a determination which in all classes of cases decides, and ought to decide, the right of fair comment.

II

When once the comment is decided to be upon a matter of public interest, there arises the question whether or not the comment is fair. The requirement of the law in regard to fairness is not based, as might be supposed, upon the consideration whether comment is mild or severe, serious or ridiculing, temperate or exaggerated; the critic is not hampered in the free play of his honest opinions; he is not prohibited from using the most stinging satire, the most extravagant burlesque, or the most lacerating invective.

In 1808, Lord Ellenborough, in Carr vs. Hood, stated the length of leash given to the critic, and the law has not since been changed. Sir John Carr, Knight, was the author of several volumes, entitled *A Stranger in France*, *A Northern Summer*, *A Stranger in Ireland*, and other titles of equal connotation. Thomas Hood was rather more deserving of a lasting place in literature than his victim, because of his sense of humor, and his well-known rapid-fire satire. According to the declaration of Sir John Carr, the plaintiff, Hood had published a book of burlesque in which there was a frontispiece entitled "The Knight leaving Ireland with Regret," and "containing and representing in the said print, a certain false, scandalous, malicious and defamatory and ridiculous representation of said Sir John in the form of a man of ludicrous and ridiculous appearance holding a pocket handkerchief to his face, and appearing to be weeping," and also representing "a malicious and ridiculous man of ludicrous and ridiculous appearance following the said Sir John," and bending under the weight of several books, and carrying a tied-up pocket handkerchief with "Wardrobe" printed thereon, "thereby falsely scandalously and maliciously meaning and intending to represent, for the purpose of rendering the said Sir John ridiculous and exposing him to laughter, ridicule and contempt," that the books of the said Sir John "were so heavy as to cause a man to bend under the weight thereof, and that his the said Sir John's wardrobe was very small and capable of being contained in a pocket handkerchief." And at the end of this declaration Sir John alleged that he was damaged because of the consequent decline in his literary reputation, and, it may be supposed, because thereafter his books did not appear in the list of the "six bestsellers" in the Kingdom.

But no recovery was allowed him, for it was laid down that if a comment, in whatever form, only ridiculed the plaintiff as an author, there was no ground for action. Said the eminent justice, "One writer, in exposing the follies and errors of another, may make use of ridicule, however poignant. Ridicule is often the fittest weapon for such a purpose.... Perhaps the plaintiff's works are now unsalable, but is he to be indemnified by receiving a compensation from the person who has opened the eyes of the public to the bad taste and inanity of his compositions?.... We must not cramp observations on authors and their works.... The critic does a great service to the public who writes down any vapid or useless publication, such as ought never to have appeared. He checks the dissemination of bad taste, and prevents people from wasting both their time and money upon trash. Fair and candid criticism every one has a right to publish, although the author may suffer a loss from it. Such a loss the law does not consider an injury, because it is a loss which the party ought to sustain. It is, in short, the loss of fame and profits to which he was never entitled."

Criticism need not be fair and just, in the sense that it conforms to the judgment of the majority of the public, or the ideas of a judge, or the estimate of a jury; but it must remain within certain bounds circumscribed by the law.

In the first place, comment must be made honestly; in recent cases much more stress has been laid upon this point than formerly. It is urged that, if criticism is not sincere, it is not valuable to the public, and the ground of public policy, upon which the doctrine of fair criticism is built, fails to give support to comment which is born of improper motives or begotten from personal hatred or malice. Yet he who seeks for cases of criticism which have been decided against the critic solely on the ground that the critic was malicious must look far. The requirement in practice seems difficult of application, since, if the critic does not depart from the work that he is criticising, to strike at the author thereof as a private individual, and does not mix with his comment false statements or imputations of bad motives, there is nothing to show legal malice, and it is almost impossible to prove actual malice. If you should conclude that your neighbor's painting which has been on exhibition is a beautiful marine, but if, because you do not like your neighbor, you pronounce it to be a dreadful mire of blue paint, it would be very hard for any other person to prove that at the moment you spoke you were not speaking honestly. Again, if the comment is within the other restrictions put by the law upon criticism, it would seem that to open the question whether or not the comment was malicious, is in effect very nearly submitting to the jury the question whether or not they disagree with the critic, since the jury have no other method of reaching a conclusion that the critic was or was not impelled by malice.

Malice, in fact, is a bugaboo in the law—and the law, especially the civil law, avoids dealing with him whenever it can. Yet it is quite certain that malice must be a consideration in determining what is fair comment; an opinion which is not honest is of no help to the public in its striving to attain high morals and unerring discernment. All the reasons of public policy that give criticism its rights fly out of the window when malice walks in at the door.

Some decisions of the courts seem to set the standard of fair comment even higher. They not only demand that the critic speak with an honest belief in his opinion, but insist also that a person taking upon himself to criticise must exercise a reasonable degree of judgment. As one English judge expressed it in charging the jury: "You must determine whether any fair man, however exaggerated or obstinate his views, would have said what this criticism has said." It would seem, however, that in many cases this would result in putting the judgment of the jury against that of the critic. To ask the jury whether this comment is such as would be made by a fair man is not distinguishable from asking them whether the comment is fair, and it sometimes happens that, in spite of the opinion of the jury,—in fact, the opinion of all the world,—the single critic is right, and the rest of the community all wrong. Does any one doubt that the comment of Columbus upon the views of those who opposed him would have been considered unfair by a jury of his time, until this doughty navigator proved his judgment correct? What would have happened in a court of law to the man who first said that those who wrote that the earth was flat were stupidly ignorant? Often the opinion or criticism which is the most valuable to the community as a contribution to truth is the very opinion which the community as a body would call a wild inference by an unfair man; to hold the critic up to the standard of a "fair man" is to deprive the public of the benefit of the most powerful influences against the perpetuity of error.

No better illustration could be found than the case of Merrivale and Wife *vs.* Carson, in which a dramatic critic said of a play: "*The Whip Hand* ... gives us nothing but a hash-up of ingredients which have been used *ad nauseam*, until one rises in protestation against the loving, confiding, fatuous husband with the naughty wife, and her double existence, the good male genius, the limp aristocrat, and the villainous foreigner. And why dramatic authors will insist that in modern society comedies the villain must be a foreigner, and the foreigner must be a villain, is only explicable on the ground that there is more or less romance about such gentry. It is more in consonance with accepted notions that your continental croupier would make a much better fictitious prince, marquis, or count, than would, say, an English billiard-maker or stable lout. And so the Marquis Colonna in *The Whip Hand* is offered up by the authors upon the altar of tradition, and sacrificed in the usual manner when he gets too troublesome to permit of the reconciliation of husband and wife and lover and maiden, and is proved, also much as usual, to be nothing more than a kicked-out croupier."

The jury found that this amounted to falsely setting out the drama as adulterous and immoral, and was not the criticism of a fair man. Granting that there was the general imputation of immorality, it seems, justly considered, a matter of the critic's opinion. Is not the critic in effect saying,

"To my mind the play is adulterous; no matter what any one else may think, the play suggests immorality to me"? And if this is the honest opinion of the critic, no matter how much juries may differ from him, it would seem that to stifle this individual expression was against public policy, the very ground on which fair criticism becomes a universal right. It does not very clearly appear that the case of Merrivale and Wife *vs.* Carson was decided exclusively on the question whether the criticism was that of a fair man, but this was the leading point of the case. The decision and the doctrine it sets forth seem open to much doubt.

III

Criticism must never depart from a consideration of the work of the artist or artisan, or the public acts of a person, to attack the individual himself, apart from his connection with the particular work or act which is being criticised. The critic is forbidden to touch upon the domestic or private life of the individual, or upon such matters concerning the individual as are not of general public interest, at the peril of exceeding his right. Whereas, in Fry vs. Bennett, an article in a newspaper purported to criticise the management of a theatrical troupe, it was held to contain a libel, since it went beyond matters which concerned the public, and branded the conduct of the manager toward his singers as unjust and oppressive.

J. Fenimore Cooper was plaintiff in another suit which illustrates the same rule of law. This author had many a gallant engagement with his critics, and, though it has been said that a man who is his own lawyer has a fool for a client, Mr. Cooper, conducting his own actions, won from many publishers, including Mr. Horace Greeley and Mr. Webb. In Cooper vs. Stone the facts reveal that the author, having completed a voluminous *Naval History of the United States*, in which he had given the lion's share of credit for the Battle of Lake Erie, not to the commanding officer, Oliver H. Perry, but to Jesse D. Elliot, who was a subordinate, was attacked by the *New York Commercial Advertiser*, which imputed to the author "a disregard of justice and propriety as a man," represented him as infatuated with vanity, mad with passion, and publishing as true, statements and evidence which had been falsified and encomiums which had been retracted. This was held to exceed the limits of fair criticism, since it attacked the character of the author as well as the book itself.

The line, however, is not very finely drawn, as may be seen by a comparison of the above case with Browning vs. Van Rensselaer, in which the plaintiff was the author of a genealogical treatise entitled *Americans of Royal Descent*. A young woman, who was interested in founding a society to be called the "Order of the Crown," wrote to the defendant, inviting her to join and recommending to her the book. The latter answered this letter with a polite refusal, saying that she thought such a society was un-American and pretentious, and that the book gave no authority for its statements. The court said that this, even though it implied that the author was at fault, was not a personal attack on his private character.

An intimate relationship almost always exists between the doer of an act which interests the public and the act itself; the architect is closely associated with his building, the painter with his picture, the author with his works, the inventor with his patent, the tradesman with his advertisement, and the singer with his song; and the critic will find it impossible not to encroach to some extent upon the personality of the individual. It seems, however, that the privilege of comment extends to the individual only so far as is necessary to intelligent criticism of his particular work under discussion. To write that Mr. Palet's latest picture shows that some artists are only fit to paint signs is a comment on the picture, but to write, apart from comment upon the particular work, that Mr. Palet is only fit to paint signs is an attack upon the artist, and if it is untrue, it is libel for which the law allows recovery.

No case presents a more complete confusion of the individual and his work than that of an actor. His physical characteristics, as well as his personality, may always be said to be presented to general public interest along with the words and movements which constitute his acting. The critic can hardly speak of the performance without speaking of the actor himself, who, it may be argued, presents to a certain extent his own bodily and mental characteristics to the judgment of the public, almost as much as do the ossified man and the fat lady of the side show.

The case of Cherry *vs.* the *Des Moines Leader* will serve to illustrate how far the critic who is not actuated by malice may comment upon the actors as well as the performance, and still be held to have remained within the limits of fair criticism. The three Cherry sisters were performers in a variety act, which consisted in part of a burlesque on *Trilby*, and a more serious presentation entitled, *The Gypsy's Warning*. The judge stated that in his opinion the evidence showed that the performance was ridiculous. The testimony of Miss Cherry included a statement that one of the songs was a "sort of eulogy on ourselves," and that the refrain consisted of these words:—

"Cherries ripe and cherries red;

The Cherry Sisters are still ahead."

She also stated that in *The Gypsy's Warning* she had taken the part of a Spaniard or a cavalier, and that she always supposed a Spaniard and a cavalier were one and the same thing. The defendant published the following comment on the performance: "Effie is an old jade of fifty summers, Jessie a frisky filly of forty, and Addie, the flower of the family, a capering monstrosity of thirty-five. Their long, skinny arms, equipped with talons at the extremities, swung mechanically, and anon waved frantically at the suffering audience. The mouths of their rancid features opened like caverns, and sounds like the wailings of damned souls issued therefrom. They pranced around the stage with a motion that suggested a cross between the *danse du ventre* and fox-trot—strange creatures with painted faces and hideous mien." This was held to be fair criticism and not libelous;

for the Misses Cherry to a certain extent presented their personal appearance as a part of their performance.

The critic must not mix with his comment statement of facts which are not true, since the statement of facts is not criticism at all. In Tabbart *vs.* Tipper, the earliest case on the subject, the defendant, in order to ridicule a book published for children, printed a verse which purported to be an extract from the book, and it was held that this amounted to a false accusation that the author had published something which in fact he had never published; it was not comment, but an untrue statement of fact. So when, as in Davis *vs.* Shepstone, the critic, in commenting upon the acts of a government official in Zululand, falsely stated that the officer had been guilty of an assault upon a native chief, the critic went far beyond comment, and was liable for defamation. Not unlike Tabbart *vs.* Tipper is a recent case, Belknap *vs.* Ball. The defendant, during a political campaign, printed in his newspaper a coarsely executed imitation of the handwriting of a political candidate of the opposing party, and an imitation of his signature appeared beneath. The writing contained this misspelled, unrhetorical sentence: "I don't propose to go into debate on the tariff differences on wool, quinine, and such, because I ain't built that way." Readers were led to believe that this was a signed statement by the candidate, and the newspaper was barred from setting up the plea that the writing was only fair criticism made through the means of a burlesque; it was held that imputing to the plaintiff something he had never written amounted to a false statement of fact, and was not within fair comment.

The dividing line between opinion and statement of fact is, however, most troublesome. Mr. Odgers, in his excellent work on *Libel and Slander*, remarks that the rule for the distinction between the two should be that "if facts are known to hearers or readers or made known by the writer, and their opinion or criticism refers to these true facts, even if it is a statement in form, it is no less an opinion. But if the statement simply stands alone, it is not defended." Applying this rule, what if a critic makes this simple statement: "The latest book of Mr. Anonymous is of interest to no intelligent man"? According to the opinion of Mr. Odgers, it would seem that such a sentence standing alone was a statement of fact, whereas it is manifest that no one can think that the critic meant to say more than that in his opinion the book was not interesting. In Merrivale and Wife *vs.* Carson, the jury found that the words used by the critic described the play as adulterous, and the court said that this was a misdescription of the play—a false statement of fact; but an adulterous play may be one which is only suggestive of adultery; and even if the critic had baldly said that the play was adulterous, many of us would think that he was only expressing his opinion.

Since the test of whether the statement is of opinion or of fact lies, not in what the critic secretly intended, but rather in what the hearer or reader understood, the question is for the jury, and, it seems, should be presented to them by the court in the form: "Would a reasonable man under the circumstances have understood this to be a statement of opinion or of fact?"

One other care remains for the critic: he must not falsely impute a bad motive to the individual when commenting upon his work. No less a critic than Ruskin was held to have made this mistake in the instance of his criticism of one of Mr. Whistler's pictures. This well-known libel case may be found reported in the *Times* for November 26 and 27, 1878. "The mannerisms and errors of these pictures," wrote Mr. Ruskin, alluding to the pictures of Mr. Burne-Jones, "whatever may be their extent, are never affected or indolent. The work is natural to the painter, however strange to us, and is wrought with utmost care, however far, to his own or our desire, the result may yet be incomplete. Scarcely as much can be said for any other picture in the modern school; their eccentricities are almost always in some degree forced, and their imperfections gratuitously if not impertinently indulged. For Mr. Whistler's own sake, no less than for the protection of the purchaser, Sir Coutts Lindsay ought not to have admitted works into the gallery in which the ill-educated conceit of the artist so nearly approached the aspect of wilful imposture. I have seen and heard much of cockney impudence before now, but never expected to hear a coxcomb ask 200 guineas for flinging a pot of paint in the public's face."

Out of all this, stinging as it must have been to Mr. Whistler, unless, since he loved enemies and hated friends, he therefore found pleasure in the metaphorical thrashings he received, the jury could find only one phrase, "wilful imposture," which, because it imputed bad motives, overstepped the bounds of fair criticism.

Mr. Odgers's treatise states the rule to be that "When no ground is assigned for an inference of bad motives, or when the writer states the imputation of bad motives as a fact within his knowledge, then he is only protected if the imputation is true. But when the facts are set forth, together with the inference, and the reader may judge of the right or wrong of the opinion or inference, then if the facts are true, the writer is protected." It is, however, difficult to see why the imputation of bad motives in the doer of an act or the creator of a work of art should in any case come under the right of fair comment, for, no matter how bad the motives of the individual may be, they are of no consequence to the public. If a book is immoral, it is immaterial to a fair criticism whether or not the author meant it to have an immoral effect; the public is not helped to a proper judgment of the book by any one's opinion of the motives of the author, and if the book is bad in its effect, it makes it no better that the author was impelled by the best of intentions, or it makes it no worse that the author was acting with the most evil designs. And if, as in most of the cases that have arisen, the imputation is one of insincerity, fraud, or deception practiced upon the public,—where, for example, the critic, in commenting upon a medical treatise, about which he had made known all the facts, said that he thought the author wrote the book, not in the interest of scientific truth, but rather to draw trade by exploiting theories which he did not believe himself,—it would seem that this charge of fraud or deception should not be protected as a piece of fair comment, but that it should be put upon an equality with all other imputations against an individual, which if untrue and damaging would be held to be libel or slander. Under Mr. Odgers's rule, in making a comment upon the acts of a public officer, one could say, "In pardoning six criminals last week the governor of the province, we think, has shown that he wishes to encourage criminality." No court would, we think, hold this to be within the right of fair comment upon public matters. If the critic had said, however, "We think that the governor of the province, in pardoning six criminals, encouraged criminality," all the true value of criticism remains, and the imputation that the public officer acted from an evil motive is stripped away. The best view seems to be that the right of fair comment will not shield the false imputations of bad motive.

Whether or not the critic may impute to the individual certain opinions does not seem to be settled, but logically this would be quite as much a statement of fact, or a criticism directed at the individual, as an imputation of bad motives. A few courts in this country have expressed a leaning to the opposite view, but the ground upon which they place their opinion does not appear.

From the legal point of view, then, we as critics are all held to a high standard of fairness. We must not comment upon any but matters of public interest. We must be honest and sincere, but we may express any view, no matter how prejudiced or exaggerated it may be, so long as it does not exceed the limits to which a reasonably fair man would go; we must not attack the individual any more than is consistent with a criticism of that which he makes or does, and we must not expect that we are within our right of comment when we make statements of fact or impute to the individual evil motives.

All the world asks the critic to be honest, careful, above spite and personalities, and polite enough not to thrust upon us a consideration in which we have no interest. The law demands no more.

HONEST LITERARY CRITICISM

BY CHARLES MINER THOMPSON

I

There are five groups interested in literary criticism: publishers of books, authors, publishers of reviews, critics, and, finally, the reading public.

An obvious interest of all the groups but the last is financial. For the publisher of books, although he may have his pride, criticism is primarily an advertisement: he hopes that his books will be so praised as to commend them to buyers. For the publisher of book-reviews, although he also may have his pride, criticism is primarily an attraction for advertisements: he hopes that his reviews will lead publishers of books to advertise in his columns. For the critic, whatever his ideals, criticism is, in whole or in part, his livelihood. For the author, no matter how disinterested, criticism is reputation—perhaps a reputation that can be coined. In respect of this financial interest, all four are opposed to the public, which wants nothing but competent service—a guide to agreeable reading, an adviser in selecting gifts, a herald of new knowledge, a giver of intellectual delight.

All five groups are discontented with the present condition of American criticism.

Publishers of books complain that reviews do not help sales. Publishers of magazines lament that readers do not care for articles on literary subjects. Publishers of newspapers frankly doubt the interest of book-notices. The critic confesses that his occupation is ill-considered and ill-paid. The author wrathfully exclaims—but what he exclaims cannot be summarized, so various is it. Thus, the whole commercial interest is unsatisfied. The public, on the other hand, finds book-reviews of little service and reads them, if at all, with indifference, with distrust, or with exasperation. That part of the public which appreciates criticism as an art maintains an eloquent silence and reads French.

Obviously, what frets the commercial interest is the public indifference to book-reviews. What is the cause of that?

In critical writing, what is the base of interest, the indispensable foundation in comparison with which all else is superstructure? I mentioned the public which, appreciating criticism as an art, turns from America to France for what it craves. Our sympathies respond to the call of our own national life, and may not be satisfied by Frenchmen; if we turn to them, we do so for some attraction which compensates for the absence of intimate relation to our needs. What is it? Of course, French mastery of form accounts in part for our intellectual absenteeism; but it does not account for it wholly, not, I think, even in the main.

Consider the two schools of French criticism typified by Brunetière and by Anatole France. Men like Brunetière seem to believe that what they say is important, not merely to fellow dilettanti or to fellow scholars, but to the public and to the mass of the public; they seem to write, not to display their attainments, but to use their attainments to accomplish their end; they put their whole strength, intellectual and moral, into their argument; they seek to make converts, to crush enemies. They are in earnest; they feel responsible; they take their office with high seriousness. They seem to think that the soul and the character of the people are as important as its economic comfort. The problem of a contemporary, popular author—even if contemporary, even if popular—is to them an important question; the intellectual, moral, and æsthetic ideals which he is spreading through the country are to be tested rigorously, then applauded or fought. They seek to be clear because they wish to interest; they wish to interest because they wish to convince; they wish to convince because they have convictions which they believe should prevail.

The men like Anatole France—if there are any others like Anatole France—have a different philosophy of life. They are doubtful of endeavor, doubtful of progress, doubtful of new schools of art, doubtful of new solutions whether in philosophy or economics; but they have a quick sensitiveness to beauty and a profound sympathy with suffering man. Not only do they face their doubts, but they make their readers face them. They do not pretend; they do not conceal; they flatter no conventions and no prejudices; they are sincere. Giving themselves without reserve, they do not speak what they think will please you, but rather try with all their art to please you with what they think.

In the French critics of both types—the men like Brunetière, the men like Anatole France—there is this common, this invaluable characteristic,—I mean intellectual candor. That is their great attraction; that is the foundation of interest.

Intellectual candor does not mark American criticism. The fault is primarily the publisher's. It lies in the fundamental mistake that he makes in the matter of publicity. Each publisher, that is, treats each new book as if it were the only one that he had ever published, were publishing, or ever should publish. He gives all his efforts to seeing that it is praised. He repeats these exertions with some success for each book that he prints. Meanwhile, every other publisher is doing as much for every new book of his own. The natural result follows—a monotony of praise which permits no books to stand out, and which, however plausible in the particular instance, is, in the mass, incredible.

But how is it that the publisher's fiat produces praise? The answer is implicit in the fact that criticism is supported, not by the public, but by the publisher. Upon the money which the publisher of books is ready to spend for advertising depends the publisher of book-reviews; upon him in turn depends the critic.

Between the publisher of books anxious for favorable reviews and willing to spend money, and the publisher of a newspaper anxious for advertisements and supporting a dependent critic, the chance to trade is perfect. Nothing sordid need be said or, indeed, perceived; all may be left to the workings of human nature. Favorable reviews are printed, advertisements are received; and no one, not even the principals, need be certain that the reviews are not favorable because the books are good, or that the advertisements are not given because the comment is competent and just. Nevertheless, the Silent Bargain has been decorously struck. Once reached, it tends of itself to become ever more close, intimate, and inclusive. The publisher of books is continuously tempted to push his advantage with the complaisant publisher of a newspaper; the publisher of a newspaper is continuously tempted to pitch ever higher and still higher the note of praise.

But the Silent Bargain is not made with newspapers only. Obviously, critics can say nothing without the consent of some publisher; obviously, their alternatives are silence or submission. They who write for the magazines are wooed to constant surrender; they must, or they think that they must, be tender of all authors who have commercial relations with the house that publishes the periodical to which they are contributing. Even they who write books are not exempt; they must, or they feel that they must, deal gently with reputations commercially dear to their publisher. If the critic is timid, or amiable, or intriguing, or struck with poverty, he is certain, whatever his rank, to dodge, to soften, to omit whatever he fears may displease the publisher on whom he depends. Selfish considerations thus tend ever to emasculate criticism; criticism thus tends ever to assume more and more nearly the most dishonest and exasperating form of advertisement, that of the "reading notice" which presents itself as sincere, spontaneous testimony. Disingenuous criticism tends in its turn to puzzle and disgust the public—and to hurt the publisher. The puff is a boomerang.

Its return blow is serious; it would be fatal, could readers turn away wholly from criticism. What saves the publisher is that they cannot. They have continuous, practical need of books, and must know about them. The multitudinous paths of reading stretch away at every angle, and the traveling crowd must gather and guess and wonder about the guide-post criticism, even if each finger, contradicting every other, points to its own road as that "To Excellence."

Wayfarers in like predicament would question one another. It is so with readers. Curiously enough, publishers declare that their best advertising flows from this private talk. They all agree that, whereas reviews sell nothing, the gossip of readers sells much. Curiously, I say; for this gossip is not under their control; it is as often adverse as favorable; it kills as much as it sells. Moreover, when it kills, it kills in secret; it leaves the bewildered publisher without a clue to the culprit or his motive. How, then, can it be superior to the controlled, considerate flattery of the public press? It is odd that publishers never seriously ask themselves this question, for the answer, if I have it, is instructive. The dictum of the schoolgirl that a novel is "perfectly lovely" or "perfectly horrid," comes from the heart. The comment of society women at afternoon tea, the talk of business men at the club, if seldom of much critical value, is sincere. In circles in which literature is loved, the witty things which clever men and clever women say about books are inspired by the fear neither of God nor of man. In circles falsely literary, parrot talk and affectation hold sway, but the talkers have an absurd faith in one another. In short, all private talk about books bears the stamp of sincerity. That is what makes the power of the spoken word. It is still more potent when it takes the form, not of casual mention, but of real discussion. When opinions differ, talk becomes animated, warm, continuous. Listeners are turned into partisans. A lively, unfettered dispute over a book by witty men, no matter how prejudiced, or by clever women, no matter how unlearned, does not leave the listener indifferent. He is tempted to read that book.

Now, what the publisher needs in order to print with financial profit the best work and much work, is the creation of a wide general interest in literature. This vastly transcends in importance the fate of any one book or group of books. Instead, then, of trying to start in the public press a chorus of stupid praise, why should he not endeavor to obtain a reproduction of what he acknowledges that his experience has taught him is his main prop and support—the frank word, the unfettered dispute of private talk? Let him remember what has happened when the vivacity of public opinion has forced this reproduction. It is history that those works have been best advertised over which critics have fought—Hugo's dramas, Wagner's music, Whitman's poems, Zola's novels, Mrs. Stowe's *Uncle Tom*.

Does it not all suggest the folly of the Silent Bargain?

I have spoken always of tendencies. Public criticism never has been and never will be wholly dishonest, even when in the toils of the Silent Bargain; it never has been and never will be wholly honest, even with that cuttlefish removed. But if beyond cavil it tended towards sincerity, the improvement would be large. In the measure of that tendency it would gain the public confidence without which it can benefit no one—not even the publisher. For his own sake he should do what he can to make the public regard the critic, not as a mere megaphone for his advertisements, but as an honest man who speaks his honest mind. To this end, he should deny his foolish taste for praise, and, even to the hurt of individual ventures, use his influence to foster independence in the critic.

In the way of negative help, he should cease to tempt lazy and indifferent reviewers with ready-made notices, the perfunctory and insincere work of some minor employee; he should stop sending out, as "literary" notes, thinly disguised advertisements and irrelevant personalities; he should no longer supply photographs of his authors in affected poses that display their vanity much and their talent not at all. That vulgarity he should leave to those who have soubrettes to exploit; he should not treat his authors as if they were variety artists—unless, indeed, they are just that, and he himself on the level of the manager of a low vaudeville house. These cheap devices lower his dignity as a publisher, they are a positive hurt to the reputation of his authors, they make less valuable to him the periodical that prints them, and they are an irritation and an insult to the critic, for, one and all, they are attempts to insinuate advertising into his honest columns. Frankly, they are modes of corruption, and degrade the whole business of writing.

In the way of positive help, he should relieve of every commercial preoccupation, not only the editors and contributors of any magazines that he may control, but also those authors of criticism and critical biography whose volumes he may print. Having cleaned his own house, he should steadily demand of the publications in which he advertises, a higher grade of critical writing, and should select the periodicals to which to send his books for notice, not according to the partiality, but according to the ability of their reviews. Thus he would do much to make others follow his own good example.

II

What of the author? In respect of criticism, the publisher, of course, has no absolute rights, not even that of having his books noticed at all. His interests only have been in question, and, in the long run and in the mass, these will not be harmed, but benefited, by criticism honestly adverse. He has in his writers a hundred talents, and if his selection is shrewd most of them bring profit. Frank criticism will but help the task of judicious culling. But all that has been said assumes the cheerful sacrifice of the particular author who must stake his all upon his single talent. Does his comparative helplessness give him any right to tender treatment?

It does not; in respect of rights his, precisely, is the predicament of the publisher. If an author puts forth a book for sale, he obviously can be accorded no privilege incompatible with the right of the public to know its value. He cannot ask to have the public fooled for his benefit; he cannot ask to have his feelings saved, if to save them the critic must neglect to inform his readers. That is rudimentary. Nor may the author argue more subtly that, until criticism is a science and truth unmistakable, he should be given the benefit of the doubt. This was the proposition behind the plea, strongly urged not so long ago, that all criticism should be "sympathetic"; that is, that the particular critic is qualified to judge those writers only whom, on the whole, he likes. Love, it was declared, is the only key to understanding. The obvious value of the theory to the Silent Bargain accounts for its popularity with the commercial interests. Now, no one can quarrel with the criticism of appreciation—it is full of charm and service; but to pretend that it should be the only criticism is impertinent and vain. To detect the frivolity of such a pretension, one has only to apply it to public affairs; imagine a political campaign in which the candidates were criticised only by their friends! No; the critic should attack whatever he thinks is bad, and he is quite as likely to be right when he does so as when he applauds what he thinks is good. In a task wherein the interest of the public is the one that every time and all the time should be served, mercy to the author is practically always a betrayal. To the public, neither the vanity nor the purse of the author is of the slightest consequence. Indeed, a criticism powerful enough to curb the conceit of some authors, and to make writing wholly unprofitable to others, would be an advantage to the public, to really meritorious authors, and to the publisher.

And the publisher—to consider his interests again for a moment—would gain not merely by the suppression of useless, but by the discipline of spoiled, writers. For the Silent Bargain so works as to give to many an author an exaggerated idea of his importance. It leads the publisher himself—what with his complaisant reviewers, his literary notes, his personal paragraphs, his widely distributed photographs—to do all that he can to turn the author's head. Sometimes he succeeds. When the spoiled writer, taking all this *au grand sérieux*, asks why sales are not larger, then how hard is the publisher pressed for an answer! If the author chooses to believe, not the private but the public statement of his merit, and bases upon it either a criticism of his publisher's energy or a demand for further publishing favors,—increase of advertising, higher royalties, what not,—the publisher is in a ridiculous and rather troublesome quandary. None but the initiated know what he has occasionally to endure from the arrogance of certain writers. Here fearless criticism should help him much.

But if the conceit of some authors offends, the sensitiveness of others awakens sympathy. The author does his work in solitude; his material is his own soul; his anxiety about a commercial venture is complicated with the apprehension of the recluse who comes forth into the market-place with his heart upon his sleeve. Instinctively he knows that, as his book is himself, or at least a fragment of himself, criticism of it is truly criticism of him, not of his intellectual ability merely, but of his essential character, his real value as a man. Let no one laugh until he has heard and survived the most intimate, the least friendly comment upon his own gifts and traits, made in public for the delectation of his friends and acquaintances and of the world at large. Forgivably enough, the author is of all persons the one most likely to be unjust to critics and to criticism. In all ages he has made bitter counter-charges, and flayed the critics as they have flayed him. His principal complaints are three: first, that all critics are disappointed authors; second, that many are young and incompetent, or simply incompetent; third, that they do not agree. Let us consider them in turn.

Although various critics write with success other things than criticism, the first complaint is based, I believe, upon what is generally a fact. It carries two implications: the first, that one cannot competently judge a task which he is unable to perform himself; the second, that the disappointed author is blinded by jealousy. As to the first, no writer ever refrained out of deference to it from criticising, or even discharging, his cook. As to the second, jealousy does not always blind: sometimes it gives keenness of vision. The disappointed author turned critic may indeed be incompetent; but, if he is so, it is for reasons that his disappointment does not supply. If he is able, his disappointment will, on the contrary, help his criticism. He will have a wholesome contempt for facile success; he will measure by exacting standards. Moreover, the thoughts of a talented man about an art for the attainment of which he has striven to the point of despair are certain to be valuable; his study of the masters has been intense; his study of his contemporaries has had the keenness of an ambitious search for the key to success. His criticism, even if saturated with envy, will have value. In spite of all that partisans of sympathetic criticism may say, hatred and malice may give as much insight into character as love. Sainte-Beuve was a disappointed author, jealous of the success of others.

But ability is necessary. Envy and malice, not reinforced by talent, can win themselves small satisfaction, and do no more than transient harm; for then they work at random and make wild and senseless charges. To be dangerous to the author, to be valuable to the public, to give pleasure to their possessor, they must be backed by acuteness to perceive and judgment to proclaim real flaws only. The disappointed critic of ability knows that the truth is what stings, and if he seeks disagreeable truth, at least he seeks truth. He knows also that continual vituperation is as dull as continual praise; if only to give relief to his censure, he will note what is good. He will mix honey with the gall. So long as he speaks truth, he does a useful work, and his motives are of no consequence to any one but himself. Even if he speaks it with unnecessary roughness, the author cannot legitimately complain. Did he suppose that he was sending his book into a world of gentlemen only? Truth is truth, and a boor may have it. That the standard of courtesy is sometimes hard to square with that of perfect sincerity is the dilemma of the critic; but the author can quarrel with the fact no more than with the circumstance that in a noisy world he can write best where there is quiet. If he suffers, let him sift criticism through his family; consoling himself, meanwhile, with the reflection that there is criticism of criticism, and that any important critic will ultimately know his pains. Leslie Stephen was so sensitive that he rarely read reviews of his critical writings. After all, the critic is also an author.

The second complaint of writers, that criticism is largely young and incompetent,—or merely incompetent,—is well founded. The reason lies in the general preference of publishers for criticism that is laudatory even if absurd. Again we meet the Silent Bargain. The commercial publisher of book-reviews, realizing that any fool can praise a book, is apt to increase his profits by lowering the wage of his critic. At its extreme point, his thrift requires a reviewer of small brains and less moral courage; such a man costs less and is unlikely ever to speak with offensive frankness. Thus it happens that, commonly in the newspapers and frequently in periodicals of some literary pretension, the writers of reviews are shiftless literary hacks, shallow, sentimental women, or crude young persons full of indiscriminate enthusiasm for all printed matter.

I spoke of the magazines. When their editors say that literary papers are not popular, do they consider what writers they admit to the work, with what payment they tempt the really competent, what limitations they impose upon sincerity? Do they not really mean that the amiable in manner or the remote in subject, which alone they consider expedient, is not popular? Do they really believe that a brilliant writer, neither a dilettante nor a

Germanized scholar, uttering with fire and conviction his full belief, would not interest the public? Do they doubt that such a writer could be found, if sought? The reviews which they do print are not popular; but that proves nothing in respect of better reviews. Whatever the apparent limitations of criticism, it actually takes the universe for its province. In subject it is as protean as life itself; in manner it may be what you will. To say, then, that neither American writers nor American readers can be found for it is to accuse the nation of a poverty of intellect so great as to be incredible. No; commercial timidity, aiming always to produce a magazine so inoffensive as to insinuate itself into universal tolerance, is the fundamental cause of the unpopularity of the average critical article; how can the public fail to be indifferent to what lacks life, appositeness to daily needs, conviction, intellectual and moral candor? At least one reason why we have no Brunetière is that there is almost no periodical in which such a man may write.

In the actual, not the possible, writers of our criticism there is, in the lower ranks, a lack of skill, of seriousness, of reasonable competence, and a cynical acceptance of the dishonest rôle they are expected to play; in the higher ranks, there is a lack of any vital message, a desire rather to win, without offending the publisher, the approval of the ultra-literary and the scholarly, than really to reach and teach the public. It is this degradation, this lack of earnestness, and not lack of inherent interest in the general topic, which makes our critical work unpopular, and deprives the whole literary industry of that quickening and increase of public interest from which alone can spring a vigorous and healthy growth. This feebleness will begin to vanish the moment that the publishers of books, who support criticism, say peremptorily that reviews that interest, not reviews that puff, are what they want. When they say this, that is the kind of reviews they will get. If that criticism indeed prove interesting, it will then be printed up to the value of the buying power of the public, and it will be supported where it should be—not by the publisher but by the people. It is said in excuse that, as a city has the government, so the public has the criticism, which it deserves. That is debatable; but, even so, to whose interest is it that the taste of the public should be improved? Honest criticism addressed to the public, by writers who study how to interest it rather than how to flatter the producers of books, would educate. The education of readers, always the soundest investment of the publisher, can never be given by servile reviewers feebly echoing his own interested advertisements. They are of no value—to the public, the publisher, or the author.

The publisher of a newspaper of which reviews are an incident need not, however, wait for the signal. If, acting on the assumption that his duty is, not to the publisher but to the public, he will summon competent and earnest reviewers to speak the truth as they see it, he will infallibly increase the vivacity and interest of his articles and the pleasure and confidence of his readers. He will not have any permanent loss of advertising. Whenever he establishes his periodical as one read by lovers of literature, he has the publishers at his mercy. But suppose that his advertising decreases? Let him not make the common mistake of measuring the value of a department by the amount of related advertising that it attracts. The general excellence of his paper as an advertising medium—supposing he has no aim beyond profit—is what he should seek. The public which reads and enjoys books is worth attracting, even if the publisher does not follow, for it buys other things than books.

If, however, his newspaper is not one that can please people of literary tastes, he will get book-advertising only in negligible quantities no matter how much he may praise the volumes sent him. Of what use are puffs which fall not under the right eyes?

If, again, his periodical seems an exception to this reasoning, and his puffery appears to bring him profit, let him consider the parts of it unrelated to literature; he will find there matter which pleases readers of intelligence, and he may be sure that this, quite as much as his praise, is what brings the publishers' advertisements; he may be sure that, should he substitute sincere criticism, the advertisements would increase.

III

The third complaint of the author—from whom I have wandered—is that critics do not agree. To argue that whenever two critics hold different opinions, the criticism of one of them must be valueless, is absurd. The immediate question is, valueless to whom—to the public or to the author?

If the author is meant, the argument assumes that criticism is written for the instruction of the author, which is not true. Grammar and facts a critic can indeed correct; but he never expects to change an author's style or make his talent other than it is. Though he may lash the man, he does not hope to reform him. However slightly acquainted with psychology, the critic knows that a mature writer does not change and cannot change; his character is made, his gifts, such as they are, are what they are. On the contrary, the critic writes to influence the public—to inform the old, to train the young. He knows that his chief chance is with plastic youth; he hopes to form the future writer; still more he hopes to form the future reader. He knows that the effect of good reviewing stops not with the books reviewed, but influences the reader's choice among thousands of volumes as yet undreamed of by any publisher.

If, on the other hand, the public is meant, the argument assumes that one man's meat is not another man's poison. The bird prefers seed, and the dog a bone, and there is no standard animal food. Nor, likewise, is there any standard intellectual food: both critics, however they disagree, may be right.

No author, no publisher, should think that variety invalidates criticism. If there is any certainty about critics, it is that they will not think alike. The sum of x (a certain book) plus y (a certain critic) can never be the same as x (the same book) plus z (a different critic). A given book cannot affect a man of a particular ability, temperament, training, as it affects one of a different ability, temperament, and training. A book is never complete without a reader, and the value of the combination is all that can be found out. For the value of a book is varying: it varies with the period, with the nationality, with the character of the reader. Shakespeare had one value for the Elizabethans; he has a different value for us, and still another for the Frenchman; he has a special value for the playgoer, and a special value for the student in his closet. In respect of literary art, pragmatism is right: there is no truth, there are truths. About all vital writing there is a new truth born with each new reader. Therein lies the unending fascination of books, the temptation to infinite discussion. To awaken an immortal curiosity is the glory of genius.

From all this it follows that critics are representative; each one stands for a group of people whose spokesman he has become, because he has, on the whole, their training, birth from their class, the prejudices of their community and of their special group in that community, and therefore expresses their ideals. Once let publisher and author grasp this idea, and criticism, however divergent, will come to have a vital meaning for them. The publisher can learn from the judgment of the critic what the judgment of his group in the community is likely to be, and from a succession of such judgments through a term of years, he can gain valuable information as to the needs, the tastes, the ideals of the public, or of the group of publics, which he may wish to serve. Accurate information straight from writers serving the public—that, I cannot too often repeat, is worth more to him than any amount of obsequious praise. That precisely is what he cannot get until all critics are what they should be—lawyers whose only clients are their own convictions.

The author also gains. Although he is always liable to the disappointment of finding that his book has failed to accomplish his aim, he nevertheless can draw the sting from much adverse criticism if he will regard, not its face value, but its representative value. He is writing for a certain audience; the criticism of that audience only, then, need count. If he has his own public with him, he is as safe as a man on an island viewing a storm at sea, no matter how critics representing other publics may rage. Not all the adverse comment in this country on E. P. Roe, in England on Ouida, in France on Georges Ohnet ever cost them a single reader. Their audience heard it not; it did not count. There is, of course, a difference of value in publics, and if these writers had a tragedy, it lay in their not winning the audience of their choice. But this does not disturb the statement as to the vanity of adverse criticism for an author who hears objurgations from people whom he did not seek to please. Sometimes, indeed, such objurgations flatter. If, for example, the author has written a novel which is in effect an attempt to batter down ancient prejudice, nothing should please him more than to hear the angry protests of the conservative—they may be the shrieks of the dying, as was the case, for instance, when Dr. Holmes wrote the *Autocrat*; they show, at any rate, that the book has hit.

Now, each in its degree, every work of art is controversial and cannot help being so until men are turned out, like lead soldiers, from a common mould. Every novel, for example, even when not written "with a purpose," has many theories behind it—a theory as to its proper construction, a theory as to its proper content, a theory of life. Every one is a legitimate object of attack, and in public or private is certain to be attacked. Does the author prefer to be fought in the open or stabbed in the dark?—that is really his only choice. The author of a novel, a poem, an essay, or a play should think of it as a new idea, or a new embodiment of an idea, which is bound to hurtle against others dear to their possessors. He should remember that a book that arouses no discussion is a poor, dead thing. Let him cultivate the power of analysis, and seek from his critics, not praise, but knowledge of what, precisely, he has done. If he has sought to please, he can learn what social groups he has charmed, what groups he has failed to interest, and why, and may make a new effort with a better chance of success. If he has sought to prevail, he can learn whether his blows have told, and, what is more important, upon whom. In either case, to know the nature of his general task, he must learn three things: whom his book has affected, how much it has affected them, and in what way it has affected them. Only through honest, widespread, really representative criticism, can the author know these things.

Whatever their individual hurts, the publisher of books, the publisher of book-reviews, and the author should recognize that the entire sincerity of criticism, which is the condition of its value to the public, is also the condition of its value to them. It is a friend whose wounds are faithful. The lesson that they must learn is this: an honest man giving an honest opinion is a respectable person, and if he has any literary gift at all, a forcible writer. What he says is read, and, what is more, it is trusted. If he has cultivation enough to maintain himself as a critic,—as many of those now writing have not, once servility ceases to be a merit,—he acquires a following upon whom his influence is deep and real, and upon whom, in the measure of his capacity, he exerts an educational force. If to honesty he adds real scholarship, sound taste, and vivacity as a writer, he becomes a leading critic, and his influence for good is proportionally enlarged. If there were honest critics with ability enough to satisfy the particular readers they served in every periodical now printing literary criticism, public interest in reviews, and consequently in books, would greatly increase. And public interest and confidence once won, the standing, and with it the profit, of the four groups commercially interested in literature would infallibly rise. This is the condition which all four should work to create.

Would it arrive if the publisher of books should repudiate the Silent Bargain? If he should send with the book for review, not the usual ready-made puff, but a card requesting only the favor of a sincere opinion; if, furthermore, he showed his good faith by placing his advertisements where the quality of the reviewing was best, would the critical millennium come? It would not. I have made the convenient assumption that the critic needs only permission to be sincere. Inevitable victim of the Silent Bargain he may be, but he is human and will not be good simply because he has the chance. But he would be better than he is—if for no other reason than because many of his temptations would be removed. The new conditions would at once and automatically change the direction of his personal interests. He and his publisher would need to interest the public. Public service would be the condition of his continuing critic at all. He would become the agent, not of the publisher to the public, but of the public to the publisher. And although then, as now in criticism of political affairs, insincere men would sacrifice their standards to their popularity, they would still reflect public opinion. To know what really is popular opinion is the first step toward making it better. Accurately to know it is of the first commercial importance for publisher and author, of the first public importance for the effective leaders of public opinion.

This new goal of criticism—the desire to attract the public—would have other advantages. It would diminish the amount of criticism. One of the worst effects of the Silent Bargain is the obligation of the reviewer to notice every book that is sent him—not because it interests him, not because it will interest his public, but to satisfy the publisher. Thus it happens that many a newspaper spreads before its readers scores upon scores of perfunctory reviews in which are hopelessly concealed those few written with pleasure, those few which would be welcome to its public. Tired by the mere sight, readers turn hopelessly away. Now, many books lack interest for any one; of those that remain, many lack interest for readers of a particular publication. Suppose a reviewer, preoccupied, not with the publisher, but with his own public, confronted by the annual mass of books: ask yourself what he would naturally do. He would notice, would he not, those books only in which he thought that he could interest his readers? He would warn his public against books which would disappoint them; he would take pleasure in praising books which would please them. The glow of personal interest would be in what he wrote, and, partly for this reason, partly because the reviews would be few, his public would read them. Herein, again, the publisher would gain; conspicuous notices of the right books would go to the right people. An automatic sifting and sorting of his publications, like that done by the machines which grade fruit, sending each size into its appropriate pocket, would take place.

But the greatest gain to criticism remains to be pointed out. The critics who have chosen silence, rather than submission to the Silent Bargain, would have a chance to write. They are the best critics, and when they resume the pen, the whole industry of writing will gain.

IV

But the critic, though liberated, has many hard questions to decide, many subtle temptations to resist. There is the question of his motives, which I said are of no consequence to the author or to the public so long as what he speaks is truth; but which, I must now add, are of great consequence to him. If he feels envy and malice, he must not cherish them as passions to be gratified, but use them, if at all, as dangerous tools. He must be sure that his ruling passion is love of good work—a love strong enough to make him proclaim it, though done by his worst enemy. There is the question again of his own limitations; he must be on his guard lest they lead him into injustice, and yet never so timid that he fails to say what he thinks, for fear it may be wrong.

I speak of these things from the point of view of the critic's duty to himself; but they are a part also of his duty towards his neighbor, the author. What that duty may precisely be, is his most difficult problem. A few things only are plain. He ought to say as much against a friend as against an enemy, as much against a publisher whom he knows as against a publisher of England or France. He must dare to give pain. He must make his own the ideals of Sarcey. "I love the theatre," he wrote to Zola, "with so absolute a devotion that I sacrifice everything, even my particular friends, even, what is much more difficult, my particular enemies, to the pleasure of pushing the public towards the play which I consider good, and of keeping it away from the play which I consider bad."

That perhaps was comparatively easy for Sarcey with his clear ideal of the well-made piece; it is perhaps easy in the simple, straightforward appraisal of the ordinary book; but the critic may be excused if he feels compunctions and timidities when the task grows more complex, when, arming himself more and more with the weapons of psychology, he seeks his explanations of a given work where undoubtedly they lie, in the circumstances, the passions, the brains, the very disorders of the author. How far in this path may he go? Unquestionably, he may go far, very far with the not too recent dead; but with the living how far may he go, how daring may he make his guess? For guess it will be, since his knowledge, if not his competence, will be incomplete until memoirs, letters, diaries, reminiscences bring him their enlightenment. One thinks first what the author may suffer when violent hands are laid upon his soul, and one recoils; but what of the public? Must the public, then, not know its contemporaries just as far as it can—these contemporaries whose strong influence for good or evil it is bound to undergo? These have full license to play upon the public; shall not the public, in its turn, be free to scrutinize to any, the most intimate extent, the human stuff from which emanates the strong influence which it feels? If the public good justifies dissection, does it not also justify vivisection? Is literature an amusement only, or is it a living force which on public grounds the critic has every right in all ways to measure? Doubtless his right in the particular case may be tested by the importance of the answer to the people, yet the grave delicacy of this test—which the critic must apply himself—is equaled only by the ticklishness of the task. Yet there lies the path of truth, serviceable, ever honorable truth.

The critic is, in fact, confronted by two standards. Now and again he must make the choice between admirable conduct and admirable criticism. They are not the same. It is obvious that what is outrageous conduct may be admirable criticism, that what is admirable conduct may be inferior, shuffling criticism. Which should he choose? If we make duty to the public the test, logic seems to require that he should abate no jot of his critical message. It certainly seems hard that he should be held to a double (and contradictory) standard when others set in face of a like dilemma are held excused. The priest is upheld in not revealing the secrets of the confessional, the lawyer in not betraying the secret guilt of his client, although as a citizen each should prefer the public to the individual; whereas the critic who, reversing the case, sacrifices the individual to the public, is condemned. The public should recognize, I think, his right to a special code like that accorded the priest, the lawyer, the soldier, the physician. He should be relieved of certain social penalties, fear of which may cramp his freedom and so lessen his value. Who cannot easily see that a critic may write from the highest sense of duty words which would make him the "no gentleman" that Cousin said Sainte-Beuve was?

But the whole question is thorny; that writer will do an excellent service to letters who shall speak an authoritative word upon the ethics of criticism. At present, there is nothing—except the law of libel. The question is raised here merely to the end of asking these further questions: Would not the greatest freedom help rather than hurt the cause of literature? Is not the double standard too dangerous a weapon to be allowed to remain in the hands of the upholders of the Silent Bargain?

Meanwhile —until the problem is solved —the critic must be an explorer of untraveled ethical paths. Let him be bold whether he is a critic of the deeds of the man of action, or of those subtler but no less real deeds, the words of an author! For, the necessary qualifications made, all that has been said of literary criticism applies to all criticism—everywhere there is a Silent Bargain to be fought, everywhere honest opinion has powerful foes.

The thing to do for each author of words or of deeds, each critic of one or the other, is to bring his own pebble of conviction however rough and sharp-cornered and throw it into that stream of discussion which will roll and grind it against others, and finally make of it and of them that powder of soil in which, let us hope, future men will raise the crop called truth.

DRAMATIC CRITICISM IN THE AMERICAN PRESS

BY JAMES S. METCALFE

A little insight into the practical conditions which surround newspaper criticism to-day is needed before we can estimate its value or importance as an institution. Venial and grossly incompetent critics there have always been, but these have eventually been limited in their influence through the inevitable discovery of their defects. They were and are individual cases, which may be disregarded in a general view. The question to be considered is, whether our newspapers have any dramatic criticism worthy of the name, and, if there is none, what are the causes of its nonexistence.

When the late William Winter lost his position as dramatic critic of the *New York Tribune*, the event marked not alone the virtual disappearance from the American press of dramatic criticism as our fathers knew and appreciated it: the circumstances of the severance of his half-century's connection with that publication also illustrate vividly a principal reason for the extinction of criticism as it used to be.

At the time mentioned the *Tribune* had not fallen entirely from its early estate. It was still a journal for readers who thought. Its strong political partisanship limited its circulation, which had been for some time declining. It had been hurt by the fierce competition of its sensational and more enterprising contemporaries. The *Tribune* could not afford to lose any of the advertising revenue which was essential to its very existence.

Mr. Winter would not write to orders. He had certain prejudices, but they were honest ones, and those who knew his work were able to discount them in sifting his opinions. For instance, he had a sturdy hatred for the Ibsen kind of dissectional drama, and it was practically impossible for him to do justice even to good acting in plays of this school.

In a broader way he was the enemy of uncleanness on the stage. For this reason he had frequently denounced a powerful firm of managers whom he held to be principally responsible for the, at first insidious and then rapid, growth of indecency in our theatre. These managers controlled a large amount of the theatrical advertising. The *Tribune* frequently printed on one page large advertisements of the enterprises these men represented, and on another page they would find themselves described, in Mr. Winter's most vigorous English, as panders who were polluting the theatre and its patrons. They knew the *Tribune's* weak financial condition and demanded that Mr. Winter's pen be curbed, the alternative being a withdrawal of their advertising patronage. What happened then was a scandal, and is history in the newspaper and theatrical world.

Mr. Winter refused to be muzzled. In spite of a half-century's faithful service, he was practically dismissed from the staff of the *Tribune*. If it had not been for a notable benefit performance given for him by artists who honored him, and generously patronized by his friends and the public who knew his work, his last days would have been devoid of comfort.

Mr. Winter's experience, although he is not the only critic who has lost his means of livelihood through the influence of the advertising theatrical manager, is in some form present to the mind of every newspaper writer in the province of the theatre. No matter how strong the assurance of his editor that he may go as far as he pleases in telling the truth, he knows that even the editor himself is in fear of the dread summons from the business office. If the critic has had any experience in the newspaper business,—no longer a profession,—he writes what he pleases, but with his subconscious mind tempering justice with mercy for the enterprises of the theatrical advertiser. This, of course, does not preclude his giving a critical tone to what he writes by finding minor defects and even flaying unimportant artists. But woe be unto him if he launches into any general denunciation of theatrical methods, or attacks the enterprise of the advertising manager in a way that imperils profits.

There are exceptions to these general statements, especially outside of New York. There are a few newspapers left where the editorial conscience outweighs the influence of the counting-room. Even in these cases the reviewer, if he is wise, steers clear of telling too much truth about enterprises whose belligerent managers are only too glad to worry his employers with complaints of persecution or injustice. In other places the theatrical advertising is not of great value, particularly where the moving-picture has almost supplanted the legitimate theatre. Here we occasionally find criticism of the old sort, particularly if, in the local reviewer's mind, the entertainment offered is not up to what he considers the Broadway standard of production. Here the publisher's regard for local pride will sometimes excuse the reviewer's affront to the infrequently visiting manager and the wares he offers.

Another exception is the purely technical critic who has no broader concern with the theatre than recording the impressions which come to him through his eyes, ears, and memory. He is safe, because he rarely offends. He is scarce, because he is little read and newspapers cannot give him the space he requires for analysis and recollection. The high-pressure life of the newspaper reader calls for a newspaper made under high pressure and for to-day. In this process there is little opportunity for the display of the scholarship, leisurely thinking, and carefully evolved judgments which gave their fame to critics of an earlier period. In the few remaining survivals of the strictly technical critic their failure to interest many readers, or exercise much influence, may argue less a lack of ability on their part than a change from a thinking to a non-thinking public. Even in the big Sunday editions of the city dailies, where the pages are generously padded with text to carry the displayed theatrical advertising, the attempts to rise to a higher critical plane than is possible in the hurried weekday review are in themselves frequent evidence that technical criticism is a thing of the past so far as the newspapers are concerned.

The close connection of the business of the newspaper with the business of the theatre accounts for the practical disappearance of the element of fearlessness in critical dealing with the art of the stage, particularly as the business control of the theatre is largely responsible for whatever decline we may discern in the art of the theatre. Of course, if criticism were content to concern itself only with results, and not to look for causes, the matter of business interests would figure little in the discussion. But when the critic dares to go below the surface and discern commercialism as the main cause of the decline that he condemns in the art of the stage, he finds himself on dangerous ground.

The theatre has always had to have its business side. Actors must live and the accessories of their art must be provided. To this extent the stage has always catered to the public. But from the days of the strolling player to those of the acting-manager the voice from back of the curtain has, until of recent years, had at least as much of command as that of the ticket-seller. Both in the theatre and in the press modern conditions have in great measure thrown the control to the material side; and just as the artist and dramatist have become subservient to the manager, the editor and critic have come under the domination of the publisher.

The need of a greater revenue to house plays and public has placed the theatre in the hands of those who could manage to secure that revenue. The same necessity on the material and mechanical side has put the power of the press in the hands of those who could best supply its financial needs. With both theatre and press on a commercial basis, it follows naturally that the art of acting and the art of criticism should both decline.

Here we have the main causes that work from the inside for the deterioration of an art and for the destruction of the standards by which that art is measured. The outside causes are, of course, the basic ones, but before we get to them we must understand the connecting links which join the cause to the effect. To-day we certainly have no Hazlitts or Sarceys writing for the American press. It might be enlightening with respect to present conditions to consider the probabilities and circumstances of their employment if they were here and in the flesh. Can any one conceive of an American newspaper giving space to Hazlitt's work, even if he treated of the things of to-day? Even if he wrote his opinions gratis and in the form of letters to the editor, it would presumably be indeed a dull journalistic day when room could be found for them.

Sarcey, writing in the lighter French vein and being almost as much a chroniqueur as a critic, might possibly have found opportunity to be read in an American newspaper, if he could have curbed his independence of thought. Starting from obscurity, it is a question whether he would ever have been able to gain opportunity to be read simply as a critic, for the processes by which newspaper critics are created or evolved seem to have nothing to do with the possession of education, training, or ability. In the majority of newspaper offices the function of dramatic critic devolves by chance or convenience, and frequently goes by favoritism to some member of the staff with a fondness for the theatre and an appreciation of free seats. One of New York's best known dailies frankly treats theatrical reviewing as nothing more than reportorial work, to be covered as would be any other news assignment. This publication and a good many others are far more particular about the technical equipment of the writers who describe baseball games, horse-races, and prize-fights, than about the fitness of those who are to weigh the merits of plays and acting. The ability to write without offending the advertising theatrical manager seems in the last case to be the only absolutely essential qualification.

With these things in mind it will be seen that there is little to tempt any one with ambition to contemplate dramatic criticism as a possible profession. The uncertainty of employment, the slenderness of return, and the limitations on freedom of expression would keep even the most ardent lover of the theatre from thinking of criticism as a life occupation. Given the education, the experience, the needed judicial temperament, and the writing ability, all these are no assurance that opportunity can be found to utilize them.

Of themselves, the conditions that surround the calling of the critic are enough to account for the absence from the American newspapers of authoritative criticism. These conditions might be overcome if the spirit of the times demanded. But there can be no such demand so long as the press finds it more profitable to reflect the moods, thoughts, and opinions of the public than to lead and direct them. When the changed conditions of producing newspapers transferred the control of their policy from the editorial rooms to the counting-rooms, the expression of opinion on any subject became of little value compared with catering to the popular love of sensation and the popular interest in the trivial.

The change does not mean that there is any ignoring of the theatre in the newspapers. The institution lends itself admirably to modern newspaper exploitation. Destroying the fascinating mystery which once shrouded life back of the curtain, for a long time made good copy for the press. There is no longer any mystery, because the great space that the newspapers devote to gossip of the theatre and its people has flooded with publicity every corner of the institution and every event of their lives. The process has been aided by managers through a perhaps mistaken idea of the value of the advertising, and by artists for that reason and for its appeal to their vanity.

Criticism has no place in publicity of this sort, because criticism concerns itself only with the art and the broad interests of the theatre. The news reporter is often better qualified to describe the milk-baths of a stage notoriety than is the ablest critic. With our newspapers as they are, and with our public as it is, the reportorial account of the milk-bath is of more value to the newspaper and its readers than the most brilliant criticism that could be written of an important event in the art of the theatre.

With "give the people what they want" the prevailing law of press and theatre, it is idle just now to look for dramatic criticism of value in our newspapers. We may flatter ourselves that as a people we have a real interest in theatrical and other arts. We can prove it by the vast sums we spend on theatres, music, and pictures. With all our proof, we at heart know that this is not true. Even in the more sensual art of music we import our standards, in pictures we are governed more by cost than quality, and in the theatre—note where most of our expenditure goes. In that institution, with the creation of whose standards we are concerning ourselves just now, consider the character of what are called "popular successes," and observe the short shrift given to most of the efforts which call for enjoyment of the finer art of the stage through recognition of that art when it is displayed.

It is no disgrace that we are not an artistic people. Our accomplishments and our interests are in other fields, where we more than match the achievements of older civilizations. With us the theatre is not an institution to which we turn for its literature and its interpretations of character. We avoid it when it makes any demand on our thinking powers. We turn to it as a relaxation from the use of those powers in more material directions. We do not wish to study our stage, its methods and its products. We ask it only to divert us. This is the general attitude of the American to the theatre, and the exceptions are few.

In these conditions it is not strange that we have no scholarly critics to help in establishing standards for our theatre, or that there is little demand for real criticism, least of all in the daily press. As we grow to be an older and more leisurely country, when our masses cease to find in the crudities of the moving-picture their ideal of the drama, and when our own judgments become more refined, we shall need the real critic, and even the daily press will find room for his criticisms and reward for his experience, ability, and judgment.

The province and profit of our newspapers lie in interesting their readers. Analysis of artistic endeavor is not interesting to a people who have scant time and little inclination for any but practical and diverting things. Until the people demand it and the conditions that surround the critic improve, what passes for criticism in our daily press is not likely to increase in quantity or improve in quality.

THE HUMOR OF THE COLORED SUPPLEMENT

BY RALPH BERGENGREN

I

Ten or a dozen years ago,—the exact date is here immaterial,—an enterprising newspaper publisher conceived the idea of appealing to what is known as the American "sense of humor" by printing a so-called comic supplement in colors. He chose Sunday as of all days the most lacking in popular amusements, carefully restricted himself to pictures without humor and color without beauty, and presently inaugurated a new era in American journalism. The colored supplement became an institution. No Sunday is complete without it—not because its pages invariably delight, but because, like flies in summer, there is no screen that will altogether exclude them. A newspaper without a color press hardly considers itself a newspaper, and the smaller journals are utterly unmindful of the kindness of Providence in putting the guardian angel, Poverty, outside their portals. Sometimes, indeed, they think to outwit this kindly interference by printing a syndicated comic page without color; and mercy is thus served in a half portion, for, uncolored, the pictures are inevitably about twice as attractive. Some print them without color, but on pink paper. Others rejoice, as best they may, in a press that will reproduce at least a fraction of the original discord. One and all they unite vigorously, as if driven by a perverse and cynical intention, to prove the American sense of humor a thing of national shame and degradation. Fortunately the public has so little to say about its reading matter that one may fairly suspend judgment.

For, after all, what is the sense of humor upon which every man prides himself, as belonging only to a gifted minority? Nothing more nor less than a certain mental quickness, alert to catch the point of an anecdote or to appreciate the surprise of a new and unexpected point of view toward an old and familiar phenomenon. Add together these gifted minorities, and each nation reaches what is fallaciously termed the national sense of humor—an English word, incidentally, for which D'Israeli was unable to find an equivalent in any other language, and which is in itself simply a natural development of the critical faculty, born of a present need of describing what earlier ages had taken for granted. The jovial porter and his charming chance acquaintances, the three ladies of Bagdad, enlivened conversation with a kind of humor, carefully removed from the translation of commerce and the public libraries, for which they needed no descriptive noun, but which may nevertheless be fairly taken as typical of that city in the day of the Caliph Haroun.

The Middle Ages rejoiced in a similar form of persiflage, and the present day in France, Germany, England, or America, for example, inherits it,—minus its too juvenile indecency,—in the kind of pleasure afforded by these comic supplements. Their kinship with the lower publications of European countries is curiously evident to whoever has examined them. Vulgarity, in fact, speaks the same tongue in all countries, talks, even in art-ruled France, with the same crude draughtsmanship, and usurps universally a province that Emerson declared "far better than wit for a poet or writer." In its expression and enjoyment no country can fairly claim the dubious superiority. All are on the dead level of that surprising moment when the savage had ceased to be dignified and man had not yet become rational. Men, indeed, speak freely and vain-gloriously of their national sense of humor; but they are usually unconscious idealists. For the comic cut that amuses the most stupid Englishman may be shifted entire into an American comic supplement; the "catastrophe joke" of the American comic weekly of the next higher grade is stolen in quantity to delight the readers of similar but more economical publications in Germany; the lower humor of France, barring the expurgations demanded by Anglo-Saxon prudery, is equally transferable; and the average American often examines on Sunday morning, without knowing it, an international loan-exhibit.

Humor, in other words, is cosmopolitan, reduced, since usage insists on reducing it, at this lowest imaginable level, to such obvious and universal elements that any intellect can grasp their combinations. And at its highest it is again cosmopolitan, like art; like art, a cultivated characteristic, no more spontaneously natural than a "love of nature." It is an insult to the whole line of English and American humorists—Sterne, Thackeray, Dickens, Meredith, Twain, Holmes, Irving, and others of a distinguished company—to include as humor what is merely the crude brutality of human nature, mocking at grief and laughing boisterously at physical deformity. And in these Sunday comics Humor, stolen by vandals from her honest, if sometimes rough-and-ready, companionship, thrusts a woe-be-gone visage from the painted canvas of the national side-show, and none too poor to "shy a brick" at her.

At no period in the world's history has there been a steadier output of so-called humor—especially in this country. The simple idea of printing a page of comic pictures has produced families. The very element of variety has been obliterated by the creation of types: a confusing medley of impossible countrymen, mules, goats, German-Americans and their irreverent progeny, specialized children with a genius for annoying their elders, white-whiskered elders with a genius for playing practical jokes on their grandchildren, policemen, Chinamen, Irishmen, negroes, inhuman conceptions of the genus tramp, boy inventors whose inventions invariably end in causing somebody to be mirthfully spattered with paint or joyously torn to pieces by machinery, bright boys with a talent for deceit, laziness, or cruelty, and even the beasts of the jungle dehumanized to the point of practical joking. *Mirabile dictu!*—some of these things have even been dramatized.

With each type the reader is expected to become personally acquainted,—to watch for its coming on Sunday mornings, happily wondering with what form of inhumanity the author will have been able to endow his brainless manikins. And the authors are often men of intelligence, capable here and there of a bit of adequate drawing and an idea that is honestly and self-respectingly provocative of laughter. Doubtless they are often ashamed of their product; but the demand of the hour is imperative. The presses are waiting. They, too, are both quick and heavy. And the cry of the publisher is for "fun" that no intellect in all his heterogeneous public shall be too dull to appreciate. We see, indeed, the outward manifestation of a curious paradox: humor prepared and printed for the extremely dull, and—what is still more remarkable—excused by grown men, capable of editing newspapers, on the ground that it gives pleasure to children.

Reduced to first principles, therefore, it is not humor, but simply a supply created in answer to a demand, hastily produced by machine methods and hastily accepted by editors too busy with other editorial duties to examine it intelligently. Under these conditions "humor" is naturally conceived as something preëminently quick; and so quickness predominates. Somebody is always hitting somebody else with a club; somebody is always falling downstairs, or out of a balloon, or over a cliff, or into a river, a barrel of paint, a basket of eggs, a convenient cistern, or a tub of hot water. The comic cartoonists have already exhausted every available substance into which one can fall, and are compelled to fall themselves into a veritable ocean of vain repetition. They have exhausted everything by which one can be blown up. They have exhausted everything by which one can be knocked down or run over. And if the victim is never actually killed in these mirthful experiments, it is obviously because he would then cease to be funny—which is very much the point of view of the Spanish Inquisition, the cat with a mouse, or the American Indian with a captive. But respect for property, respect for parents, for law, for decency, for truth, for beauty, for kindliness, for dignity, or for honor, are killed, without mercy. Morality alone, in its restricted sense of sexual relations, is treated with courtesy, although we find throughout the accepted theory that marriage is a union of uncongenial spirits, and the chart of petty marital deceit is carefully laid out and marked for whoever is likely to respond to endless unconscious suggestions. Sadly must the American child sometimes be puzzled while comparing his own grandmother with the visiting mother-in-law of the colored comic.

II

Lest this seem a harsh, even an unkind inquiry into the innocent amusements of other people, a few instances may be mentioned, drawn from the Easter Sunday output of papers otherwise both respectable and unrespectable; papers, moreover, depending largely on syndicated humor that may fairly be said to have reached a total circulation of several million readers. We have, to begin with, two rival versions of a creation that made the originator famous, and that chronicle the adventures of a small boy whose name and features are everywhere familiar. Often these adventures, in the original youngster, have been amusing, and amusingly seasoned with the salt of legitimately absurd phraseology. But the pace is too fast, even for the originator. The imitator fails invariably to catch the spirit of them, and in this instance is driven to an ancient subterfuge.

To come briefly to an unpleasant point: an entire page is devoted to showing the reader how the boy was made ill by smoking his father's cigars. Incidentally he falls downstairs. Meanwhile, his twin is rejoicing the readers of another comic supplement by spoiling a wedding party; it is the minister who first comes to grief, and is stood on his head, the boy who, later, is quite properly thrashed by an angry mother—and it is all presumably very delightful and a fine example for the imitative genius of other children. Further, we meet a mule who kicks a policeman and whose owner is led away to the lockup; a manicured vacuum who slips on a banana peel, crushes the box containing his fiancée's Easter bonnet, and is assaulted by her father (he, after the manner of comic fathers, having just paid one hundred dollars for the bonnet out of a plethoric pocketbook); a nondescript creature, presumably human, who slips on another banana peel and knocks over a citizen, who in turn knocks over a policeman, and is also marched off to undeserved punishment. We see the German-American child covering his father with water from a street gutter; another child deluging his parent with water from a hose; another teasing his younger brother and sister. To keep the humor of the banana peel in countenance, we find the picture of a fat man accidentally sitting down on a tack; he exclaims, "Ouch!" throws a basket of eggs into the air, and they come down on the head of the boy who arranged the tacks. We see two white boys beating a little negro over the head with a plank (the hardness of the negro's skull here affording the humorous *motif*), and we see an idiot blowing up a mule with dynamite. Lunacy, in short, could go no further than this pandemonium of undisguised coarseness and brutality—the humor offered on Easter Sunday morning by leading American newspapers for the edification of American readers.

And every one of the countless creatures, even to the poor, maligned dumb animals, is saying something. To the woeful extravagance of foolish acts must be added an equal extravagance of foolish words: "Out with you, intoxicated rowdy!" "Shut up!" "Skidoo!" "They've set the dog on me." "Hee-haw." "My uncle had it tooken in Hamburg." "Dat old gentleman will slip on dem banana skins," "Little Buster got all that was coming to him." "Aw, shut up!" "Y-e-e-e G-o-d-s!" "Ouch!" "Golly, dynamite am powerful stuff." "I am listening to vat der vild vaves is sedding." "I don't think Pa and I will ever get along together until he gets rid of his conceit." "Phew!"

The brightness of this repartee could be continued indefinitely; profanity, of course, is indicated by dashes and exclamation points; a person who has fallen overboard says, "Blub!" concussion is visibly represented by stars; "biff" and "bang" are used, according to taste, to accompany a blow on the nose or an explosion of dynamite.

From this brief summary it may be seen how few are the fundamental conceptions that supply the bulk of almost the entire output, and in these days of syndicated ideas a comparatively small body of men produce the greater part of it. Physical pain is the most glaringly omnipresent of these motifs; it is counted upon invariably to amuse the average humanity of our so-called Christian civilization. The entire group of Easter Sunday pictures constitutes a saturnalia of prearranged accidents in which the artist is never hampered by the exigencies of logic; machinery in which even the presupposed poorest intellect might be expected to detect the obvious flaw accomplishes its evil purpose with inevitable accuracy; jails and lunatic asylums are crowded with new inmates; the policeman always uses his club or revolver; the parents usually thrash their offspring at the end of the performance; household furniture is demolished, clothes ruined, and unsalable eggs broken by the dozen. Deceit is another universal concept of humor, which combines easily with the physical pain *motif*; and mistaken identity, in which the juvenile idiot disguises himself and deceives his parents in various ways, is another favorite resort of the humorists. The paucity of invention is hardly less remarkable than the willingness of the inventors to sign their products, or the willingness of editors to publish them. But the age is notoriously one in which editors underrate and insult the public intelligence.

Doubtless there are some to applaud the spectacle,—the imitative spirits, for example, who recently compelled a woman to seek the protection of a police department because of the persecution of a gang of boys and young men shouting "hee-haw" whenever she appeared on the street; the rowdies whose exploits figure so frequently in metropolitan newspapers; or that class of adults who tell indecent stories at the dinner-table and laugh joyously at their wives' efforts to turn the conversation. But the Sunday comic goes into other homes than these, and is handed to their children by parents whose souls would shudder at the thought of a dime novel. Alas, poor parents! That very dime novel as a rule holds up ideals of bravery and chivalry, rewards good and punishes evil, offers at the worst a temptation to golden adventuring, for which not one child in a million will ever attempt to surmount the obvious obstacles. It is no easy matter to become an Indian fighter, pirate, or detective; the dream is, after all, a day-dream, tinctured with the beautiful color of old romance, and built on eternal qualities that the world has rightfully esteemed worthy of emulation. And in place of it the comic supplement, like that other brutal horror, the juvenile comic story, which goes on its immoral way unnoticed, raises no high ambition, but devotes itself to "mischief made easy." Hard as it is to become an Indian fighter, any boy has plenty of opportunity to throw stones at his neighbor's windows. And on any special occasion, such, for example, as Christmas or Washington's Birthday, almost the entire ponderous machine is set in motion to make reverence and ideals ridiculous. Evil example is strong in proportion as it is easy to imitate. The state of mind that accepts the humor of the comic weekly is the same as that which shudders at Ibsen, and smiles complacently at the musical comedy, with its open acceptance of the wild-oats theory, and its humorous exposition of a kind of wild oats that youth may harvest without going out of its own neighborhood.

In all this noisy, explosive, garrulous pandemonium one finds here and there a moment of rest and refreshment—the work of the few pioneers of decency and decorum brave enough to bring their wares to the noisome market and lucky enough to infuse their spirit of refinement, art, and genuine humor into its otherwise hopeless atmosphere. Preëminent among them stands the inventor of "Little Nemo in Slumberland," a man of genuine pantomimic humor, charming draughtsmanship, and an excellent decorative sense of color, who has apparently studied his medium and makes the best of it. And with him come Peter Newell, Grace G. Weiderseim, and Condé,—now illustrating *Uncle Remus* for a Sunday audience,—whose pictures in some of the Sunday papers are a delightful and self-respecting proof of the possibilities of this type of journalism. Out of the noisy streets, the cheap restaurants with their unsteady-footed waiters and avalanches of soup and crockery, out of the slums, the quarreling families, the prisons and the lunatic asylums, we step for a moment into the world of childish fantasy, closing the iron door behind us and trying to shut out the clamor of hooting mobs, the laughter of imbeciles, and the crash of explosives. After all, there is no reason why children should not have their innocent amusement on Sunday morning; but there seems to be every reason why the average editor of the weekly comic supplement should be given a course in art, literature, common sense, and Christianity.

THE AMERICAN GRUB STREET

BY JAMES H. COLLINS

I

New York's theatres, cafés, and hotels, with many of her industries, are supported by a floating population. The provinces know this, and it pleases them mightily. But how many of the actual inhabitants of New York know of the large floating population that is associated with her magazines, newspapers, and publishing interests?—a floating population of the arts, mercenaries of pen and typewriter, brush and camera, living for the most part in the town and its suburbs, yet leading an unattached existence, that, to the provincial accustomed to dealing with life on a salary, seems not only curious but extremely precarious—as it often is.

The free-lance writer and artist abound in the metropolis, and with them is associated a motley free-lance crew that has no counterpart elsewhere on this continent. New York's "Grub Street" is one of the truest indications of her metropolitan character. In other American cities the newspaper is written, illustrated, and edited by men and women on salaries, as are the comparatively few magazines and the technical press covering our country's material activities. But in New York, while hundreds of editors, writers, and artists also rely upon a stated, definite stipend, several times as many more live without salaried connections, sometimes by necessity, but as often by choice. These are the dwellers in Grub Street.

This thoroughfare has no geographical definition. Many of the natives of Manhattan Island know as little of it as do the truck loads of visitors "seeing New York," who cross and recross it unwittingly. Grub Street begins nowhere and ends nowhere; yet between these vague terminals it runs to all points of the compass, turns sharp corners, penetrates narrow passageways, takes its pedestrians up dark old stairways one moment and through sumptuous halls of steel and marble the next, touching along the way more diverse interests than any of the actual streets of Manhattan, and embracing ideals, tendencies, influences, and life-currents that permeate the nation's whole material and spiritual existence. Greater Grub Street is so unobtrusive that a person with no affair to transact therein might dwell a quarter-century in New York and never discover it; yet it is likewise so palpable and vast to its denizens that by no ordinary circumstances would any of them be likely to explore all its infinite arteries, veins, and ganglia.

Not long ago there arrived on Park Row for the first time in his life a newspaper reporter of conspicuous ability along a certain line. In the West he had made a name for his knack at getting hold of corporate reports and court decisions several days in advance of rival papers. Once, in Chicago, by climbing over the ceiling of a jury-room, he was able to publish the verdict in a sensational murder trial a half-hour before it had been brought in to the judge. A man invaluable in following the devious windings of the day's history as it must be written in newspapers, he had come to Park Row as the ultimate field of development for his especial talent. To demonstrate what he had done, he brought along a thick sheaf of introductory letters from Western editors. There was one for every prominent editor and publisher in the New York newspaper field, yet after all had been delivered it seemed to avail nothing. Nobody had offered him a situation.

"The way to get along in New York is to go out and get the stuff," explained a free lance whom he fell in with in a William Street restaurant. "Get copy they can't turn down—deliver the goods."

In that dull summer season all the papers were filled with gossip about a subscription book that had been sold at astonishing prices to that unfailing resource of newspapers, the "smart set." Charges of blackmail flew through the city. Official investigation had failed to reveal anything definite about the work, which was said to be in process of printing. In twenty-four hours the newcomer from the West appeared in the office of a managing editor with specimen pages of the book itself. Where he had got them nobody knew. No one cared. They were manifestly genuine, and within two hours a certain sensational newspaper scored a "beat." At last accounts he was specializing in the same line, obtaining the unobtainable and selling it where it would bring the best price.

This is one type of free lance.

At the other end of the scale may be cited the all-around scientific worker who came to the metropolis several years ago, after long experience in the departments at Washington. Lack of influence there had thrown him on the world at forty. Accustomed to living on the rather slender salary that goes with a scientific position, and knowing no other way of getting a livelihood, he set out to find in New York a place similar to that he had held in the capital. He is a man who has followed the whole trend of modern scientific progress as a practical investigator—a deviser of experiments and experimental apparatus, a skilled technical draughtsman, a writer on scientific subjects, and a man of field experience in surveying and research that has taken him all over the world. New York offered him nothing resembling the work he had done in Washington; but in traveling about the town among scientific and technical publishers he got commissions to write an article or two for an encyclopedia. These led him into encyclopedic illustration as well, and then he took charge of a whole section of the work, gathering his materials outside, writing and drawing at home, and visiting the publisher's office only to deliver the finished copy. Encyclopedia writing and illustration has since become his specialty. His wide experience and knowledge fit him to cope with diverse subjects, and he earns an income which, if not nearly so large as that of the free-lance reporter, is quite as satisfactory as his Washington salary. As soon as one encyclopedia is finished in New York, another is begun, and from publisher to publisher go a group of encyclopedic free-lances, who will furnish an article on integral calculus or the Vedic pantheon, with diagrams and illustrations—and very good articles at that.

II

Who but a Balzac will take a census of Greater Grub Street, enumerating its aristocrats, its well-to-do obscure bourgeois, its Bohemians, its rakes and evil-doers, its artisans and struggling lower classes? Among its citizens are the materials of a newer *Comédie Humaine*. The two personalities outlined above merely set a vague intellectual boundary to this world. In its many kinds and stations of workers Grub Street is as irreducible as nebulæ. Its aristocracy is to be found any time in that "Peerage" of Grub Street, the contents pages of the better magazines, where are arrayed the names of successful novelists, essayists, and short-story writers, of men and women who deal with specialties such as travel, historical studies, war correspondence, nature interpretation, sociology, politics, and every other side of life and thought; and here, too, are enlisted their morganatic relatives, the poets and versifiers, and their showy, prosperous kindred, the illustrators, who may be summoned from Grub Street to paint a portrait at Newport. This peerage is real, for no matter upon what stratum of Grub Street each newcomer may ultimately find his level of ability, this is the goal that was aimed at in the beginning. This is the Dream.

Staid, careful burghers of the arts, producing their good, dull, staple necessities in screed and picture, live about the lesser magazines, the women's periodicals, the trade and technical press, the syndicates that supply "Sunday stuff" to newspapers all over the land, the nameless, mediocre publications that are consumed by our rural population in million editions. The Bohemian element is found writing "on space" for newspapers this month, furnishing the press articles of a theatre or an actress the next, running the gamut of the lesser magazines feverishly, flitting hither and thither, exhausting its energies with wasteful rapidity, and never learning the business tact and regularity that keep the burgher in comfort and give his name a standing at the savings bank. The criminal class of Grub Street includes the peddler of false news, the adapter of other men's ideas, and the swindler who copies published articles and pictures outright, trusting to luck to elude the editorial police. The individual in this stratum has a short career and not a merry one; but the class persists with the persistence of the parasite. Grub Street's artisans are massed about the advertising agencies, producing the plausible arguments put forth for the world of merchandise, and the many varieties of illustration that go with them; while the nameless driftwood which floats about the whole thoroughfare includes no one knows how many hundreds of aspirants whose talents do not suffice for any of these classes, together with the peddler of other men's wares on commission, who perhaps ekes out a life by entering as a super at the theatres, the artists' models, both men and women, who pose in summer and are away with a theatrical company in winter, the dullard, the drone, the ne'er-do-well, the palpable failure. At one end, Art's chosen sons and daughters; at the other, her content, misguided dupes.

The free lance is bred naturally in New York, and thrives in its atmosphere, because the market for his wares is stable and infinitely varied. The demand he satisfies could be appeased by no other system. The very life of metropolitan publishing lies in the search for new men and variety. Publishers spend great sums upon the winnowing machinery that threshes over what comes to their editors' desks, and no editor in the metropolis grudges the time necessary to talk with those who call in person and have ideas good enough to carry them past his assistants. Publicly, the editorial tribe may lament the many hours spent yearly in this winnowing process. Yet every experienced editor in New York has his own story of the stranger, uncouth, unpromising, unready of speech, who stole in late one afternoon and seemed to have almost nothing in him, yet who afterwards became the prolific Scribbler or the great D'Auber. Not an editor of consequence but who, if he knew that to-morrow this ceaseless throng of free lances, good, bad, and impossible, had declared a Chinese boycott upon him and would visit his office no more, would regard it as the gravest of crises.

New York provides a market so wide for the wares of the free lance that almost anything in the way of writing or picture can eventually be sold, if it is up to a certain standard of mediocrity. A trained salesman familiar with values in the world of merchandise would consider this market one of the least exacting, most constant, and remunerative. And it is a market to be regarded, on the whole, in terms of merchandise. Not genius or talent sets the standards, but ordinary good workmanship. Magazines are simply the apex of the demand—that corner of the mart where payment is perhaps highest and the byproduct of reputation greatest. For each of the fortunate workers whose names figure in the magazine peerage, there are virtually hundreds who produce for purchasers and publications quite unknown to the general public, and often their incomes are equal to those of the established fiction writer or popular illustrator.

New York has eight Sunday newspapers that buy matter for their own editions and supply it in duplicate to other Sunday newspapers throughout the country under a syndicate arrangement. Perhaps an average of five hundred columns of articles, stories, interviews, children's stuff, household and feminine gossip, humor, verse, and miscellany, with illustrations, are produced every week for this demand alone; and at least fifty per cent of the yearly $150,000 that represents its lowest value to the producers is paid to free-lance workers. The rest goes to men on salary who write Sunday matter at space rates. This item is wholly distinct from the equally great mass of Sunday stuff written for the same papers by salaried men. Several independent syndicates also supply a similar class of matter to papers throughout the United States, for both Sunday and daily use. This syndicate practice has, within the past ten years, made New York a veritable journalistic provider for the rest of the nation. The metropolis supplies the Sunday reading of the American people, largely because it has the resources of Grub Street to draw upon. Syndicate matter is cheaper than the provincial product, it is true; but not price alone is accountable for this supremacy of the syndicate. By the side of the workmanlike stories, articles, skits, and pictures supplied by Greater Grub Street, the productions of a provincial newspaper staff on salary grow monotonous in their sameness, and reveal themselves by their less skillful handling.

The Sunday-reading industry provides a market, not only for writers and artists, but also for photographers, caricaturists, cartoonists, makers of squibs and jokes, experts in fashions, devisers of puzzles, men and women who sell ideas for novel Sunday supplements, such as those printed in sympathetic inks, and the like. It is a peculiarity of our country worth noting, that all our published humor finds its outlet through the newspapers. Though England, Germany, France, and other countries have a humorous press distinctly apart, the United States has only one humorous journal that may be called national in tone. An overwhelming tide of caricature and humor sweeps through our daily papers, but the larger proportion is found in the illustrated comic sheets of the leading New York dailies; and these are syndicated in a way that gives them a tremendous national circulation. The Sunday comic sheet, whatever one wishes to say of its quality, was built in Greater Grub Street, and there, to-day, its foundations rest.

In Grub Street, too, dwells the army of workers who furnish what might be called the cellulose of our monthly and weekly publications—interviews, literary gossip, articles of current news interest, matter interesting to women, to children, to every class and occupation. As there are magazines for the servant girl and clerk, so there are magazines for the millionaire with a country estate, the business man studying system and methods, the woman with social or literary aspirations, the family planning travel or a vacation. To-day it is a sort of axiom in the publishing world that a new magazine, to succeed, must have a new specialty. Usually this will be a material one, for our current literature deals with things rather than thought; it is healthy but never top-heavy. Each new magazine interest discovered is turned over to Greater Grub Street for development, and here it is furnished with matter to fit the new point of view, drawings and photographs to make it plain, editors to guide, and sometimes a publisher to send it to market.

Then come, rank on rank, the trade and technical periodicals, of which hundreds are issued weekly and monthly in New York. These touch the whole range of industry and commerce. They deal with banking, law, medicine, insurance, manufacturing, and the progress of merchandise of every kind through the wholesale, jobbing, and retailing trades, with invention and mechanical science, with crude staples and finished commodities, with the great main channels of production and distribution and the little by-corners of the mart. Some of them are valuable publishing properties; more are insignificant; yet each has to go to press regularly, and all must be filled with their own particular kinds of news, comment, technical articles, and pictures. Theirs is a difficult point of view for the free lance, and on this account much of their contents is written by salaried editors and assistants. Contributions come, too, from engineers, scientists, bankers, attorneys, physicians, and specialists in every part of the country. Foremen and superintendents and mechanics in some trades send in roughly outlined diagrams and descriptions that enable the quick-witted editors to see "how the blamed thing works" and write the finished article. The American trade press is still in an early stage of development on its literary side. It has grown up largely within the past two decades, and still lacks literary workmanship. To hundreds of free-lance workers this field is now either unknown or underestimated. Yet year after year men disappear from Park Row and the round of Magazinedom, to be found, if any one would take the trouble to look them up, among the trade journals. Some of the great properties in this class belong to journalists who saw an opportunity a decade ago, and grasped it.

III

The trade journals lead directly into the field of advertising, which has grown into a phenomenal outlet for free lance energies in the past ten years, and is still growing at a rate that promises to make it the dominant market of Grub Street. A glance through the advertising sections of the seventy-five or more monthly and weekly magazines published in New York reveals only a fraction of this demand, for a mass of writing and illustration many times greater is produced for catalogues, booklets, folders, circulars, advertising in the religious, agricultural, and trade press, and other purposes. Much of it is the work of men on salary, yet advertising takes so many ingenious forms and is so constantly striving for the novel and excellent, that almost every writer and illustrator of prominence receives in the course of the year commissions for special advertising work, and fat commissions, too. Often the fine drawing one sees as the centre of attraction in a magazine advertisement is the work of a man or woman of reputation among the readers of magazines, delivered with the understanding that it is to be published unsigned.

The advertising demand is divided into two classes—that represented by business firms which prepare their own publicity, and that for the advertising agencies which prepare and forward to periodicals the advertising of many business houses, receiving for their service a commission from the publishers. It is among the latter especially that the free lance finds his market, for the agencies handle a varied mass of work and are continually calling in men who can furnish fresh ideas. One of the leading advertising agencies keeps in a great file the names and addresses of several hundred free-lance workers—writers, sculptors, illustrators, portrait painters, translators, news and illustrating photographers, fashion designers, authorities in silver and virtu, book-reviewers, journalists with such specialties as sports, social news, and the markets. Each is likely to be called on for something in his particular line as occasions arise.

This concern, for example, may receive a commission to furnish a handsomely bound miniature book on servants' liveries for a clothing manufacturer, or a history of silver plate to be privately printed and distributed among the patrons of a great jewelry house. For a simple folder to advertise a brand of whiskey, perhaps, the sporting editor of a leading daily newspaper is asked to compile information about international yacht-racing. From Union Square may be seen a large wall, upon which is painted a quaint landscape of gigantic proportions. It is a bit of thoroughly artistic design, fitting into the general color scheme of the square, and its attractiveness gives it minor advertising value for the firm that has taken an original way of masking a blank wall. This decoration was painted from a small design, made for the above advertising agency by a painter of prominence. The same agency, in compiling a catalogue of cash registers some time ago, referred to their utilitarian ugliness of design. The cash register manufacturers protested that these were the best designs they had been able to make, whereupon the advertising agency commissioned four sculptors, who elaborated dainty cash-register cases in the *art nouveau* manner, for installation in cafés, milliners' shops, and other fine establishments.

Advertising requires versatility of a high order. A newspaper writer, so long as he makes his articles interesting to the widest public, is not required to give too strict attention to technicalities—he writes upon this subject to-day and upon one at the opposite pole to-morrow. A writer for a trade journal, on the other hand, need not give pains to human interest if his technical grasp of the iron market, the haberdashery trade, or the essentials of machine-shop practice is sure. Moreover, each year's experience in writing for a trade journal adds to his knowledge of its subject and makes his work so much the surer and simpler. But the writer of advertising must combine human interest with strict accuracy; his subject is constantly changing, unless he is a specialist in a certain line, taking advertising commissions at intervals. To-day he studies the methods of making cigars and the many different kinds of tobacco that enter therein; to-morrow he writes a monograph on enameled tin cans, investigating the processes of making them in the factory; and the day after that his topic may be breakfast foods, taking him into investigations of starch, gluten, digestive functions, diet and health, and setting him upon a weary hunt for synonyms to describe the "rich nutty flavor" that all breakfast foods are said to have. All the illustrative work of an advertising artist must be so true to detail that it will pass the eyes of men who spend their lives making the things he pictures. The Camusots and Matifats no longer provide costly orgies for Grub Street, sitting by meekly to enjoy the flow of wit and banter. They now employ criticism in moulding their literature of business. It was one of them who, difficult to please in circulars, looked over the manuscript submitted by an advertising free lance with more approval than was his custom. "This is not bad," he commented; "not bad at all—and yet—I have seen all these words used before."

An interesting new development of advertising is the business periodical, a journal published by a large manufacturer, usually, and sent out monthly to retail agents or his consuming public. In its pages are printed articles about the manufacturer's product, descriptions of its industrial processes, news of the trade, and miscellany. Many of these periodicals are extremely interesting for themselves. There must be dozens of them in New York— none of the newspaper directories list them. Writers who are not especially familiar with the product with which they deal often furnish a style of matter for them that is valued for its fresh point of view and freedom from trade and technical phraseology. These publications range from journals of a dozen pages, issued on the "every little while" plan for the retail trade of a rubber hose manufacturer, to the monthly magazine which a stocking jobber mails to thousands of youngsters all over the land to keep them loyal to his goods.

This, then, is the market in its main outlines. But a mass of detail has been eliminated. In groups large and small there are the poster artists who work for theatrical managers and lithographers; the strange, obscure folk who write the subterranean dime-novel stories of boyhood; the throngs of models who go from studio to studio, posing at the uniform rate of fifty cents an hour whether they work constantly or seldom; the engravers who have made an art of retouching half-tone plates; the great body of crafts- and-arts workers which has sprung up in the past five years and which leads the free-lance life in studios, selling pottery, decorated china, wood, and metal work to rich patrons; the serious painters whose work is found in exhibitions, and the despised "buckeye" painter who paints for the department stores and cheap picture shops; the etchers, the portrait painters, and the "spotknockers" who lay in the tones of the crude "crayon portrait" for popular consumption—these and a multitude of others inhabit Greater Grub Street, knowing no regularity of employment, of hours, or of income.

IV

While its opportunities are without conceivable limitation, Grub Street is not a thoroughfare littered with currency, but is paved with cobblestones as hard as any along the other main avenues of New York's life and energy. The Great Man of the Provinces, landing at Cortlandt or Twenty-third Street after an apprenticeship at newspaper work in a minor city, steps into a world strangely different from the one he has known. For, just to be a police reporter elsewhere is to be a journalist, and journalism is the same as literature, and literature is honorable, and a little mysterious, and altogether different from the management of a stove foundry, or the proprietorship of a grocery house, or any other of the overwhelmingly material things that make up American life. Times have not greatly changed since Lucien de Rubempré was the lion of Madame de Bargeton's salon at Angoulême, and this is a matter they seem to have ordered no better in provincial France. To be a writer or artist of any calibre elsewhere breeds a form of homage and curiosity and a certain sure social standing. But New York strikes a chill over the Great Man of the Provinces, because it is nothing at all curious or extraordinary for one to write or draw in a community where thousands live by these pursuits. They carry no homage or social standing on their face, and the editorial world is even studied in its uncongeniality toward the newcomer, because he is so fearfully likely to prove one of the ninety-nine in every hundred aspirants who cannot draw or write well enough. The ratio that holds in the mass of impossible manuscript and sketches that pours into every editorial office is also the ratio of the living denizens of Grub Street. The Great Man of the Provinces is received on the assumption that he is unavailable, with thanks, and the hope that he will not consider this a reflection upon his literary or artistic merit.

So he finds himself altogether at sea for a while. No Latin Quarter welcomes him, for this community has no centre. His estimates of magazine values, formed at a distance, are quickly altered. Many lines of work he had never dreamed of, and channels for selling it, come to light day by day. To pass the building where even *Munsey's* is published gives him a thrill the first time; yet after a few months in New York he finds that the great magazines, instead of being nearer, are really farther away than they were in the provinces. Of the other workers he meets, few aspire to them, while of this few only a fraction get into their pages. He calls on editors, perhaps, and finds them a strange, non-committal caste, talking very much like their own rejection slips. No editor will definitely give him a commission, even if he submits an idea that seems good, but can at most be brought to admit under pressure that, if the Great Man were to find himself in that neighborhood with the idea all worked up, the editor *might* be interested in seeing it, perhaps even reading it—yet he must not understand this as in any way binding ... the magazine is very full just at present ... hadn't he better try the newspapers, now? For there are more blanks than prizes walking the Grub Street paving, and persons of unsound minds have been known to take to literature as a last resort, and the most dangerous person to the editor is not a rejected contributor at all, but one who has been accepted once and sees a gleam of a chance that he may be again.

If the Great Man really has "stuff" in him, he stops calling on editors and submits his offerings by mail. Even if he attains print in a worthy magazine, he may work a year without seeing its notable contributors, or its minor ones, or its handmaidens, or even its office-boy. Two men jostled one another on Park Row one morning as they were about to enter the same newspaper building, apologized, and got into the elevator together. There a third introduced them, when it turned out that one had been illustrating the work of the other for two years, and each had wished to know the other, but never got around to it. An individual circle of friends is easily formed in Grub Street, but the community as a whole lives far and wide and has no coherence.

What ability or skill the Great Man brought from his province may be only the foundation for real work. There will surely be extensive revising of ideals and methods. A story is told of a poet who came to the metropolis with a completed epic. This found no acceptance, so after cursing the stupidity of the public and the publishers, he took to writing "Sunday stuff." Soon the matter-of-fact attitude of the workers around him, with the practical view of the market he acquired, led him to doubt the literary value of the work he had done in the sentimental atmosphere of his native place. Presently a commission to write a column of humor a week came to him, and he cut his epic into short lengths, tacked a squib on each fragment, and eventually succeeded in printing it all as humor, at a price many times larger than the historic one brought by *Paradise Lost*. Another newcomer brought unsalable plays and high notions of the austerity of the artistic vocation. Three months after his arrival he was delighted to get a commission to write the handbook a utilitarian publisher proposed to sell to visitors seeing the metropolis. This commission not only brought a fair payment for the manuscript on delivery, but involved a vital secondary consideration. The title of the work was "Where to Eat in New York," and its preparation made it necessary for the author to dine each evening for a month in a different café at the proprietor's expense.

This practical atmosphere of Grub Street eventually makes for development in the writer or artist who has talent. It is an atmosphere suited to work, for the worker is left alone in the solitude of the multitude. False ideals and sentimentality fade from his life, and his style takes on directness and vigor. Greater Grub Street is not given to reviling the public for lack of ideals or appreciation. The free lance's contact with the real literary market, day after day, teaches him that, as soon as he can produce the manuscript of the great American novel, there are editors who may be trusted to perceive its merit, and publishers ready to buy.

V

This free-lance community of the metropolis is housed all over Manhattan Island, as well as in the suburbs and adjacent country for a hundred miles or more around. An amusing census of joke-writers and humorists was made not long ago by a little journal which a New Jersey railroad publishes in the interest of its suburban passenger traffic. It was shown, by actual names and places of residence, that more than three fourths of the writers who keep the suburban joke alive live in Suburbia themselves.

New York has no Latin Quarter. As her publications are scattered over the city from Park Row to Forty-second Street, so the dwellings of free-lance workers are found everywhere above Washington Square. There are numerous centres, however. Washington Square is one for newspaper men and women, and in its boarding-houses and apartment hotels are also found many artists who labor in studios near by. Tenth Street, between Broadway and Sixth Avenue, has a few studios remaining, surrounded by the rising tide of the wholesale clothing trade, chief among them being the Fleischmann Building, next Grace Church, and the old studio building near Sixth Avenue. More old studios are found in Fourteenth Street; and around Union Square the new skyscrapers house a prosperous class of illustrators who do not follow the practice of living with their work. On the south side of Twenty-third Street, from Broadway to Fourth Avenue, is a row of old-time studios, and pretty much the whole gridiron of cross streets between Union and Madison squares has others, old and new. Thence, Grub Street proceeds steadily uptown until, in the neighborhood of Central Park, it may be said to have arrived.

Look over the roofs in any of these districts and the toplight hoods may be seen, always facing north, as though great works were expected from that point of the compass. Grub Street is the top layer of New York, and dislikes to be far from the roof. A studio that has been inhabited by a succession of artists and writers for twenty, thirty, forty years, may be tenanted to-day by a picturesque young man in slouch hat, loose neckerchief, and paint-flecked clothes, who eats about at cheap cafés, and sleeps on a cot that in daytime serves as a lounge under its dusty Oriental canopy. The latter ornament is the unfailing mark of that kind of studio, and with it go, in some combination, a Japanese umbrella and a fish-net. This young man makes advertising pictures, perhaps, or puts the frames around the half-tone illustrations for a Sunday newspaper. By that he lives, and for his present fame draws occasional "comics" for *Life*. But with an eye to Immortality, he paints, so that there are always sketching trips to be made, and colors to putter with, and art, sacred art, to talk of in the terms of the technician. Or such an old studio may shelter some forlorn spinster who ekes out a timid existence by painting dinner cards or the innumerable whatnots produced and sold by her class in Grub Street.

In the newer studios are found two methods of working. Prosperous illustrators, writers, and teachers may prefer a studio in an office building, where no one is permitted to pass the night, conducting their affairs with the aid of a stenographer and an office boy. Others live and work in the newer studios that have been built above Twenty-third Street in the past decade. Few of the traditions of Bohemia are preserved by successful men and women. The young man of the Sunday supplement, and the amateur dauber, once he succeeds as a magazine illustrator, drops his slouch hat, becomes conventional in dress, and ceases to imitate outwardly an artistic era that is past. Success brings him in contact with persons of truer tastes, and he changes to match his new environment. This is so fundamental in Grub Street that the ability of any of its denizens may be gauged by the editor's experienced eye; the less a given individual dresses like the traditional artist or writer of the Parisian Latin Quarter, the nearer he is, probably, to being one.

Women make up a large proportion of the dwellers in Grub Street, and its open market, holding to no distinctions of sex in payment for acceptable work, is in their favor. Any of the individual markets offers a fair field for their work, and in most of them the feminine product is sought as a foil to the staple masculine.

What is the average Grub Street income? That would be difficult to know, for the free lance, as a rule, keeps no cash-book. Many workers exist on earnings no larger than those of a country clergyman, viewed comparatively from the standpoint of expenses, and among them are men and women of real ability. Given the magic of business tact, they might soon double their earnings. Business ability is the secret of monetary success in Greater Grub Street. One must know where to sell, and also what to produce. It pays to aim high and get into the currents of the best demand, where prices are better, terms fairer, and competition an absolute nullity. Even the cheapest magazines and newspapers pay well when the free lance knows how to produce for them. Hundreds of workers are ill paid because they have not the instinct of the compiler. Scissors are mightier than the pen in this material market; with them the skillful ones write original articles and books—various information brought together in a new focus.

While untold thousands of impossible articles drift about the editorial offices, these editors are looking for what they cannot often describe. A successful worker in Grub Street divines this need and submits the thing itself. Often the need is most tangible. For two weeks after the Martinique disaster the newspapers and syndicates were hunting articles about volcanoes—not profound treatises, but ordinary workmanlike accounts such as could be tried out of any encyclopedia. Yet hundreds of workers, any one of whom might have compiled the needed articles, continued to send in compositions dealing with abstract subjects, things far from life and events, and were turned down in the regular routine. Only a small proportion of free lances ever become successful, but those who do, achieve success by attention to demand, with the consequence that most of their work is sold before it is written.

This community is perhaps the most diversified to be found in a national centre of thought and energy. Paris, London, Munich, Vienna, Rome— each has the artistic tradition and atmosphere, coming down through the centuries. But this Grub Street of the new world is wholly material,—a "boom town" of the arts,—embodying in its brain and heart only prospects, hopes. Its artistic rating is written plainly in our current literature. There is real artistic struggle and aspiration in it all, undoubtedly, but not enough to sweeten the mass.

Greater Grub Street is utilitarian. That which propels it is not Art, but Advertising—not Clio or Calliope, but Circulation.

JOURNALISM AS A CAREER

BY CHARLES MOREAU HARGER

I

In a recent discussion with a successful business man concerning an occupation for the business man's son, a college graduate, some one suggested: "Set him up with a newspaper. He likes the work and is capable of success."

"Nothing in it," was the prompt reply. "He can make more money with a clothing store, have less worry and annoyance, and possess the respect of more persons."

This response typifies the opinion of many fathers regarding a newspaper career. It is especially common to the business man in the rural and semi-rural sections. The dry-goods merchant who has a stock worth twenty thousand dollars, and makes a profit of from three thousand dollars to five thousand dollars a year, realizes that the editor's possessions are meagre, and believes his income limited. He likewise hears complaints and criticisms of the paper. Comparing his own placid money-making course with, what he assumes to be the stormy and unprofitable struggle of the publisher, he considers the printing business an inferior occupation.

For this view the old-time editor is largely responsible. For decades it was his pride to make constant reference to his poverty-stricken condition, to beg subscribers to bring cord-wood and potatoes on subscription, to glorify as a philanthropist the farmer who "called to-day and dropped a dollar in the till." The poor-editor joke is as well established as the mother-in-law joke or the lover-and-angry-father joke, and about as unwarranted; yet it has built up a sentiment, false in fact and suggestion, often accepted as truth.

To the younger generation, journalism presents another aspect. The fascination of doing things, of being in the forefront of the world's activities, appeals to young men and young women of spirit. Few are they who do not consider themselves qualified to succeed should they choose this profession. To the layman it seems so easy and so pleasant to write the news and comment of the day, to occupy a seat on the stage at public meetings, to pass the fire-lines unquestioned.

Not until the first piece of copy is handed in does the beginner comprehend the magnitude of his task or the demand made upon him for technical skill. When he sees the editor slash, blue-pencil, and rearrange his story, he appreciates how much he has yet to learn. Of this he was ignorant in his high school and his college days, and he was confident of his ability. An expression of choice of a life-work by the freshman class of a college or university will give a large showing for journalism; in the senior year it will fall to a minor figure, not more than from three to seven per cent of the whole. By that period the students have learned some things concerning life, and have decided, either because of temperament, or as did the business man for his son, for some other profession.

To those who choose it deliberately as a life-work, obtaining a position presents as many difficulties as it does in any other profession. The old-time plan by which the beginner began as "devil," sweeping out the office, cleaning the presses, and finally rising to be compositor and writer, is in these days of specialization out of date. The newspaper business has as distinct departments as a department store. While a full knowledge of every part of the workings of the office is unquestionably valuable, the eager aspirant finds time too limited to serve a long apprenticeship at the mechanical end in order to prepare himself for the writing-room.

Hence we find the newspaper worker seeking a new preparation. He strives for a broad knowledge, rather than mechanical training, and it is from such preparation that he enters the newspaper office with the best chances of success. Once the college man in the newspaper office was a joke. His sophomoric style was the object of sneers and jeers from the men who had been trained in the school of actual practice at the desk. To-day few editors hold to the idea that there can be no special preparation worth while outside the office, just as you find few farmers sneering at the work of agricultural colleges. It is not uncommon to find the staff of a great newspaper composed largely of college men, and when a new man is sought for the writing force it is usually one with a college degree who obtains the place. It is recognized that the ability to think clearly, to write understandable English, and to know the big facts of the world and its doings, are essential, and that college training fits the young man of brains for this. Such faults as may have been acquired can easily be corrected.

Along with the tendency toward specialization in other directions, colleges and universities have established schools or departments of journalism in which they seek to assist those students who desire to follow that career. It is not a just criticism of such efforts to say, as some editors have said, that it is impossible to give practical experience outside a newspaper office. Such an opinion implies that news and comment can be written only within sound of a printing-press; yet a vast deal of actual everyday work on the papers themselves is done by persons outside the office.

About twenty colleges and universities, chiefly in the Middle West and Northwest, have established such schools. They range in their curriculum from courses of lectures by newspaper men continued through a part of the four-years' course, to complete schools with a systematic course of study comprehending general culture, history, and science, with actual work on a daily paper published by the students themselves, on which, under the guidance of an experienced newspaper man, they fill creditably every department and assist in the final make-up of the publication. They even gain a fair comprehension of the workings of linotypes, presses, and the details of composition, without attempting to attain such hand-skill as to make them eligible to positions in the mechanical department.

These students, in addition to possessing the broad culture that comes with a college degree, know how to write a "story," how to frame a headline, how to construct editorial comment, and they certainly enter the newspaper office lacking the crudeness manifested by those who have all the details of newspaper style to learn. This sort of schooling does not make newspaper men of the unfit, but to the fit it gives a preparation that saves them much time in attaining positions of value. That a course of this kind will become an integral part of many more colleges is probable.

In these schools some of the most capable students enroll. They are the young men and young women of literary tastes and keen ambitions. They are as able as the students who elect law, or science, or engineering. From months of daily work in a class-room fitted up like the city room of a great newspaper, with definite news-assignments and tasks that cover the whole field of writing for the press, they can scarcely fail to absorb some of the newspaper spirit, and graduate with a fairly definite idea of what is to be required of them.

II

Then there comes the question, where shall the start be made? Is it best to begin on the small paper and work toward metropolitan journalism? or to seek a reporter's place on the city daily and work for advancement?

Something is to be said for the latter course. The editor of one of the leading New York dailies remarked the other day: "The man who begins in New York, and stays with it, rises if he be capable. Changes in the staffs are frequent, and in a half-dozen years he finds himself well up the ladder. It takes him about that long to gain a good place in a country town, and then if he goes to the city he must begin at the bottom with much time wasted." This is, however, not the essential argument.

Who is the provincial newspaper man? Where is found the broadest development, the largest conception of journalism? To the beginner the vision is not clear. If he asks the busy reporter, the nervous special writer on a metropolitan journal, he gets this reply: "If I could only own a good country paper and be my own master!" Then, turning to the country editor, he is told: "It is dull in the country town—if I could get a place on a city journal where things are happening!" Each can give reasons for his ambition, and each has from his experience and observation formed an *ex parte* opinion. Curiously, in view of the glamour that surrounds the city worker, and the presumption that he has attained the fullest possible equipment for the newspaper field, he is less likely to succeed with satisfaction to himself on a country paper than is the country editor who finds a place in the city.

The really provincial journalist, the worker whose scope and ideals are most limited, is often he who has spent years as a part of a great newspaper-making machine. Frequently, when transplanted to what he considers a narrower field, which is actually one of wider demands, he fails in complete efficiency. The province of the city paper is one of news-selection. Out of the vast skein of the day's happenings what shall it select? More "copy" is thrown away than is used. The *New York Sun* is written as definitely for a given constituency as is a technical journal. Out of the day's news it gives prominence to that which fits into its scheme of treatment, and there is so much news that it can fill its columns with interesting material, yet leave untouched a myriad of events. The *New York Evening Post* appeals to another constituency, and is made accordingly. The *World* and *Journal* have a far different plan, and "play up" stories that are mentioned briefly, or ignored, by some of their contemporaries. So the writer on the metropolitan paper is trained to sift news, to choose from his wealth of material that which the paper's traditions demand shall receive attention; and so abundant is the supply that he can easily set a feast without exhausting the market's offering. Unconsciously he becomes an epicure, and knows no day will dawn without bringing him his opportunity.

What happens when a city newspaper man goes to the country? Though he may have all the graces of literary skill and know well the art of featuring his material, he comes to a new journalistic world. Thus did the manager of a flourishing evening daily in a city of fifty thousand put it: "I went to a leading metropolitan daily to secure a city editor, and took a man recommended as its most capable reporter, one with years of experience in the city field. Brought to the new atmosphere, he was speedily aware of the changed conditions. In the run of the day's news rarely was there a murder, with horrible details as sidelights; no heiress eloped with a chauffeur; no fire destroyed tenements and lives; no family was broken up by scandal. He was at a loss to find material with which to make local pages attractive. He was compelled to give attention to a wide range of minor occurrences, most of which he had been taught to ignore. In the end he resigned. I found it more satisfactory to put in his place a young man who had worked on a small-town daily and was in sympathy with the things that come close to the whole community, who realized that all classes of readers must be interested in the paper, all kinds of happenings reported, and the paper be made each evening a picture of the total sum of the day's events, rather than of a few selected happenings. The news-supply is limited, and all must be used and arranged to interest readers—and we reach all classes of readers, not a selected constituency."

The small-town paper must do this, and because its writers are forced so to look upon their field they obtain a broader comprehension of the community life than do those who are restricted to special ideas and special conceptions of the paper's plans. The beginner who finds his first occupation on a country paper, by which is meant a paper in one of the smaller cities, is likely to obtain a better all-round knowledge of everything that must be done in a newspaper office than the man who goes directly to a position on a thoroughly organized metropolitan journal. He does not secure, however, such helpful training in style or such expert drill in newspaper methods. He is left to work out his own salvation, sometimes becoming an adept, but frequently dragging along in mediocrity. When he goes from the small paper to the larger one, he has a chance to acquire efficiency rapidly. The editor of one of the country's greatest papers says that he prefers to take young men of such training, and finds that they have a broader vision than when educated in newspaper-making from the bottom in his own office.

It is easy to say, as did the merchant concerning his son, that there are few chances for financial success in journalism. Yet it is probable that for the man of distinction in journalism the rewards are not less than they are in other professions. The salaries on the metropolitan papers are liberal, and are becoming greater each year as the business of news-purveying becomes better systematized and more profitable. The newspaper man earns vastly more than the minister. The editor in the city gets as much out of life as do the attorneys. The country editor, with his plant worth five thousand dollars or ten thousand dollars, frequently earns for his labors as satisfactory an income as the banker; while the number of editors of country weeklies who have a profit of three thousand dollars or more from their papers is astonishing.

It is, of course, not always so, any more than it is true that the lawyer, preacher, or physician always possesses a liberal income. When the city editor makes sport of the ill-printed country paper, he forgets under what conditions the country editor at times works. A prosperous publisher with sympathy in his heart put it this way:—

"The other day we picked up a dinky weekly paper that comes to our desk every week. As usual we found something in it that made us somewhat tired, and we threw it down in disgust. For some reason we picked it up again and looked at it more closely. Our feelings, somehow or other, began to change. We noted the advertisements. They were few in number, and we knew that the wolf was standing outside the door of that little print-shop and howling. The ads were poorly gotten up, but we knew why. The poor fellow didn't have enough material in his shop to get up a good ad. It was poorly printed—almost unreadable in spots. We knew again what was the matter. He needed new rollers and some decent ink, but probably he didn't have the money to buy them. One of the few locals spoke about 'the editor and family.' So he had other mouths to feed. He was burning midnight oil in order to save hiring a printer. He couldn't afford it. True, he isn't getting out a very good paper, but at that, he is giving a whole lot more than he is receiving. It is easy to poke fun at the dinky papers when the waves of prosperity are breaking in over your own doorstep. Likely, if we were in that fellow's place we couldn't do as well as he does."

The profession of the publicist naturally leads to politics, and the editor is directly in the path to political preferment. The growth of the primary system adds greatly to the chance in this direction. One of the essentials of success at a primary is that the candidate have a wide acquaintance with the public, that his name shall have been before the voters sufficiently often for them to become familiar with it. The editor who has made his paper known acquires this acquaintance. He goes into the campaign with a positive asset. One western state, for instance, has newspaper men for one third of its state officers and forty per cent of its delegation in Congress. This is not exceptional. It is merely the result of the special conditions, both of fitness and prominence, in the editor's relation to the public.

This very facility for entering politics is perhaps an objection rather than a benefit. The editor who is a seeker after office finds himself hampered by his ambitions and he is robbed of much of the independence that goes to make his columns of worth. The ideal position is when the editor owns, clear of debt, a profit-making plant and is not a candidate for any office. Just so far as he departs from this condition does he find himself restricted in the free play of his activities. If debt hovers, there is temptation to seek business at the expense of editorial utterance; if he desires votes, he must temporize often in order to win friendships or to avoid enmities. Freedom from entangling alliances, absolutely an open way, should be the ambition of the successful newspaper worker. Fortunate is the subordinate who has an employer so situated, for in such an office can be done the best thinking and the clearest writing. Though he may succeed in other paths, financially, socially, and politically, he will lack in his career some of the finer enjoyments that can come only with unobstructed vision.

III

It is not agreed that everyday newspaper work gives especial fitness for progress in literature. The habit of rapid writing, of getting a story to press to catch the first edition, has the effect for many of creating a style unfitted for more serious effort. Yet when temperament and taste are present, there is no position in which the aspirant for a place in the literary field has greater opportunity. To be in touch with the thought and the happenings of the world gives opportunity for interpretation of life to the broader public of the magazine and the published volume. Newspaper work does not make writers of books, but experience therein obtained does open the way; and the successes, both in fiction and economics, that have come in the past decade from the pens of newspaper workers is ample evidence of the truth of this statement.

It is one of the criticisms of the press that it corrupts beginners and not only gives them a false view of life, but compels them to do things abhorrent to those possessed of the finer feelings of good taste and courtesy. The fact is that journalism is, to a larger degree than almost all other businesses or professions, individualistic. It is to each worker what he makes it. The minister has his way well defined; he must keep in it or leave the profession. The teacher is restrained within limits; the lawyer and physician, if they would retain standing, must follow certain codes. The newspaper worker is a free lance compared with any of these.

The instances in which a reporter is asked to do things in opposition to the best standards of ethics and courtesy are rare—and becoming rarer. The paper of to-day, though a business enterprise as well as a medium of publicity and comment, has a higher ideal than that of two decades ago. The rivalry is greater, the light of competition is stronger, the relation to the public is closer. Little mystery surrounds the press. Seldom does the visitor stand open-eyed in wonder before the "sanctum." The average man and woman know how "copy" is prepared, how type is set, how the presses operate. The newspaper office is an "open shop" compared with the early printing-offices, of which the readers of papers stood somewhat in awe. Because of this, there is less temptation and less opportunity for obscure methods. The profession offers to the young man and young woman an opportunity for intelligent and untainted occupation. Should there be a demand that seems unreasonable or in bad taste, plenty of places are open on papers that have a higher standard of morals and are conducted with a decent respect for the opinions and rights of the public.

Nor is it necessary that the worker indulge in any pyrotechnics in maintaining his self-respect. The editor of one of the leading papers of western New York quietly resigned his position because he could not with a clear conscience support the nominee favored by the owner of the paper. He did nothing more than many men have done in other positions. His action was not proof that his employer was dishonest, but that there were two points of view and he could not accept the one favored by the publisher. Such a course is always open, and so wide is the publishing world that there is no need for any one to suffer. Nor can a paper or an editor fence in the earth. With enough capital to buy a press and paper, and to hire a staff, any one can have his say—and frequently the most unpromising field proves a bonanza for the man with courage and initiative.

In a long and varied experience as editor, I have rarely found an advertiser who was concerned regarding the editorial policy of the paper. The advertiser wants publicity; he is interested in circulation—when he obtains that, he is satisfied. Instances there are where the advertiser has a personal interest in some local enterprise and naturally resents criticism of its management, but such situations can be dealt with directly and without loss of self-respect to the publisher. Not from the advertiser comes the most interference with the press. If there were as little from men with political schemes, men with pet projects to promote, men (and women) desiring to use the newspaper's columns to boost themselves into higher positions or to acquire some coveted honor, an independent and self-respecting editorial policy could be maintained without material hindrance. With the right sort of good sense and adherence to conviction on the part of the publisher it can be maintained under present conditions—and the problem becomes simpler every year. More papers that cannot be cajoled, bought, or bulldozed are published to-day than ever before in the world's history. The "organ" is becoming extinct as the promotion of newspaper publicity becomes more a business and less a means of gratifying ambition.

Publishers have learned that fairness is the best policy, that it does not pay to betray the trust of the public, and journalism becomes a more attractive profession exactly in proportion as it offers a field where self-respect is at a premium and bosses are unconsidered. The new journalism demands men of high character and good habits. The old story of the special writer who, when asked what he needed to turn out a good story for the next day's paper, replied, "a desk, some paper, and a quart of whiskey," does not apply. One of the specifications of every request for writers is that the applicant shall not drink. Cleanliness of life, a well-groomed appearance, a pleasing personality, are essentials for the journalist of to-day. The pace is swift, and he must keep his physical and mental health in perfect condition.

That there is a new journalism, with principles and methods in harmony with new political and social conditions and new developments in news-transmission and the printing art, is evident. The modern newspaper is far more a business enterprise than was the one of three decades ago. To some observers this means the subordination of the writer to the power of the publisher. If this be so in some instances, the correction lies with the public. The abuse of control should bring its own punishment in loss of patronage, or of influence, or of both. The newspaper, be it published in a country village or in the largest city, seeks first the confidence of its readers. Without this it cannot secure either business for its advertising pages or influence for its ambitions. Publicity alone may once have sufficed, but rivalry is too keen to-day. Competition brings a realizing sense of fairness. Hence it is that there is a demand for well-equipped young men and clever young women who can instill into the pages of the press frankness, virility, and a touch of what newspaper men call "human interest."

The field is broad; it has place for writers of varied accomplishments; it promises a profession filled with interesting experiences and close contact with the world's pulse. It is not for the sloth or for the sloven, not for the conscienceless or for the unprepared. Without real qualifications for it, the ambitious young person would better seek some other life-work.

BIBLIOGRAPHY

1. Books on Principles of Journalism

Adams, Samuel Hopkins. The Clarion. A novel. 1914.

Bleyer, W. G. Newspaper Writing and Editing. The Function of the Newspaper, pp. 331–389. 1913.

Hapgood, Norman. Everyday Ethics. Ethics of Journalism, pp. 1–15. 1910.

Holt, Hamilton. Commercialism and Journalism. 1909.

Proceedings of the First National Newspaper Conference. University of Wisconsin. 1913.

Reid, Whitelaw. American and English Studies. Journalistic Duties and Opportunities, v. 2, pp. 313–344. 1913.

Rogers, Jason. Newspaper Building. 1918.

Rogers, J. E. The American Newspaper. 1909.

Scott-James, R. A. The Influence of the Press. 1913.

Thorpe, Merle, *editor*. The Coming Newspaper. 1915.

2. What Typical Newspapers Contain

Wilcox, Delos F. The American Newspaper: A Study in Social Psychology. Annals of the American Academy, v. 16, p. 56. (July, 1900.)

Garth, T. R. Statistical Study of the Contents of Newspapers. School and Society, v. 3, p. 140. (Jan. 22, 1916.)

Tenney, A. A. Scientific Analysis of the Press. Independent, v. 73, p. 895. (Oct. 17, 1912.)

Mathews, B. C. Study of a New York Daily. Independent, v. 68, p. 82. (Jan. 13, 1910.)

3. What the Public Wants

Thorpe, Merle, *editor*. The Coming Newspaper, pp. 223–247; Symposium: Giving the Public What It Wants, by newspaper and magazine editors. 1915.

Independent Chicago Journalist, An. Is an Honest and Sane Newspaper Possible? American Journal of Sociology, v. 15, p. 321. (Nov. 1909.)

What the Public Wants. Dial, v. 47, p. 499. (Dec. 16, 1909.)

Haskell, H. J. The Public, the Newspaper's Problem. Outlook, v. 91, p. 791. (April 3, 1909.)

Stansell, C. V. People's Wants. Nation, v. 98, p. 236. (March 6, 1914.)

Newspapers as Commodities. Nation, v. 94, p. 236. (May 9, 1912.)

Scott, Walter Dill. The Psychology of Advertising, pp. 226–248. 1908.

Bennett, Arnold. What the Public Wants. A play. 1910.

4. What Is News?

What Is News? A Symposium from the Managing Editors of the Great American Newspapers. Collier's Weekly, v. 46, p. 22 (March 18, 1911); v. 47, p. 44 (April 15, 1911); v. 47, p. 35 (May 6, 1911); v. 47, p. 42 (May 13, 1911); v. 47, p. 26 (May 20, 1911).

Irwin, Will. What Is News? Collier's Weekly, v. 46, p. 16. (March 11, 1911.)

What Is News? Outlook, v. 89, p. 137. (May 23, 1908.)

What Is News? Scribner, v. 44, p. 507. (Oct. 1908.)

Brougham, H. B. News—What Is It? Harper's Weekly, v. 56, p. 21. (Feb. 17, 1912.)

5. The Reporter and the News

Irwin, Will. "All the News That's Fit to Print." Collier's Weekly, v. 47, p. 17. (May 6, 1911.)

Irwin, Will. The Reporter and the News. Collier's Weekly, v. 47, p. 21. (April 22, 1911.)

Münsterberg, Hugo. The Case of the Reporter. McClure's Magazine, v. 36, p. 435. (Feb. 1911.)

Strunsky, Simeon. Two Kinds of Reporters. Century, v. 85, p. 955. (April 1913.)

Gentlemanly Reporter, The. Century, v. 79, p. 149. (Nov. 1909.)

Dealing in Scandal. Outlook, v. 97, p. 811. (April 15, 1911.)

Seldes, G. H. and G. V. The Press and the Reporter. Forum, v. 52, p. 722. (Nov. 1914.)

6. Effects of News of Crime and Scandal

Fenton, Francis. Influence of Newspaper Presentation upon the Growth of Crime and Other Anti-social Activity. 1911. Also in American Journal of Sociology, v. 16, pp. 342 and 538. (Nov. 1910, and Jan. 1911.)

Phelps, E. B. Neurotic Books and Newspapers as Factors in the Mortality of Suicides and Crime. Bulletin of the American Academy of Medicine, v. 12, No. 5. (Oct. 1911.)

Newspapers' Sensations and Suggestion. Independent, v. 62, p. 449. (Feb. 21, 1907.)

Tragic Sense. Nation, v. 87, p. 90. (July 30, 1908.)

Danger of the Sensational Press. Craftsman, v. 19, p. 211. (Nov. 1910.)

Howells, W. D. Shocking News. Harper's Magazine, v. 127, p. 796. (Oct. 1913.)

Irwin, Will. "All the News That's Fit to Print." Collier's Weekly, v. 47, p. 17. (May 6, 1911.)

Responsibility of the Press. Independent, v. 53, p. 2248. (Sept. 19, 1901.)

Our Chamber of Horrors. Outlook, v. 99, p. 261. (Sept. 30, 1911.)

The Newspaper as Childhood's Enemy. Survey, v. 27, p. 1794. (Feb. 24, 1912.)

Lessons in Crime at Fifty Cents per Month. Outlook, v. 85, p. 276. (Feb. 2, 1907.)

The Man Who Ate Babies. Harper's Weekly, v. 51, p. 296. (March 2, 1907.)

Lawlessness and the Press. Century, v. 82, p. 146. (May 1911.)

Newspaper Responsibility for Lawlessness. Nation, v. 77, p. 151. (Aug. 20, 1903.)

Newspaper Invasion of Privacy. Century, v. 86, p. 310. (June 1913.)

Newspaper Cruelty. Century, v. 84, p. 150. (May 1912.)

Newspapers and Crime. Journal of Criminal Law, v. 2, p. 340. (Sept. 1912.)

7. Yellow and Sensational Journalism

Irwin, Will. The Fourth Current. Collier's Weekly, v. 46, p. 14. (Feb. 18, 1911.)

Irwin, Will. The Spread and Decline of Yellow Journalism. Collier's Weekly, v. 46, p. 18. (March 4, 1911.)

Thomas, W. I. The Psychology of the Yellow Journal. American Magazine, v. 65, p. 491. (March 1908.)

Brooks, Sydney. The Yellow Press: An English View. Harper's Weekly, v. 55, p. 11. (Dec. 23, 1911.)

Whibley, Charles. The American Yellow Press. Blackwood's, v. 181, p. 531 (April 1907); also in Bookman, v. 25, p. 239. (May 1907.)

Brisbane, Arthur. Yellow Journalism. Bookman, v. 19, p. 400. (June 1904.)

Brisbane, Arthur. William Randolph Hearst. North American Review, v. 183, p. 511 (Sept. 21, 1906); editorial comment on this article, by George Harvey, on p. 569.

Commander, Lydia K. The Significance of Yellow Journalism. Arena, v. 34, p. 150. (Aug. 1905.)

Brunner, F. J. Home Newspapers and Others. Harper's Weekly, v. 58, p. 24. (Jan. 10, 1914.)

Pennypacker, S. W. Sensational Journalism and the Remedy. North American Review, v. 190, p. 587. (Nov. 1909.)

Curb for the Sensational Press. Century, v. 83, p. 631. (Feb. 1912.)

8. Inaccuracy

Smith, Munroe. The Dogma of Journalistic Inerrancy. North American Review, v. 187, p. 240. (Feb. 1908.)

Collins, James H. The Newspaper—An Independent Business. Saturday Evening Post, v. 185, p. 25. (April 12, 1913.)

Kelley, Fred C. Accuracy Pays in Any Business: New York World's Bureau of Accuracy and Fair Play. American Magazine, v. 82, p. 50. (Nov. 1916.)

New Credulity. Nation, v. 80, p. 241. (March 30, 1905.)

Fakes and the Press. Science, v. 25, p. 391. (March 8, 1907.)

Newspaper Science. Science, v. 25, p. 630. (April 19, 1907.)

Gladden, Washington. Experiences with Newspapers. Outlook, v. 99, p. 387. (Oct. 14, 1911.)

Irwin, Will. The New Era. Collier's Weekly, v. 47, p. 15. (July 8, 1911.)

Print the News. Outlook, v. 96, p. 563. (Nov. 12, 1910.)

Falsification of the News. Independent, v. 84, p. 420. (Dec. 13, 1915.)

9. Faking

Faking as a Fine Art. American Magazine, v. 75, p. 24. (Nov. 1912.)

Bok, Edward. Why People Disbelieve the Newspapers. World's Work, v. 7, p. 4567. (March 1904.)

Offenses Against Good Journalism. Outlook, v. 88, p. 479. (Feb. 29, 1908.)

Lying for the Sake of War. Nation, v. 98, p. 561. (May 14, 1914.)

Wheeler, H. D. At the Front with Willie Hearst. Harper's Weekly, v. 61, p. 340. (Oct. 9, 1915.)

Russell, Isaac. Hearst-made War News. Harper's Weekly, v. 59, p. 76. (July 25, 1914.)

Hearst-made War News. Harper's Weekly, v. 59, p. 186. (Aug. 22, 1914.)

Dream Book. Outlook, v. 111, p. 535. (Nov. 3, 1915.)

Hall, Howard. Hearst: War-maker. Harper's Weekly, v. 61, p. 436. (Nov. 6, 1915.)

Pulitzer, Ralph. Profession of Journalism: Accuracy in the News. Pamphlet published by the New York World. 1912.

10. Coloring the News

Irwin, Will. The Editor and the News. Collier's Weekly, v. 47, p. 18. (April 1, 1911.)

Irwin, Will. Our Kind of People. Collier's Weekly, v. 47, p. 17. (June 17, 1911.)

Irwin, Will. The New Era. Collier's Weekly, v. 47, p. 15. (July 8, 1911.)

Irwin, Will. The Press Agent. Collier's Weekly, v. 48, p. 24. (Dec. 2, 1911.)

Confessions of a Managing Editor. Collier's Weekly, v. 48, p. 18. (Oct. 28, 1911.)

Tainted News as Seen in the Making. Bookman, v. 24, p. 396. (Dec. 1906.)

Baker, Ray Stannard. How Railroads Make Public Opinion. McClure's Magazine, v. 26, p. 535. (March 1906.)

How the Reactionary Press Poisons the Public Mind. Arena, v. 38, p. 318. (Sept. 1907.)

11. Suppression of News

Irwin, Will. The Power of the Press. Collier's Weekly, v. 46, p. 15. (Jan. 21, 1911.)

Irwin, Will. Advertising Influence. Collier's Weekly, v. 47, p. 15. (May 27, 1911.)

Irwin, Will. Our Kind of People. Collier's Weekly, v. 47, p. 17. (June 17, 1911.)

Irwin, Will. The Foe Within. Collier's Weekly, v. 47, p. 17. (July 1, 1911.)

The Patent Medicine Conspiracy against the Freedom of the Press. Collier's Weekly, v. 36, p. 13. (Nov. 4, 1905.)

Silencing the Press. Nation, v. 76, p. 4. (Jan. 1, 1903.)

Stansell, C. V. Ethics of News Suppression. Nation, v. 96, p. 54. (Jan. 16, 1913.)

A Real Case of Tainted News. Collier's Weekly, v. 53, p. 16. (June 6, 1914.)

Seitz, Don C. The Honor of the Press. Harper's Weekly, v. 55, p. 11. (May 6, 1911.)

Can the Wool Trust Gag the Press? Collier's Weekly, v. 46, p. 11. (March 18, 1911.)

Holt, Hamilton. Commercialism and Journalism. 1909.

12. Editorial Policy and Influence

Kemp, R. W. The Policy of the Paper. Bookman, v. 20, p. 310. (Dec. 1904.)

Blake, Tiffany. The Editorial: Past, Present, and Future. Collier's Weekly, v. 48, p. 18. (Sept. 23, 1911.)

The Editorial Yesterday and To-day. World's Work, v. 21, p. 14071. (March 1911.)

Editorialene. Nation, v. 74, p. 459. (June 12, 1902.)

Irwin, Will. The Unhealthy Alliance. Collier's Weekly, v. 47, p. 17. (June 3, 1911.)

Shackled Editor. Collier's Weekly, v. 51, p. 22. (April 12, 1913.)

Fisher, Brooke. The Newspaper Industry. Atlantic Monthly, v. 89, p. 745. (June 1902.)

Porritt, Edward. The Value of Political Editorials. Atlantic, v. 105, p. 62. (Jan. 1910.)

Haste, R. A. Evolution of the Fourth Estate. Arena, v. 41, p. 348. (March 1909.)

We. Independent, v. 70, p. 1280. (Jan. 8, 1911.)

Bonaparte, Charles J. Government of Public Opinion. Forum, v. 40, p. 384. (Oct. 1908.)

Ogden, Rollo. Journalism and Public Opinion. American Political Science Review, Supplement, v. 7, p. 194. (Feb. 1913.)

Williams, Talcott. The Press and Public Opinion. American Political Science Review, Supplement, v. 7, p. 201. (Feb. 1913.)

13. The Associated Press and the United Press

Beach, H. L. Getting Out the News. Saturday Evening Post, v. 182, p. 18. (March 12, 1910.)

Noyes, F. B. The Associated Press. North American Review, v. 197, p. 701. (May 1913.)

Stone, Melville E. The Associated Press. Century, vv. 69 and 70. (April to Aug. 1905.)

Irwin, Will. What's Wrong with the Associated Press? Harper's Weekly, v. 58, p. 10. (March 28, 1914.)

Is There a News Monopoly? Collier's Weekly, v. 53, p. 16. (June 6, 1914.)

Stone, Melville E. The Associated Press: A Defense. Collier's Weekly, v. 53, p. 28. (July 11, 1914.)

Mason, Gregory. The Associated Press: A Criticism. Outlook, v. 107, p. 237. (May 30, 1914.)

Kennan, George. The Associated Press: A Defense. Outlook, v. 107, p. 240. (May 30, 1914.)

The Associated Press as a Trust. Literary Digest, v. 48, p. 364. (Feb. 21, 1914.)

The Associated Press Under Fire. Outlook, v. 106, p. 426. (Feb. 28, 1914.)

Criticisms of the Associated Press. Outlook, v. 107, p. 631. (July 18, 1914.)

Irwin, Will. The United Press. Harper's Weekly, v. 58, p. 6. (April 25, 1914.)

Roy W. Howard, General Manager of the United Press. American Magazine, V. 75, p. 41. (Nov. 1912.)

Howard, Roy W. Government Regulation for Press Association in Thorpe's The Coming Newspaper, pp. 188–204. 1915.

14. Ethics of Newspaper Advertising

The Patent Medicine Conspiracy against the Freedom of the Press. Collier's Weekly, v. 36, p. 13. (Nov. 4, 1905.)

Adams, Samuel Hopkins. The Great American Fraud. A series of articles in Collier's Weekly, vv. 36 and 37. (Oct. 7, 1905, to Sept. 22, 1906.) Published as a book, with the same title, in 1906.

Creel, George. The Press and Patent Medicines. Harper's Weekly, v. 60, p. 155. (Feb. 13, 1915.)

Roberts, W. D. Pursued by Cardui. Harper's Weekly, v. 60, p. 175. (Feb. 20, 1915.)

Waldo, Richard H. The Second Candle of Journalism, in Thorpe's The Coming Newspaper, pp. 248–261. 1915.

Roosevelt, Theodore. Applied Ethics in Journalism. Outlook, v. 97, p. 807. (April 15, 1911.)

The Lure of Fake Sales. Current Opinion, v. 56, p. 223. (March 1914.)

Adams, Samuel Hopkins. Tricks of the Trade. Collier's Weekly, v. 48, p. 17. (Feb. 17, 1912.)

Millions Lost in Fake Enterprises. Outlook, v. 100, p. 797. (April 13, 1912.)

Brummer, F. J. The Home Newspaper and Others. Harper's Weekly, v. 58, p. 24. (Jan. 10, 1914.)

Houston, H. S. New Morals in Advertising. World's Work, v. 28, p. 384. (Aug. 1914.)

Stelze, Charles. Publicity Men in a Campaign for Clean Advertising. Outlook, v. 107, p. 589. (July 11, 1914.)

15. Dramatic Criticism

Confessions of a Dramatic Critic. Independent, v. 60, p. 492. (March 1, 1906.)

Armstrong, Paul, and Davis, Hartley. Manager *vs.* Critic. Everybody's Magazine, v. 21, p. 119. (July 1909.)

Cudgeling the Dramatic Critics. Literary Digest, v. 48, p. 321. (Feb. 14, 1914.)

Serious Declaration of War Against the Dramatic Critic. Current Opinion, v. 57, p. 328. (Nov. 1914.)

Trials and Duties of a Dramatic Critic. Current Literature, v. 39, p. 428. (Oct. 1905.)

William Winter's Retirement. Independent, v. 67, p. 487. (Aug. 26, 1909.)

The Newspaper and the Theatre. Outlook, v. 93, p. 12. (Sept. 4, 1909.)

16. Book-Reviewing in Newspapers

Perry, Bliss. Literary Criticism in American Periodicals. Yale Review, v. 3, p. 635. (July 1914).

Grocery-shop Criticism. Dial, v. 57, p. 5. (July 1, 1914.)

Reviewing the Reviewer. Nation, v. 98, p. 288. (March 19, 1914.)

Varieties of Book-Reviewing. Nation, v. 99, p. 8. (July 2, 1914.)

Haines, Helen E. Present-Day Book-Reviewing. Independent, v. 69, p. 1104. (Nov. 17, 1910.)

Benson, A. C. Ethics of Book-Reviewing. Putnam's, v. 1, p. 116. (Oct. 1906.)

Matthews, Brander. Literary Criticism and Book-Reviewing, in Gateways to Literature, pp. 115–136. 1912.

Woodward, W. E. Syndicate Service and Tainted Book-Reviews. Dial, v. 56, p. 173. (March 1, 1914.)

Book-Reviewing *à la Mode*. Nation, v. 93, p. 139. (Aug. 17, 1911.)

17. Newspaper Style

Journalistic Style. Independent, v. 64, p. 541. (March 5, 1908.)

Newspaper English. Literary Digest, v. 47, p. 1229. (Dec. 20, 1913.)

Scott, Fred Newton. The Undefended Gate. English Journal, v. 3, p. 1. (Jan. 1914.)

Bradford, Gamaliel. Journalism and Permanence. North American Review, v. 202, pp. 239–241. (Aug. 1915.)

Henry James on Newspaper English. Current Literature, v. 39, p. 155. (Aug. 1905.)

Boynton, H. W. The Literary Aspect of Journalism. Atlantic Monthly, v. 93, p. 845. (June, 1904.)

Perils of Punch. Nation, v. 100, p. 240. (March 4, 1915.)

Mr. Hardy and Our Headlines. World's Work, v. 24, p. 385. (Aug. 1912.)

Lowes, J. L. Headline English. Nation, v. 96, p. 179. (Feb. 20, 1913.)

18. Newspapers and the Law

Schofield, Henry. Freedom of the Press in the United States. Papers and Proceedings of the American Sociological Society, v. 9, p. 67. 1914.

Grasty, C. H. Reasonable Restrictions upon the Freedom of the Press and Discussion. Papers and Proceedings of the American Sociological Society, v. 9, p. 117. 1914.

White, Isaac D. The Clubber in Journalism, in Thorpe's The Coming Newspaper, pp. 81–90. 1915.

Bourne, Jonathan. The Newspaper Publicity Law. Review of Reviews, v. 47, p. 175. (Feb. 1913.)

Newspapers Opposing Publicity. Literary Digest, v. 45, p. 607. (Oct. 12, 1912.)

Smith, C. E. The Press: Its Liberty and License. Independent, v. 55, p. 1371. (June 11, 1903.)

Garner, J. W. Trial by Newspapers. Journal of Criminal Law, v. 1, p. 849. (Mar. 1911.)

Keedy, E. R. Third Degree and Trial by Newspapers. Journal of Criminal Law, v. 3, p. 502. (Nov. 1912.)

Gilbert, S. Newspapers as Judiciary. American Journal of Sociology, v. 12, p. 289. (Nov. 1906.)

O'Hara, Barratt. State License for Newspaper Men, in Thorpe's The Coming Newspaper, pp. 148–161. 1915.

Lawrence, David. International Freedom of the Press Essential to a Durable Peace. Annals of the American Academy, v. 72, p. 139. (July 1917.)

19. The Country Newspaper

White, William Allen. The Country Newspaper. Harper's Magazine, v. 132, p. 887. (May 1916.)

Tennal, Ralph. A Modern Type of Country Journalism, in Thorpe's The Coming Newspaper, pp. 112–147. 1915.

Bing, P. C. The Country Weekly. 1917.

20. Newspapers of the Future

Irwin, Will. The Voice of a Generation. Collier's Weekly, v. 47, p. 15. (July 29, 1911.)

Low, A. Maurice. The Modern Newspaper as It Might Be. Yale Review, v. 2, p. 282. (Jan. 1913.)

Thorpe, Merle, *editor*. The Coming Newspaper, pp. 1–26. 1915.

Munsey, Frank A. Journalism of the Future. Munsey Magazine, v. 28, p. 662. (Feb. 1903.)

Ideal Newspaper. Current Literature, v. 48, p. 335. (March 1910.)

Murray, W. H. An Endowed Press. Arena, v. 2, p. 553. (Oct. 1890.)

Payne, W. M. An Endowed Newspaper, in Little Leaders, p. 178–185. 1902.

Endowed Journalism. Literary Digest, v. 45, p. 303. (Aug. 24, 1912.)

Holt, Hamilton. Plan for an Endowed Journal. Independent, v. 73, p. 299. (Aug. 12, 1912.)

Taking the Endowed Newspaper Seriously. Current Literature, v. 53, p. 311. (Sept. 1912.)

Municipal Newspaper, The. Independent, v. 71, p. 1342. (Dec. 14, 1911.)

Municipal Newspapers. Survey, v. 26, p. 720. (Aug. 19, 1911.)

Slosson, E. E. The Possibility of a University Newspaper. Independent, v. 72, p. 351. (Feb. 15, 1912.)

NOTES ON THE WRITERS

ROLLO OGDEN became a member of the editorial staff of the *New York Evening Post* in 1891, and has been editor of that paper since 1903. He edited the *Life and Letters of Edwin Lawrence Godkin*, published in 1907. His article on "Some Aspects of Journalism" was published in the *Atlantic Monthly* for July, 1906.

OSWALD GARRISON VILLARD, whose article, entitled "Press Tendencies and Dangers," appeared in the *Atlantic* for January, 1918, is a son of the late Henry Villard, who owned the *New York Evening Post* and the *Nation*, and a grandson of William Lloyd Garrison, the great emancipator and editor of the *Liberator*. He succeeded his father as president of the *New York Evening Post* and of the *Nation*, to both of which he frequently contributes editorials and special articles.

FRANCIS E. LEUPP was actively engaged in newspaper work for thirty years, from the time that he joined the staff of the *New York Evening Post* in 1874 until 1904. During half of that time, from 1889 to 1904, he was in charge of the Washington bureau of the *Post*. Since retiring from that position, he has been doing literary work. His article on "The Waning Power of the Press" was published in the *Atlantic* for February, 1910.

H. L. MENCKEN was connected with Baltimore newspapers for nearly twenty years, part of the time as city editor and later as editor of the *Baltimore Herald*, and for the last twelve years as a member of the staff of the *Baltimore Sun*, from which he has recently severed his connection. He is now one of the editors of *Smart Set*. "Newspaper Morals" was printed in the *Atlantic* for March, 1914.

RALPH PULITZER, who wrote his reply to Mr. Mencken's article for the *Atlantic* for June, 1914, is a son of the late Joseph Pulitzer of the *New York World* and the *St. Louis Post-Dispatch*. He began newspaper work in 1900, and since 1911 has been president of the company that publishes the *World*. He takes an active part in the direction of the editorial and news policies of that paper.

PROFESSOR EDWARD A. ROSS has been an aggressive pioneer in the field of sociology in this country and has written many books on social problems. His study of the suppression of news, the results of which were published in the *Atlantic* for March, 1910, grew out of his interest in the newspaper as a social force.

HENRY WATTERSON, who takes issue with Professor Ross in his article on "The Personal Equation in Journalism," in the *Atlantic* for July, 1910, is the last of the great editorial leaders of Civil War days. For half a century his trenchant editorial comments in the *Louisville Courier-Journal*, of which he has been the editor since 1868, have been reprinted in newspapers all over the country.

AN OBSERVER has seen much service as the Washington correspondent of an important newspaper. "The Problem of the Associated Press" was printed in the *Atlantic* for July, 1914.

MELVILLE E. STONE, who defends the Associated Press, has been its general manager for twenty-five years. Previous to his connection with that organization he was associated with Victor F. Lawson in the establishment and development of the *Chicago Daily News*. He has written a number of articles on the work of the Associated Press.

"PARACELSUS" sketches briefly his own career in journalism in his "Confessions of a Provincial Editor," published in the *Atlantic* for March, 1902.

CHARLES MOREAU HARGER, as head of the department of journalism at the University of Kansas from 1905 to 1907, was one of the first college instructors of journalism in this country. At the same time he was editor of the *Abilene* (Kan.) *Daily Reflector*, which he has published for thirty years. "The Country Editor of To-day" is taken from the *Atlantic* for January, 1907, and "Journalism as a Career," from that for February, 1911.

GEORGE W. ALGER, author of the article on "Sensational Journalism and the Law," in the *Atlantic* for February, 1903, has been engaged in the practice of law in New York City for many years. He has taken an active part in the framing of New York state laws protecting workers. Two books of his, *Moral Overstrain*, 1906, and *The Old Law and the New Order*, 1913, deal with the relation of the law to social, commercial, and industrial problems.

RICHARD WASHBURN CHILD, although a lawyer, is best known to the reading public as the author of novels and short stories, many of which have been published in magazines. His article on "The Critic and the Law" appeared in the *Atlantic* for May, 1906.

CHARLES MINER THOMPSON, editor-in-chief of *Youth's Companion*, has been a member of the staff of that periodical since 1890. Previous to that time he was literary editor of the *Boston Advertiser*. "Honest Literary Criticism" was published in the *Atlantic* for August, 1908.

JAMES S. METCALFE has been dramatic editor of *Life* for nearly thirty years. In 1915 he established the Metcalfe dramatic prize at Yale University, his alma mater. His article on "Dramatic Criticism in the American Press" appeared in the *Atlantic* for April, 1918.

RALPH BERGENGREN has been cartoonist, art critic, dramatic critic, and editorial writer on various Boston newspapers, and is a frequent contributor to magazines. "The Humor of the Colored Supplement" is taken from the *Atlantic* for August, 1906.

JAMES H. COLLINS, whose article on "The American Grub Street" appeared in the *Atlantic* for November, 1906, is a New York publisher, best known as the writer of articles on business methods published in the *Saturday Evening Post*.

www.ingramcontent.com/pod-product-compliance
Ingram Content Group UK Ltd.
Pitfield, Milton Keynes, MK11 3LW, UK
UKHW041943131224
452403UK00004B/392